# RIVER EAST,
# RIVER WEST

## AUBE REY LESCURE

DUCKWORTH

First published in the United Kingdom by Duckworth in 2024

This paperback edition published by Duckworth in 2024

First published in the United States in 2024 by William Morrow,
an imprint of HarperCollins Publishers

Duckworth, an imprint of Duckworth Books Ltd
1 Golden Court, Richmond, TW9 1EU, United Kingdom
www.duckworthbooks.co.uk

For bulk and special sales please contact info@duckworthbooks.com

A catalogue record for this book is available from the British Library

Designed by Elina Cohen

Printed and bound in Great Britain by Clays Ltd, Elcograf S.p.A.

Paperback ISBN: 978-0-7156-5562-7
eISBN: 978-0-7156-5540-5

**Aube Rey Lescure** is of French and Chinese heritage, and grew up between Provence, northern China and Shanghai. She worked in foreign policy before turning to writing and editing full-time. Her work has appeared in *Guernica*, *Best American Essays*, *Litro* and elsewhere, and she is the deputy editor if *Off Assignment*. She lives in Massachusetts.

'In this beautiful debut, familiar narratives of adolescence are scrambled across lines of class, race, and national difference. *River East, River West* portrays, too, the powerlessness of our loves against the riptides of history'                    **Garth Greenwell, author of *Cleanness***

'"River east, river west" comes from a Chinese saying which suggests that people's destinies are in constant change, and there is no fixed path of rise, fall, honour or disgrace. Aube Rey Lescure has represented this idea brilliantly in her novel'                    **Xinran, author of**
**_The Good Women of China_**

'Compelling and thought-provoking. A vivid portrait of China and the uneasy relationships of class and family history'                    **Catherine Cho,**
**author of *Inferno***

'*River East, River West* is a beautifully expansive tale of new beginnings – and the pasts we can't extricate ourselves from. Bright human insights shine through unforgettable characters fighting for their autonomy, often straining against familial bonds for a glimpse of freedom. Aube Rey Lescure deftly illuminates the difficult choices we make to save ourselves and each other'                    **Thao Thai, author of *Banyan Moon***

'At once tender and unflinching, *River East, River West* is a staggering, immersive coming-of-age set irresistibly amid the glamour and grime of a changing Shanghai. Aube Rey Lescure has crafted a vast, yet intimate, novel about performance and belonging, power and identity. I loved every word'
**Katie Gutierrez, author of**
**_More Than You'll Ever Know_**

TO ANDRÉE REY LESCURE AND LI GUIHUA

曾经沧海难为水

—元稹

FOR ONE WHO HAS SEEN THE VAST OCEAN, ALL ELSE
CAN HARDLY BE CONSIDERED WATER.

—*Yuan Zhen*

# PART I

# ALVA

SHANGHAI, 2007

A man called Lu Fang stole Alva's mother in Grand Ballroom B of Shanghai's Imperial Hotel. The 88,888-yuan luncheon wedding came with five cold appetizers, two soups, four meat dishes, three seafood dishes, plus Western-style black pepper steak, sugar-cream cake, and artificial flower bouquets. So expensive, yet so tasteless, Alva thought as she took in the windowless function room, the musty red-and-gold carpeting, the fabric petals scattered over each banquet table. Nothing like the white and pastel weddings of American movies, the candles and gazebos, the bridesmaids in their flowing gowns. Then again, her mother wasn't that kind of bride.

Alva didn't know any of the guests—they were all Lu Fang's acquaintances. Her mother had wanted a big wedding, and he'd managed to fill the space with his business connections. Alva was at the VIP table with some longtime clients of Lu Fang's and their plus-ones, some so conspicuously young they were obviously little honeys and not wives. Along with the plus-ones came a glinty display of Chanel and Louis Vuitton bags—slung over chairs negligently, though not negligently enough to hide their logos.

"I heard the bride's well-connected in America," a woman said, leaning into her neighbor.

"I heard she used to be a movie actress," the other woman, a business wife with tattooed eyebrows, replied.

"A famous one?"

"Never heard of her before today."

"Still. Lu Fang was born with some blind luck. An American actress. Why is she with *him*?"

Lu Fang stood onstage beneath an arch of pink balloons, his three-piece suit fitting him like sausage casing. The grease on his nose shone under the spotlight.

"Where is she?" one of the guests at Alva's table whispered.

The preset meal was growing cold. Several suited men had started smoking; another stealthily shoved a pork cube in his mouth.

She's going to make you wait and savor her entrance, Alva thought. Even if it means entering a smoky room crammed with strangers gawking at the Chinese man waiting for his foreign bride.

Alva couldn't understand why, out of all the men Sloan had been with over the years, it was Lu Fang who'd made the cut. He was in his fifties, chewed with his mouth open, wore suits with cheap satin sheens. He liked quoting poems in his thick Dongbei accent. Alva had noticed these traits with the distant condescension of a teenage girl when he'd come to their apartment for regular checkups. Technically, he'd been their landlord, a businessman leasing a spare property in Pudong. In the two years they'd been renting his apartment, Alva had seen him five or six times at most. Clearly, for her mother, it'd been a different story.

The business wife continued, "I heard the *laowai* is no spring chicken. She already has a kid."

"That's her right there," the other woman hushed, jutting her chin toward Alva.

"The mixed-blood? Can she understand Chinese?"

Alva focused on staring vacantly at the stage, where the emcee was pacing in front of Lu Fang, smiling with practiced joviality and repeating into the microphone, "The bride is arriving soon, soon!"

"I guess she doesn't understand," the other woman said.

"She looks more Chinese," the business wife declared, switching from Mandarin to Shanghainese. "Not one of those lucky mixes with big eyes and white skin."

"Pity," replied the other.

Alva took a gulp from her Wangzai milk. She loved this canned milk-flavored drink as a kid. Today, though, it tasted like syrup, cloying, neither milk nor cream. Half-and-half, just like herself. She wanted to say, I was made and raised in China, you old hags, and I understand Shanghainese perfectly. Yet they were right about the unlucky mix. She was half-and-half, white-Chinese, but with the wrong distribution of ingredients. Black hair, single-lidded eyes, slightly olive skin. To this day, she really did look nothing like her mother.

"Sad, that she's the only family. I thought there'd be more Americans. What about Lu Fang's relatives?" the business wife asked.

The other woman shrugged. "I heard he's from some small town close to North Korea. Maybe he doesn't want his poor relations here."

"You think his family *disapproves?*"

"Of the laowai? I wouldn't care if I were him. His company is exporting prefab housing parts to America."

"Then she's good for business." They laughed, loose behind the presumed safety of a linguistic wall. Alva was tearing the fabric petal to shreds, digging her nails into the glue dewdrops. This was all a joke to them, a business transaction, idle gossip, but it was Alva's life. It was Alva's *mother.*

The music cut abruptly to something orchestral. "The American bride!" the emcee shouted.

Sloan was finally here. Age forty-six and a bride for the first time, she glided along the red carpet in a lace-accented silk *qipao*. The emcee led a rhythmic clap that died down once she'd reached center stage, where Lu Fang stood beaming. Sloan's ash-blond hair fell pin-straight down her back and her cheekbones glowed with shiny dust, sparkles on white marble. She's beautiful, Alva thought.

"Tight dress, eh? Western women aren't afraid to show skin," the business wife whispered.

Sloan slowly turned to face the crowd. Her eyes scanned the tables, looking for someone. Alva raised her hand and gave her mother a small wave, a signal there was still time to escape. The door's that way! But Sloan's gaze swept past her, past the rows of business guests, and fell to the back corner of the room. The videographer stood there next to his tripod. He made the thumbs-up signal. Sloan threw back her blond mane and gave the crowd her best Hollywood smile.

A round of clapping followed the ring exchange. Her mother repeated "I do" (我愿意, more like *I'm willing*) after the emcee. It was official. Alva used to think that Sloan would leave China, that one day she'd give in to Alva's pleas. "We'll move to L.A.," Alva would say. "We'll rent a tiny apartment with a communal pool. We'll watch matinees and drive to the Pacific, just like you used to when you lived there."

"Maybe, maybe," her mother had said.

There was a flurry of camera flashes. Now Sloan was a proper *taitai* here in China, anchored by a husband and an apartment. Her arms encircled Lu Fang as they posed for photos, pointing to a distant mold stain on the ceiling. He clutched her waist, bloated, red-faced, clearly overwhelmed.

"Let's toast to the newlyweds, and a new era of Sino-American friendship!" the emcee said. Everybody scuttled up, raised their porcelain shot glasses.

"May your hair whiten till your golden age! May your love be deeper than the sea!" they cooed.

The emcee green-lighted the dinner's commencement, and the screen of cigarette smoke thickened as waitstaff poured and replenished bottles of Maotai and Great Wall. Alva reached for a chicken wing and gnawed it ragefully. In the din of the reception hall, amid burps and cheers and hollers, the business wives' gossip grated against her ears.

"I heard the laowai raised the kid in Shanghai by herself."

"You said she had family money?"

"I don't know. She must." The woman whispered more closely. "At this age, she can't be living off her looks, if you know what I mean."

Lu Fang and Sloan were making their way to Alva's table in fits and starts, stopping to greet this manager and that taitai. Alva had never known her mother like this, expertly knocking back *baijiu* toasts like she'd been on the banquet circuit her entire life. The Sloan she knew would have called this the Convention of Tycoons and Gold Diggers, mimed cocking a gun to her head for every one of the emcee's cheesy jokes. But not today. Sloan was perfectly focused, her performance devoid of irony. She had a captive audience of hundreds, a makeup artist, and a videographer. Lu Fang had delivered it all. Sloan was the star of the room and she knew it.

Alva set down her chicken bones, cleared her throat until the whole table stared. "I heard—" Alva said in Shanghainese, loudly.

The women stiffened, their conspiratorial expressions suddenly alert.

"I heard she's marrying him for his money," Alva continued.

The business wives went bug-eyed, and a suited man coughed uncomfortably. "This child is funny . . ." one of the women began, then paused. Lu Fang and Sloan had finally reached their table and were pulling out the seats next to Alva.

"It's the truth," Alva murmured in Shanghainese.

"Partner!" Sloan exclaimed as she gave Alva a sideway embrace. "Having fun?"

"We've just met . . . your wife's daughter," the business wife said to Lu Fang in a pinched voice.

Lu Fang swiveled toward Alva. "My wife's daughter? Oh. Manager Feng, we're all family. Alva is my daughter now too." He squeezed out a tentative smile.

Alva winced. "I'm not your daughter," she said.

Lu Fang stiffened in his sausage suit. Sloan glared at Alva, then said to the table, "This child lived in China her whole life, but somehow still doesn't know how to speak."

Everyone rattled out dry chuckles. Manager Feng paused for a second before saying, "Your Chinese is so good."

Sloan murmured the traditional deflection, "Too high of a compliment."

That was her mother's special trick, how she could shift attention to herself in any setting: her Chinese was *so good*, a fact that usually spooled out the requisite ceremony of niceties. "Where did you learn it?" "Here, in China." "How long have you been in China?" "Twenty-two years now." "What? You're practically an honorary Chinese!" And Sloan would toss her blond hair over her shoulder, laugh, and say with an insouciance that made Alva cringe, "Yes, I'm basically Chinese."

Manager Feng now said in a honeyed tone, "Sloan, your linguistic skills will be very useful for Manager Lu's business, I'm sure."

"Oh, I know nothing of business," Sloan said.

"No matter. Clients love an international consultant," a suited man said.

Sloan studied her teacup. "I suppose I could go on some business trips."

"Absolutely," Lu Fang said. "You know how poor my English is."

"Very poor," Alva muttered.

Lu Fang went on, oblivious. "There are many factories to visit down in Dongguan. Manager Feng and I are talking about some big expansions, aren't we? Sloan can help me evaluate manufacturing properties, from a Western perspective."

"Is that how you and Sloan met?" the other business wife asked. "Real estate dealings?"

"In a sense," Sloan said.

Manager Feng smiled. "Your daughter was telling us that it's going to be . . . very good business for everyone."

Lu Fang's gaze was flitting from his associates to Alva. He spread his arms grandiosely. "Should we toast? If we're all going to be doing business together . . ."

Sloan turned toward Alva. "Alva, pour Manager Feng and the other guests some Maotai."

"That's a good idea," Lu Fang said. He handed Alva the bottle. With stiff hands, she received it. She knew she was too deep in this game of debts and favors. It was a heightened art form, hidden dimensions folded into appeasement, flattery, and camaraderie, so opaque you emerged feeling like a debtor without knowing the reason. She poured the pungent alcohol into their outstretched cups. No one thanked her—only Manager Feng emitted a triumphant little "humph."

Lu Fang raised his Maotai and smiled pleasantly toward Sloan and Alva. "To new family."

Alva scrunched the mangled fabric petals in her palm. Around her, the perm-haired women and fat-necked men echoed the disingenuous toast. Sloan held Lu Fang's hand, her long white fingers interlaced with his thick, yellow-nailed ones. A sickening sight, those wedding rings. And yet the gesture seemed natural, almost instinctual. Was it so easy, Alva wondered, to pretend yourself into another life, even when the rest of the world knew it was a farce?

Sloan had told Alva about Lu Fang's proposal on a late spring evening in early May. They were lying on the cool balcony tiles of their rented apartment, listening to crickets and the intermingling sounds of televisions drifting from high-rise windows. Sloan pressed her cold Tsingtao bottle against Alva's cheek. "Lu Fang asked me to marry him, and I said yes."

"What?" Alva sat up so fast she'd knocked the Tsingtao sideways.

She barely knew him. When they'd started leasing Lu Fang's apartment two years ago, Sloan had introduced him as the landlord. There were times when Alva had come home from school and found him on their couch, taciturn. Sloan sat across from him in the big armchair by the banyan plant. Mr. Lu came to look at the air conditioner, she'd say. Or the water heater.

Alva didn't especially take notice. It seemed unlikely this terse, fleshy man had become her mother's "friend." Although in the past, Sloan had many "friends" that Alva seldom met. The "friends" were, for some reason, always Chinese. In Sloan's stories so-and-so always approached her, accosted her, bought her a drink. When Alva was younger, Sloan had a rule that she'd never spend the night away: "Mommy will be home when you wake up tomorrow." And she'd pay a neighborhood *ayi* a pittance to watch her daughter. Alva overheard these neighborhood ayis talking in Shanghainese, calling her mother an easy woman. ("The state she comes home in. Stinking. What do you think she does out there all night?") But Sloan always kept her promise. When Alva woke up, Sloan was there next to her, even if her breath was stinking of rotten eggs and something sour.

Alva knew to never think too much about these "friends." They came and went. She and her mother were partners.

Sometimes, when Sloan had a "friend," their lives would get better for some months. Sloan's wallet fatter with pink Mao bills, and they'd go on "splurge" trips to the supermarket—Alva always went straight for the imported cereals, Honey Nut Cheerios and Lucky Charms. But these boons, like the friendships, were short-lived. "They don't actually like *me*, partner," Sloan once explained to Alva. "They like foreigners. And I don't like it when they take advantage of me." Alva didn't quite understand what advantage was being taken when the "friends" were usually so generous, almost unfailingly Chinese businessmen who frequented the two or three Bund-side bars her mother loved most. She could imagine Sloan doing the Hollywood actress thing, laughing loudly with the bartender in Chinese, smudging lipstick on glass rims, drunk on attention and imported chardonnay, daring the businessmen to approach her.

When Lu Fang conducted his landlord visits, Sloan displayed flowers and fresh fruit on the dining room table—an attempt to evoke a more put-together lifestyle, so he wouldn't think they lived like slobs, which they did. They spent entire weekends in their underwear. They boiled instant noodles in cardboard cups most dinners. That's how they used to live anyway, in tiny rentals in Shanghai's older, more decrepit neighborhoods in Puxi, where they shared a mattress on the floor. These habits were hard to shake, even after they moved into his two-bedroom in the upper-middle-class neighborhood of Century Park. Everything in Pudong was newly developed—the streets wider, the buildings shinier. It'd been a patchwork of empty fields only a decade ago, and now it was where well-to-do Chinese families rushed to buy property.

About a year after Lu Fang began his intermittent landlord visits, Sloan had asked, "What do you think of him?"

"I don't know him," Alva had said.

"This apartment, this neighborhood, your new school—aren't they better?"

"Yeah."

"That's because Lu Fang is giving us a very good deal."

"Okay."

But Alva had always thought Lu Fang would meet the fate of Sloan's other "friends." He was so average, and silent, not particularly friendly with Alva. When her mother tired of him, the only pity would be that they'd probably have to move out.

"Marrying him can make our lives a lot easier," Sloan said that night in May as she broke the news, avoiding Alva's panicked eyes in the balcony's darkness.

"Mom, we don't need him. We can move again."

"We've never had a life as comfortable as this one, partner."

True enough, their pantry was always stocked with big, colorful boxes of Cheerios and Cocoa Puffs and Special K. And Alva's new school, Mincai, had shiny red rubber tracks.

"Mom, we're fine." The spilled beer trickled along Alva's leg. "We don't need him."

Sloan's eyes were closed. "Sometimes, partner," she said, "when an opportunity presents itself, you have to play the part. Sometimes you can't say no."

And Alva said no, no, no, but the matter had already been settled without her.


From the hallway, Alva watched the bosses and taitais file out the door, many wobbly from drink. The banquet hall was booked for another wedding that night. The staff was already clearing away detritus and spills. The emcee stood onstage making the final staid jokes—forecast of a Pacific rainstorm in the bedroom, ha ha—to disband the straggling guests.

At the last occupied table, Sloan was nodding along to some manager's story, her eyelids drooping. Lu Fang had lit a cigarette and was tapping its ashes onto the peels of a clementine. He forced a laugh at something the manager said, but when he glanced down, his smile slipped for an instant.

When Sloan and Lu Fang finally left the Grand Ballroom, Alva followed them onto the street. The bellboy, a shriveled old man with stained teeth, hailed a taxi to take them home.

Lu Fang passed out in the front seat, snoring loudly, mouth agape. Sloan looked out the window, turned away from Alva. They crossed the river eastward by way of Nanpu Bridge. Skyscrapers along the Pudong shore glistened in the mist. The river, opaque and mud-colored, roiled beneath them, engorged by a week of drizzling rain.

Neither Alva nor her mother liked this kind of mist. Sloan used to take Alva outside to chase epic downpours, sheets of water cascading with a thunderous pitter-patter, diffusing the sticky humidity of Shanghai summers. Now, Alva cracked open her window to air out the adults' alcohol breaths and meat fumes. But the wind whooshed loudly, and Lu Fang let out a startled snort. Sloan said, "Close the window, partner."

And Alva said, "Maybe you should stop calling me that."

Sloan widened her eyes, the foundation cracking at their corners. There was an immediate churn in Alva's stomach. She didn't want her mother to be mad. Not today, not with this man in the car. The rolls of skin on his neck were all Alva could see, the tiny black hair buzzed short, the slightly yellowed shirt collar, his entire body an unfamiliar mass in this car, in their apartment, in their lives.

The taxi driver turned the radio knob, filling the car's frozen silence. As they descended the elevated highway off the bridge, Alva reached across the car seat for Sloan's hand, a wordless apology. For a moment it seemed like Sloan would ignore her. Then she let her hand fall against the leather, accepting Alva's grasp, the ring cold and sharp-edged between their fingers.

# 2

Steam rose from the soy milk of breakfast carts. The first street vendors were rolling out their tarps, setting up displays of plastic trinkets, fake handbags, crate after crate of bootleg movies. Alva nodded to the DVD man, who raised a cigarette in silent salute. With My Chemical Romance blaring from her earbuds, Alva could almost forget she was walking to school at 7 A.M. on a Monday morning, away from the apartment she now shared with the strange man.

Pirated CDs and DVDs were her lifeline to adolescence across the Pacific. Over the years Alva had amassed a wealth of them, ten-yuan discs she and Sloan purchased in bundles from street vendors, iridescent soundtracks and tales of blond cheerleaders and Upper East Side parties, loners and stoners and prom. She coiled her earpods and hid them in her pocket before she reached the gates of Mincai Experimental School, where no electronics were allowed. She straightened her Communist Young Pioneers red kerchief and joined the swarm of kids in the same hideous yellow-and-green polka-dot tracksuits. Alva silently cursed the sadistic uniform designer for the Shanghai public school system, this expert on neutering hormonal yearnings. For the same reason, hair could not hang loose on girls, lest the boys be distracted. A row of Discipline Delegates lined the school entrance, ready to write up any student who exhibited the slightest deviation from the appearance rulebook.

Alva slunk dejectedly toward her classroom, Nine (1). She'd been nominated as a Homework Delegate this semester: a shit job. It meant turning a blind eye to the frenzied copying sweeping through the class-room at 7:43 A.M., collecting the booklets at 7:45 A.M., reporting any homework stragglers by 8:00 A.M. Alva's best friend in the class, Li Xinwei, was one of the few who enjoyed such duties. Li Xinwei wore a badge with three red stripes, meaning she was a school-level captain of the Communist Young Pioneers. Every morning she helped Alva file through the rows and collect the booklets.

Li Xinwei was already at her desk. "Was it that bad?" she asked after one look at Alva.

"He's moved in."

"To your mother's bedroom?"

"Yeah. And there's pee on the toilet seat now."

"Please don't tell me that."

"And he wears long underwear around. Instead of turning up the heat. He says that's what they do in northern winters."

"Maybe he's trying to save money."

They started filing through the rows. "But he's rich," Alva said.

"Third strike this month, Zhang Shao," Li Xinwei announced to a cowering girl. Then she shrugged at Alva. "Well, he does own the place."

"He does." Alva sighed as she put an X over Zhang Shao's name.

They had come to the desk of Gao Xiaofan, a boy who was asleep every morning until one of them poked him with a pencil. Gao Xiaofan was the tallest boy in class and played basketball during lunch break. He returned with sweat-matted hair and visible veins on his forearms. That made him the closest thing Mincai had to a jock, albeit a renegade one. Gao Xiaofan was always summoned to the teachers' office. He hung out with rich boys who snuck Game Boys into school and were rumored to drink and get into fights.

Alva knocked on Gao's desk, right next to his head. His eyes opened, filmy.

"Homework," she said.

Gao Xiaofan closed his eyes. "Another strike," Li Xinwei said. "You're hanging by next to nothing, Gao Xiaofan." He stayed slumped, ignoring them. His shoulders filled out the yellow-and-green uniform. When Li Xinwei wasn't looking, Alva quickly erased the X next to Gao's name.

Only three subjects mattered for the Big Test—Chinese, math, and English. This was ninth grade, the last grade in the Chinese middle school system, which served little purpose besides yearlong prep for zhongkao, the high school entrance exam.

The teachers made deals so that the day's art class turned into math practice, PE into English cram sessions, and geography into double Chinese. Today they were reading Ba Jin's "Starry Night," about the author's journey at sea, the night silent and soft as he stared at the sky above. As they read aloud in unison, Alva closed her eyes and imagined being on the dark ocean, floating toward the greater world, away from the overcrowded classroom.

During the last period, Ms. Song, who was also Nine (1)'s homeroom teacher, walked in with a stack of graded history exams. She returned them by reading each score aloud, from highest to lowest. Alva got a 92. Four points had been deducted from a multiple-choice question she'd been sure she'd gotten right. It read:

**Why did the Japanese capitulate during WWII?**

   a) The American atomic bombs

   b) The threat of a Soviet land invasion

   c) The relentless courage of the Chinese Communist Party

   d) All of the above

Alva had, diplomatically, circled *d*. But Ms. Song was now explaining the correct answer was *c*, and *c* only. Alva seethed through the rest of class, snapping into alertness when the bell rang, and Ms. Song held them for additional announcements.

"School authorities are urging anyone with information on the circulator of corrupt materials to come forward."

"HentaiLord," someone whispered, and the class broke into murmurs.

"There will be consequences for all who are found to have kept silent," Ms. Song said somberly. "And don't pack up yet," she added before nodding to the math teacher, who'd come in with another round of practice exams.

It was already dark by the time they left school. Li Xinwei's compound was called the Age of Romance, while Alva lived in the Garden of Heavenly Peace. All around were towering residential buildings with names like Prosperous and Beautiful Family and Lavish Years of United Oceans. A banner outside the compounds read "Socialism with Chinese Characteristics," but in this neighborhood there was little discernible socialism and lots of capitalist imports—an outdoor mall, a Carrefour supermarket, Nike stores, private gyms.

"They're serious about hunting down HentaiLord," Alva said to Li Xinwei as they walked by a breast-beauty spa promising massages and ointments for "fuller, softer chests." As always, her friend looked away from the foreign model's décolletage on the storefront poster. "You think they know?"

"They think it's a boy," Li Xinwei said.

"That's so sexist. As always, they underestimate us."

"It wasn't us, it was *you*." Li Xinwei's eyes were narrow.

Li Xinwei was the only person who knew Alva was HentaiLord. Earlier in the semester, Alva had gone down an internet rabbit hole of *Naruto* fan fiction and found a trove of pornographic links. The panels were full of wet, slobbery breasts and massive veined penises. Alva had made a fake username, HentaiLord, and posted all the porn links on their class Baidu forum. The next day every boy in class was freaking out, asking who HentaiLord was with feverish reverence. At first it was hilarious. Then some Goody-Two-shoes girls told the teachers, and school authorities began a panicked hunt for the "corrupter."

"Why did you do it?" Li Xinwei had wailed when Alva told her. She took pride in her three-striped badge, the symbol of the captain of the Communist Young Pioneers, and the captain was supposed to report all wrongdoing to the school discipline officer, Supervisor Liu.

"It's only a little crack in the routine," Alva had said, shrugging. "We deserve a diversion."

What she didn't say was how alien and violent those sex scenes had seemed to her, and posting the links felt like an assertion of power, turning her unease into the thrill of disseminating the forbidden. She had no idea how close those nasty hentai comics were to the real thing and hoped they weren't. Sex education didn't exist at their school, for that would imply sex existed, and that was the last thing Mincai wanted their students thinking about.

"Let's go to the Starbucks," Alva said. They'd all opened on the square in recent years—a Starbucks, a McDonald's, a KFC, and a Subway. But Li Xinwei said, "It's too expensive. And my dad won't let me drink coffee. Let's go to FamilyMart."

The FamilyMart was overrun by kids in uniforms and smelled like fish ball stew. "If I were you, I'd surf the web less and focus on the zhong-kao," Li Xinwei said, examining a box of matcha chocolate sticks.

"I'm dying from all the practice tests. Aren't you?"

"No," Li Xinwei said. "That's the difference between the strong and the weak. I can't allow myself to think like that."

"Right." Alva filled a paper cup with brown broth and shrimp ball brochettes. "Huadong No. 2 High School, overseas high-school exchange, then Oxbridge."

Li Xinwei had been obsessed with Oxbridge ever since receiving the purple Oxford English textbooks in first grade. She still loved repeating after the British-accented tapes, echoing the children with foreign names: Alice, Kitty, Ben. Emigration was an all-consuming, silent fever in Shanghai. Many of their richer classmates planned to apply abroad for college, too, though few said it out loud.

"And you'll end up in America," Li Xinwei said defensively.

"My mom wouldn't move back, even before she was married. Now, with Lu Fang . . . it's hopeless."

"You always see the bad side of things."

"What's the good side?"

The bell jingled as they exited FamilyMart. Li Xinwei shrugged. "My dad spends half his paycheck on New Oriental supplemental classes, Alva. I share a bedroom with my grandma. Is it that bad to have a rich stepdad?"

When she came home to Lu Fang's empty apartment, Alva turned on all the lights, then dialed up the heat to maximum. Burn, burn, burn. It was Lu Fang's money, and no one else was home to care.

She dropped her backpack on the floor and surveyed the space she used to think was hers. The apartment wasn't only cold in temperature. It was also the decor—nude white walls, spindly redwood furniture, a scratchy navy couch that belonged to an office lobby. Nothing looked cheap, but nothing felt like home. Yet two years ago, when they'd first moved in, Alva had been grateful for all the space, for a bed with legs, for her own private room, for a nonsquatting toilet. It didn't matter that they didn't have enough belongings to fill the rooms, to decorate. *We get to live here?* She hadn't believed their luck.

Alva was sprawled on the couch doing homework, the canned laughter of *Friends* blaring on the flat-screen TV, when the key turned in the lock. It was Lu Fang, coming home from work. "You're here," Lu Fang mumbled, as if she could be anywhere else.

"Where's my mom?"

"A hair appointment."

"Oh."

"What are you watching?"

"Nothing."

"It's a little loud," he said. He turned down the thermostat. "Is in front of the TV the best place for homework?"

Alva turned off the TV. After that, they sat without speaking until Sloan returned, her long blond hair blown out like a mermaid's. "Dinner!" she announced too loudly and cheerfully. She'd brought takeout from a nearby restaurant, mu'er mushrooms swimming in oil with tenderized meat of unknown provenance. "Want to set the table, Alva?" Sloan asked.

"I have homework," Alva said and took the white polyester container to her room.

She could hear the ceramic bowls clinking on the dining table. She opened her laptop, an old Lenovo ThinkPad Lu Fang had given her after the engagement, and logged on to QQ messenger. Gao Xiaofan was on there as 笑傲江湖, Smiling and Proud Wanderer, after the Jin Yong novel. His little dot shone green. She clicked on his name.

HentaiLord: are you going to the class trip

笑傲江湖: depends. What is it?

HentaiLord: ice-skating

笑傲江湖: there's no ice in shanghai

HentaiLord: it's at the mall, stupid

She'd started talking to Gao on QQ about a month ago, after Hentai-Lord had become a household name at Mincai. Not once had Gao Xiaofan talked to Alva in real life, but she'd known he would respond to a fellow rebel. And he did.

笑傲江湖: will you be there?

HentaiLord: Maybe, maybe not

笑傲江湖: who are you? I promise I won't tell

There was a rap at the door and Alva slammed the ThinkPad shut. It was only her mother, poking her head in. "We're gonna watch a movie," Sloan said. "*I Am Legend*. It comes out next month in America. Wanna join?"

"No, thank you," Alva said. "I've already seen it." She didn't turn around and the door closed behind her with a soft, disappointed clink.

# 3

For the class trip, Alva wore tight black jeans, a neon pink tank top, a fishnet shirt, and a Dodgers baseball cap she'd bought at a fake market. A class outing was, after all, a very titillating occasion: for once her male classmates would see her in something other than a yellow-and-green tracksuit uniform.

"It's not a costume contest," Li Xinwei said when they met at the gates of Age of Romance.

Alva knew Li Xinwei's outfit had also been carefully selected—the pink ruffles of her collar spilled out of a new camel peacoat.

They shared a taxi that smelled like stale cigarettes to the gold-pillared gates of Super Brand Mall. It was Alva who'd pleaded with Li Xinwei to go to the mall for the class ice-skating trip. American movies had proven malls to be high-voltage locales of courtship and intrigue. Plus, Super Brand Mall was a mecca for Alva. It was where, upon its mid-2000s opening, she'd first met the holy trifecta of H&M, Zara, and Sephora. It was where she watched a nonsensical screening of *Pirates of the Caribbean 3* that removed many of the scenes featuring Chow Yun-Fat, the main villain. Alva loved this inexplicably Egypt-themed top-floor cinema. Here, in this mall, she could stroll from the sandstone replicas of Abu Simbel to Toys"R"Us, to foreign bookstores, to Burger King. Alva loved this mall. You could experience the whole freaking world in this mall.

When they got to the ice-skating rink, clumps of girls from their class were already gliding in circles, guffawing and holding hands. Hardly any boys were on the ice, save for a few pimply class monitors groveling to be in Li Xinwei's good graces.

Alva advanced in little stabs on her skates. She wanted the space to be dark, the stereo loud, for any of the lanky, sporty boys who didn't turn in their homework to be there. She wanted varsity jackets, Budweiser, the entire cast of *American Pie*. All the excitement Sloan must have had growing up in America. She'd begged Sloan many times to consider a summer trip to the States and was told it'd be too expensive. Anything her mother didn't want to do was always too expensive.

Alva launched toward the railing and let herself crash against the soft pad.

That's when she saw the arcade adjacent to the rink. Some boys in her class were there, glued to video screens, jerking handles frantically. Gao Xiaofan's skeletal frame hunched over a machine advertising flames, blood, and women with breasts exploding out of Tomb Raider outfits.

Back on the ice rink, Li Xinwei was skating with great concentration and gusto. No one was paying any mind to Alva. She advanced into the arcade until she reached the fake motorcycle next to Gao. He didn't notice her. Since she didn't have tokens to start the game, Alva took out her phone, though of course there were no messages. Her mother was the only person who ever texted her.

"Mission accomplished," a man's voice said in English, startling Alva. Gao Xiaofan set down the rifle and felt for something in his pockets, then swore under his breath.

"Out of tokens?" Alva asked.

Seeing her, he didn't show surprise, or even recognition. She'd put on mascara, her hair was down underneath the Dodgers cap. Still, he looked past her, toward two boys, his friends Teng Xin and Doggy. They both had fat stacks of tokens beside them. Alva knew Gao was one of the few students in their grade who didn't live in posh Century Park. His father, driving an old Yamaha moped, dropped him off every morning after commuting from the edge of the school district. Today, without the uniform, Gao's nylon track pants and denim jacket looked shabby. Only his feet were fashionable; the leather of his bright red Nikes gleamed. He must've cleaned them carefully to keep them so new, because he'd worn them every day for the past two years.

Alva fished out a ten-yuan bill crumpled in her pocket. "You want this for tokens? You could teach me how to play."

Gao finally faced her. "Who are you?" he said.

"Ho . . . Homework Delegate," Alva fumbled.

He shrugged. "Maybe another time." Then he slunk toward Teng and Doggy.

Idiot! They talked every day! Alva wanted to shout after him. But if it got out that she was HentaiLord, then what? Someone would report her, and her years of good grades would crumble. The corrupter's head would roll, the crack would be painted over, the routine would carry on. The arcade's neon enclosure narrowed around her, airless. Alva slid the bill back into her pocket and, saying goodbye to none of her classmates, took the elevator down into the bowels of Super Brand Mall.

On the ground floor, she paused to admire the red swooshy font of the two letters: H&M. It was soothing to know things could be the same, standardized, everywhere in the world. The mannequins of white faceless plastic, the clothes made in Bangladesh. When she was younger, she and Sloan used to come to H&M and try on outfits like a makeover montage, strutting around the changing rooms, knowing they wouldn't buy any of them. The clothes they could afford were in the fake-goods market underneath the Shanghai Science and Technology Museum station, stretchy T-shirts that spelled CHRISTIN DIOR and GUCCHI in plastic studs.

In H&M, Alva scooped up hangerfuls of furry and frilly things and locked herself in a dressing room. She stripped down to her underwear, wiggled into a pair of acid-washed skinny jeans, and paused midhoist to contemplate her reflection. In the past year, her hips had stretched out obscenely. In the harsh fluorescent light, the skin on her buttocks was dimpled where it used to be smooth. She couldn't even look at her breasts. She was fighting with the jean clasp when she heard a shrill laugh in the room next to hers.

"Ouch! Scoot!"

"Oh my god, this is *so* cute."

Shuffled footsteps. Two people, maybe even three. Speaking English, with the unmistakable inflection of American teenagers.

"Don't you think the shoulders are weird?"

"Danny Merchant didn't even *look* at Rebecca."

"Ugh, I'm so fat."

"You're not."

"And Rebecca was flipping out, you should have seen her, she was so drunk—"

Alva held her breath. Three girls, three American girls. She had never been this close; she was practically in the stall with them.

"I promise, it's cuuuute. Go look at yourself in the big mirror outside." More shuffling. A lock clicking. The voices now outside. "I don't know. It's so tight."

Alva pulled on a strappy, silky top that flowed amply over the unclasped jeans. She opened her own door. The three girls were in the hallway in front of the big mirror. They all had brown hair—they were less beautiful than Alva had imagined. One of the girls had severe acne, another was chubby, the third freakishly tall. They were all trying on short bodycon dresses. They clocked Alva waiting and made no effort to move from the mirror. Their gazes drifted over her face like the shadow of a plane on flyover land. Why? Alva thought.

Then it dawned on her. They think I'm Chinese.

She took a step forward and said loudly in English to the tall one, "You look so pretty."

The girl swiveled, surprised. "Oh," she said. "Thank you."

Now the other two stepped aside to make space for Alva in the mirror. The four of them in its reflection. American teenagers. The one with acne said to Alva, "I like the top." The price tag was dangling out of Alva's armpit. One hundred twenty-nine yuan.

Alva forced the kind of easy, half-committed smile that said, Yeah, I might buy it. "You guys have a dance coming up?" she asked, trying to sound natural.

"Winter formal," the tall one said. Then, after a pause, she added, "Which school do you go to?"

Alva had stood in front of this very mirror before, sashaying while Sloan shouted cues in their game of pretend. In the reflection, she could be anyone.

"The Shanghai American School," Alva said.

"No way! We go to SAS too. Pudong or Puxi campus?"

Alva swallowed. It was a 50-50 chance. Shanghai's two main districts were named after the Huangpu River that bisected it, and Puxi, "River West," was the old colonial zone. Pudong, or "River East," with its rabid housing development and family-friendly malls, was the Chinese equivalent to suburbia. "Pudong," she said.

The girls exchanged looks. "Makes sense," the acned one said. "We go to Puxi. You getting that top?"

They changed back into their original outfits and walked toward the checkout counter together, Alva half a step behind, cradling the silk tank. It was so thin, almost sheer. She would never have a reason to wear it in public, not at Mincai, not in Century Park. The cashier waved her over. Alva slid the top across the counter and fumbled for her wallet. She didn't have 129 yuan. She pretended to count her bills, knowing full well they fell short. "A hundred twenty-nine yuan," the cashier repeated, not bothering to touch the small bills Alva set down. The chubby American girl was at the next counter and caught Alva's grimace. She said, "What's wrong?"

"I must have lost the hundred I had . . ." Alva said.

The girl took a hundred-yuan bill, with its hot pink Chairman Mao, from her own wallet. "Here," she said. "Don't sweat it."

Alva saw there was a thick wad of pink Maos still in there. She took the bill and said, "Thanks." The cashier folded the camisole and handed it to Alva in a plastic bag. The three girls ambled toward the exit and Alva followed them, greedily soaking in their conversation. So it was true: there were dances and boys and alcohol, but also lexicon Alva hadn't heard in the movies—ABC, chauffeur, open bar. She wanted to ask them what an ABC was, but the crowd on the mall floor was like a swift-moving current, and the girls weren't slowing down to include her: it seemed they'd already forgotten about her. Past the metal detectors, the three American girls disappeared into the human wave surging out the doors of Super Brand Mall. Alva stood there, dumbly, the silk tank top soft and beige and weightless in her bag.

# 4

After the American girls, Alva took the subway and walked home in the cold. She found the apartment empty. Sloan and Lu Fang were off on a business trip tonight, visiting a factory in Dongguan. Someone had left a pink Mao on the table.

The bill filled Alva with rage. Were Sloan and Lu Fang delusional? Not even a note, so smug in their presumption that she'd take care of herself, do her homework, and sit around while they jetted south and stayed in hotels with plush, starched beds. Did they know what happened in the movies when teenagers were left home alone? They trashed the house. They threw ragers. She bet the girls at Super Brand Mall did it all the time. It didn't even cross her mother's mind to worry about that.

A plan was percolating in her head. She'd throw a house party and invite . . . well, she'd throw a house party for herself. She didn't even need a fake ID. She could stroll right into FamilyMart and buy booze and no one would bat an eye. She used to be eight when Sloan started dispatching her to corner markets for beer.

She pocketed the hundred yuan and headed out.

FamilyMart kept its tiny selection of wine and spirits on a small shelf by the checkout desk. A bottle of Ballantine's whiskey was only forty-six yuan. The girl working behind the counter barely glanced at Alva's basket when she set it down. "And a pack of Hong Ta Shan too," Alva said, emboldened. The girl turned around and snatched a pack of cigarettes off the shelf.

Alva handed over the hundred-yuan bill. When she walked out, the automatic doors opened with an electric jingle. Alva waited to hear "Thank you for your patronage," which FamilyMart employees were supposed to say to every customer. But the girl was quiet, staring out the window to the already darkened streets.

Alva hurried past the security kiosk on her way back into Heavenly Peace, worried the compound guards might spot the bottle through the plastic bag. The man on duty gazed at her blankly and said nothing.

At home, she opened a Pepsi-Cola Lu Fang kept in the fridge. He'd moved in the weekend before, and his soft drink collection was one of the few signs of his presence. Fridge doors stocked with forgotten bottles of Pepsi, Fanta, 7Up, a graveyard of flattening American sodas. Besides that, there were few traces of Lu Fang in the apartment. He kept a pair of ostentatious red Nike sneakers on the shoe rack, a flashy vintage model similar to the ones Gao Xiaofan wore. Further proof of Lu Fang's lack of taste—the Nike craze had swept through the boys at her school, but it was a bizarre vanity for a businessman over fifty.

She filled half a glass with Ballantine's and poured in the mixer. The whiskey's edge was soft behind the Pepsi's fizzy sweetness. She pulled off her shirt and slunk on the silky camisole. It felt like wearing air.

She unwrapped the new Linkin Park album she'd bought from the DVD man the week before. Even its cover art was a perfect replica of the one she'd seen online. She put the CD in the player, and eyes closed, she swayed to the music, imagining bodies all around her, red Solo cups sloshing. She danced over to the master bedroom. The curtains there were drawn and the air smelled foreign, like a man's sweat. She knew Sloan kept the Box of Important Things somewhere in the dresser. Alva had to shove Lu Fang's clothes aside to reach it. In the second drawer, he kept a stack of button-downs and two soccer jerseys still in plastic wrap. Besides this stack Alva found the Box. She took it back to the living room and set it on a clean patch on the table.

The Box of Important Things had accompanied her and her mother in every move crisscrossing Shanghai. They had few physical possessions, no furniture, only cardboard boxes and ratty suitcases. For as long as Alva could remember, though, Sloan had always held on to the Box of Important Things.

It was an old tin that once housed British shortbread cookies. At the very top was a cardboard DVD sleeve. Sloan's favorite movie: *Thelma & Louise*. Alva eased the disc out of its plastic pouch. They'd watched it together so many times. The dust and sepia of the Southwest, a road bisecting the screen. "That's where I grew up," Sloan said. She came from a place where trucks lined the road, where everyone wore flannel and cowboy hats.

Alva pushed the play button and the familiar opening greeted her like a well-worn memory. Louise the neat one. Thelma the wild one. The women in the movie wore bright red lipstick and drank like her mother, like Alva right now.

The whiskey warmed her insides. Sloan had always told her they were partners, just like Thelma and Louise, and Alva loved to role-play the famous bar scene. "Let's go to Johnny Moo's and pretend to be Thelma and Louise!" she would beg on her birthdays. Johnny Moo's was a real, bona fide imitation American diner that'd opened a few years ago across from the supermarket. They wore jean cutoffs and black sleeveless tops with embellished skulls and roses, big sunglasses and shiny lip gloss. They ordered black coffee and cheeseburgers.

The Box of Important Things also contained print ads Sloan had done in her twenties, photo shoots for Chinese companies, one for a skin-whitening cream, the other for an English dictionary box set. Alva used to marvel at these pictures, which implied her mother was famous. At one time, Sloan was not only a model but also an actress, a real movie character. She said she used to travel with movie crews, all around the world and then stayed in Asia. She was even a lead once, a film set in Indochina, but it was never released.

Sloan didn't talk too much about the lead-up to her acting days: she'd moved to L.A. as a teenager after her parents died. Alva knew Sloan was fourteen when she lost her parents in a car accident. This, to Alva, seemed both incredibly glamorous and incredibly tragic, a movielike fate that could only befall someone as extraordinary as her mother. Alva couldn't imagine the sadness of losing your parents, of being adrift in a big city, and she understood why Sloan didn't like to talk about that time, or America. "All I know," Sloan would say, "is I'm glad to have broken free of the US of A."

Alva didn't see how living in their old grimy apartments, where the toilets didn't flush, was freedom. But her mother had a wildness about her. On good days she was a dazzling, feral creature, prowling the streets of Shanghai as if she could mark the whole city as hers. That wildness used to exhilarate Alva, like when they snuck into Jinjiang Park, boarded the ricketiest roller coaster, and screamed at the top of their lungs. Or when six-year-old Alva said she wanted pets and Sloan bought some sugary Taiwanese sausages, threw them at the stray cats, and said, "Pick one!"

But there were bad days too. Sloan often came home dog-tired from her shifts teaching English classes, kicked off her heels to reveal reddened feet, cracked open a Tsingtao, and stationed Alva in front of the TV. Then, curtains drawn, she'd feed one DVD after another into the player, measuring time by ninety-minute increments, while Sloan nursed two six-packs of Tsingtao and provided running commentary, words increasingly slurred. The movies were always American. When Alva looked alternately at her mother drifting into stupor and the saturated landscapes on-screen, she felt like a character in a dramatic sequence, a secret life. She knew this wasn't how her classmates lived.

The mornings after nights like these, which had become increasingly frequent over the years, Alva quietly opened the windows before leaving for school to let out the stale smell. Later Sloan would be waiting at the school gates, showered, perfumed, in heels and makeup, handing Alva a jumbo-size pearl milk tea. And Alva's little schoolmates would whisper excitedly, "Your mom looks like a movie star!"

Though most treasures in the Box of Important Things were artifacts of Sloan's past, there was another piece of crinkly paper, a certificate Alva had gotten for achieving the highest marks in fourth grade. Sloan had attended the ceremony in sunglasses, her left eye swollen and colored like an eggplant. She'd fallen and crashed into the kitchen counter three nights before. For that reason, she missed two days of work, and Alva knew her mother couldn't afford to get fired from another job. After Alva had returned from the podium, Sloan kissed her forehead and said, "I'm proud of you, partner." It was then that Alva realized as long as she got good grades, as long as one of them kept a baseline of order, they would somehow survive. In contrast to the chaos of weekends, school was an organizing principle, a relief. It made clear what was wanted of Alva: follow the rules, study hard, and nothing too terrible would happen to her or her mother.

But now there was a man, a stranger. Alva lit a cigarette and exhaled through her nostrils in what she assumed was a chic way before collapsing into coughs. It had the same tarry taste as the secondhand smoke from Lu Fang's Double Red Happiness, official brand of Chinese graft. Li Xinwei's words resurfaced in her head: *Is it that bad to have a rich stepdad?*

Alva paused the movie, walked to her bedroom, and fumbled through the stack of contraband literature she kept in her closet. Two glossy magazines—*That's Shanghai* and *City Weekend*. The expat magazines featured restaurant reviews, bars and concert recommendations, and places where foreigners could find one another in China. Alva took them to the couch and flipped to the page she'd dog-eared. An advertisement for the Shanghai American School, multiracial children with gleaming white teeth and even whiter lab coats, the campus grounds green as a prairie.

Sloan had explained to her that these magazines were the Coca-colonization of China. People were kidding themselves if they thought colonialism was over, when it was all around them in Shanghai, as advertised by the mags. Embassy parties, French Concession bars, international schools.

The teenagers at Super Brand Mall went to the Shanghai American School. So why couldn't Alva, a legal American teenager, go there too? A foreign passport—that's all one needed. A foreign passport and money.

At the bottom of the cookie tin were two neat booklets, dark blue. Golden eagles shimmered on their covers. Alva opened hers. Alva Collins, nationality: United States of America. She knew the blue passport was something others coveted. To even obtain a study visa, Li Xinwei would have to scale a mountain of paperwork. Whereas Alva, with this passport, could go to the American school tomorrow, if somebody paid for it.

She flipped through the pristine pages, studied the drawings of forefathers and presidents. This is my *real* country, she thought. But immediately she felt a twinge of guilt, and an eerie sense of exposure. Hundreds of windows looked onto Lu Fang's apartment. She leapt up and pulled the curtains closed, concealing the TV screen and cigarette butts, the empty whiskey glass and the precious blue passport.

Her eyelids drooped dangerously. This is what drunkenness feels like, she thought. This heaviness, Lu Fang's apartment spinning slightly around her. She surveyed the mess she'd made, the impromptu ashtrays, the ramen cup coated with grease, the remainder of the whiskey uncapped on the table. As a final touch, she walked over to the door and nudged one of the red Nikes off the rack.

Alva's forehead met the couch cushion. She closed her eyes. She remembered what her mother always said: "I'll be home when you wake up, partner, I promise." And so Alva waited.

## 5

The jingling keys in the door jolted her awake the next morning. From the couch, her glazed eyes took in Lu Fang, squatting by the rack. He picked up the knocked-over Nike shoe and placed it delicately next to its twin. Then his nostrils flared at the cigarette butts in the ashtray. This was, Alva thought, how you created conditions for a bargain: a behavior to be stopped in exchange for a concession.

Sloan's suitcase thudded against the walnut floors. "Damn it, Alva. What happened in here?"

"Had a little party," Alva said.

"What?"

"You drink," Alva said, jutting her chin at the whiskey bottle, then at Lu Fang. "He smokes."

"You are fourteen," Sloan gasped. "And what are these!" She'd spotted the Box of Important Things, its guts spilling out on the table. And then the expat magazines, open to the glossy school ads.

"You left me alone," Alva said. She switched to English. "You didn't come back."

"You knew I was going on a business trip," Sloan said. She inhaled deeply. "You're going to clean this up."

"I'm done with cleaning," Alva said.

"What?"

"I haven't been the one making the messes until now."

"Don't talk to me in that tone!"

Her mother had never put on this act before, shrill and onerous, and it made Alva furious. It was clearly for Lu Fang's benefit. She tugged the drooping strap of her camisole back in place.

"Stop," she said. "Stop acting like you're the dutiful mother."

Lividness overtook her mother's face. "Go to your room. Now."

Alva brushed past Lu Fang on her way out. He was leaning against the wall, his face ashen, looking once again monumentally tired.

Alva slammed the door and threw herself down on her pink alphabet bedspread. She'd never been grounded. Furious tears crept into her eyes. Alva used to cry incessantly after anyone died in a movie, until one day Sloan took her by the shoulders and said very seriously, "Partner, that isn't real. You shouldn't cry about made-up things."

Her mother was only playing a role, and there was no use being sad about something that wasn't real. That was what Sloan had promised, wasn't it?

Alva spent the day holed up in her room. At one point she heard the vacuum through the door, though somehow she doubted it was her mother. In the distance, cars honked lazily but otherwise the night was quiet, calm made possible only by their distance from the city's heart.

If Alva opened her bedroom window and leaned out slightly, she could see the edge of the balcony. Lu Fang was there, smoking. He hunched, his cumbersome body curved. The ashes he tapped against the balustrade flew like snow onto the downstairs neighbor's balcony.

In the compound parking lot below, a car crawled into the lot, slightly swerving. Alva recognized it: Teng Xin, likely coming to pick up Doggy. He did that some weekends, stole his family's car for a joyride. From the balcony, Lu Fang seemed to be watching the white Mercedes too. It almost hit another vehicle, then ground to a stop. Three figures emerged, walking in zigzags. One lamppost dimly illuminated the lot. She saw the third person: a lanky boy with bright red shoes. Gao Xiaofan.

She was leaning so far out the window that Lu Fang spotted her and waved. "Come to the balcony," he called.

*I'm grounded*, Alva mouthed.

"Come."

Alva crossed the apartment, pulled open the glass doors, and stood next to him, shivering. He was looking out onto the compound, not at Alva. The boys were still loitering around the car. "Look at them," he said. "These are what we Chinese call fox and dog friends."

Alva realized she'd never had a real conversation with Lu Fang before. She hated that the few times he spoke, it was in riddles and proverbs. "Meaning?" she asked.

"For Westerners, to be young and to disobey rules—it's *ku*. Cool, no? But those children down there, who are drunk, we call them *society* kids. Problem youth."

"Okay," she said. She rested her hands on the balustrade. "So?"

"I know it can take time to adjust to change, that you and your mother have been on your own a long time. But the rules apply to you, too, in China."

Alva narrowed her eyes. "You think I don't know about rules?"

"I know you haven't had . . . a father."

He looked embarrassed uttering that word, and she felt embarrassed for him. "It doesn't matter," she said. When she was young she used to say her dad was dead, like it was the most romantic thing that could happen to someone. When she said that—hoarsely, lowly, *he's dead*—she always pictured herself wearing a black trench coat. There was no grief.

Her biological father might as well be dead. Her mother refused to talk about him, and once, when Alva had asked too persistently as a kid, Sloan had exploded, "Why do you care where a squirt of sperm comes from? Am I not the one raising you?" But the truth was he did matter to Alva. She hated to think that she came from a spin of a Chinese roulette, some accident along a string of "friends," that 50 percent of her half-and-half was an inconsequential unknown. If her father didn't matter, then why were her eyes singled-lidded, why was she born in a hospital across the river in Puxi and not in Los Angeles, why did she have to prepare for the zhongkao exam and learn about the unrelenting courage of the

Communist Party revolutionary martyrs? Alva would never admit it to Sloan, but sometimes she wished for a father, someone to tell her why she was here, trace back which of China's fifty-six ethnicities one-half of her came from, so she might tell her classmates: *I'm not just a laowai.* Still, she wasn't desperate enough to need this greasy businessman to play father.

"We are a three-person unit now. We can help each other. But this doesn't serve you," Lu Fang was saying. "Being rude to guests at our wedding, making this shared living space a mess, drinking, smoking cigarettes—"

The boys downstairs were hooting. Around her, she could imagine countless neighbors watching, tsk-tsking, pulling back their curtains, turning to catch a glimpse of their sleeping children, reassured they wouldn't grow up to be fox and dog friends. These boys, these problems.

"You think I'm like them." Alva pointed at the boys.

"That's not what I am saying." Lu Fang sighed.

"I can stop being a problem. We can 'live in harmony.' If you do something for me."

He looked surprised. "What would that be?"

"Mom was never able to afford international school. But I have a passport. I have the grades. I just need the tuition. I promise I won't ask for anything else. I'll stay out of your way with my mother."

Lu Fang lit another cigarette. He exhaled slowly. "The heart of the ox beats to an odd rhythm," he finally said. "You're offering a deal?"

"Yes," Alva said. She held out a hand, ready for a handshake.

He didn't take it. Instead, slowly, he shook his head. "We both know your mother is against those schools. You have to accept that I am your mother's partner. And I have to stand by her decisions."

Alva's hand hung limp in the air. "So you're saying no to the deal."

"I'm saying no."

To hear him put it so plainly stung worse than any opaque excuse. It confirmed they were a sham family, one she had no power in. The words left her mouth before she could think. "She's got zero connections there, you know, no family. You're not going to get to America by marrying her."

Lu Fang turned to face her, his expression almost pained. "Alva," he said gravely. "Your mother and I love each other."

Was he really so pathetically stupid? "She had many 'friends,' many like you," she spat. "Don't think you can act concerned and tell me what to do." Then, seeing him flinch, she added, "You'll be gone as soon as she has no more use of you."

Lu Fang blinked, the next proverb stuck in his throat. Alva took this as the opening to push open the doors, pull on her shoes, and speed out of the apartment.

Let him watch her leave. This was a game of chicken, and she wouldn't swerve. Here, in Century Park, it had seemed to her that everyone's life was equally bound within a neutering test factory, but maybe she had been blind to the adolescence happening all around her. Those boys— they had a car! They were drunk! What was the point of her wimpy mutinies if she was still a good student, following orders? She'd done it for her mother, but now her mother had someone else to care for her. Someone who gave Sloan everything she wanted, and when it came to Alva, the terms were clearly different.

In the elevator, Alva tried to calm her breathing. Outside, when her eyes made out the shape of the irregularly parked car, she started running toward it. She didn't want to look up at the balcony. This apartment, this nice neighborhood—she wouldn't have wanted any of it if she knew he came with it. When she reached the white Mercedes, she saw that the boys were inside, Teng nodding his head to muffled music.

Yes, she would be a problem. She would be a problem until someone gave in.

Alva tapped on the driver's-side window.

What came next happened in a flash: Teng stirred, saw Alva, and panicked. He jabbed Doggy and turned on the ignition. Gao Xiaofan was passed out across the back seat.

Alva looked up toward the eighth-floor balcony of Lu Fang's building. A red dot glowed, very still.

Right as the car started to move, she opened the passenger door and jumped in.

# PART II

# LU FANG

QINGDAO, 1985

## 6

On most days Lu Fang swam for over two hours. On this windless August afternoon, the waves were clement, and he went out farther than usual in the Yellow Sea. The clear water revealed a school of jellyfish gliding a few meters below him, unhurried. They wouldn't sting unless threatened. He had his lane and the jellyfish had theirs.

In the winter, he swam for shorter periods. Men who grew up by the northern coastline knew how to plunge into the cold ocean, bracing against the icy waves. The best swimmers were rotund, insulated like seals. Lu Fang didn't have an ounce of excess meat on his body. His shoulders had broadened with years of daily exercise; the muscles in his back were strong and tight.

He was far from the coast. He knew it was behind him, Mount Lao rising from the horizon. He always swam straight into the sea, far enough that humans or structures blurred into the sand and hills, as far as he could estimate the half-life of his strength to be.

The sea wasn't a border. Lu Fang had grown up on a river in Liaoning Province, where the Yalu River divided North Korea to the east and China to the west. Guards at Chinese military outposts along the Yalu watching tightly for river crossers. The North Koreans came at night. They said that a defector's family, close and distant, would be executed. When he was eight, on his morning walk to school, Lu Fang saw a man in rags throw himself into the Yalu River, swimming toward

China in a frenzied crawl; there was the sound of two quick gunshots and the man's body was swallowed into the fold of the brown current.

North of Harbin, a river separated China and Russia. Mongolia, Kazakhstan—those were land borders, more westward than he'd ever been. Narrow lines you could not cross. But the sea wasn't a border, and no one was here to stop you from swimming out a little farther each day. The only border here was the limitation of his own body.

He turned and began swimming back toward shore.


The rocks on Dali Beach were a popular gathering place for young people. Green glass bottles in hand, they waited for nightfall in their white button-downs, most of them students from the university.

As Lu Fang swam closer to shore and the rocks came into focus, he saw the yellow hair. He choked on a gulp of seawater. A dot of yellow in a cluster of black, unmistakable. Fifty strokes forward and Lu Fang could see it was a woman, a foreign woman.

He'd left his backpack against the rocks, not far from the group of young people and the woman. He draped his towel around his waist as he changed into dry pants. A guitar was lazily strummed. A few voices joined together in an English song. Already he could tell which voice was the woman's—though she had a smoker's rasp, the words rolled into the music with ease.

After Lu Fang changed, he sat against the rocks and lit a cigarette. He would not be a gawker, but he wanted to listen. He'd heard the song they were singing on the radio before and understood pieces of the lyrics: *It doesn't matter much to me . . . let me take you down . . .* the little English he could remember was rusty, though he always kept a Chinese-English dictionary on his desk. He'd learned some new words: *tanker, strait, load.*

When the cigarette burned to a stub, he allowed himself another look at the woman. She was young, laughing with her mouth closed. Lu Fang eviscerated the cigarette against the rock.

At thirty-six, he was too old to be one of the university students with their beers and guitar. The yellow-haired foreigner's eyes briefly met his and looked away unfazed, like someone accustomed to being stared at. A male student handed her a new bottle of Tsingtao. She searched around for an opener, which disturbed the guitar-playing. Finally, the student who'd handed her the beer took it back and opened the bottle with his teeth.

Lu Fang reflexively touched his own lips. The foreigner stood up, held the bottle's thin neck, and drank without breathing until the liquid leaked and dripped down her chest. The students all watched and cheered. When she finished, the foreigner wiped her mouth and looked straight at Lu Fang, then sat back down. Or he thought she looked at him. It was getting dark. After that they started singing Qi Yu's 1979 hit, "Olive Tree." A drifter keeps seeing an olive tree in her dreams. Lu Fang had heard the songwriter originally intended the drifter to dream about a little gray donkey. That wouldn't be the same, he thought. Olive trees weren't meant for China; they could appear only in dreams, and one had to be content for even this brief apparition.

When the woman's yellow hair melted into the darkness, Lu Fang stood and walked toward the bus stop to head home.

## 7

In their one-bedroom apartment on Anwei Road, Lu Fang found Ciyi soaking her bloated ankles in a plastic bucket. "A Fang, it's too late," she said as soon as he walked in the door.

"Too late for what?"

"The milk."

"Oh." He checked his watch. "Huang's kiosk is closed now. I'm sorry, I swam for longer than usual."

He squatted in front of the basin and poured more hot water from the thermos. He held his wife's feet. "You've ruined them again?"

She had the nervous tic of shredding the flesh of her soles, picking at a callus until she could pull off a strip of hard skin. His thumbs ran over the lacerated soles, the edges of the rips mollified by water.

"I don't like those calluses," she said. "I don't like how they won't go away."

She rubbed her hand over her stomach. For two months now, she'd stopped going to her cleaning jobs downtown. It'd become too hard to hunch over a mop or kneel on a lacquered floor. Pregnant women were supposed to be deities, especially if they carried a boy—and Ciyi said she was sure it was a boy; a fortune teller she consulted at a temple fair had told her so. He also sold her a jade charm to ward off evil spirits, for the nonnegligible price of eighteen yuan. That was half her monthly salary as a maid. Lu Fang wished his wife didn't have to clean offices, but she told him she was good at it and kept getting referrals, and that any labor was proud labor.

Lu Fang rose from the plastic basin. "I'll get you an extra pouch of milk tomorrow," he said.

The milk had been his idea. He had heard from a colleague that the Chinese were shorter and skinnier than Westerners because they lacked calcium. His colleague had a cousin who lived abroad, in Canada. "The people are enormous there," his colleague had relayed. "Their thumb and index could wrap around my leg. It's because they drink cow milk every day!"

Lu Fang had never tasted cow milk growing up. His bulky swimmer's body was the result of years of exercise. But his son—his son would grow up to be as big and strong as any Westerner, no calcium spared.

Lu Fang sat down at the kitchen table. A cold bowl of egg and tomato noodles awaited. He turned on the radio and tuned it to the one station that played foreign music.

Ciyi didn't like it when he played 洋 songs. "A Fang, put on *Story Hour* instead," she called from the armchair. He considered telling her about the foreigner he saw today, then decided against it. Ciyi referred to foreigners on newsreels as devils. "They're so white," she'd say. "Like dead people."

He listened to the strange words of the song for a few more seconds before turning the dial. They fuzzed into Chinese, a strange hybrid tongue, then faded out.

## 8

He'd met a Westerner once. Lu Fang had only been seventeen then, studying for his first—and, though he didn't know then, only—year at Renmin University. He'd heard rumors there was a white man at school, an American soldier who'd defected during the Korean War.

In Lu Fang's hometown, Dandong, there was a broken bridge that stopped midriver, bombed by American fighter jets during the war. Lu Fang was too young to remember the aerial raids conducted by Americans along the Chinese–North Korean border, but he knew it was because of them that his father, who'd been conscripted into the volunteer army to help the North Koreans, came home with an infected stump for a leg. The infection spread throughout his body, and the disability checks were barely enough to pay for new bandages. His mother, a nurse, took on night shifts at the hospital, and, at a very young age, Lu Fang was left to tend to his father and study by oil lamp as his baby brother played on the dirt floor. Still, every time he walked past the broken bridge as a teenager, he did not think to blame his family's misery on the American devils. They were formless and faceless, though it bewildered him to think they had machinery that could travel as far as his backwater city. He knew it was wrong to feel so little hatred, especially because he equally failed to muster any adoration for Marx and Engels and Lenin. Their illustrated portraits in his textbooks only made him aware of the existence of worlds outside his city, worlds with wide streets and shiny black cars like the ones in Shanghainese movies.

At school, he kept these thoughts to himself and shouted the slogans about the new China as loudly as his classmates. In truth, he preferred the classical texts, had always been drawn to poems describing epic battles, dynastic collapses, legendary drunken nights, the rise and falls of heroic men. When schoolteachers ordered the class to stand pin-straight in military stance and recite poetry in unison, barking at the top of their lungs, Lu Fang and forty other skinny boys and girls took on the might of an ancient battalion. When he shouted out "Reminiscence at the Red Cliffs," he lost himself alongside Lord Zhou of the Three Kingdoms, back against the cliff wall, the Yangtze River's raging waves *pounding the banks, spraying like snow*. More so than looking at the framed portrait of the chairman above the blackboard, Lu Fang felt then, swelling within him, a great romance for the history of their people, for their potential to take on the world.

Most of all, he saw that potential in himself. His grades were the highest in the province, and the neighbors whispered that the eldest Lu boy was like an imperial scholar who'd travel further with each examination, showering his hometown with glory. When their father died after eight bedridden years, Lu Fang's younger brother started skipping school to collect metal for the scrapyard and told Lu Fang, "Ge, you study and be the big man. You're going to study your way to the Imperial City." And when Lu Fang passed the entrance exam for Renmin University in Beijing, his whole street killed chickens and drank plum wine to celebrate. Even Lu Fang drank until his head spun, and when the neighbors asked what he'd study he said business, international business. And maybe, later, he'd get a scholarship to study economics outside of China. In 1965, when he bid Dandong goodbye and boarded a train for the capital, he felt like the train was speeding toward a future that knew no bounds.

It was halfway through spring semester at Renmin University when Lu Fang saw the white man in the cafeteria, scooping congee from a metal tub. The man didn't have yellow hair or blue eyes, but rather ordinary brown hair and brown eyes, and at first Lu Fang was disappointed. But the American's nose was large and arched, his eyes sunk into his skull, and he was a head taller than the other men on campus. Lu Fang was a lanky boy then, with a wild mop of hair and too-big uniform pants he belted high on his waist. It took him weeks to work up the courage to address the man. One day the American was sitting alone and Lu Fang set his metal tray down next to him, ignoring his classmates' stares.

"Hello," Lu Fang said in English. "My name is Alexander."

Lu Fang had practiced this sentence thousands of times. He'd whispered it to himself in his bed, in the shower, walking from class to class. He'd started learning English this semester, from an ancient professor who'd studied in the West before the war. Lu Fang had been excited to receive a name from the professor: Alexander. Lu Fang went to the library's foreign languages wing and learned from the dictionary that he shared a name with Alexander the Great, Alexandre Dumas, Alexander Hamilton. The professor himself had learned English through an exchange scholarship in the 1920s, at a university in a place called O-something in America. Lu Fang found a list of American states in the dictionary: Ohio, Oregon, Oklahoma. Perhaps one day he'd study there, like the old professor, or the students sent to learn engineering in the Soviet Union. The Soviet Union was too close, though, just north of his hometown of Dandong, and he'd already memorized Leninist Thought in his classes. He wanted to cross an ocean, any ocean, and see how people lived and studied on the other side. After all, even premier Zhou Enlai had spent years in France, Germany, Britain. Lu Fang wrote in his notebook: *The Adventures of Alexander in Oklahoma*. And when he received a near perfect score on the last vocabulary exam, the old professor had handed his stack back with an especially approving nod.

"Alexander?" The American soldier looked amused. "I'm Zhang," he continued in Chinese, picking up a strand of pickled radish with his chopsticks. "The younguns here call me Old Zhang."

"I hear you used to live in America," Lu Fang said, switching to Chinese with a mix of relief and disappointment. "Have you been to O . . . Oklahoma?"

Old Zhang scoffed. "No."

"I'm going to study there one day," Lu Fang said, surprised by his own bravado.

"Good for you. But no good if you don't know how to drive."

Lu Fang felt stung. "How do you know I don't?"

"Don't meet many Chinese men who can. What did you say your name was? Alexander?"

"Yes."

"And what's your actual name?"

"Lu Fang." Of course no one would believe he could be an Alexander.

"Fang, which character? The one that means square?"

"Yes."

Old Zhang dipped his index finger in the brown sauce in his tray. He drew a square on the table: 口.

"You don't ever need an English name."

"口 is the character for mouth," Lu Fang said.

"I know. But watch. This here is the character for man, yeah?" Old Zhang drew a 人 with soy sauce on the table. A stick figure person with two long legs, next to the 口. "And when you put the man in the coop here—"

He drew a 人 again, this time inside the 口. It made a 囚. This was the Chinese character for prisoner.

"I learned this when I was a prisoner in the war. I didn't need to speak Chinese to understand it back then."

Lu Fang shifted in his seat uneasily. He rarely thought about the literal depictions of characters, just like Old Zhang probably never thought about the English alphabet, never thought about his cars in America.

"You are free now," Lu Fang said.

"I am," Old Zhang said. "Free to go back to my metal factory and my beautiful Chinese wife." He smirked, scraped the last of his millet congee from his metal bowl. "Listen, here's a word of advice before you go to Oklahoma: get acquainted with something called disappointment. And learn to drive. Otherwise you'll be this little man in the coop."

Then Old Zhang excused himself and left for class. Lu Fang wiped the 囚 in soy sauce off the table with the last piece of his *mantou*. You never knew what the next person who saw it might think. Old Zhang was an American defector, so he was on the right side of history, but he should know better than going around campus writing 囚.

After that, when Lu Fang crossed paths with the hunched giant at the cafeteria or on campus, they exchanged nods. Lu Fang remembered thinking that Old Zhang was a crazy man, choosing to stay here in China rather than go back to America and drive his cars. Lu Fang decided not to use the name Alexander to refer to himself until he wouldn't look foolish doing so. All semester he stayed up reading the English dictionary in the dorm hallway's dim light, well past curfew. At the end of winter term, he had the highest marks in the year.

That spring of 1966, when the first denunciation posters appeared on campus, Lu Fang saw Old Zhang in the marching crowds. In June, a professor jumped into a river. Then a vice-principal at a neighboring school was beaten to death by Red Guards. Classes stopped, committees were formed, students asked to stay on campus over the summer to partake in the revolution. Lu Fang waited for the new school year to start, but it did not. He spent those blood-filled months hiding in his dorm or trying to melt into the crowds, watching the beatings and shaming processions, terrified of being recruited into the Red Guards, even more terrified someone would say he wasn't doing enough. He would never forget the day the old English professor was found hanging from a beam in his apartment. Then came word that committees were planning to dispatch the students for rural reeducation, under the encouragement of Chairman Mao and Premier Zhou Enlai. Lu Fang was called into a makeshift headquarters, handed a red-stamped document: he'd been assigned to the tobacco fields of Chuanxi, he would leave on the first train in the New Year, and, needless to say, he would never call himself Alexander again, never cross any ocean to study international economics, never drive a car in places whose names were already fast-fading words from a dictionary.

## 9

The day after he saw the foreign woman, instead of his usual after-work swim, Lu Fang took the bus to the northeastern side of the city. Qingdao University's main campus was a spattering of ugly yellow buildings behind gates. They'd planted rows of sickly pines to beautify the campus, but the recent decade of abandon filled its every edge. Now students strolled around carefree, girls holding hands, shoulders sagging with heavy backpacks. There was a kiosk at the entrance where a guard was laboriously cleaning his teeth with a toothpick.

Lu Fang stood in the shade of the bus stop. Ten minutes passed and still he did not see what he wanted—a speck of yellow down a campus path, or bursting through the gates. What an odd sight that would be, almost two decades after his own university years. That they should be *here*, this seaside city in northeastern China.

The guard in the kiosk lit a cigarette and cracked open a window. Lu Fang crossed the street and pulled out a smoke from the pack in his shirt pocket. He knocked on the glass.

"Brother, you have a light?"

The guard frowned before sizing him up. Lu Fang was in the clean shirt Ciyi washed every other night, his hair cut by a street barber during lunch. The guard produced a plastic lighter from his pocket and handed it to Lu Fang without a word.

"Thanks, brother. Summer break now, is it?"

"School's started," the guard said.

Lu Fang rolled his thumb over the lighter's little wheel. "Say, do you have exchange students here? I saw some foreigners . . ."

The guard interrupted him with a sudden swing of his arm and pointed to a sign on the kiosk wall. It read: IDLE PEOPLE MAY NOT LINGER. "Light up and move along, brother," the guard said.

Lu Fang sensed the heat rising to his face. A gawker and stalker, that was all he was to the guard. He handed the lighter back through the kiosk. "I've troubled you," he said.

As he walked away he heard the guard say, "The devils are here all right."

Lu Fang waited for the bus that would take him up the coast. That night he went farther out than ever in the black waves, turning around last minute to dim lights flickering in the hills.

He was a 囚, four borders enclosing him, even if those borders stretched for thousands of kilometers, even if they were invisible. They were his laughable monthly paycheck, the university degree he'd never earned, the visa he could never afford, the openness to life he had lost at seventeen, all because he was born in the wrong decade, because a few high-up men's whims were enough to change the course of a generation. The borders around him were the refrain of sitting at his shipyard clerk's desk, waiting for the clock to expire so he could board a bus, wade into the Yellow Sea, swim until his mind went as dark as the skies. All while a pregnant woman waited for her husband to come home, so they could eat, the dishes could be done, the bamboo mat could be laid out on the bed, and the husband could briefly close his eyes before awakening in the predawn darkness to do it all again.

Ciyi was asleep when he got home. He put his ear against her stomach and waited for his son to kick.

At Dali Beach, Lu Fang couldn't stop himself from scanning the rocks to see if the university students had returned, if she was among them. He knew it was irrational to hope to see one person in a city of millions, but it seemed like the laws of probability would bend from his sheer wishfulness. He desperately wanted to see her. To remind himself China was changing, foreign entities were coming in, markets and borders were opening, the unexpected was still possible. The unexpected was within touching distance.

He would have returned to the university gates, but in the end, he didn't need to—the woman with yellow hair was sitting on the rocks when he returned from another day's swim, this time with only the male student who'd opened the beer with his teeth. They looked like they were arguing. At some point the student stood and left. Lu Fang wondered if this scrawny boy was her lover. He took longer than usual patting himself dry with the towel—stolen from one of Ciyi's old cleaning jobs. For a moment he felt proud of his swimmer's body.

Then she stood and walked straight toward him. He tied the towel around his waist apprehensively. Immediately, he thought she knew about the visit to the university, that the guard had provided her with a minute physical description of him, a dangerous stalker. He forgot to worry about the fact that they probably could not have a conversation at all, because his English was not up to par.

But she spoke to him in Chinese.

"You swim very far," she said, "so far that at some point I can no longer see you."

No one had ever spoken to Lu Fang this way. Dumbly, Lu Fang repeated, "You can no longer see me?"

"Isn't it dangerous? You must be good."

"At swimming?"

"Yes."

"I do it every day," he said.

"I know," she replied. "I've been watching you every day, to find out if you'll come back."

Together, they walked toward the snack stand where the 804 bus usually stopped. The foreign girl said her name was Sloan. It was easy enough for Lu Fang to pronounce. Her Mandarin was heavily accented but confident.

Sloan asked for Lu Fang's name and he said, "A— Lu Fang." When the bus came, she dropped into a seat by the window and watched his indecision. Finally, he sat down beside her. At a tight turn, her knee touched his. Lu Fang's slacks were wet because he'd kept his swimsuit on underneath. He hugged his backpack in his lap. The only other passenger was an old woman whose eyes had remained on them since they'd sat down.

"I wish I could swim like you, in the open," Sloan said. "I grew up with backyard pools."

"Where?"

"美国. America."

It made sense that she was American. Those were the stereotypes his colleagues circulated—British people were elegant, French were romantic, and Americans were hot and emotional. It may be true. Sloan was very much like Old Zhang—openly irregular.

"If you had pools, then why can't you swim?" Lu Fang asked.

"You're funny."

From this close she looked very young. She had an upturned nose and freckles. Her thighs were white and he could see every hair follicle. She was wearing a dress Chinese women would find too short. Maybe the male student had taken her to the rocks to confess his feelings and she'd refused his advances. Lu Fang liked the idea of it, because she'd come straight to him afterward.

Her bare knee touched his again. They were getting closer to the city. "I think your stop is the next one, if you're getting off at the university," he said gently.

"How do you know I'm getting off there?"

"Oh." Lu Fang clutched his backpack, a gesture he hadn't made since he was a schoolboy. "I saw you with the guy in the uniform."

"I'm an English teacher there," she said. "I like coming to the beach with Chinese students, to practice speaking. But today was a little awkward."

"The guy?"

"The guy," she said, then shrugged, like it went without saying she always had to turn down men.

The bus was rounding the corner to her stop. She drew in her breath like she was hesitating.

"Lu Fang—I was wondering—if you wouldn't mind if I came by the beach again and, you know, swam with you. Not as far. I'm not a good swimmer but you could teach me?"

She spoke fast, almost like she was nervous. He'd thought that maybe he'd been someone to practice Chinese with on the way home, but now it dawned on him there was something else. She'd really *seen* him swim; she'd been waiting to talk to him. She was getting up and smoothing her dress, not looking him in the eye. The effect of this shyness was torrential. "Of course," he said. "I can teach you."

He got up to let her pass and watched her hop off the bus. He felt immensely woozy, barely registering the old woman's beady eyes, which were glued to him. He changed lines at May Fourth Square and arrived home right before Huang closed his corner store. He bought two pouches of milk. "Good day?" Huang asked, smoking by the oil lamp at his desk. "Still hasn't given birth, has she?"

"Still some time away," Lu Fang said. He was still beaming stupidly when he climbed the stairs.


"This is a cursed weekend," Ciyi declared on Sunday. They'd been locked indoors since the typhoon made landfall in Japan. Outside their window, the shrubs in the communal court bent in submission to the winds. A newscaster's report fuzzed in and out from the radio: "Deng Xiaoping affirms we must rank Chairman Mao's contributions first, and his errors second. Without Chairman Mao, the Chinese people would have groped in the dark even longer."

"Or found the light switch much sooner," Lu Fang said.

Ciyi hushed him. "Don't disrespect. The skies have ears."

Lu Fang could sense Ciyi getting more superstitious as her stomach grew. She wore the pendant bought from the fortune teller around her neck at all times. She'd even stopped referring to the baby as a son, as if a jinx would result in a last-minute gender reversal. After all, they had no guarantee—only their own wishful thinking, a potential charlatan's predictions, and the courtyard matrons' insistence that Ciyi's belly was shaped like a boy. At the hospital, they hadn't been allowed to ask about the gender. They heard the crackdown of the one-child policy was strict. They knew of couples paying hush money to "get rid" of the baby the second it was born if it turned out to be female. It'd be declared a stillbirth; the couple could try again. Ciyi and Lu Fang had never discussed this option. They couldn't afford to get in trouble, not with Lu Fang's past as a reeducated "intellectual," and they didn't have any money for a bribe. They would follow the rules.

"The radio won't work anymore." Ciyi turned the dial. Distorted voices sputtered.

"We'll live without the news for a day."

"I like the news. Keeps me company."

"You have company." He sighed.

"Barely. I'm lucky the storm is keeping you home. I don't know why you're so irritated."

Lu Fang had told her he might go for a swim today. But with the typhoon outside, the waves were too wild. The gray clouds rumbled and he lay morose in their sheets, undressed. Four walls, a 囚, per the skies' wishes, no swimming lesson today. He lit a Double Red Happiness, a pack he'd found on the floor after a banquet at the shipyard.

Ciyi set the radio flat on her stomach. "You shouldn't smoke in bed," she said. "It could catch fire. That's what happened to my dad's comrade. He fell asleep and burned to a crisp."

"Your dad's comrades always perish in educational examples."

Ciyi frowned. He couldn't even speak to her in jest; she saw her parents as sacred. Her father was the party secretary of Chuanxi village, nestled in the ass crack of two forgotten mountains. Still, Ciyi took pride in this bureaucratic aristocracy, even when the unshakable country accent that distorted her Mandarin instantly sold her out as a rural migrant. Even when she scrubbed office workers' shit out of sanitary ditches, even as she wiped the meat grease off a rich man's sink.

"My dad and his comrades are the generation that built the new republic," she said. "So we can live the good life."

"Yes, a very good life."

Lu Fang didn't like to be reminded of it. Although there must have been millions of party secretaries in towns big and small across the republic, without the Chuanxi party secretary, Lu Fang would not be here. He'd have wasted away in reeducation, working the tobacco farms of Yunnan until the central authorities decided he'd been sufficiently neutered. He remembered the night the party secretary sat him on a stone bench after dinner and handed him a smoke. Lu Fang had always been the man's favorite among the university students exiled to Chuanxi. The party secretary liked that Lu Fang was from the North Korean border and that his father had been a soldier. The party secretary had also fought in the war against the Americans in the '50s. He liked telling Lu Fang war stories about killing devils. Lu Fang stayed quiet and listened. But this night the party secretary wanted to talk about his daughter, Ciyi. Lu Fang knew she was the girl who sat in the first row at the village-wide Mao Zedong Thought study sessions. She had round cheeks and two braids, and though she hadn't gone to middle school or high school, her eyes were alive and perceptive. At the cafeteria, they smiled at Lu Fang through the service window.

"Here she will be a farm laborer. She has no prospects in Chuanxi. Even I, the party secretary—am I not just a farmer, after all?" Ciyi's father had said.

That's true and untrue at the same time, Lu Fang had thought. But he only nodded.

"You were in one of the country's best universities," the party secretary continued. "I know you think of it bitterly now, but the political situation will not last forever. You are a man with ambition, Little Lu." He flashed his yellow teeth. "You'd treat our Ciyi well, wouldn't you?"

"I..."

"She's not educated like you, but she is smart. Here she is a frog at the bottom of a well. Our new China is going to open, I tell you, but it will be years before the wealthy tides of the coast seep into our backwater mountains." He set down his metal mug with a clang, cleared his throat as he looked with melancholy toward the tobacco fields and the craggy hills beyond. In the twilight, the landscape emanated a bleak beauty. "You young people have no years to waste here. Your productivity will serve our nation better elsewhere."

Lu Fang held the party secretary's gaze, uncertain. "The papers say I have to serve indefinite reeducation here until discharged."

"A letter of discharge for a man who has learned his errors, who is part of a hardworking couple, an eager unit of production waiting to serve in the industrial northeast. That wouldn't be hard to arrange." The party secretary's voice softened. "Our Ciyi is lovely, isn't she?"

Lu Fang finally understood. "Yes," Lu Fang said. "She is."

After that the family hadn't taken long to arrange the courtship. Ciyi and Lu Fang took walks along the tobacco fields, hand in hand. She let loose her braids and her shiny black hair was wavy like Vivien Leigh's in *Gone With the Wind*, one of the many Western movies Lu Fang had eagerly watched in the university projection room. The Chinese translation for *Gone With the Wind* was only one word: 飘. It meant "float" and consisted of 票, a ticket, and 风, wind. Since talking to Old Zhang Lu Fang had started paying closer attention to the wisdom of characters. When someone handed you a ticket, you took it. Lu Fang had looked at Ciyi's beaming face through her red bridal veil at the village wedding and tried not to think too hard about his decision. The next year, he was discharged, and took his bride on a five-day train journey to Qingdao, a northern port city thousands of miles away from Chuanxi. During Chinese New Year, they made the trip to Lu Fang's hometown of Dandong, which was much closer, a few hours by bus. Lu Fang's mother never said what she thought of this poor peasant girl from the mountains, only studied her stomach, and said she was glad Lu Fang was home. Ciyi was stick-thin for eleven years, sickly upon arriving to the North. She said she had to get used to the food and climate, but Lu Fang suspected it was homesickness. Then her cheeks caved in and her muscles became wiry from long hours of sweeping and scrubbing, and just when they thought her body would never be hospitable for a baby, she got pregnant.

Ciyi was now staring at the storm clouds outside the window. "Boy or girl," she said, "I'd like to use the name Min. After my father."

Min—the people. Ciyi's father had legally changed his name after his promotion in the local party branch. "The fortune teller said it would fit," Ciyi added.

"Is the fortune teller a party member?" Lu Fang smirked.

Before she could retort, something whacked the window and they both jumped. It was only stray garbage swept up by the winds. The radio fizzed, then white noise again.

"Could we leave for the hospital if we needed to?" Ciyi asked, her face pale. "How long is the storm going to last?"

"It'll pass soon," he said, though he had no idea. All morning he'd been wishing the winds away so the next day would be placid and sunny—a good day, a safe day for a swim.

"I have a bad feeling," Ciyi said, and he could see it was the truth. Something in him softened. He climbed out of bed and crouched next to the lone armchair.

"Min is good." He placed his hand on her stomach. "Minmin. The heavens will protect a child of the people." It was the kind of declaration Ciyi liked to hear.

# 10

The storm had strewn the beach with torn branches and stinking kelp. The sea was a murky greenish color. Lu Fang didn't care. It only mattered that she'd kept her word. Sloan waved to him from the water, and he raised a hand in response. Once damp, her hair was a darker yellow, almost brown. He undressed and folded his work clothes with extreme care, taking his time, his breathing shallow.

Anyone could see them and say, Who is that man with the foreign girl? Isn't that Lu Fang, the shipyard clerk?

No, he was not that important. He wasn't at all important.

"I felt like a caged animal after that typhoon," she said when he reached her. The navy straps of her swimsuit and her freckled shoulders bobbed above the water. "I stayed in my room and read books and banged on the walls so my idiot hallmates—they're British—would keep their record player down. How was your weekend?"

"Oh," he said. He didn't really understand the question. "I did not have work. I stayed home."

"I'm so rude for not having asked yet. What do you do?"

"I do . . . business," he said. He planted his feet on the ocean floor and swung his arms back and forth in the water. "International business," he added.

"Where do you live in the city?"

"By Hexi District." It was an industrial zone, workers' compounds. She would never have a reason to visit. "Close to the old refrigerator factory."

Sloan was squinting at the sun above Lao Mountain. "Maybe we could go steal one," she said. "There's only one refrigerator in our whole dorm building."

"Good idea," Lu Fang said. His panic was slowly receding, his eyes growing accustomed to the glare on the water, looking at her and past her at the same time. "I could use one too."

She raised her eyebrows and he thought, Kao. *An international businessman would own a refrigerator.* But she only asked, "What do you do with your food?"

"I . . . buy it fresh every day, make something simple." He was removing Ciyi from his domestic picture—why didn't he mention her? Then it'd be in the open. Yet he was enjoying being a person with unknown contours.

"What swimming style do you know?" he asked.

"Only the breaststroke. I want to learn how you swim. The crawl. What do you call it in Chinese? Freedom style?"

"The freedom swim."

He ignored the soft, distorted curves of her torso disappearing into the ocean. "You do freedom swim this way," he said. He extended one arm and leaned sideways into the water. He could feel his bicep tensing. With his other arm, he mimicked a wave. "Then you come down, like this."

Sloan followed his gestures, frowning with concentration. He swam a few strokes forward. She tried, but couldn't stay afloat long. "Again," Lu Fang said. "Like scissors."

"You're"—she was coughing up water—"too tough of a teacher."

"Again," he repeated. "Breathing will become instinctual."

She disappeared into the water and made a show of emerging, forehead up, hair slicked back. He followed after her, so at ease that he flipped into a backstroke. The clouds were wispy. Glugs of waves crashed against his ears. Still, he was careful not to steer too close, not to brush against her. They swam in perfect parallel for some time.

On the bus ride back into town Sloan was talking about pools again. "We had a small round one in our yard, just enough to soak in."

A house, a yard, a pool, a car. With what disdain would she judge his apartment if she ever set foot there? There were black stains on the ceiling, a squat toilet they flushed with a water bucket. Ciyi tore out color images from newspapers and taped them to the walls: city skylines, landscapes. Advertisements for electronics and medicine. A fashion ad with a foreign couple in low-waisted jeans, embracing, their upper halves naked—not something that struck Ciyi, surprisingly, as dirty. They were so foreign they might as well be alien, a different species, a decorative component in a collage of random images. Lu Fang, for his part, had hung a single picture he found in a used bookstore downtown: a print of a Chevrolet. It was next to the sink mirror, and he looked at it every morning when he shaved.

"My dad saved up to buy that pool after I complained about all my friends having one," Sloan said. "Still, I never swam in it. It was above-ground, and I was ashamed."

She shivered. Her clothes were damp and the bus windows were open, letting the night air gush in.

"You must miss them," Lu Fang said. "Your parents." It occurred to him that he'd never said the same to his own wife, whose hometown was also thousands of miles away. His wife, who hadn't crossed an ocean, and yet also spoke Mandarin with an accent. He put her out of his mind.

"When are you going home?" he asked.

"I may never go back." Sloan said it like a child making a petulant threat.

"Why not? Are you a runaway? A bank robber, like Bonnie and Clyde?"

She giggled. "How do you know Bonnie and Clyde?"

"I watched many American movies when I was in university."

"I loved movies growing up. I wanted to be a movie star, but my mother said I wasn't pretty enough."

"Oh," he said. "But you are."

"Here in China I am." She smiled deflectively, and he was embarrassed to realize she could have construed his comment as an advance. The words had rushed out of his lips.

The bus jerked to a stop, and she was up. "Thanks, Coach. See you again."

"See you again." He nodded.

After Sloan got off, Lu Fang immediately put his hand on the plastic seat where she'd been sitting. It was still warm and slightly damp. He smelled his hand. He couldn't help himself. He was at once amazed the past few hours had occurred at all and also left with a terrible solitude, like not nearly enough had transpired.


The next day, he logged inventory of cargo containers for the shipping company. The merchandise was Tsingtao Beer. Over to southern Chinese ports, some to Korea. The Japanese didn't care for it.

Lu Fang's colleague, Qi, traveled to Incheon twice a year. Qi was younger than Lu Fang, and he had a university degree from Dalian Maritime Academy. After every trip, he returned with jars of kimchi, rice cakes, and porno magazines he loaned to the other men on the floor.

Once, Lu Fang asked his manager if there was room for another employee to join on the trip.

"Do you speak Korean? Or English?" the manager asked.

"I can speak . . . a little English." Lu Fang said.

"Xiao Qi is a university graduate," the manager said simply. He clasped his hand on Lu Fang's back paternally. "You do a good job where you are. Learning to be content—that is wealth in itself."

The sentence had the gravity and wisdom of an ancient proverb, except it wasn't one. But Lu Fang understood that unless he could produce a forged degree or an adequate bribe, he would have to make himself happy with indefinite days of number-crunching as a lowly clerk.

Unlike Xiao Qi or the students at Dali Beach singing the Beatles, Lu Fang had never completed an education, never become the pride of his hometown. His ambitions had been snuffed out, his path redrawn with such banality, one of millions with such stories. But this was a new era. Ports were busy once again, cargo containers filled with traveling goods. On the wall by his desk, he'd hung a map of the company's shipping routes. He traced his fingers along the pale ocean lanes, as fine as veins on porcelain skin.

When Sloan missed their lesson for the next two days, Lu Fang could no longer swim his usual route, toward the ocean's heart. He was afraid he wouldn't see her arrive. Instead he patrolled the length of the coast, close to shore. The waves here were, in fact, more turbulent.

On Thursday, finally, he found her waiting on the rocks. She was drinking beer from a green Tsingtao bottle. Once they were in the water, he found that she'd regressed in her form. "Did you forget everything already?" he asked.

He tried to demonstrate the nestling of the skull.

She said, "It'd be much easier if you could correct me directly."

He approached her cautiously, circling his fingers around her wrists. She bent in the direction he willed. To help her stay afloat, he held his hand under her abdomen, where it met the bottom of her rib cage. He felt the slippery material of her swimsuit and, underneath, hard muscle. He held her aloft with one hand and didn't dare move. He felt the rhythm of her heart against his palm, her white shoulder blades cresting the water, her damp blond hair spreading loose and grazing his forearm. Then she flutter-kicked and was off.

## 11

To Ciyi, everything outside was a danger: the heat, an irregularity in the road, a germ she might inhale. Inside the apartment, Lu Fang was becoming increasingly suspect; he brought in impurities from the outside world. His swimsuit might carry rare ocean bacteria, his breath smelled like nicotine, he was coming home later; and for what reason, pray tell, was he getting off a bus line he'd never used before? One of the courtyard matrons had seen him.

"You need fresh air," he told her. "You used to laugh at those gossipy hags. Now they're what—your informants? Your best friends?"

"I have no friends," Ciyi said. "My friends are in Chuanxi."

She walked down the three flights of stairs on the condition that he held her closely, lest she slipped. Outside she wouldn't release his arm. They had to stop every other step because Ciyi would strike up a conversation with an idle neighbor and discuss her due date.

"It's next month," she told Auntie Wu. "I can feel every turn, every kick, and they're strong!"

"He'll be a CEO!" the aunties said. "He'll be a movie star! Look at his handsome father. Look at his beautiful mother."

As they shuffled along the residential compound, Ciyi said, "Did you hear? Beautiful. That's not a word you've ever called me."

And because it was true, Lu Fang felt an odd pang of guilt. He'd never thought of Ciyi as beautiful, though maybe she was. In the village she'd been considered pretty, but here in the city no one gave her a second look—her skin was too dark and ruddy compared to the city taitais whose houses she cleaned. Once a taitai had given Ciyi an expired tube of whitening lotion that had burned Ciyi's skin and made it peel. She didn't grow any whiter.

He stroked Ciyi's arm. "It's because it needs no saying."

She snorted, leaned more of her weight on him.

They walked past factory barracks and the wet market until they reached the shoddy district school. Children were screaming like monkeys in a jungle, kicking up clouds in the dirt schoolyard.

"This is where our child will go to school," Ciyi said.

"I hope not," Lu Fang said. "By then we'll be in a better apartment, in a better district. Our child will get the best education around." He believed in his words and felt emotional about his vision. "That is the only way out."

He contemplated the educations of both women currently on his mind. In an offhand discussion of her Chinese classes, Sloan had referred to the great poet Su Shi as "sushi," as in Japanese for raw fish on rice. But at least she knew who he was. Ciyi had never properly studied anything. Yet he had always liked the kind of childlike practicality with which she saw the world, the way she intuited human emotions. Now it made Lu Fang nervous. He knew she had sensed a shift within him. He could see it on her face each night as she chewed and stared at him from across the table, open-mouthed, eyes narrowed, fondling her jade pendant.

Presently, Ciyi said, "A Fang, I don't mind our apartment or our district. We are already so far away from where we started. My parents would be proud."

But he could hear the nostalgia in her voice. He heard it in the voices of all the migrants who'd come to the coast, carrying their old sorrows, crowding the streets like ghosts.

After his third swimming lesson with Sloan, she invited Lu Fang to a bierhaus in the old German district, not far from St. Michael's Cathedral.

He said yes and tried to not read into it: Americans liked going to bars. The menu was written on a chalkboard in both Chinese and English. Most customers here were men Lu Fang's age, some with the gold-wire glasses businessmen wore to keep up with the Hong Kong trends.

Sloan ordered them big pints full of something amber-colored, thankfully not Tsingtao. "He brews it himself," she told Lu Fang, pointing to the barman. The barman looked to be in his midfifties, a Chinese man in a funny, loose shirt, with long hair past his ears. In some ways, he didn't look Chinese at all. "Jim used to live in Europe and came back a few years ago, after the reform," Sloan said.

Lu Fang took a sip of his beer. It was bitter, thick. Not unpleasant, a bit like medicine, but not revolting like cow milk. The word *Jim* reminded him of the name he once had, for a year when he was seventeen— Alexander. Why was this man allowed to be a Jim? Instantly, he felt a strong dislike toward him.

"Women here don't really drink alcohol, do they?" Sloan said.

"It's not seen well here," Lu Fang said.

"I don't care about not being seen well." Sloan tossed her yellow hair over her shoulder. It was voluminous from the salt, uncombed.

"With you, it's different," Lu Fang said.

She sighed with satisfaction, like he'd paid her a compliment. The beer seeped through his empty stomach, and he felt like a younger, different person, although his youth had never included beer or flirtations. "There's something I wanted to ask you about America," he said. "Did you have a car?"

She squinted in mock suspicion. "That's what you wanted to ask?"

"I thought everybody had one there."

"My parents had one. I never had my own."

"But you know how to drive?"

"Yes."

"Maybe one day, in exchange for the swimming lessons, you'll teach me."

She sighed, and immediately Lu Fang felt foolish for asking. She drained her beer and turned toward the bar, holding up two fingers to

Jim. Then she faced Lu Fang again, slowly, but she was smiling. "In exchange, huh? I suppose that's better than what most people want in exchange."

Lu Fang hoped his face wasn't splotchy, like so often when he drank. "What do they want?"

"You know. They think foreigners are loose."

Lu Fang coughed up his beer. Sloan continued, "Or that I can get them abroad. Like it's that easy. Like that's all I'm good for."

For the next minute they sipped their beers quietly. He tried not to look at the freckles on her pale chest. If he were young with an open future like the university students at Dali Beach, he might be one of those men who asked her too. It was hard to be next to her and not think about it. Wasn't that exactly what Sloan had done, leaving America to see what was outside? "What would your parents say if you brought home a Chinese man?" he asked.

"They would say nothing. They died a long time ago. In a car crash."

"Oh." Lu Fang felt his shoulders hunch, his bravado evaporate. "I'm sorry."

"I was a teenager when it happened. They didn't leave me with much. I moved to L.A.," Sloan said without blinking. "I started auditioning. No one was there to tell me I couldn't. I got small parts for years. Then I was cast for this movie, a big production about Indochina."

Lu Fang wanted to reach across the table and take her hand. "I'm sorry," he said again. "About your parents."

"The movie never came out," she continued. "Studio disagreements. I liked Southeast Asia, but it was too fraught—unexploded bombs from the war, all that. I wanted to go somewhere Westerners hadn't yet touched."

"I'm not sure it's untouched here," Lu Fang said. They were sitting in the historical colonial district in a city known for its German breweries.

"No, I know, the spheres of influence, all that. But that was before. The new China, I mean. It's so . . . different, unspoiled, authentic. That's how I decided. I enrolled in a Chinese language class. It took *months* to apply for a teacher's visa, an eternity, but—"

"Months," Lu Fang repeated. That hardly seemed like an eternity. "Was it a hard visa to get?"

"Not really." She lowered her voice. "I lied and said I was enrolled at a university in California, and the agency handling the visa didn't ask too many questions. They said many Chinese universities were hungry for foreign teachers."

"And now you're here."

"Yes. And I like it. America feels small in comparison."

The frosted glass had left condensation on their table. Lu Fang dipped his finger into the water and traced a 口 on the table. It was an old habit. He drew himself into the square: 囚. He felt sorry for her, for her dead parents, for the aborted movie. But how could America be too small? How could it be so easy for her to come to China, and not for him to get out? Lu Fang realized he was drunk.

"And you?" She leaned in. "Why do you swim so far every day?"

He wasn't sure what she was asking, but he could see the top of her cleavage bulging from her T-shirt. He closed his eyes so he wouldn't stare.

"To see how far I can get away," he said.

"Get away from what?"

He drank his beer. This was a question he could not answer. Not here, not out loud, not with her. Not even with himself.

She pushed. "You don't like it here?"

"It's not that," he said. He thought about her question. He did love the green hills that gave the city its name, the smell of roasted yams in the northern winter, the shores of the Yellow Sea at dusk, the roaring laughter at comedy performances at old teahouses, the poems traded on drunken nights with his colleagues. These were the very small pleasures woven into the fabric of his memories, but they did not make a life when his life could have been so much bigger.

Sloan was studying him. "You have this—reservation about you," she said. "Like you want to be careful. Careful about not crossing a line. And, look, I appreciate it. But in the end I know nothing about you."

"There's not much to know," he said. She was looking at him eagerly, an eagerness he wanted to reciprocate, so he tried. "I was born by the North Korean border, across the strait from here. My dad was a soldier and my mother a nurse. I have a younger brother. I only see my mother and brother during Spring Festival. I studied economics at Renmin University." And of course he couldn't go on.

"How old are you?"

"Thirty-six," he said. "I was born in 1949, the year the People's Republic was founded. I'm as old as the new China. I must seem ancient to you."

She leaned forward, lowering her voice. "Being as old as the new China is *amazing*. So you experienced the Great Leap Forward and the Cultural Revolution? Were you sent to the countryside? Did you ever see . . . something bad?"

With his own eyes, Lu Fang had witnessed three killings. The first was the shooting of the defector in the Yalu River, when he was a boy. The second was his mother mixing the crushed powder into his father's bowl, when his father was so sick all his limbs were engorged logs. The third was the beating of a crops thief in Chuanxi, ordered by Ciyi's father, the party secretary. No doubt this listing was exactly what Sloan was awaiting, her gaze fixated hungrily on his face. Americans were so open. They held back nothing, wanted you to do the same. It would please her if he told her these stories. But when he tried to arrange the words in his head, he felt only shame about his desire to forget. He had witnessed, but also closed his eyes and kept moving. That was the only way forward.

He shook his head. "Nothing to speak of."

Lu Fang knew it was late. Outside the windows, night had fully fallen. It was past ten, and Ciyi would resent him for each passing minute. Lu Fang thought about his son—separated from the world only by bodily fluid and membrane, resisting his official entry into the squalid existence his parents shared. Sloan was dancing by herself in a small open area near the bar. All the men were staring at her. But it was to Lu Fang that she returned at the end of the song. She cupped her hand around his ear and said, "Let's go."

He handed Jim the only large bill in his wallet and told him to keep the change. They ascended the stairs to the street, where there was the scent of something filthy, old urine intermingling with kitchen fumes. Sloan said, "Let's go to a massage parlor."

He didn't want to leave her yet. He thought of the Chinese word for future: 未来, that which hasn't arrived. They wandered down the streets trying to find a sauna or a parlor. Lu Fang knew these were the kinds of places some of his colleagues went, popular after-drinking spots that operated twenty-four hours a day.

"This one," Sloan said, pointing at a large, cubical building with neon signs advertising FOOT THERAPY MASSAGE SAUNA STEAMROOM.

She told the receptionist they wanted foot massages. They were taken to a dim private room with two reclining massage chairs. Across from the chairs, on a traditional redwood table, was a bulky television. They each reclined in their chairs and waited.

Two masseuses came in, one a pretty young woman with severe eyes, the other a dark and lanky teenager. The teenager sat on the stool in front of Lu Fang. The severe girl turned on the television and chose a channel with an old Hong Kong soap. The actors' voices were shrill and exaggerated, the music a mix of plaintive Chinese instruments. The masseuses poured hot water into buckets. Lu Fang thought of the footbaths Ciyi took to relieve her swollen ankles. The girl massaging Sloan asked if the pressure level was to her liking. Lu Fang noticed the masseuse had a small lily tattoo on her wrist. The teenager repeated the other masseuse's question to Lu Fang, in the exact same wording, her accent from Heilongjiang Province, he guessed, and he said yes, it was fine.

The girls started washing their feet, the teenager a few beats behind the other girl, obviously an apprentice. They kneaded their soles, dug into their arches, pulled on each of their toes until they cracked. Not once did they speak to each other. The soap entered its end-of-episode score. Lu Fang was asleep but not asleep. The teenager's hands kneaded into his calf muscles, which were tight and unused to probing. On the reclining chair beside him, Sloan's eyes were closed. The girls moved so they could massage their thighs, using their thumbs and index fingers like pincers.

They did this for a while until the girl with the lily tattoo spoke for the second time. She whispered, "Additional?" The teenager was looking at Lu Fang in terror. He turned toward Sloan. Her eyes were still closed. She looked both asleep and completely, molecularly awake. She nodded. "And you?" the older girl turned toward him. He shook his head. The teenager tried to neutralize her expression, but he could see immense relief, even though she was in near darkness, backlit by the television. The older girl motioned for the teenager to keep massaging his legs. She took the edges of Sloan's skirt and pulled it upward. Underneath Sloan was wearing the same navy swimsuit. The girl held the elastic fabric aside with one hand, revealing Sloan's pubic mound. The girl started stroking down its length, opening its pink lips. Lu Fang's masseuse was watching as well, her own movements faltering. The girl's lily tattoo kissed the mound rhythmically as the girl's fingers worked their way inside, disappearing into the now slick, swollen flesh. Sloan's eyes were closed, but her muscles were tense. Everyone was quiet, the only sounds the soap opera's murmurs. Then Sloan quivered, and her hand flailed across the gap between them and grabbed Lu Fang's arm. Her eyes were open now, looking straight up at the ceiling. "Okay?" the masseuse asked, and Sloan nodded again. The masseuse cleaned her hands on a towel and resumed massaging Sloan's legs. He caught the dark-skinned teenager looking at him, smiling strangely, the halo of light behind her stretching and receding as another episode played on the old television.

After the two girls left, Sloan remained in her chair. Lu Fang knew it was already too late. "Open your eyes," he said. His entire body was burning. "Take off your swimsuit."

She wriggled it down, and her breasts were as firm and white, her stomach as pale and flat as he'd imagined. He took off his own clothes. She lay on the reclining chair, scanning first his erection, then his face, goose bumps on her breasts. She shivered, watching him watch her. And then her lips stretched into a defiant smile, like a dare.

"Get on your hands and knees," he said, his voice taking on a foreign authority, and he recognized it as the one he used during her swimming lessons.

She did. His hands were shaking as they clutched her hips. He entered her this way, standing. They both shuddered while he thrust, and he held on to her hair like it was a bridle of gold.

For the past twelve years, Lu Fang had been a man of his word. He'd made a promise to the Chuanxi Communist party secretary, father of Li Ciyi, concerning the well-being of his daughter. In exchange, approval was exceptionally stamped onto Lu Fang's Certificate of Discharge. Lu Fang wanted to be a businessman, and businessmen made deals.

On his walk home from the massage parlor, Lu Fang was assaulted by an acute wave of nausea. Sloan had flagged a taxi and waved him goodbye like an old friend. Were they lovers now, he and Sloan? If so, she loved a rich, successful international businessman, not a poor, uneducated clerk with a pregnant wife. He chased the thought away, focusing instead on the memory of the dim massage parlor, the fever amid the misery. He imagined her going back to America at the semester's end, asking him to go with her. He could see himself at seventeen again, a boy holding a thick English dictionary in a dim university hallway, tracing the curve of an O, studying the atlas's shades of blue and green. A boy who'd taken a long train ride from a border town, who was a student in the nation's capital, who dreamed of one day occupying a glass-walled office and delivering commands in perfect dignified English, of having a fast car and driving as far as he wanted to, where no one told him to be content.

He was nearing home now, and sobering. No doubt Ciyi was waiting for him. He'd say Xiao Qi dragged him out and got him drunk. He'd say he swam too far and lost sight of Dali Beach, and then, and then—

Even before he unlocked his apartment door, he sensed that someone was pacing on the other side, ready to leap at him. It was Auntie Wang, their downstairs neighbor. "Lu Fang!" she yelped. "They took her away at dusk. We called your office and they said you were gone. Oh, where were you, we were going mad! Get to the hospital—"

He stood looking at her, dazed. "She . . . she had the baby?" he asked.

"There are complications," Auntie Wang said. "I don't know anything else."

"It's not time yet," he repeated. "It's not—"

"Go!" The old woman slapped his arm. "Don't just stand here. Go now!"

He stumbled back down the stairs. She stood on the landing, muttering, "The heavens are watching."

PART III

SHANGHAI, 2007

## 12

From the car window, Alva could still see the red dot of Lu Fang's ciga-rette on the balcony. Without it, she wouldn't be able to discern his dark silhouette amid the tight slabs of the apartment tower. The boys in the car were shouting at her.

"She got in!" Doggy screamed, his nose quivering like a snout.

"Just drive," Alva said, leaning forward. Teng Xin blinked in the driv-er's seat and slammed on the gas pedal. The car lurched toward the com-pound gates. Throughout the commotion Gao Xiaofan had remained slumped across the back seat.

"What do you want?" Teng Xin craned his neck toward her.

"You were loud. People were watching. Someone could have called the security guards."

"We're not afraid of motherfucking guards," Doggy said. "Right, Teng Ge?"

Ge was the honorific title for "big brother." Doggy was a grayhound-like boy with crooked teeth who rarely left Teng's side.

Gao moaned and opened his eyes. "What's happening?" he asked, pasty-mouthed.

"The laowai's joining the ride," Teng Xin said.

The compound's salmon-colored buildings receded in the rearview mirror. Was Lu Fang still up there on the balcony? Would he rush down, call a taxi, chase their car? Parents didn't let their teenage daugh-ters disappear into the night. Only now did Alva consider the possible consequences of her escape—he'd shake Sloan awake, and maybe her mother would panic, call the authorities. Alva would be in a lot of trouble. It was a prickly, dangerous feeling. She'd never been in real trouble before. But now she would be like these boys, fearless.

"You know about HentaiLord?" she asked.

The two boys up front exchanged a glance. "Why, you like his links?" Doggy asked.

"They were okay," Alva said.

Doggy hollered and slapped the dashboard. "So you did read them!"

Teng Xin smirked. "Laowai girls are open-minded, Doggy."

There was a jittery mood in the car, something unkind beneath their snickers. Alva didn't like how they called her laowai. They're drunk, she told herself. She wanted to be drunk herself.

"HentaiLord did a brave thing," Gao Xiaofan said. "He stirred things up."

Alva repressed a smile. Gao played it so cool on QQ, but the Smiling and Proud Wanderer stood up for HentaiLord when it mattered.

"He's an idiot," Teng Xin said.

"But maybe he won't get caught," Alva said, tilting as they turned a corner, her thigh grazing Gao's. No one was wearing their seat belts.

"He wants to get caught," Teng Xin said. "It's a matter of time."

They rode along Century Park until they pulled up to a compound called Luxury Beautiful Dynasty. Teng Xin took off his uniform jacket, underneath which he wore a white tank. His arms were thick and muscular, probably toned at the Will's Private Gym Club they'd passed.

They descended into a subterranean parking lot and Teng pulled into a reserved space. Alva exhaled with relief when her feet touched solid ground. Teng Xin was the first person she knew to actually own a car. It was strange and nonfunctional to have your own vehicle in this city, where subway lines were as dense as spider veins and taxis were cheap. The sole purpose of owning a car was, seemingly, to own a car. To drive it around Century Park, fifteen and rich.

Gao Xiaofan leaned against the wall and swayed lightly as they waited for the elevator. Nobody was telling Alva to leave anymore, so she followed them.

"I hope the maid went home," Teng Xin said. "She's a snitch, a stupid countryside cow. I could bribe her to keep her mouth shut, but my dad already counterbribed her more."

It clicked in Alva's mind that Teng's father was the owner of a restaurant chain, leagues wealthier than Lu Fang, and Doggy's mother was rumored to be a starlet on mainland sitcoms. People at Mincai were secretly rich like that, except for anomalies like Gao Xiaofan and Alva, though it could be said that her situation had changed now.

The apartment was enormous, with floor-to-ceiling bay windows overlooking the dark forest of Century Park. The living room was dominated by a flat-screen TV, a sleek console system, and a modern leather couch. The imitation wood on the floor was milky white. "My parents don't live here," Teng said. "They bought the apartment just for me."

"Where are they?" Alva asked.

"Shuttling between Taipei and Shenzhen. We have restaurants all over."

He pulled out a pack of cigarettes and held one between his lips. He didn't offer to share any. Gao started walking toward the Xbox, and Teng said, "Fire." Gao came back and fiddled out a plastic lighter, which he brought to Teng Xin's dangling Marlboro. He jerked the wheel three times before the flame caught.

"Brother, you really need to get a better lighter." Teng laughed, exhaling a plume of smoke. Gao didn't respond and turned back to the Xbox. Doggy slumped on the couch. Alva lowered herself onto a large footrest. For a few moments nobody said anything. There was only the sound of footsteps on crunchy leaves, Gao Xiaofan's avatar running through a ghostly forest. Then Doggy asked, "Teng Ge, do you have Sprite or Fanta? My mouth is so fucking dry."

"In the fridge," Teng said. "Bring us all some."

He stretched his arms around the couch ledge, eyes resting on Alva.

"The Homework Delegate," Teng said.

Alva shifted, crossed her legs to look relaxed. She was still wearing the sheer silky top. Doggy returned holding a bottle of Sprite.

"Drink with us, and we'll be among friends."

"Fine," Alva said. She wasn't afraid of alcohol. In her controlled experiment with the Ballantine's whiskey yesterday, she'd handled herself perfectly.

Doggy poured the Sprite into three plastic cups. When Alva took a sip, her tongue burned with a searing, greasy spirit, maybe rum. Gao's avatar fell off an edge with an electronic gurgle of dissolution. Without skipping a beat he hit the play button again.

The rum burned down Alva's insides. She wouldn't drink too quickly. In Shanghainese bars, the girls always lapped like kittens. A performed, measured, titillating drunkenness: slightly flushed cheeks, watery eyes, increased touchiness. The opposite of Sloan on her bad nights, when she hiccuped and burped and stumbled. Alva didn't want to be like that—a sad, sloppy drunk like her mother. She'd remain in control. Maybe she could go sit next to Gao. His sinewy muscular arms were on full display in a sleeveless Chicago Bulls jersey.

"*Ganbei*," Teng said, and he and Doggy threw their heads back and drained their cups, Adam's apples bobbing. Teng finished first and wiped his mouth. "What's wrong?" he asked Alva, eyeing her cup. "You don't like the taste?"

A guest could not disrespect the host. So she closed her eyes and drank until the cup was empty. When she opened them again, Teng was smiling and stroking a small Siamese kitten in his lap.

"It's your cat?" she asked.

"Are you scared, kitty-kitty?" Teng lifted the kitten by the neck. It let out a little meow.

Doggy refilled their three cups to the brim. "Have you seen that cat torture video?" he said.

She knew the one they were referring to—a pretty woman had put on her highest heels and filmed herself trampling a kitten to death. It was everywhere on the Chinese internet. Teng was shaking the Siamese kitten and speaking to it in a baby voice. "We wouldn't want that to happen to you, would we?"

Alva wasn't sure if this was one of their inside jokes. Gao remained mum, shooting at enemies in the video game. Teng set the kitten down and it darted from the room in a panicked flash. Then he leaned back against the couch, twirling his cigarette. "Everyone in class knows you've got your eye on Gao Xiaofan, Homework Delegate," he said. "But did you know his father is a line cook at Undersea Emporium in Thumb Plaza?"

Alva's cheeks were burning. "No," Alva said. Thankfully Gao was still completely absorbed in the video game.

"And do you know who owns the Undersea Emporium?"

"No."

"My father."

"Oh."

Teng traced a line between him and Gao with his cigarette. "My father wanted to reward his father. For being a good . . . worker. So my father pulled strings to let Gao Xiaofan into Mincai, even if he's a migrant. And told me to take good care of him, like a little brother. Isn't that right, little Gao?"

"Yes, Teng Ge." This time Gao's response was immediate, shot out of tight teeth.

"That's right," Teng said. "So if someone wants to take a bite of my little Gao, they pass through me first."

Alva shifted in her seat. She tried laughing. "I don't want to take a bite."

"Product inspection." Teng turned to Doggy slowly. "Doggy. B, C, or D, you figure?"

"Hmm," Doggy said. "I'd say C."

Another inside joke, Alva thought. Then she realized they were staring at her chest. "Really?" Teng said. "I don't know. I heard the American average was at least a double-D."

"Ha ha," she said and hugged her arms around her sheer top.

Teng leaned in toward Alva, propping his elbows on his knees. "Is it true? About the American average?"

"I don't know. I've never been there."

Doggy laughed shrilly. "What kind of laowai are you?"

"I've been there five times," Teng said. "For vacation. New York, L.A.,

Houston, Miami, Sun Valley, Idaho. I know it well. Americans act like they own the world, but show them a nice wad of crisp cash. They'll be eating out of your hand."

Doggy snorted emphatically.

"But they don't respect us," Teng continued. "You see it in their eyes. They think they're better than us, right as they put on their fake smiles and take our Chinese money."

Doggy cracked his knuckles and pushed a refilled cup of Sprite toward Alva. Every time she took a sip, he topped her off.

"What do you think of that, laowai?" Teng asked.

"My dad's Chinese. You don't have to call me laowai."

"But your mom's a laowai," Teng said. "I've seen her." He brought his hands to his chest like he was clutching melons. "That's where you get it from."

Doggy and Teng were laughing again, and Gao stared mutely at the screen. Alva was infuriated by their dumb laugh. "I was born here. We live here. I'm not a laowai."

"But your nationality?"

It was American, there was no denying it. Alva once overheard Sloan tell a "friend" on the phone that no, she never considered getting her daughter Chinese nationality. It was better not to box oneself in, no?

"I have a residency permit," Alva said.

Doggy snorted again. "There you go," Teng said. "Not Chinese. Why don't you go back where you came from?"

"I didn't choose to be in your country," Alva said.

She didn't know why she said your country, not our. Or just: China. Teng narrowed his eyes.

"What are you doing, then, in our country, if it's so bad?" he asked.

"I didn't say it was bad," Alva said.

But Teng continued as if he hadn't heard her. "So many of you here now. You think you can just walk into my home. And climb into my car. You know who else gets into a car like that? Whores my father picks up on street corners. You think you're one of us because you go to our school, wear our uniform?"

Alva tried to stand, but before she could, Teng reached across the table and clenched his hand around her shoulder, pressing her back down. His thumb dug into the ridge below her collarbone, beneath the tank top's hemline, where the soft flesh of her chest began. Doggy laughed like a hyena. Alva felt the hot prickle of tears, which she absolutely could not let fall, and looked toward Gao Xiaofan. He had paused the game and was staring at them, blinking like he'd only just realized she wasn't an apparition. Alva hoped he remembered all the times she erased the X from the homework tracking sheet. "RESUME PLAYING?" the TV screen asked.

"Teng Ge, I think this remote is broken," Gao said.

Teng let go of Alva's shoulder and waved his hand like he was shooing a fly. "That's impossible," he said. "The set is brand-new."

Doggy pushed Alva's Sprite cup farther toward her. "Keep up," he said jovially.

She hoped the maid was still here, somewhere. There was a bowl of fruit on the dining room table, apples, pears, and oranges too saturated and round to be real.

"Teng Ge," Gao called out again.

"We're busy here," Teng said. "Doggy, see what's going on with our friend Gao's console. It was very expensive, much more than what he could repay."

"Xbox, American brand," Doggy winked at Alva. He took the remote from Gao's hands. "It's working fine. Come on, Teng Ge, we'll play a game."

Teng was still staring at Alva. He licked his teeth, then moved toward the Xbox. Gao Xiaofan walked over and hunched over the table, fidgeting with the Sprite and a plastic cup. "Rich brats," he said under his breath.

Alva rubbed the spot beneath her collarbone. "Why are you with them?" she whispered.

He didn't answer. They both looked toward the console, where Teng and Doggy had started playing. Gao's Chicago Bulls jersey was red, the synthetic fabric shiny and cheap. But the prized Nikes on his feet were, as always, immaculate. The other two boys wore similar shoes, though their models were newer. It's always money, Alva thought.

"You should go," Gao said. "This one is for the homework passes." Then he turned and said loudly, "Teng, count me in."

He had forgotten to say ge. Teng took a giant gulp of Sprite and set his cup down with a thump. The liquid fizzed on the floor. Doggy cracked his knuckles again. "You want to play?" Teng said. He waved Gao over. "Then we'll play."

Doggy stood cross-armed behind the two players. Alva stayed on the footrest, not yet daring to move. Gao's avatar was a ninja and Teng's a hirsute Viking. The ninja and the Viking zoomed around in a cacophony of *cling*s and *clang*s and *bzzzot*s and *whoosh*es while Teng and Gao sat immobile save for their fingers, which moved like the legs of a tarantula. The ninja was blown to pieces. "Tough," Doggy said, and Gao merely said, "Again." Like a moth to fire the ninja ran at the Viking and was blown to pieces on the roof, blown to pieces in the mines, blown to pieces in the tavern. None of the boys were speaking, and Alva realized this was her exit, that Teng wouldn't torment her when absorbed in this systematic, iterated destruction of Gao. She got up quietly.

They weren't looking at her. The gunfire from the console intensified. Somewhere from the guts of the apartment came a feeble meow. Doggy's lean frame was dark against the window. She was almost at the door when Gao's ninja avatar jumped from a ledge and unleashed a torrent of deafening shots. Teng's Viking blinked once, twice, then faded to nothingness.

"Uh-oh," Teng Xin said.

That was the last thing Alva heard before closing the door behind her. Then she ran for the elevator.

There was almost no traffic on this Sunday night, only the blue glare of TV screens blinking from high-rises. The icy air burned Alva's lungs. She ran down the track along Century Park, all the way back toward the north-side compounds, until she was at the gates of Heavenly Peace. She folded over, hands on knees, every breath a gasp.

She'd never been more aware of her skin, her breasts, of an emptiness rising from her abdomen. Why had she run? Had she really been in any danger?

She reached the base of her building. It was past midnight, and blackness engulfed the grid of windows. Her own eighth-floor apartment was dark. And then she saw it again. A glowing red dot on the balcony.

Alva dashed into the building and pushed the elevator button. So Lu Fang was waiting. She readied herself for a commotion. Once she was outside the apartment door she put her ear against it—silence. No panicked voices, no Sloan. He had waited alone.

She tiptoed inside. Maybe he wouldn't talk to her, would let her slip back to her room, a disgruntled landlord keeping tabs on an ill-behaved tenant. He intercepted her in the living room. She couldn't read his expression; it wasn't fury as she'd feared. His eyes simply scanned her from head to toe, evaluating for defects, and she felt dirtier than ever, her body damaged from the assumptions of what had been done to it.

"Nothing happened," she said. "We just played video games."

"A strange hour for video games," Lu Fang said.

She didn't answer.

"The legal driving age in this country is eighteen."

"I can't drive!" She threw her hands over her head. "The boy who owned the Mercedes—he drove."

"If you want to live here," Lu Fang said slowly, "you cannot break laws."

"If I want to live here?" Alva stared at him. Was this a fatherly chastising? She nearly giggled. "I don't want to live here. I told you what I wanted."

There were goose bumps on her arms, the apartment once again too cold. Its furniture too spare, the surrounding towers closing in, claustrophobic. "I was happy before you came," she said.

Lu Fang didn't respond. He was looking at something beyond her head. Alva turned around and saw her. Sloan was standing at the threshold of the living room, barefoot, in a nightdress, contemplating Alva with wide, inexpressive eyes.

"Your daughter is drunk," Lu Fang said.

"Mom doesn't mind, right?" Alva said. "She knows *drunk*." It was cruel, even if it felt good to say it. All those years of the yellow beer gurgling down her mother's throat, of yeasty breath, of acrid bathrooms. Lu Fang knew nothing about it.

"Sloan," Lu Fang said. "Say something."

Finally her mother spoke. "This is miserable."

And in her stricken face Alva saw that it was true, this was miserable. Her mother turned around and disappeared down the hallway. Lu Fang sighed heavily and went after her, leaving Alva alone once again.

Strangely, she felt like the victory was hers. Across the black treetops of Century Park, there was a little kitten on the sixteenth floor. That world was an edge of Shanghai's infinite edges, and she'd found it. Maybe these edges had been what her mother was on the hunt for all these years. Alva knew it now. When Sloan would come home late at night, turn on the shower, and stand underneath it, water so hot steam spilled out from the crack under the door like a spirit exorcised. The shower's pitter-patter resembling steady rain, an unchanging rhythm, as if Sloan was standing very, very still. It was the stillness of someone who'd just traveled to the edge and back.

# 13

Alva's alarm blared at 6:30 A.M. Monday morning meant school, even if her temples clenched from last night's rum. In the opposite building, room after room lit up among a thousand slots, glowing in the morning fog. Except it wasn't fog. The news blamed the warm spell for the floating dust particles—but no CCTV anchor would ever utter the word *pollution*. So they called it smog.

She tied the red kerchief around her collar, looping the synthetic silk in a movement ingrained in muscle memory, and walked the few short blocks to school.

When Alva sat down at her desk, Li Xinwei immediately came over.

"I heard a strange rumor. You went to Teng Xin's apartment."

Alva considered denial, but Li Xinwei wasn't asking a question. "I didn't know you knew him," Li Xinwei said.

Alva straightened her kerchief. "Who told you?"

"Yu Chentian from class Nine (6) heard from one of Teng Xin's friends that their hangout was crashed by this—well, they used a mean word. I won't repeat it, but it's a synonym of prostitute. I couldn't figure out who they were talking about for the longest time." Li Xinwei's eyebrows rose in a cruel, innocent arc. "Then I realized it was you."

Alva clutched the homework tracking notepad, a grid of names and dates, checkmarks and Xs. Alva was the master of that grid, the pettiest of rule enforcers in a party apparatus with power divided, subdivided, and sub-subdivided. She started her rounds, with Li Xinwei following close behind her. "It's not a good idea to mix with those students. They are delinquents. Teng, Doggy, Gao Xiaofan. Do you know he's the worst of them?" She lowered her voice. "He's completely addicted to gaming, and maybe worse. Like, drugs worse."

"A good citizen does not spread rumors," Alva said.

"Yeah? Then where is he now?"

Alva had been avoiding the back corner of the classroom, and now saw that Gao's desk sat empty. Teng Xin and Doggy were there, though, throwing paper shreds at each other. They sniggered when Alva came over.

"Homework," she said coolly.

"Look who it is," Teng Xin's eyes widened in mock surprise. "The face of authority and discipline."

"Oh no," Doggy falsettoed. "Are we in trouble?"

"If you don't hand it in, I'll mark it as late," Alva said. She could feel Li Xinwei watching the exchange. Alva lowered her voice. "What are you telling people about me?"

"Why, you scared of them knowing the truth?" Teng Xin said. "I just said you invited yourself to my house. Laowai chicks are *sao*—you don't know the concept of shame."

A slow fury crept into Alva's chest. Sao was what the neighborhood ayis had called her mother—offering herself up, shameless. A word hissed on the street when Sloan's neckline scooped below the Y crevasse of her breasts.

"Where's Gao Xiaofan?" she asked, trying to sound calm.

Teng Xin shrugged. Alva marked big thick Xs next to his and Doggy's names, but she knew they did not care. She couldn't even take revenge with her bottom-rung bureaucratic powers. Li Xinwei's voice rang out from the front of the classroom, "It's morning calisthenics time," and they all lined up outside in the hall.

Alva let herself be folded into the human flow. Out on the field, they stood in a sea of uniforms, spread along a grid of equidistant dots. Altogether, they launched into jumping jacks to the rhythm of classical music and commands of "one, two, three, four" broadcast by the loudspeakers.

There was safety in numbers. Here no one would point at her and say she's a sao laowai or ignore her for having a too-Chinese face. She was one small player within a mass movement. She wouldn't be singled out unless she waved her limbs too wanly, a beat out of sync, enough to create a glitch in the disciplinary patroller's field of vision.

When Ms. Song came in and told the boys to draw down the shades, it was clear today was the day. They all knew of the Nanjing Massacre as the greatest atrocity of the past century; the cruelest and most shameful war crime, the great butchering TV pundits, newspapers, political speeches, and movies never failed to invoke when it came to WWII. They all knew its horror was unspeakable, and that was precisely why there was a mix of jitters and apprehension as they neared the Nanjing Massacre chapter in history class. Everybody had already flipped to those pages in the textbook to see the photos.

Ms. Song didn't say anything that whole hour; she only clicked through the pictures on the projector. The images were black and white and grainy. It took a few seconds to understand what was blood or guts or severed body parts. There were mothers with their bellies sliced open. There were dead, premature fetuses. There were mass graves, piles of naked bodies. Sobs erupted across the classroom. They had thought they wanted to see, but this was too much. Even the boys had tears streaming down their faces. Alva's stomach clenched, like she was going to throw up. Then Ms. Song turned off the projector, and everybody looked around, stunned. "Fucking devils," someone said.

Two years ago, crowds had gathered in Shanghai's city center and burned Japanese cars to protest a new edition of textbooks in Japan denying war crimes. Alva hated them too—those in Japan who humiliated China, who worshipped at shrines of war criminals, who claimed the evidence they'd all just seen didn't exist. The Chinese part of her, from what her mother called a squirt of sperm, hated them. And she'd never known this kind of hatred before, not against her mother during their biggest fights, not even against Lu Fang when he invaded their lives. This was hatred that stemmed from the craziest kind of love—love for your country. She felt it trapped in her heaving chest and she knew that she, too, would carry this collective memory, no matter what boys like Teng Xin said.

And then they had a double-math period, and it was like history class had never happened. People blew their noses and went to the bathroom and the math teacher strolled in with a stack of practice problems. Alva tried to catch Li Xinwei's eye but her friend was staring straight ahead at the blackboard, breath still shaky, ready to attack the day's work.

When Gao Xiaofan finally showed at school that day, it was close to noon. His face was badly bruised, with a black eye and a torn lip.

"Maybe his father beat him up again," Li Xinwei said, materializing next to Alva's desk. "It's happened before. After he caught Gao Xiaofan on one of his cybercafe binges."

"Maybe," Alva said. She noticed that Teng Xin and Doggy weren't talking to Gao Xiaofan, weren't even looking at him.

"He shouldn't have come to school," Li Xinwei said. "His injuries are distracting the other students. I don't know why he bothers at this point. He doesn't belong here."

"Because he's from Gansu?" Alva asked, more sharply than she'd intended.

"Because every spot is precious," Li Xinwei said. "They shouldn't be wasted on people who don't want them."

When Alva asked Gao for his homework booklet, he stared at her and said nothing. She wanted to ask about his injuries. Not here, though, not with Teng Xin a few rows back. She added a checkmark next to Gao's name on the homework booklet and showed it to him. His swollen eye twitched, almost like a wink.

After school Li Xinwei and Alva walked home together. Li Xinwei said she had to hurry to a secret marathon cram camp in Xuhui, one that taught participants to game a perfect TOEFL score. "Don't tell anybody," Li Xinwei said. "My dad would kill me if he knew I babbled. He doesn't want my competitors to copy my extracurricular classes."

"I won't tell," Alva said.

"My dad thinks you're not going to take the high school entrance exam anyways," Li Xinwei ventured, kicking a plastic wrapper. They were passing the corner with the overcrowded FamilyMart and the DVD vendor, except the man was now sitting in the back of a white minivan full of flowers.

"Pssst, girls," he hissed.

"You sell flowers now?" Alva asked.

The man produced a stack of cardboard-wrapped DVDs from behind two pots of hydrangeas. "They're cracking down so I had to adapt. I have something you'd like." His fingers fluttered expertly along the stack, until he pried one away and handed it to Alva. The cover had a white-faced person in Beijing Opera makeup. The English title read *Farewell My Concubine*. "Banned in China," the man said.

"How much?" Alva asked.

"Usually ten. But for an old customer, eight."

Alva paid for the movie under Li Xinwei's disapproving gaze. "Your mother lets you watch anything," she said. "But you didn't answer. Are you taking it?"

"Taking what?"

"The high school entrance exam."

"Why wouldn't I?"

Li Xinwei stopped walking. "I thought maybe you'd found other options."

"Other options?"

"Your stepdad won't pay for international school?"

"No," Alva said grimly.

Li Xinwei's face grew wan. Alva imagined her reporting these answers back to her father, him annotating a thick dossier. She looked away from Li Xinwei's captain badge, the three red stripes on her bicep. How proud Li Xinwei must feel when she pins that badge on her uniform each morning. Sure, everyone wore a red Communist Young Pioneer kerchief, but that was merely part of the uniform. Three stripes was the real deal. It was *leadership*. It came with school officials' trust, with oaths and a test on Mao Zedong Thought. "Do you believe in that stuff?" Alva had asked Li Xinwei the previous semester when she was memorizing lines from a book of Mao quotes. Li Xinwei had shrugged. "I guess. I mean, it's all theory. None of it has anything to do with our lives." But now Li Xinwei was glowering, and it had everything to do with their lives.

"Why do you care so much?" Alva said. "If I take that exam. Or if I spend time with problem students. You can choose not to see."

"I care because I'm supposed to report it," Li Xinwei said. "And I don't, because I'm your friend. You don't even realize what you are doing. Only *you* can post a bunch of porn online and act like you've done everyone a favor, then say you did it because you were bored with practice exams. Only *you* can run off with delinquents and come in the next morning complaining that being Homework Delegate is a chore. And it's all because you have an American mom."

"What does my mom have to do with it?"

"Because you *are* a laowai, Alva. You can leave anytime you want. That makes you *entirely* different from me, from the rest of us!"

Li Xinwei had never called her a laowai to her face before. Alva said, "But you're leaving too. You always talk about Oxbridge—"

"*If* they—or any school in their country—take me. If my scores are high enough. If my English is not too accented for them. If I get the visa. If my dad gets a loan to pay for international tuition. And it's all just so that I can get a degree and come back, and be slightly more competitive in the job market."

"You never said you'd come back."

Li Xinwei sneered. "My family is here. I want to see what's outside, but Shanghai is my home."

"It's my home too," Alva said.

"It's not *home* for you the way it is for me, Alva. People like you and your mom, you can *choose* to make Shanghai your home. It's all tempo-rary, and when you tire of it you can take off. If you decide to leave Mincai tomorrow, you can, and I'll still be here." Something was distorting Li Xinwei's voice. She turned away before it broke completely. "I have to get to my TOEFL class."

Once more Alva turned right toward Garden of Heavenly Peace, and Li Xinwei left toward Age of Romance. Alva trudged home in a rage, speeding by FamilyMart. It hurt, what Li Xinwei said about home. What else could Shanghai be, when it was the only city Alva had ever known? She thought of all the times she and Li Xinwei had run the rubber tracks of Century Park at night to prepare for a PE fitness test, or taken the subway to Wenmiao's weekend temple fairs to buy glitter gel pens and shengjian pork buns, crispy-bottomed and glistening with oil. Li Xinwei lived in a gargantuan residential tower pushing skyward, like Alva did. They'd pestered the neighborhood ayis at the compound party office to get their community service stamp together, they'd gone to ComicCons and gawked at the cosplay costumes together. She used to think of Li Xinwei as her one best friend, a fellow trenchmate, and she wanted to say it was the stress of the looming zhongkao that was spoiling everything, but she also hated the truth in what Li Xinwei had spoken. She remembered the giggles of the three American girls squeezed into one stall at H&M, how close and intimate their bodies were, their lazy gossip. She bet that at the American school, exams didn't ruin friendships.

In the empty apartment, Alva watched *Farewell My Concubine* before the adults got home. The movie was about two young men in an opera troupe. She didn't understand why the vendor had suggested it for her. She always told him she wanted more American movies, and last time he'd given her *Eyes Wide Shut*. She'd read about its strange non sequitur scenes and something called alienation effect, which reminded audiences they were watching something fake. She'd offhandedly mentioned it to the man, saying she wanted more like it, but this was not it. In *Farewell My Concubine*, the beautiful, effeminate opera singer was played by Hong Kong actor Leslie Cheung. His eyes were so sad, his features so fine, his reckless love so convincing. Alva felt the prickle of tears at the end, when

Cheung's character slits his throat with the same motion he'd performed countless times onstage as Yu Concubine. Then she reminded herself: it wasn't real.

This was a banned movie, but there was no sex, no nudity. Everything was implied, horrible things the camera cut away from—the young singer's sexual abuse by an older patron, a ghoulish eunuch chasing the boy around a room. Was that unshown sex like the wet, violent mess of naked bodies in the *Naruto* hentai? It felt dirty, like the sao she was accused of being for climbing into Teng's car, for having her mother's breasts.

Naked bodies didn't always need to be sao. When she was small, her mother used to take her to public baths, complexes where you paid a few yuan for a plastic bracelet and a rusting locker key. There were mazes of wet floors and clapping slippers. Alva still remembered the naked women in the shower room, women with shiny scars slashed along their bellies, round bruises covering their backs, stretch marks like weeping willows down their thighs, women who touched her mother's hair, a matted brown-yellow when wet. They scrubbed Sloan's back with rough towels and periodically, with a flick, discharged shards of skin that flowed with the small rivers on the floor toward a drain, everyone's skin merging into the same gray clumps, all swallowed by the same hungry, frothing mouth.

In the bathroom mirror, Alva stripped to her underwear and examined herself for stretch marks. She was expanding, taking up more space. Soon, this body would no longer contain her. Her body too sao for Chinese school, but surely not skinny enough for American school. Half-and-half, but *entirely* different from the rest of *us*, as Li Xinwei had said.

She heard keys turning, then Sloan's and Lu Fang's muffled voices outside the bathroom. Alva quickly threw on her uniform tracksuit. There were footsteps, then silence. She could feel her mother's presence on the other side of the bathroom door.

Finally Sloan's voice came through, "Come out. We need to talk. About what you said to Lu Fang."

✦ ✦ ✦

"You tried to make a *deal* with him? By asking him to pay for *international* school?" Sloan was pacing Alva's bedroom. Alva sat on her pink alphabet bedspread, counting the ABCDs. At least this was happening in the privacy of her room, while Lu Fang was out in the living room watching a movie on high volume, some American "big Hollywood" flick with the *whack-whack-whack* of helicopters and secret agents in stupid sunglasses. He hadn't even glanced at Alva when she'd walked by, a stripe of his flabby midriff exposed as he reclined on the couch.

"You told him I had *many friends*? Alva!" Her mother smacked her own temple. "Have you lost your mind?"

"But isn't it true?" Alva said. "He thought you two were in love. I mean, that's cruel. If you let him believe that."

Her mother stopped pacing. "What do you know about it?"

"He can make our lives comfortable. That's what you said. And do you know what his guests were saying at the wedding? That you're good for business. Maybe you two don't care about using each other. But him saying *love* . . . that grosses me out, and him trying to be my father? That makes me sick."

"Oh, Alva." Sloan sat down on the bed, inches from Alva, though they didn't touch. "I know you don't need a father. But I thought this would be good for you. Some stability."

"Good for me? Just me?"

"Everything I do is for you."

" Do you still teach English lessons?"

"That was never a real job—"

"Yes or no."

"No," Sloan said. "I don't teach anymore. I help with Lu Fang's company."

"As an international consultant? That has a nice ring to it, Mom."

Her mother's mouth disappeared into a line. Finally, she said, "Every paycheck I earned for the past fifteen years went toward housing and feeding you, Alva."

"And something else."

"What?"

"Maybe you could've held down a real job if you'd bought less beer."

She might as well have slapped her mother. Sloan's jaw hung open, the pigments in her cheeks turned red, and then she pointed at the door.

"If all I've done for you means nothing, then go. Don't live here. Find your own place to stay."

Alva couldn't tell if her mother was bluffing. Maybe she meant it. Maybe she did want Alva to leave. After all, Sloan had run away to L.A. when she was a teenager. Sloan had fended for herself.

Alva stood up. "Fine," she said. "I'm going."

Before she could deflate, she grabbed her schoolbag and stormed out the bedroom door. Her mother rose slowly and followed her. Passing by Lu Fang on the couch, Alva spat out "Happy now?" and he looked at her, bewildered.

"Where are you going?" he said.

"Let her go," Sloan said. "She wants to run off all night with boys from her class? She wants to find another apartment to wreck? Let her see what it's like to not have a home."

Alva let the apartment door slam behind her, shutting out her mother's words. She wanted to kick something, punch something, a super-charged mix of fury and exhilaration. She could officially be an outcast now—Teng Xin and the problem crew didn't take her seriously, Li Xinwei secretly hated her guts, her own mother had chosen a strange man with money over her. She'd never had a single room, a single apartment that was really her own, so what did it matter if she was exiled from Lu Fang's? She'd find somewhere else to spend the night.

Walking into the darkness of Garden of Heavenly Peace, she took a mental inventory of the crumpled bills in her wallet. Not enough for a room at the Motel 168 across the street. She could hardly show up at Age of Romance and knock on Li Xinwei's door. She thought of Teng Xin and the Siamese kitten across the park, but even the idea made her shudder. FamilyMart was open twenty-four hours, though it was un-likely they'd let her sit all night at one of their fluorescent-lit tables.

God, she was stupid for not thinking of it sooner: of course. Gao Xiaofan and his notorious cybercafe binges. That was why Gao Xiaofan always showed up to class with dark circles under his eyes. The twenty-four-hour cybercafe on the seedier edge of Century Park, where he was rumored to spend his nights. That was the place for Chinese teenagers who didn't have anywhere else to go.

Alva would find him there. They were alike, there was no doubt in her mind. Outsiders. All right, he was a migrant, and she had an American passport, but he'd stood up for her that night at Teng Xin's—and he admired HentaiLord. In the cyberworld they were both glorious rebels, final bosses. And in the real world she, like him, needed a place to spend the night for cheap.

# 14

A taped sign on the door warned UNDER 18 STRICTLY PROHIBITED, but the place was milling with minors still in their school uniforms. An obese man shelled a stack of sunflower seeds at the front desk.

"Hourly or all-night, girl?"

Alva scanned the room. There were so many teenage boys, their black hair tamed down by the cybercafe's massive headsets. Then she caught sight of the familiar Chicago Bulls jersey. "Girl, hourly or all-night?" the man repeated.

"How much's all night?"

"Fifteen yuan."

She gasped at how cheap it was. The man returned five salt-coated one-yuan coins. "Pick any monitor," he said. "Except for the back row. That's mature-only."

The man waved her off, and she made her way toward Gao Xiaofan. His fingers fluttered along the clunky keyboard like those of a mad pianist. She tapped Gao's arm and he jerked violently on his swivel chair.

"What the fuck? What are you doing here?"

"My mom kicked me out," she said, sinking into the chair next to his.

His left eye was still swollen with a purply-red bruise. His right eye looked her up and down. "Homework Delegate," he said. "How you've fallen."

Alva pushed the on button of her CPU. A film of grease covered her mouse. The crevasses of the keyboard were filled with cigarette ashes, crumbs, grime. "What happened to your eye?" she asked.

He shrugged. "A fight."

"Teng Xin and Doggy?"

He shrugged again.

"It was nice of you," she said. "Helping me with Teng Xin."

"You should be more careful," Gao said. "Following around that kind of guy."

Alva flushed and pretended to be distracted by the worn, soft leather of the headset. "I didn't know. I don't like *him*. That's not why I got into the car."

She wanted Gao to ask why she'd jumped into that Mercedes. But she didn't even know if he'd heard her, because he had already plugged back into the video game.

She watched him play. The ninja, the pixelated man, the present gun barrel—that was the world Gao lived in, more than the one made of bones and tissue and muscles and flesh. When he finished the round, she tapped him again.

"How many nights have you been here?"

"It's my eleventh."

She tried not to seem alarmed, to scan the room again just to make sure it was possible to live in its stuffy confine. Eleven nights! Could *she* spend eleven nights here? Some of the patrons were literal children, straight out of elementary school. Many crowded around the best players, chirping directions. Their prepubescent voices lilting, merging like birdsong into the pitter-patter of keys, the pulling of aluminum tabs and fizzing of soft drinks, the hoarse cacophony of *fuckfuckfuck* and *gogogogogo*s sputtered by the older players.

"Do you ever sleep?" she asked.

"Sleep is for school," Gao said.

Alva laughed. "Zhongkao practice is the best sleep medicine."

Gao Xiaofan leaned back against his swivel chair. "My parents think that after Mincai I'll go to a tech school and become an IT guy. They don't know I'm flunking."

"You probably don't need tech school to become an IT guy." Alva gestured at the myriad windows open on his screen.

He smiled. "You want to see what I *really* want to do?"

"Sure."

He clicked on a new tab, pulled up a forum called CityX, and pressed play on a video. The shaky camera panned around a top-down view of an industrial cityscape. Voices spoke in a harsh foreign tongue. Then the video zoomed in on a pair of legs, standing on the ledge of the tower. One foot lifted, wiggled over the city. Trees like dots, gray roads like streams, cranes of construction sites like silhouettes of prehistoric birds.

"Rooftopping," Gao Xiaofan said. "They're doing it in Russia. And it's starting in Shanghai."

Alva didn't like it at all, the reckless flaunting of the height, the implication of the hovering feet. "It's not real footage," she said.

"It's real," Gao said. "Have you ever been on the roof of a skyscraper?"

"No."

"Neither have I. But I want to. When you're up there, you must be the baddest motherfucker in the city. You *own* it."

They heard a loud sigh. In the next row, a boy clutched a giant Sprite bottle to his crotch, guiding the stream of his urine in with one hand while his other kept playing the game. Gao Xiaofan winked at Alva and stood up. "I'll use the bathroom." Alva sank back in her seat. She didn't want to watch the rooftopping video still playing on his screen.

Minutes later, Gao returned with a spring in his step. He sniffed loudly. "Better now," he said, and Alva remembered what Li Xinwei had said about the drug rumors. It could be true. It was midnight, and the fuel of the cybercafe all-nighter was becoming clear to her. An entire separate economy existed within these walls, sugar and leaves and crystals, commodities of awakeness. There was a line of boys outside the bathroom.

"You *own* it," Gao repeated, like no time had passed at all. "And it doesn't matter that it's illegal. Up there, on top of the skyscrapers, rules and laws don't exist. It doesn't matter if you're in Russia or China. There's only one rule: slip and you die. Once you let go of fear, once you hover over the drop, that's when you're completely, utterly free."

The fat man by the entrance was dozing off. Gao was leaning into her. There were possibilities in the darkness. He was so close that she could contemplate the enormity of his pupils.

"Do you ever think of leaving China?" Alva asked.

His eyelids peeled open. His enormous pupils took her in.

"Leaving China?" he said. "Let's see. For people like me, there are no study abroad packages. No visas. How would I do it? I've heard the stories. Travel south, to Fujian and Guangdong. Get on a small boat crammed full of people. And if the boat makes it far out enough, get onto a bigger boat with other illegals from Vietnam, Philippines, Bangladesh. And if this boat is able to cross the Pacific without sinking—and they sink all the time—dock in Mexico. And survive the heat, the exhaustion, until we're in the Great America, and scatter off, but then what? Live like cockroaches, if we haven't managed to die a million deaths in between. No thank you. I prefer to die in my own country."

Asking him that question had been sheer stupidity. She felt cold, despite the droning AC sputtering warm air so dry it made her lips crack. Soon the glow of daybreak would come through the front door. She took in the stink of the place: cigarette smoke, meat fumes and caffeinated burps, and urine and the sweat of sixty people stewing in the same room. The stink of collective, electronic freedom. Gao Xiaofan, with whatever he took in the bathroom still coursing through him, had turned away from her, watching yet another rooftopping video, shaky cameras and howling winds and feet on the tiny ladder of a TV tower high above a city. She rubbed her eyes.

"I think I need some fresh air," she said.

"Go home, Homework Delegate." Gao swiveled back toward her. "Go to school. This isn't for you."

She shook her head. "Stop saying that. I hate being Homework Delegate. I hate Mincai."

"Then do something." He was leaning close again, his face inches from hers. He smelled of sweat, but his was a scent she liked. "Then blow it wide open."

"How?" she asked.

"What are you afraid to lose?"

"Nothing," she said.

"Then I dare you. You're a laowai. Play the card the rest of us cannot."

The QQ chatbox was on the bottom right corner of his screen, the Smiling and Proud Wanderer next to a glowing green dot, HentaiLord top among his chats. He knew her more than he realized. Slowly, Alva nodded. "See you in school," she said, rising from her chair.

Gao didn't answer. His eyes were almost closed, only a line of white, staring down at the rooftop view of the metropolis on his screen.

Alva walked back toward Heavenly Peace as the pale sun rose behind the smog. The wide streets were empty save for a thin stream of cars, soon to be thickened with the mopeds of the earliest commuters.

Inside the apartment, Lu Fang and Sloan were both at the living room table. Within seconds, her mother's face morphed from worry to a cold, distant anger. Lu Fang, ready for work in a crumpled shirt, was the first to speak.

"You're back."

"Of course she's back," Sloan said.

He put a hand on her forearm, pressed gently but firmly. Sloan looked down.

"It's almost time for school," Lu Fang said.

Alva gave him what she knew was a demented smile. "I would never be late," she said. He and Sloan exchanged a glance, though neither said anything further. No one wanted to disturb the equilibrium of this pretend family. The only comfort Alva took was in their waxy, tired faces, betraying that they'd slept little or not at all.

She showered, pulled on a clean uniform, fluffed her red kerchief into a billowing dash of red. She ate a bowl of Special K with Guangming milk, as she always did, and walked back out the door at 7 A.M., as she always did. Collected the homework, saluted the flag, performed the calisthenics, as she always did.

History class that morning was on the eruption of the Chinese Civil War. The smog outside the windows made it feel as if their classroom was floating in a cloud as Ms. Song launched into a dramatic reading of their textbook: "The Nationalists had only one goal: to decimate the Communists. Chairman Mao knew he faced a battle for China's soul"— and here Ms. Song's voice quivered an octave higher—"Whether China would be rebuilt into a new democracy led by the proletariat class, or whether it remained a half-colonial half-feudal state."

Alva yawned. The quote from Mao Zedong that Ms. Song had written on the board swam like squiggly tadpoles:

*We will build China into an independent, free, democratic, unified, and prosperous new country.*

—Mao Zedong, April 24, 1945

A large pop came from the corner of the classroom, and Alva turned to see Teng Xin blowing a giant bubble. Ms. Song ignored the disturbance and continued, "The Nationalists shamelessly tore up the peace agreement and attacked the Communists. Jiang Jieshi's troops were flown by *American aircrafts* to the front lines of the civil war."

Alva felt a few eyes on her, a collective reflex whenever the word *American* was mentioned, and she sat very still. This was her chance. Ms. Song went on, "The Nationalists were equipped with the latest military technology provided by *Americans*, while the Communist Party only had millet and rifles. Despite the stark inequality of this fight, we all know the outcome—"

"Did they really *only* have millet and rifles?"

Alva had posed the question out loud, and every head in the classroom swiveled in her direction. Ms. Song lowered the textbook. "What?"

Alva drew a deep breath. "I mean, is that a fact? Or is that a myth? Like how the Japanese were defeated *only* because of the Communist Party's relentless courage. Is that a fact?"

Two rows away, Li Xinwei rolled her eyes. But the other students were watching Alva with great interest now. "The laowai is going ballistic!" Alva heard someone whisper.

"Quiet!" Ms. Song barked.

"Doesn't it bother you?" Alva stilled the quiver in her voice and spoke louder. The *trouble* she was getting herself in! After years of silent eye rolls through CCP drivel, this was the moment when the heroine makes an impassioned speech. "What are you doing?" Li Xinwei hissed.

"No one here feels like this textbook is insulting our intellects? No one here . . ."

Most of her classmates' faces had morphed from entertainment to annoyance. They scoffed, perhaps because only a laowai would think of making a ridiculous, self-righteous scene about the half-truths they were fed. Ms. Song was now telling two male class delegates, "Take her outside." When Alva tried to catch Li Xinwei's eye, her friend looked away, as if Alva's disgrace was contagious. In the back corner of the room, a slight smile crept onto Gao Xiaofan's lips. He was the one who'd dared her: *blow things wide open.* There was only one thing left to do. The two delegates were advancing toward her. Alva closed her eyes.

"Don't touch me!" she said. "I am HentaiLord!"

There was a silence, most classmates merely sitting in shock, then some girls started whispering and laughing. Ms. Song shouted, "Quiet! Quiet!" The two male delegates were upon Alva now, pulling her toward the classroom door. "I am HentaiLord!" she repeated, louder. She wished the classroom would erupt, people would rise from their desks, spill into the hallway, and chant "HentaiLord! HentaiLord!" after her. Instead, there were only low mutterings, "It's her." "It's a girl." "Of course it's the laowai."

"Order!!" Ms. Song shouted, and the classroom fell silent again.

With the two delegates iron-clawed on her sides, Alva made her way toward the exit. No one was meeting her gaze. Alva knew there was no turning back. She was out; this could only mean expulsion. As she was led down the hallway, she heard Ms. Song start again, in a shrill falsetto, "In 1945, the Chinese Nationalist Party . . ." And Alva knew that in most ways that mattered, nothing would change. But she *had* blown things wide open—for herself.

## 15

You got expelled," Lu Fang repeated.

Before they came home, Alva had been sitting on the couch, rereading the QQ message she'd gotten from Smiling and Proud Wanderer: *HentaiLord, you did it. The freedom of letting go.* It was a small comfort, this word: *freedom.* It almost made her smile. But when she heard the apartment door's lock turn, she tried to make herself cry.

"They said I incited unrest." She blinked innocently. "When all I did was ask a question in history class!"

"I cannot believe you," Sloan said. She sat cross-armed in the chair by the banyan. "You know better. You did it on purpose. They said you were circulating corrupt materials online? Disseminating Western pornography to fellow students?"

"It was Japanese," Alva said.

"It's not funny. Not funny at all." Sloan was fiddling with a bracelet on her wrist, an emerald-green chain of peacock stone. Alva had never seen it before. "You sabotaged yourself out of the most decent school in the district. Now what?"

Alva worked on making her face mournful, resolute. "I didn't sabotage myself. I got tired of sitting through all this hero worship the party passes as facts. I don't know why I'm going through it in the first place."

That hit a nerve. Red splotches creeped onto her mother's cheeks. "You think I could afford something other than public school all these years? Even if it has its quirks, it built your character. Though now I don't know what kind of character it built."

"You can say things like 'quirks' because you didn't have to go through it," Alva said. "Remember when you used to tell me to ignore 'all the silliness' in my textbooks? It's not silly when all we learn in history class is how foreigners are set on humiliating China. Hearing that day in, day out, does it make you think, *I'm* the foreigner."

Sloan's nostrils flared. "Oh, Alva. That's a load of bullshit. Those kids always welcomed you."

Lu Fang turned to Alva, cracking his knuckles, his fingers swollen from too many banquets. "I imagine that next, you'll say you want to go to international school."

"No child of mine is going to one of those rich expat schools," Sloan said.

Now she was proffering the perfect opening. Alva had come prepared. She pulled out her passport and set it on the table. "I am an American citizen," she said. "I have a right to those schools. I demand safe haven there."

Sloan howled. "Safe haven? You think it's an embassy?"

"It's my right to attend," Alva said. "If I'm going to be in America one day, when I turn eighteen. It never made sense for me to go through the zhongkao or gaokao. International school—that's where kids like me go. I just need the funding to do it." She looked meaningfully at Lu Fang.

"There's no 'right to' anything," Sloan said. "You never understood a thing about America. And you are fourteen. You're not going anywhere without me." She stood and whipped her blond hair behind her shoulder. Alva wanted to follow her down the hall, curl against her, and say, *Don't you get it, this way, we both get what we want.* But Lu Fang was still sitting there. Lu Fang who could make it happen.

He was staring at the blue passport. "It was a very stupid thing you did," he said.

She hated the way he was leaning slightly backward, as if trying to peer into her. Not with urgency or concern, but with an eerie detachment. She reached for her passport, pulled it into the safety of her lap.

"I've looked at all the transfer papers. If you're willing to pay, I only need a parent's signature."

"A parent's?"

She winced, remembering her bratty proclamations—"I don't need a father." But her mother would never sign this paper. She thought of Li Xinwei's father, the folders he kept and how he spared no expenses for his daughter's education. She needed Lu Fang to play the part.

"A guardian's signature, then," she said.

His gaze drifted to the shoe rack, where Alva's sneakers leaned against Lu Fang's own pair of Nikes. Maybe he was imagining her standing at the threshold, ready to leave.

"Did you know that I never graduated from university?" Lu Fang reached for his pack of Double Red Happiness. "I went to school in the late sixties. Just in time for the 文革. Bad luck, eh?"

"I didn't know," Alva said in a small voice. She knew he was older, but she'd never thought to do the math. People always referred to the Cultural Revolution in passing. She knew some intellectuals and poets had committed suicide during that era, that *someone* had done something wrong, but the unit on it in history was very short. It boiled down to: mistakes were made, let's focus on the good.

"One day you're in a classroom, the next you're not," Lu Fang said. "The future you thought you had—gone. Do you know the feeling of not having a choice?"

He sighed deeply. Alva thought back to all the glossy ads in *That's Shanghai* and *City Weekend*, the green lawns and multiracial children in lab coats, the giggling girls in the H&M stall. They seemed like a mirage, one dissipating as Lu Fang spoke. She knew what he'd say next—that she'd sabotaged herself and didn't deserve any of it.

"And that's why I'll talk to your mother," Lu Fang said.

Alva nearly dropped her passport from shock. He continued, "Forcing you to stay where you have no desire to be . . . it'll corrode you, make you compromise yourself until you are nothing but a cutout of regrets. You'll only be thinking about the choices you were denied. That's the reason I'm helping you. Let this be the last time you compromise yourself."

She knew that she should nod, emphatically, repentantly. He sighed again. "What is the name of this place you want so badly?"

"The Shanghai American School," she said.

He nodded. "Okay."

She squirmed in her seat. "You'll really pay for it?"

"I really will." He slumped back in his chair and lit a Double Red Happiness. "This is not a reward," he said. "So don't smile like that." He waved his cigarette in a vague crescent motion. When she left him he was still swaying his fingers left and right, unconscious of the ash falling on the table, gaze lost in the direction of the shoe rack, the door.

The red neckerchief, unwashed for days, curled and blackened at its edges. Alva caught Ms. Song staring. She nudged the transfer papers forward.

"Ten thousand yuan, and an expulsion becomes a transfer," Ms. Song susurrated. "You have a nice stepfather, don't you?"

Her hand hovered above a dotted line, withholding a stamp wetted with red ink, making Alva wait. Then it came down with a thud, the school's official approval, Alva's liberation. She took off her red neckerchief, balled it in her fist.

"Where are you off to now?" Ms. Song blinked at Alva, chewing on a bloated sterculia flower from her thermos. "Somewhere to wash that dirty brain of yours, I hope."

"I'm going to international school," Alva said. She folded the transfer documents. The red ink had bled through the recyclable paper. "They teach actual history there."

Ms. Song took a minuscule sip of tea, her motion calm, though her eyes took on a hard glint. "You think foreign textbooks are the authorities of 'actual' history? I choose to teach children to respect themselves as citizens of China, even when the rest of the world does not."

The red stamp and transfer papers separated them. Alva leaned backward, emboldened. "Teacher Song, do you believe what you teach?"

Ms. Song screwed back the lids of her thermos. She spoke softly, not looking at Alva. "You are so confident that what you know is the truth. Don't be so sure of yourself, Alva. What do you know of the world?"

With that, Ms. Song waved her hand, her final dismissal.

For one last time Alva exited the school gates of Mincai Experimental. The midafternoon streets of Pudong were eerily quiet. Alva moved slowly toward Lu Fang's apartment, where her mother would come home later that night, pull out a beer, and slam the fridge door. Sloan was mad about the American school, though she'd agreed to it after Lu Fang spoke to her in hushed tones for hours. Alva didn't know how he convinced her to relent. But it was only fair. Only fair that Alva would get as close as she could to the America inside of China. Sloan had always spoken so highly of reinvention, of being whoever one wanted to become. That's what Alva would do now, on her own terms.

The familiar white van was parked on the street corner, the DVD man hauling a heavy rubber plant onto the sidewalk. He didn't betray any surprise at seeing Alva out at this truant hour.

"Want some new movies, girl?"

For the first time she took in his caved-in cheeks, missing teeth, hair buzzed short to stubble. She stopped in front of the van's green interior, breathed in the scent of a hundred plants. "Why did you recommend that movie last time—*Farewell My Concubine?*"

The man scratched his head. "You said you liked the alienation effect, no?"

"But it was a Chinese movie."

"Damn right." The man cackled, turned his head to spit a loogie into one of the potted plants. "Girl, I've watched a thousand movies a year for the past decade. I know a thing or two about film. The guy who came up with this alienation business, the German, first wrote about it after watching Beijing Opera. And guess which opera?" He squatted in front of a bush of peace lilies, pulled out a stash of DVDs, tapped his yellow nail on Leslie Cheung's painted face.

"*Farewell My Concubine*," Alva said.

The man nodded. "The Chinese invented the alienation effect. You know you're putting on a show, but you still get lost in it. Sometimes too lost. Like the actor who plays the Yu Concubine in this movie and ended up dead."

"In the movie," Alva said.

The man stared at her blankly. "No, girl. In real life. You haven't heard what happened to Leslie Cheung?"

Alva shook her head.

The man sighed. "It can be dangerous to lose yourself to fantasies, girl," he said, and leaned back into the van's foliage.

# PART IV

# LU FANG

QINGDAO, 1985

## 16

Stumbling down the spare corridors of the Qingdao hospital, Lu Fang scanned the floor for suspicious stains, blood, or body fluids. It could only be bad news. Auntie Wang had said she didn't know what was wrong with Ciyi, that she may be giving birth early. Much too early. As he approached the nurses' station he tried to steady his footing. That was the kind of man he'd become: a drunk father holding his premature baby after returning from an adulterous night. Or perhaps he'd be holding no baby at all.

"Your wife is healthy." The night nurse handed him a clipboard to sign. "We set her up in a temporary cot."

"So it was nothing?" Lu Fang scribbled a hasty signature.

"Maybe she experienced false contractions, and they stopped by the time she arrived." The nurse pursed her lips.

"There's no baby then."

The nurse halted their advance down the hallway. Her nostrils flared as if she could smell the alcohol and cheap incense on Lu Fang. "Your wife said her husband wasn't home. She had to come here by herself."

"I was at a late-night shift at work," Lu Fang said.

"The hospital is not a place of play," the nurse said. She stood in front of a poster with the slogan: *Lovable farmers are the backbone of our nation.* "Tell your wife she shouldn't come for the slightest irregularity next time. Countryfolk don't realize we have more serious business to take care of here."

He wanted to say, Countryfolk business is never serious to you. But instead he nodded. "I'll make sure to tell her."

When Lu Fang entered the room, Ciyi yanked the sheet off her still-enormous stomach and slid her legs toward the ground.

"My colleagues—" he began.

"We aren't going to speak about it," she said, not looking at him. "Help me up."

He did, and she clutched her stomach when her feet hit the floor. "My shoes," she said. He got on his knees and lowered his face to the filthy floor to reach the pair of canvas slippers.

"There's nothing to *not* speak about," he said, stuffing her swollen feet into the shoes. "My colleagues and I went out for a drink and got carried away. You know Xiao Qi and his love for erguotou."

"No, I don't know Xiao Qi and his love for erguotou," she said.

"What did they say about the baby?"

"Does Xiao Qi want to know so he can plan his next drinking session?"

"I'm sorry," he said softly.

In the taxi home, Lu Fang took Ciyi's hand and massaged her knuckles. She was so helpless, always awaiting his arrival from work, relying on him for most things. So he was surprised when, before they stepped back into their apartment, Ciyi said, "I had Auntie Wang call my parents last night. My mother is going to make the trip from Yunnan to come help me."

"From Yunnan?" he repeated. The party secretary's wife was one of the last people he wanted in his house. "We talked about this—my mother can come from Dandong. It's much closer. And she was a nurse."

"I prefer my own mother, thank you," Ciyi said. A furious red wetness crept into her eyes. He'd been waiting for the tears. She must have been imagining all kinds of scenarios for his absence tonight, lurid stories like the serialized radio programs she loved, popular tales of depravity and deceit, in which justice was always served, and wronged simpletons prevailed over the cunning of the universe.

"Of course," he said. "Just as well."

"And don't get in bed until you wash off," she said. "You stink like sour milk."

## 17

He needed to tell Sloan that once was enough before things took on a momentum he could no longer control. He found her at their usual meeting place, on the rocks, waiting in her navy bathing suit. Dali Beach was brimming with beachgoers enjoying one of the last warm days of the fading summer.

"Hey." She waved a beer bottle at him. She was always drinking Tsingtaos, even if it was only late afternoon.

"Put on your clothes," Lu Fang said. "Let's go somewhere more private."

She took a long look at him, stood, and pulled on her dress. She grabbed her shoes by the straps. After they'd walked away from the rocks, she said, "Is there a problem?"

Lu Fang didn't respond. He quickened his pace. They walked toward the entrance of Lao Mountain Park. There was dense foliage there, a pathway ascending steeply into the forest.

"It's not—" he began. He tried again. "I have a wife, and a baby on the way."

She stopped walking. He waited for her to be angry, disgusted. She let out a sigh. "And?" she said.

"What do you mean, and?"

She crossed her arms over her chest. A mosquito was biting the soft, white interior of her bicep. He could have swatted it away, but he didn't want to risk touching her. He watched a bump form on her flesh.

Finally she said, "Do you love your wife?"

"We never—we were never a fit," Lu Fang said. "She's a peasant. I went to university."

Sloan nodded, like that information was sufficient. She began climbing the stone steps and he followed. They reached a pagoda halfway up the mountain. It wasn't ever cleaned or maintained; the floor was littered with wrappers and blackening chicken bones.

"Still, I have duties to her," Lu Fang said.

Sloan laughed. "Don't be dramatic," she said.

She was taking the steps two by two. He couldn't believe how unfazed she was. If she meant to sting him by playing their night together as nothing of significance, then she had succeeded. When they reached a small concrete plaza that looked out to the blue-green sea, she discovered the fresh mosquito bite and started manically scratching it. "So you'll be a father. When?"

"I'm not sure," he said. "Mid-September. It could be two weeks, three weeks."

Before he could say anything else, she put her arms around him, pressed herself against his chest. And of course he was defenseless. The wind whooshed wildly on the exposed plaza. They were the only ones there. He didn't know if any conclusions had been reached—it felt, rather, like his marriage had been gently set aside and out of consideration. As he took off his shirt and laid it onto the concrete ground, so her fine freckled skin would not be dirtied or scraped, he willed himself to forget the starting point of this conversation. It only mattered that she wanted him again, even if it was here under the flight of crying seagulls, in broad daylight, in complete exposure.

The duffel bags announced the arrival of his mother-in-law. Large pouches woven out of plastic strands, held together by flimsy zippers. A row of these bags overtook the space where Ciyi usually set out their stolen hotel slippers. Immediately, his nose detected the aroma of ripe fruit, fermented soy, and—roasted fowl. An inspection of the kitchen confirmed the presence, hiding inside a lidded casserole, of three rotisserie chickens wrapped in grease-soaked papers.

"Hello? Anybody home?" he shouted toward the hallway.

The woman had brought three chickens on a three-day train journey, across thousands of kilometers. Did she think chicken didn't exist in the north? Did she think he couldn't afford to feed her daughter? He slammed a cabinet door.

"A Fang!" The party secretary's wife appeared from the darkness of the hall. More shrunken than ever in the decade since he last saw her, gray hair clipped short, heavily bagged eyes darting like a mouse. "A Fang, A Fang, let me look at you."

His mother-in-law took his hands and peered up at him as if he were a mountain. There were calluses in her grip. He must have flinched unconsciously because she released his hands and spread her palms open. Hard, yellow mounds colonized every phalange.

"The tobacco harvest season just ended," she said. "It was a good year. All the people of Chuanxi pitched in. You remember how it is."

He nodded compliantly. "Ma, it's a long journey to trouble you with."

His mother-in-law sat down in their single plastic-wrapped armchair. "For my baby daughter, no distance is too far. It's a boy, don't you think? Ciyi is napping. She's had a big scare with that false labor. I could tell she was shaken up as soon as I got here."

"Yes, it was a shock. For us both."

"I hate to think of her in that hospital, alone. What panic." His mother-in-law was examining the wooden beads on her bracelet.

"She'll be in good hands with you here. With my long hours at the shipyard, I—"

"I know. Long hours. Look at the time. Past nine, isn't it?" She motioned to a nonexistent clock on the wall. "You must be exhausted. Have you eaten?"

"I— No. I'm not hungry."

She shook her head. "A tall, strong man like you has to eat. Oh, you look so healthy, strong like an ox! You were a stickbug back then, when you came to us. It's that white-collar life, isn't it? I brought chickens."

"Ma, you did not have to carry them all this way."

"Farm chicken from the good province of Yunnan. Raised in my own backyard. Ciyi's favorite. Don't worry, they are very fresh. I killed them myself."

She patted his arm as she talked, brushed a speck of dirt off his sleeve. "Go, go. Ma will make sure her children are fed."

In the bedroom Lu Fang found Ciyi listening to her radio on low. She glanced sideways at him. "You're home late. Xiao Qi wanted to drink again?"

"I was swimming."

A laugh track erupted on the program. Lu Fang sat down on the bed. "Your mother seems to be in good health. She carried all those bags by herself?"

"She wouldn't have had to if you took the trouble to ask when her train arrived."

"I thought you had it arranged—"

"I did. I sent Auntie Wu to the train station. She said Ma was waiting on the quay, and a policeman was shouting at her. To move along. Shouting like she was garbage, calling her a stinking peasant."

Lu Fang made no answer. *Lovable farmers*, he thought, *backbone of our nation.*

"And when she got here, I . . . we just couldn't stop crying. It'd been so long."

He reached over to stroke Ciyi's hair. It was jet black, oily from lack of washing. He could sense her body responding to him like a cat uncertain of a stranger's petting.

"Was she upset?"

"Of course. She said she told him she was a party secretary's wife in Chuanxi. He laughed in her face." Ciyi looked out the window, down to a group of matrons in the courtyard practicing an evening dance. "I told my mom that's one bad seed in a million. That the city people are so nice, usually. She just doesn't know. How it feels to be condescended to all the time."

The party secretary and his wife didn't know about Ciyi's cleaning job. Lu Fang's mother-in-law was under the impression that Ciyi worked part-time in office towers. Ciyi was illiterate, so Lu Fang didn't know how she got her parents to believe this story. But they did—believed their daughter was living a more refined life, working in offices in an East Coast city, just as they'd made Lu Fang promise she would.

His mother-in-law had cooked more food than the small table could fit: scallion omelettes, fried peppers and potatoes, all three of the chickens divided by a meat cleaver into chunks of bone and meat, and, as the centerpiece, silkworm larvae, freshly sizzled and squirming.

"So fresh they're still alive," his mother-in-law said.

"Ma, this is a feast," Ciyi said. "What will we do with all the leftovers?"

"We're getting a fridge next year," Lu Fang said. "I'm working on it."

"Very good," his mother-in-law said. "There will be three of you, remember."

They bowed their heads and dug into the steaming plates. Lu Fang bit into a silkworm larvae. Its skin broke and a hot yellow substance oozed into his mouth.

"Lu Fang, do you like the worms?" his mother-in-law asked. "Eat them all. Still lively, aren't they?"

"Squirming," he said. His mouth was full of larvae and he spit out their brown shells. The bowl was piled high with writhing, stir-fried silkworms. They kept crawling over each other toward the top, as if they knew, dumb liquid masses that they were, that this way they'd meet their end sooner.

Across the table, Ciyi shoveled her rice wordlessly, and he tried to tell himself he could learn from her. To be content with the cards dealt. She'd be a good mother. But there weren't three of them yet. Before becoming a father, a man could stay out drinking with colleagues, a man could swim late. A man could be an international businessman with a foreign lover, for just a while longer.

## 18

The doctor had projected Ciyi's due date to be the Mid-Autumn Festival, when the moon was the fullest. Lu Fang and Sloan watched the moon grow rounder every night. She let him in from a campus side entrance where no guard stood watch. They made love in empty classrooms, dark open spaces. On the patchy grass of the soccer field, Lu Fang told Sloan about the tale of Chang'e.

"She's the woman on mooncake packages," he said. "A great, sorrowful beauty in flowing robes. Usually she's holding a white rabbit, her only companion."

"She stole a pill from her husband?" Sloan asked. "I think I've heard this story."

"It starts with Houyi, Chang'e's husband," he began. "In ancient times, ten suns appeared in the sky at once. The crops died and the earth cracked. A hero called Houyi climbed Kunlun Mountain and, using his supernatural strength, shot down nine suns with his bow and arrow. As a reward, the Empress of Heavens gave him a pill she promised could make him instantly rise to the celestial realms and become a deity."

"Sounds like a pill I know," Sloan said.

"Houyi had a beautiful wife named Chang'e. This is where the story diverges. In one common version, Houyi gives her the precious pill to keep, because he can't bear the thought of becoming a god and leaving her behind. A disciple of Houyi called Feng Peng sees the pill and becomes overcome by greed. On a day when Houyi is out hunting, Feng Peng ambushes Chang'e and forces her to give him the pill. As a last resort, she swallows it so the bad man cannot have it, and instantly becomes so light that she floats upward toward the skies. In her despair, she latches on to the closest celestial body—the moon. She becomes doomed to live there alone. But it is said that on the day the moon is fullest, Houyi would spread a feast in his court and toast to his wife, far up in the Moon Palace, hoping to catch a glimpse of his beloved. That's the version where Chang'e is a martyr who sacrifices herself for the greater good."

"And what's the other version?"

"In other versions, there is no Feng Peng. Chang'e cannot resist the pill's temptation and wants it for herself. She swallows it, only her fate as a deity is to be exiled alone in the bleak Cold Palace on the moon."

Sloan was ripping little fistfuls of the dry grass on the field. "She can be a deity, but she must live in exile."

Lu Fang went on. "Human weakness would be too unhappy a conclusion for a national holiday. So it's about melancholia, about what is out of reach. Looking at the moon and missing those you cannot be with—this is a very Chinese sentiment. All the great poets have written about it."

"Yeah?" Her voice was distant.

Lu Fang closed his eyes as he remembered.

"One knows not what year it is
tonight in the moon palace.
I yearn to return, riding the wind,
yet fear the towers of crystal and jade.
The cold can be too much to bear in high places."

"It's nice." She sounded sleepy. "It's by that poet you like?"

"Su Shi," Lu Fang said. "This type of poem—it's called a *ci*. Cis come with set templates, and this one is called 'Water Melody.' Chairman Mao liked to write his own cis, too, especially the ones made famous by Su Shi. He wrote his version of 'Water Melody,' and titled it 'Swimming.'"

Sloan laughed lightly. "And is it any good?"

"'I drank the water of Changsha, I ate the fish of Wuchang.' Well, it was published in the preeminent poetry periodical of the time."

She squinted at the moon overhead. "Do you know the American story about the moon?"

"The American one?" He thought for a few seconds. "I don't think so."

"It's that we've been there."

Lu Fang found this unbearably funny. He laughed so loudly he curled to his side, hugging his ribs.

"What?" Sloan asked, laughing too. "You don't believe that instead of a greedy pill-swallowing woman, the person waving up there is our very own Neil Armstrong?"

Lu Fang wiped the tears from the creases of his eyes. "I believe it," he said.

They looked at the craters on the pale orb. She played with one button of his shirt, unbuttoning, rebuttoning. "Why do you love those old stories and poems so much?" she asked.

He had to think about it. Against the dark outlines of tree branches across the field, he imagined swaying bodies, the quiet campus overtaken by shouts. "Because it's harder to tell stories nowadays."

Sloan lifted her head from the nook of his shoulder. "Times are changing," she said. "Things are getting better. The students I teach—they think so. They are circulating petitions about liberal reforms."

"They are young," Lu Fang said.

"You're not old. You could be a part of it."

"A part of what?"

"A movement," Sloan said.

Rumbles of laughter shook him again. "This is not America," he said. "Here you do not ask, you say thank you. Here entire fates change with one wrong word, one unlucky instant. That's what these young people don't understand. They should count their blessings and survive."

Sloan made a contrite sound. "Believe me, China is opening up. They let me in," she said.

He turned over and trapped her beneath his chest. He composed his face so that his smile was easy, so that this conversation might conclude. "They did," he said. "They've poached America's greatest movie star." She giggled, slid her hand down the waistband of his too-loose slacks. "And

America's greatest movie star met China's greatest international businessman," she said. She was laughing as they melted into each other, two dark silhouettes on a patchy soccer field, beneath the white moon.

These were a happy stretch of days, with only one minor issue: Sloan still failed to directly mention his wife, his child, what would happen after the birth. At first, he hoped it was out of avoidance or jealousy. But he soon began to wonder how casual this affair was for her. She said she wasn't seeing other men, that Lu Fang was different from them. But what did that mean? Did she even think of his family, the supposed taitai of an international businessman, carrying their business heir? He imagined Sloan like an actress on those Hong Kong soaps, begging him to divorce his unloved wife. But maybe Sloan didn't even need to see Ciyi's sallow face or hear her uncouth accent to feel secure in being the most cherished woman. Maybe she never talked about their future to protect his feelings, because a future together was a laughable idea. He was sure that despite all her talk about staying in China, she'd go back to America and get an American husband.

"You ever think of getting married?" he asked her one day.

She kicked a crushed soda can from the sidewalk. "Maybe. If I have to, I guess."

What did he think she was going to say—yes, and to you? They were walking in a neighborhood in the southern part of town, crowded with stalls selling mechanical parts. He felt the vendors' eyes on them. "Sir, sir," they hissed. If he hadn't been walking next to Sloan, they would never have used the honorific. He wouldn't be mistaken for a man of grander stature. But inside he felt like a silkworm larvae, swirling liquids held up by a carapace.

"Why do you ask?" she asked.

He sensed she was interested in his answer with a certain ferocity. He didn't want to say the wrong thing. "You're young. Maybe you'll soon want other things, like a husband or a family." It hurt to say, because it was so obviously to his exclusion. But it also made it sound like he wanted nothing from her, which he now realized was perhaps why she was with him at all. Because he never asked a future of her.

"Do you see me becoming a wife and a mother?" she said.

"The pale heavens' arrangements are obeyed as they come," he replied.

She squinted at him, then sighed. "Sometimes I think Chinese proverbs were only invented to obfuscate."

The next week Sloan showed up in a boxy Samochód Polonez, a Polish car popularized in China since the Reform. Lu Fang circled the vehicle, caressed it with disbelief. They were in a leafy residential neighborhood not far from the university. Sloan sat in the driver's seat, sunglasses perched on her nose.

"How did you get this car?" Lu Fang leaned into the driver's window.

"You can come inside, you know."

He got in. The engine hummed noisily, and she hit the gas pedal.

"Sloan!" he cried, scrambling to yank on the seat belt.

"I borrowed it for the afternoon," she said.

"Whose is it?"

"My friend's father. He's a driver for the municipal government."

"Where are we going?"

"An adventure," she said.

It was an early autumn dusk. Sloan drove north along the coastal highway. The climate of the peninsula had given rise to megafarms in recent years, and the rows of trees rolled past like stripy optical illusions. Eventually, she slowed and turned onto a bumpy dirt road. "This is a good spot," she said, and parked the Polonez at the edge of a pear orchard. The engine went off with a sputter.

She took off her summer dress. The car was small. It was awkward for her to climb over him and straddle him. The Polonez creaked and rattled as they rocked, and after they were done she opened the passenger door and stepped onto the loose soil, still naked.

"There could be farmers around. They might see you," Lu Fang said. He grabbed the dress and threw it at her; she caught it laughing.

"I am Chang'e," she said, "alone on my moonscape. You think I could play that part?"

Her blond hair was radiant in the fading light. "Yes, you are a goddess. You don't have a care in the world," he said. "Now put your dress on, for heaven's sake."

She smiled at him. "I will, if you get in the driver's seat."

"What?"

"I'm teaching you how to drive."

"Oh, Sloan," he said.

He stepped out, kissed her, circled around the hood, and sat in the driver's side. The steering wheel felt toylike in his hands. Sloan climbed back into the car and explained the gears to him. She told him how to put the car into drive. She told him he could keep his feet pressed hard on the brake pedal if he felt nervous.

"You understand?" she asked.

"Yes."

"Then drive."

He shifted into gear. It was happening, the car was moving, they were creeping along the edge of the orchard. "Now turn the wheel," she said, and they veered left, toward a skinny pear tree. "More, more, more," she said. The car traced the shape of a U. He drove them back down the length of the dirt strip. "Now do that again, and faster," she said. He was laughing at every bump, laughing as the Polonez zigzagged on the pockmarked country road. The sound of his own laughter surprised him.

After a few laps he put the car into park. "Thank you," he said. "Genuinely."

"We made a deal: if you taught me how to swim, I'd teach you how to drive."

"That's true," he said. "Though I hadn't imagined it to be so soon. Not here, not like this."

"Where and how, then?" she asked softly.

Where and how? In America, on a smooth highway. Instead he said, "I guess I never thought about it."

"This is the best we can do, right?" she said.

The orchards were dim in the twilight, leaves rustling in a breeze that'd grown cold. He rolled up the window and said, "Maybe it's time to go. It'll be dark soon."

"Yes, it's time," she said. They exchanged seats again.

On the way back they were quiet. Lu Fang's hand rested on Sloan's thigh and she drove with her free hand on his. They could have been on any road in the world. Night fell by the time they reached the city's edge. Finally, she said, "So were you happy to learn how to drive?"

"It made me very happy," he said.

"Really?"

"It will be one of my happiest memories."

At that she looked at him and made no answer. A few minutes later she said, "Well, I'm honored."

They reached the neighborhood behind the university. After she turned off the ignition, they sat inside the car on the darkened street.

"I do sometimes wonder," she said, "what it would be like if you didn't have a wife and a child on the way." The words came out a whisper. "We could go on trips like this every day."

It was all he had ever wanted to hear from her. The moonlight that night was strong, nearing its full potency. A shiver passed through him. "I thought you liked that about me," he said. "That I had a family, a separate life."

"And soon you'll return to them," she said.

He didn't know how to answer. It was shocking how lonely, all of a sudden, she seemed. For a moment he thought she was going to ask him something that would be impossible to refuse.

But she only took his hand and pressed her face into his palm. "It's only the melancholia of mid-autumn," she said. "I am experiencing a very Chinese sentiment."

## 19

Lu Fang was out inspecting crates when a young clerk ran over to him, breathless. Someone had called the shipyard; his wife was at the hospital. This is the day, Lu Fang thought to himself. He lodged his clipboard under his arm and walked straight along the glimmering harbor, in the direction of Qingdao People's Hospital. He knew he should be running. His footsteps were leaden. He stopped for a moment to look out over the harbor's choppy waves. Gargantuan cargo ships emitted slow wails to announce their departure, sorrowful beasts carrying China's new riches toward distant shores and foreign lands.

At the hospital, Lu Fang found his mother-in-law sitting in the blue plastic chairs of the maternity floor. "They are cutting her open," she said, then returned to muttering a prayer, "Buddha protect her."

"It will be all right," Lu Fang said, though he wasn't sure himself. The doctor hadn't mentioned the possibility of a cesarean. He knew this was a medical procedure. He had a terrible thought: if something went wrong with the operation, if something happened to Ciyi and the baby, he would be a free man. The fact that he was capable of entertaining this notion even for a moment horrified him, even if a part of him saw the merit in it. The greatest men in history did not rely on such easy morality—the generals who ordered slaughters, the kings who sacrificed their own sons. Exceptionality was forged by tolerance of loss. He could see himself in this narrative: tragic widower, victim of yet another sense-less governmental policy, exiled abroad, seeking a second chance with a young American woman. He wondered whether Ciyi had worn her jade pendant to the operating theater. If gods did exist, he'd be doomed to the eighteenth layer of hell for thinking these thoughts.

"A Fang, look at what a beautiful little girl she was."

His mother-in-law clutched his sleeve, tugging his attention to the black-and-white picture she held, of Ciyi in a padded cotton outfit. It was tattered at the corners. It was obvious his mother-in-law had been carrying this picture for many years.

"She will be a good mother," his mother-in-law said. "She's always had so much love. Despite everything that happened, the famine and the sacrifices we had to make, I made sure she felt loved."

She tugged at his sleeve again, like she was worried he hadn't heard her.

"Me and Ciyi's dad—we thank you. We know you've worked hard. Now that she'll be raising a child, it's going to be all on you. We are grateful."

"Ma, it's my duty," he said.

"I want you to know"—she leaned toward him—"that if you ever find yourself momentarily in need, well, we're here, and we would be happy to give you a loan."

"That won't be necessary."

"The tobacco harvests have been good," his mother-in-law said. "Very good."

They were entering the decade, Lu Fang thought, where harvests were always good when one was party secretary.

From her jacket she pulled out a red envelope. "It's Dad's well wishes, to celebrate the birth of his grandchild."

"I won't accept it," Lu Fang said. The harshness of his own tone surprised him.

"You can save it. It may be useful on a bad day."

"We are managing fine. Your well wishes are received. I can't take it."

"Oh, Lu Fang." His mother-in-law unceremoniously shoved the envelope in his lap. "Well wishes aren't our concern. I've seen how late you've been staying out. We wouldn't want you to be too strained with your duties to . . . provide." Unlike her voice, which had been a perfect performance of in-law generosity, her eyes were harsh, derisive. "I'm afraid there isn't a choice for you but to take it."

It was Lu Fang who lowered his gaze first. "Please relay my thanks to Dad," he said.

"I most certainly will," his mother-in-law said.

A nurse came out of the operating room, and Lu Fang's mother-in-law quickly turned away from him and leapt up to greet her. "Is it a boy?" she squawked in Yunnanese, then caught herself and repeated the question in Mandarin.

"The mother is recovering," the nurse said, taking a step away from his mother-in-law. The nurse spoke slowly and too loudly, as if to someone deaf and dumb. "It is a boy."

The mother-in-law turned to Lu Fang. "The heavens are good," she said.

They were allowed to see Ciyi after she awoke from the anesthesia. The baby was not in the room; he'd been taken away by the nurses while the mother rested. Ciyi was in a hospital gown, her hair a mess against the pillow. Ciyi's mother rushed to her side to smooth the black strands. "Are you in pain?" she whispered.

"Yes, no," Ciyi said. Her voice was hoarse. Lu Fang stood by the door. He didn't know whether he should praise her or comfort her. He'd always felt superior about the amount of mental pain he'd suffered in comparison to Ciyi, but he could never claim to know what it was like to be cut open, to have another body pulled from your insides.

"When we go home Ma will take good care of you," his mother-in-law said.

The nurse returned to the room to administer an injection to Ciyi. "What is it?" Lu Fang asked.

"Morphine. The first dose must be wearing off. The second operation took a bit longer."

"The second operation?" his mother-in-law asked.

"The sterilization," the nurse said blankly. "We'll bring the baby in a minute."

Ciyi looked toward the door, at Lu Fang. "The sterilization," she said, dazed.

"I guess they were quick with it," Lu Fang said.

"What?" the mother-in-law cried.

"It's the law, Mama," Ciyi said. "One child only."

"They went into her abdomen and sealed up her tubes," Lu Fang said.

Lu Fang watched his mother-in-law's lips go white. Perhaps the decree wasn't in full effect in the countryside yet, but when it spread, she and the party secretary would be the ones responsible for enforcing it. She was shocked now, Lu Fang thought. Soon she would be used to it. She would be the one dragging women to rural operation clinics by force. Complicity became easy with practice.

"Good heavens," Ciyi's mother said. She lifted Ciyi's hospital gown, and Ciyi squirmed, though she didn't resist.

They all stared at Ciyi's stomach, swollen above diaperlike cotton underwear. It was bloated and raw, heavily bandaged, the cotton pads a darker pale yellow in some spots. He heard his mother-in-law stifle a sob.

"Ma," Ciyi said. Her voice was weak. "It's what must be done. There isn't a choice."

"Of course, of course," her mother said, then shuffled out of the room, sniffling loudly.

After the door shut Ciyi closed her eyes. Lu Fang rested his forehead against her bedpost. He didn't dare touch her. "You did well," he whispered.

There was a knock at the door. It was the nurse, carrying a small bundle. She looked at Lu Fang, then Ciyi, and handed the bundle to Ciyi.

"Our son," Ciyi said. "Minmin. After my father."

There was a face in the middle of the bundle, a red, scrunched-up, button-nosed little face. It didn't look like Lu Fang, it didn't look like Ciyi, it didn't look like anyone. Lu Fang could only dumbly repeat, "Minmin."

A wave in him was rising, of wonder, of dread. He thought of a word his own mother used when she explained why she wouldn't spoil Lu Fang or his brother—she called it *ni'ai*, love that drowns.

The character for "drown" looked like this: 溺

氵 represented three drops of water; 弱 was the character for weakness. The weak in the water drown. The kind of love being asked of him was an act of mercy. To be given a chance, to be carried to shore safely, because the love Lu Fang felt for the American woman was too all-consuming, a raging flood. He resolved to keep this love, this love that drowns, at bay within himself. Looking at his son, he thought, This being has no choice. Ciyi had no choice, he himself had no choice. The very idea of choice was monstrous. He was heaving now, the breaths coming short, and felt like in the end he did suffer a great tragic loss. It was the loss of a future he'd briefly allowed himself to imagine.

# 20

He mailed the invitation to her dorm, with no return address. He imagined her surprise at the formality of this colonial hotel. It was the opposite of empty science buildings and seaweed-strewn coves, the kind of place he'd envisioned taking her in a different life. It was the kind of place an international businessman could afford.

"You're dressed up," she said when she met him in the lobby. He'd worn his best white shirt, a blazer he'd bought secondhand years ago. In truth he knew it looked cheap.

"I am inviting you to dinner—" Lu Fang began. He was finding it difficult to speak in a normal voice. "A proper dinner." Never before had they eaten together. "I made a reservation at the restaurant here."

"Lu Fang!" Sloan's eyes widened. "This is a very expensive restaurant."

"It is the best Western restaurant in the city. I thought you might enjoy a taste from home."

Sloan considered the dark interior of the restaurant. "Yes," she said after a few beats. "A taste from home would be nice."

"Please," Lu Fang said. His steps were shaky as he approached the maître d'hôtel, a man in a sharp black suit, much better-fitting and expensive-looking than Lu Fang's. "Under Mr. Lu," Lu Fang said.

The man looked at Sloan and bowed. Lu Fang couldn't remember the last time a Chinese man had bowed to him. "Of course," the man said. "Mr. Lu."

They were seated at a table that looked out onto the gardens. "Lu Fang, this is such a production," Sloan murmured. "Have you come here before?"

"No," Lu Fang said. "I mean, it's not my usual. But you, you belong here. You deserve to be in a place like this. To make up for the past few weeks."

"What do you mean, to make up for?"

Lu Fang opened the leather-bound menu. "The sneaking around," he said. "I imposed that on you. Because of my . . . situation."

Sloan turned the menu pages carefully. "Has your situation changed?"

The dining room was mostly unoccupied. Lu Fang noticed one elderly foreign man in a far corner, dining alone with a near-empty martini glass. Other than that, the few diners were Chinese men in suits talking in hushed business tones.

"My situation—it's still essentially what I told you," he said quickly. "Let's not talk about that right now. What looks good here? They have steak. I don't believe I've ever had steak before."

The menu was written in fancy cursive letters in English. Below each item there was a smaller-fonted Chinese translation.

"Or salmon?" Lu Fang said. "Salmon is very popular in Japan. And they have Italian noodles here too. It's the best Western restaurant," he repeated.

"Yes, I don't doubt it," Sloan finally said.

"Did you go to places like this in Hollywood?"

"What?"

"When you were an actress," he said.

She unfolded the stiff napkin and placed it on her lap. "Sure. From time to time," she said.

"Get the steak," Lu Fang said. It was the most expensive item on the menu, at nearly one hundred yuan. He realized he had no idea what she liked to eat. He was afraid she would say something like, *I don't eat meat.* He'd heard that not eating meat was an ideological trend in the West.

"I will order the steak," she said.

A skinny young man approached their table. His back was querulously bent, as if he were trying to appear shorter. "She will have the black pepper sauce steak," Lu Fang said.

The waiter nodded at Sloan, then turned to Lu Fang. "What degree of doneness would she prefer?"

"Rare," Sloan said in Chinese.

"Very well," the waiter said. "And you, sir?"

He glared at the waiter. "I'll have, I'll have—" He didn't know anything about the dishes on the menu.

"There is a selection of Chinese-style dishes on the last page," the waiter said.

"I'll have the steak as well."

"Yes, of course," the waiter said. "And the doneness?"

Lu Fang didn't understand what doneness meant. "Like hers," he said.

The waiter nodded. "To drink, I recommend the Château Lafite '76."

Sloan was pale, even whiter than usual. It was the odd lighting in the restaurant, he thought. It had no cheer about it.

"Lu Fang, it is very expensive," Sloan said.

"We'll have it," Lu Fang told the waiter.

The waiter took a few steps, back bowed, like a eunuch exiting an imperial court. "Your Chinese is so very good," he told Sloan.

For a flash she looked pleased, before her attention returned to Lu Fang, and her smile immediately dropped.

The waiter returned with a bottle of red wine, which he uncorked expertly. They were both poured generous amounts of the inky-red liquid.

"Ganbei," Lu Fang said and drained his glass. It tasted like earthy vinegar water. "Do you think this place is nice? It was built by foreigners for foreigners. Do hotels in America look like this?"

"For the most part, not at all," she said.

Their steaks arrived, steaming on black plates. A gelatinous brown sauce covered clumps of boiled broccoli and potatoes. He picked up his fork and knife indecisively, mimicking Sloan's movements. He'd never used such utensils before. He sawed off a chunk of the steak, revealing a tendony cross section. Under the pressure of the fork, the meat oozed bloodied liquid and grease.

No matter how hard he chewed, the bite of steak refused to be shredded. He was flattening it and folding it with his teeth and tongue. Finally he swallowed it whole, a hard lump down his throat.

Sloan reached for her wine constantly, washing down every morsel. Soon Lu Fang had to refill her glass.

"Do you like the meat?"

"It's a bit tough," she said.

"Tough?" He couldn't continue watching her chew. He waved over the waiter. "We'll also have the salmon, the Italian noodles, and the classic American-style hamburger," he said, reciting every item he remembered from the menu.

Sloan looked flushed. She pushed her barely eaten steak to the side and folded her arms. Then she said, "It is the first week of October."

"Yes."

"It is past your wife's due date."

"I wanted to take you somewhere nice."

"But why?" she said. "Don't you think this will bring attention to us? I thought you were scared of being seen."

"No one I know would ever come here," Lu Fang said. "These businessmen here, they admire me for being with you. But they would never look at me twice otherwise."

"You can't afford this," Sloan said. "You're not an international businessman."

"No, of course not," Lu Fang said.

She smiled bitterly and shook her head.

"I'm a clerk at the shipyard," he said.

"I have no appetite." She threw the napkin onto the table. "You only want to show me off before you get rid of me."

They were interrupted by the arrival of the salmon and pasta and classic American-style hamburger. Their table was crowded with dishes now, the way it would look at a Chinese restaurant.

"You misunderstand," Lu Fang said quietly. "I need you to understand this."

"I think I do," she said.

"I am beholden to my situation," he said. "My father-in-law is the party secretary of the town where I was sent for reeducation. A small fry and a bully, but these people have the power of life and death in this country. My wife—she is not a bad person. I made a promise to her parents. I want to give our child a good life. A life unlike mine. And with you, it is too painful."

He looked up. Sloan's eyes had pooled with tears.

"Your child," she said. "Boy or girl?"

"Boy," he said.

"And his name?"

"Lu Min."

"Congratulations," she said.

She slowly stood. The waiter lurched forward to help pull back her chair.

"I'm going," she announced. She lingered, as if she were holding something back. Or, it occurred to him, she was waiting for him to change his mind, to say he couldn't be without her. He wanted to stand and envelop her, like she always enveloped him. But he did not move. He tasted blood, which he thought was from the rare meat, then realized he'd been biting down too hard on his own lip. When it became obvious he wasn't going to respond, she let out a peal of laughter. "Every day I wake up in this country, I am an outsider, a novelty," she said. "Was I a novelty to you? A taste of the West, like this dinner?"

Not a muscle in his face moved. It took so much stillness to maintain dignity.

"Don't think you're making a noble sacrifice, Lu Fang," she said. "When the truth is that you're an opportunist, like the rest of them. Another man who thinks I'm an easy American, to be discarded after use."

He wanted to say, *You are the least easy opportunity of my life*. But the words choked in his throat.

Sloan turned around and walked out. He was certain he would never see her again. He no longer had the strength to sit. He wanted to sink down onto the green carpet and puddle into the fibers. But the armor of his body held him upright. It had to carry him up, out, home. To his bedroom on Anwei Road plastered with posters of happy, smiling babies dressed like flowers.

The plates spread out before him, uneaten, their intermingling smells creamy and meaty, fishy and rich. He waited long enough for Sloan to have disappeared, far away, wherever she'd go next. He motioned for the waiter, who no longer cared to hunch, to bring over the bill. The eyes of the other men in the dining room darted away when he glanced up. The bill came to upward of a thousand yuan. He set the red envelope on the table and left.

PART V

# ALVA

SHANGHAI, 2008

## 21

Today, her new life would begin. Alva avoided the stray leaves and bruised fruit left over from the morning produce market—she didn't want to sully her new shoes, cream-colored flats with iridescent rhinestones. She steered clear of the breakfast stalls, so the smoke from the fried dough sticks would not seep into her teased-and-sprayed hair. A few stray commuters shot her a look. Without her uniform, there was no way they knew that only a few weeks ago, she'd been a Mincai student. Alva stood at the street corner, waiting for a bus, though not a public one—hers would bear a laminated sign, SHANGHAI AMERICAN SCHOOL BUS 9.

From Yingchun Road, she could see Mincai Experimental enclosed within its fence. It was time for the flag-raising ceremony and calisthenics. Uniformed students in red kerchiefs marched in formation to patriotic music. She knew that Li Xinwei was among them, along with Gao Xiaofan and Teng Xin and Doggy and all her old classmates. She herself had once been among them.

A strange thought occurred to her—she'd never *seen* the march from afar, never appreciated what years of training and calisthenics yielded from a distance. From where she stood, she had to admit this single, disciplined mass movement held power. The swings of arms a vigorous 180-degree pendulum, straight legs kicking to 45 degrees with each crisp step.

Yet power existed only for the beholder. How she'd loathed being part of that routine, the command of "one-two-three-four." How freeing it was to slouch here, against the bus stop, refusing to move her limbs. When the national anthem began to thunder, she did not stand to attention, did not salute the flag with fingers grazing temple. And this felt like heresy.

The shiny green SAS bus pulled up to the curb. It was scary, how eager she was to step on board. How fast Alva felt like she wasn't one of the uniformed students inside the fence, that she'd never really been one of them at all.

But when she climbed the stairs and was faced with row upon row of blond heads and light eyes and screams in English, she felt she wasn't one of them, either. "Name?" a Chinese woman with permed hair asked from the front seat.

"早上好," Alva said. "我的名字是, 呃, Alva Collins."

The woman's features immediately softened. She nodded and checked Alva's name off the clipboard.

"Your Chinese is so good!" she called out as Alva slunk toward the back row.

There had been so many preparations for this day. Another hierarchy ruled over pockets of Western adolescence on Chinese soil, and Alva would not enter an outsider. Alva had rewatched *Gossip Girl* and repeated every one of Serena's flat, cool-girl intonations. She'd raided Super Brand Mall—leggings from H&M, a handbag from Zara, Marc Jacobs perfumes from Sephora. Over break, she made a pile of the gaudy clothes she and Sloan had bought at the fake-goods market over the years. As Alva bagged them for the donation bins, she imagined Chinese Red Cross trucks on newly constructed highways driving to distant provinces, the children there wearing tight polyester shirts with GUCCHI and CHRISTIN DIOR printed in glittery letters. Her mother made no comment when the shirts materialized in the trash can.

Sloan had no leverage with her own brand-new wardrobe of tailored dresses and silk blouses. She bit her tongue as Lu Fang handed over one pink Mao Zedong bill after another to Alva. Sloan's nails, once peeling and gnawed, were now perfectly French-manicured. She had a slight tan from their southern factory trips.

Sloan was so good at playing taitai. In her L.A. days, she'd taken classes on method acting. She'd told Alva about it while ten beers deep one night. "I'd drive every Thursday night to a strip mall in El Segundo, and this old actor would teach us about the Stanislavski system. You become the character, you inhabit their world, their skin, their subconscious. He told me I was his only student with real talent for the Method. He's the one who got me the audition for that movie in Cambodia."

Sloan was so good at the Method that the previous version of herself was fading fast, even in Alva's memory. The version who'd gotten fired from English teaching gigs, who rimmed her eyes in a compact mirror, fumigated the room with cheap hair spray as she ran crablike fingers through bleached hair. Who lined up the empty Tsingtaos by the sink, said she felt sick, then drank some more. At least the business taitai did less of that.

Alva was going to reinvent herself too. She'd be a true American teenager, shedding fourteen years of shape-shifting indoctrination from the news and school, from her own too talented, too special, too chameleon-like mother.

Alva would have a Method too.

She'd read the obscure film journals. "Alienation" wasn't the correct English translation for what Bertolt Brecht intended. The original German word meant something closer to distancing, or estrangement. Regardless, the point of Brechtian alienation was for the performer to notice the strangeness of their own act. To embrace artificiality, to see the fakeness of appearances as virtue, not shame.

As a first step, Alva decided to dye her hair blond. Why not? All her life she'd watched Sloan do it, hunched over the sink, yellow water gurgling down the drain, until she married Lu Fang and started going to a high-end salon in Jinqiao. Plenty of girls at the Shanghai American School would be blondes, and fake ones too.

A five-hour session at Coiffure de Parris at Thumb Plaza was all it took. Alva's hair was clipped into little foil pockets and rubbed with a sulfurous chemical that burned her scalp. The black strands became limp and yellow, the overall effect wiglike. The hairdresser said the color may take a few days to settle, but an extra 888-yuan keratin take-home treatment would ensure it looked natural. Alva said that wouldn't be necessary. She didn't want natural.

When Sloan saw the new hair, she set down her copy of *Entrepreneurial China*. "Oh, Alva. What have you done?"

She was curled up on the couch against Lu Fang. "Honey," Sloan said. "It looks horrible. Blond hair doesn't suit Asians."

Alva's still-raw scalp tingled. "Not everyone can afford your ten-thousand-yuan coloring sessions," she said.

Lu Fang's fingers, which had been twirling the curls along Sloan's neck, froze for a nanosecond.

In the bathroom, standing before the mirror, Alva brushed the frizzy, haylike strands. Sloan was right: it was ugly, unnatural. But there was a nobility inherent to Asian blondness. It was unsettling, mutinous. It screamed: SO WHAT, MOTHERFUCKERS. Alva wondered what else didn't suit Asians.

The Shanghai American School bus made its rounds past the eastern bounds of Century Park, past the expat enclave of Jinqiao with its Carrefour and Decathlon and Starbucks, past sprawling compounds of identical villas, with their foreign mothers in yoga pants, past migrant maids handing off a light-haired child before hurrying home to clean breakfast dishes, past the enormous economic development zone factories of Zhangjiang Hi-Tech Park, rural satellite townships, dirt brown fields, and concrete barracks, until the bus came all the way east, to the land's edge against the Yellow Sea, and suddenly they were on the grounds of the Shanghai Links Golf and Country Club. Alva had never seen grass so green in her entire life. Across sweeping meadows and artificial lakes, there was a red-roofed mansion, a lighthouse, buildings she recognized from the brochures. The Shanghai American School was literally built on a golf course.

The white walls of the building gleamed, not a trace of soot, and even the Yellow Sea shimmered blue in the distance. Alva hadn't expected a school with an ocean view. She hadn't expected a baseball field, a performance arts center, a two-story lounge with black leather armchairs. And the laowais—there were so many white teachers and teenagers walking around blithely. She could be on a safari, watching a rare species gathered in great numbers, grazing and preening in their natural habitat. But there weren't only foreigners—many students looked ethnically Chinese, some Korean, though all visually distinct from Alva's old schoolmates. It was hard to explain. You could instantly tell a local Chinese apart from an expat Chinese. Perhaps it was the way they dressed or carried themselves. The light jeans, the Hollister hoodies, the overall performative teenage languor in their gait. They talked in Valley English full of likes and oh-my-gods and I-can't-evens. Their eyes glazed past Alva, pausing only on the bleached hay-hair, their glances devoid of the avid curiosity of her old schoolmates, when she was a mixed-looking child lost deep in old-fashioned Shanghainese districts. *Laowailaowailaowai*, the other children would say, crowding around her. She knew she had an unspoken pull back then, the special power of being foreign. Now no one looked at her twice.

Earlier that morning, she'd crossed paths with Sloan outside the bathroom. Her mother was still puffy-eyed from a late-night banquet. She flashed a fast scowl when Alva emerged, having just ironed the frizz out of her atrocious new hair. Sloan reached to lift a limp strand off her collar.

"This capillary massacre won't help you blend in, you know."

"I'm not trying to blend in."

"Then why did you do this?"

"Same reason you do it," Alva said.

Sloan cocked her head. "And what would that be?"

"Hiding true colors."

"What?"

"Some parents would wish their child a happy first day of school."

Lu Fang's heavy footsteps came down the hallway, the familiar sound of his morning belly scratch, nails against woolen fabric. Alva was out the door fast, though not fast enough to miss her mother say, "Some children should be grateful to have parents at all."

The homeroom teacher was a Texan woman called Beverly Steward, whose protruding eyelids gleamed with baby-blue eyeshadow. "So, *guys*," Ms. Steward said, clapping her hands with overdone enthusiasm. She surveyed the room—so happy, so great, so awesome, so psyched to see y'all. "How were your winter breaks? Should we go around and share?"

Alva shifted in her seat. She hadn't heard a teacher use this tone since kindergarten. A girl sitting near Alva, with chipmunk cheeks and an aggressive amount of perfume that Alva recognized as Miss Dior Chérie, announced, "My family went to Jackson Hole."

"Lucky!" Ms. Steward cooed. "Love the Grand Tetons!"

Ms. Steward offered individualized commentary for each vacation destination: Club Med in Phuket? *Love* their nightly dress code. Visited family in Taipei? The street food is to *die* for! Thermal springs in Hokkaido? Japanese shiatsu is my *favorite* massage at Dragonfly. Stayed in Shanghai? So did I, but isn't the city so much more *breathable* with everyone gone for Chinese New Year?

Alva didn't want Ms. Steward's attention, as it swept along the rows, to fall on her. Breaks had never meant vacations for her and her mother. Two weeks ago, for their first Chinese New Year with Lu Fang, he'd suggested a traditional dinner of *jiaozi*—except no one wanted to make them at home, so he'd gone to FamilyMart and returned with two packs of frozen Wanzai dumplings. Sloan guzzled through her beer reserve too fast and complained of a headache before midnight. Alva said she was tired and retreated to her room, where she kept her own stash of cheap supermarket liquor and watched seven episodes of *Survivor*. Lu Fang rang in the New Year alone. Alva might have felt bad, but he'd already made the wire transfer for the Shanghai American School tuition, so she didn't need to feel *that* bad.

Ms. Steward was before her. "How about you, Alva? Go anywhere fun this break?"

"Not really," Alva fumbled, then she remembered they did technically have vacation plans. Lu Fang and Sloan's honeymoon, which he'd delayed until summer so Alva could join. "Later this year, we're going to Sanya, on Hainan Island."

Vacant stares. Ms. Steward smiled confusedly. Clearly nobody here had ever heard of Sanya, the Chinese business community's domestic resort haven. "Wow!" Ms. Steward said. "That sounds great!"

Alva's face burned. She should have made up something that sounded glamorous to Americans: Maui! St. Barts! Martha's-fucking-Vineyard! But Ms. Steward had already chirpily moved on to another student, a rail-thin white girl in a hoodie. "Zoey, please put that hood down. Did you go anywhere?"

The girl's features were pinched, severe, her eyebrows faint. "Churchill, Manitoba," she said.

Ms. Steward choked down a sound of reprobation. "Well! Is that a ski resort?"

"No," Zoey said.

Ms. Steward sighed and moved onto other matters: spring sport sign-ups and TX-84 calculators. Alva rubbed her temples. Calculators! You'd never hear of that in a Chinese classroom. What was the point of studying math if you could punch all of it into a machine?

During free time after homeroom, the girl at the desk in front of Alva pivoted toward her. "I'm Jiyoon," she said. "Where did you transfer from?"

"A school in Pudong," Alva said.

The girl wearing too much Miss Dior Chérie also turned their way. "Dulwich? Concordia?" She was Asian but spoke perfect American English.

"Mincai Experimental."

Miss Dior Chérie frowned. "I don't think I know it."

"Wait," Jiyoon said. "Is that a *local* school?"

It was the first time Alva became aware of the particular tinge *local* had when coming out of the mouth of expats. "I guess," she said, "if you mean that it's a Chinese school."

"Yeah. Like, a school for locals."

"Then yes."

"Oh my god!" Miss Dior Chérie gasped. "So everything was in Chinese?"

"Yes." Alva frowned. What was so surprising about a Chinese person (or half a Chinese person) going to a Chinese school in China? She looked around and realized it was true that there were no *locals* in this classroom. Even she herself would never count as one, not with her hay-blond dye job and the passport copy she'd dropped off at the administrative office this morning.

At noon, Alva picked up her textbooks for the semester: *Huckleberry Finn*, algebra, biology, and world history, all with thick, glossy pages printed with color ink. They felt heavy and expensive, unlike the tomes of thin recycled paper at Mincai. The teachers didn't cold-call or ask her to stand; they were young, pearly-toothed, light-eyed, cardigan-clad, upbeat. By the end of third period, Alva dipped to her locker to take a sip from her thermos. She'd filled it with a finger of whiskey that morning, in case she needed some liquid courage, as Sloan liked to call it. Theater actors took shots before going onstage, didn't they? No one knew her baseline personality here. Last night she'd taken the Myers-Briggs test five times online and managed to achieve five different results. You weren't actually an ISTJ or an ENFP. You were whoever you wanted to be.

Alva Baidued "Churchill, Manitoba" on her new Lu Fang–sponsored smartphone. It was a town at the edge of the Hudson Bay, with no access roads, where supplies had to be airlifted.

She chewed peppermint gum to get rid of the whiskey smell.

During lunch period, Ashley—that was Miss Dior Chérie's name— took it upon herself to show Alva around the cafeteria, which looked a lot like a hotel buffet. Glass bowls of rosemary croutons and applewood-smoked bacon adorned the salad bar.

"If you get sick of these options, you can totally bring your own lunch here. Honestly, it's like the third time we had caesar salad this month," Ashley said, nose scrunched. "Jiyoon, for example, prefers to bring her own Korean food."

Jiyoon opened her lunchbox, an elaborate two-layer contraption with subcompartments filled with kimchi, fried fish, sesame-crusted tofu. "I only eat food from home," she explained.

"Jiyoon's mom got her ayi, like, perfectly trained in Korean cooking. It's like going to a restaurant every time I go to their house," Ashley said. She bit decisively into a green apple. Alva waited for her to touch the rest of her lunch. She didn't.

"You're one to talk." Jiyoon daintily lifted a small fried fish with heavy silver chopsticks. "Dinners at your place are nuts. Your ayi goes crazy. And you have a lazy Susan, like, built-in."

"My dad got it, like, for when we had guests. We have a lot of his clients over."

Alva took a bite of a potato roll smothered with mayo. "Susan who?" she asked.

Ashley giggled. "A lazy Susan! You don't know what that is?"

"No."

"But you've been in China for so long! It's, like, the spinning thing on the tables of Chinese restaurants."

"Oh," Alva said. "I've never heard it be called Susan."

"I've looked into this," Jiyoon said. "A white woman holds the patent for inventing the lazy Susan. And guess what? Her name wasn't even, like, Susan. It was Elizabeth."

Alva tried to eke out a laugh. "Like, no wayyyy," she said, with the sluggish vocal fry both girls had been using. In this case, there was actually no fucking way. It was like she had to learn everything about China all over again.

When she escaped from the cafeteria to the bathroom for another sip from her thermos, Alva found the skinny white girl in the hoodie, Zoey, in front of the mirrors, putting on pink Chap Stick. Alva went into a stall, even though she didn't have to pee. She stood there, flushed, then walked back out. Her gaze crossed the girl's in the mirror. It reminded her of a scene in *Twin Peaks*, where one girl is painting her lips in a high school bathroom and another walks in, lights a cigarette, and says, *I've been doing some research. In real life, there is no algebra.*

"Hey," Alva said.

Zoey swiped the Chap Stick along her bottom lip, then said, "Hey."

"So, math was dumb."

"Hmm."

Alva knew this wasn't going to be easy. She scanned her brain for *Gossip Girl* and *Mean Girls* wisdom. The key to American bathroom socializing, she remembered, was throwing someone not present under the bus.

"Ashley and Jiyoon have been showing me around."

"Uh-huh."

"So what's their deal?"

Zoey gathered her hair up in a ponytail, let it fall. But she was looking at Alva with more interest now. "They like claiming the new students, I guess."

"They do this with everyone?"

"Not with me."

"Why not?"

"They haven't told you about me?"

Alva pressed the faucet to wash her hands. The water here turned hot instantaneously and didn't smell like rust. "No," she finally said.

There was a little eagle embroidered on Zoey's hoodie, one with open claws, ready to clutch its prey. "Maybe they'll tell you when they come in here to puke their guts out in a few minutes," Zoey said.

Alva pumped the soap five times. It smelled like liquid cherry blossoms. It was becoming clear that Ashley, despite her heavy perfume and apple-only lunch, or perhaps precisely because of these things, was not someone Alva should befriend. Zoey was.

"Yeah, they're chewing off my earlobes." Was that the right expression? Alva shook her thermos. "Want some of this?"

"Um . . . what?" Zoey blinked. "What is it?" She lifted the thermos and sniffed.

"Just a little postlunch digestif." Digestif was Sloanian vocabulary: apéritivo, digestif, hair of the dog, island syrup, barley juice, anything but *alcohol*.

"I better not," Zoey said. But she took a sip from the thermos and handed it back to Alva. There was a pink, waxy smudge where her lips had been.

"I looked up Churchill, Manitoba, by the way," Alva said. "You didn't actually go there, right?"

"Obviously not," Zoey said.

Alva smiled, for real this time, and shoved the thermos in her bag. She walked back through the cafeteria, where Ashley and Jiyoon were still sitting, waiting for her. The browning apple core was on a napkin in front of Ashley. Ashley waved at Alva. Alva waved back, then kept walking, not even making up some kind of excuse. She didn't want her new life to start with perfume headaches and pickled radish. She wanted it to start with the white girl in the American Eagle hoodie who'd lied about going to Churchill, Manitoba, who slouched onto her desk, her tank top so tight you could see her rib cage. Here, Alva thought, was a proper American teenager.

# 22

Zoey was chewing bubble gum, blowing and popping it from her lacquered lips. It was the end of the first week of school, and she'd stopped by Alva's desk with a piece of paper. "I wrote this essay for Chinese class. Could you look it over? My grade last semester was a B and I ran out of ways to kiss the teacher's ass."

"You take Chinese?" Alva asked.

"Yeah. The college counselor said it'd look the best on my transcript."

"Why?"

"'Cause we're in China, duh," Zoey said. "Gotta cash in."

Alva started reading the paper. Zoey's Chinese was rudimentary, obviously translated by software in places. It was titled:

### IF I HAD TO LIVE ANYWHERE IN THE WORLD

If I had to live anywhere in the world, I'd live in a town in Canada called Churchill.

Churchill is at the edge of a sea of ice. The food is brought in by helicopters. There are many polar bears. Once a year, there are more polar bears than people. Sometimes the polar bears stalk people who are walking outside. Some people who are attacked die.

During polar bear season tourists fly to Churchill and go on buses to take pictures. They pack the town's two hotels. The polar bears have

tried breaking into the hotels. To the bears, the hotels are like cans of
SPAM, fat processed American meat in a cheap metal box. I wish the
bears could eat all the tourists. I would stay inside and laugh.

"Chinese teachers usually want more metaphors," Alva said. "Proverbs.
A quote from Winston Churchill himself, to throw them off. Flower it up."

Zoey scanned her paper, biting her lip. Alva made a mental note to
practice that in front of the mirror later, the biting. Zoey sighed. "It's like
I can't ever get it. The right tone to strike."

"Make it more poetic. Talk about why you want to go there so bad."

"I saw it on Animal Planet," Zoey said.

"You get Animal Planet at home?"

"Yeah. We have an international cable bundle. CNN gets cut out
sometimes."

"That's nice," Alva said. "I've never seen those channels."

A bubble stretched, popped, and was vacuumed back into Zoey's
lips. "I live really close. Right here in the Club, actually. You want to come
over after school?"

"Sure," Alva said.

Zoey nodded and walked back to her desk. It was like they'd gotten
over the leap toward a first date. Zoey's family must be loaded to live
at the country club. Alva had heard rumors about Zoey's father being
a finance bigwig. Girls' bathroom talk, whines from other stalls: "Zoey
Cruise is such a *bitch.*" But Alva didn't ask anyone what Zoey had done.
She was content being Zoey's new best friend, and she didn't need to
know why the job was open.

For the rest of the day, her mind lingered on Zoey's strange essay, on
the sparsely populated frozen tundras, where beasts hunted men in their
own streets, where predators outnumbered prey.

She'd miss the school bus tonight if she went to Zoey's, but that
was fine. Gao Xiaofan was in a cybercafe somewhere, and Li Xinwei
was shut inside Mincai. Fortunes in Shanghai changed in a blink, and
now she'd go to Zoey Cruise's house and watch American channels and

maybe if CNN did cut out at the most suspicious of times, a scrambled signal right as some inconvenient truth about the Middle Kingdom was mentioned, Alva wouldn't mind. Maybe it didn't concern her after all.

A driver came to pick up Zoey, even though she lived only a few minutes away from campus. "It's because of the shantytowns right outside," Zoey explained. "My parents don't want me walking around by myself, in case some desperate peasant attacks me."

"Has anything happened before?"

"No, they're crazy," Zoey said. "The club's security is basically militarized. They're paranoid about a native riot or something."

The family's car was a black Range Rover with creamy leather seats. Alva had never experienced a less bumpy ride, raised high above the usual dents and potholes of Chinese asphalt, along the wide lanes surrounding the golf course. Three minutes later they were parked in front of an opulent turreted villa with faux sun-kissed Tuscan walls.

Alva unbuckled her seat belt. Zoey put her hand on her arm.

"Wait," Zoey said. "Feng comes to open it."

The driver, a Chinese man who hadn't uttered a word thus far, leapt out of the car and was already by Zoey's door.

"Every time?"

"It's one of my dad's rules."

Feng brusquely pulled Alva's car door open, not meeting her eyes. Zoey didn't thank him, so neither did Alva. He climbed back in the parked car. Did he spend his days inside the car, staring at the golf course?

They walked up the porch stairs and Zoey buzzed the intercom. It rang and rang with no answer. "Is there no one home?" Alva asked.

"There's always someone home." Zoey pushed the buzzer again with obvious irritation. "We have a live-in maid."

They heard a scuffle and footsteps. The door pulled open, and a woman with tan skin and red watery eyes bowed her head. "Sorry, Miss Zoey," she said. "I did not hear over the vacuum cleaner."

The maid's smooth English took Alva by surprise. The woman was clearly not Chinese—maybe Filipina or Malaysian. "Seriously, Girlie?" Zoey asked. The maid couldn't be more than five feet tall. Both Zoey and Alva towered over her. "We were out there for, like, five minutes."

The maid pulled out two pairs of fluffy white slippers and set them before Alva and Zoey. "Sorry, Miss Zoey," she said again. But Zoey stormed off, slipperless, to the staircase—a real prom-picture staircase, curved around the foyer—and shouted, "Mom? MOM?"

"Madam Julia is exercising," the maid said.

"Let's go to my room," Zoey said. Alva followed her upstairs, through a hallway lined with equidistant abstract paintings. Zoey's room had its own lounge area, like a hotel suite.

Alva stretched out on the velvety couch. Zoey turned on the TV and zapped through the channels. They were all in English. "There's nothing good," she said. She settled for a rerun of *American Idol* auditions in Milwaukee. "I've seen this before," she told Alva. "These people are fucking awful. But Simon Cowell is my spirit animal."

There was a rasp at the door. "It's just Girlie," Zoey said. "I can tell from the knock." The maid came in with a tray laden with miniature Evian bottles, cranberry almond crisps, and Boursin cheese.

"Madam Julia said to bring you snacks," Girlie said.

"She's done with her workout?"

"She saw you and your friend from the intercom screen in the home gym."

"Okay," Zoey said. "You can go now, Girlie."

After the maid left, Zoey rolled her eyes. "My mother must be thrilled I've brought a friend."

"You don't invite people over?" Alva asked carefully.

"Haven't you figured it out? I'm an outcast."

Alva had never seen anyone actually be mean to Zoey—she didn't look like someone easily bullied. But it was true not many people talked to her.

"I heard that your family had to move from Hong Kong," Alva said. "And that you don't really hang out with anyone at SAS."

Zoey narrowed her eyes. "Whatever," she said. "I have friends. They're just in college already."

"Friends from your old school?"

"Yeah. We were in Hong Kong for three years before this. My dad asked to transfer to Singapore but his company only had an opening here. My mom was so pissed about having to go to *mainland* China, but she wasn't in any position to bitch. The company gave us a really good package to make up for it."

"What company does your dad work for?" Alva asked.

Zoey spat out a long string of men's names. "He's vice president in the China office now."

"And you moved for his job?"

"No," Zoey said. She hesitated, then sighed. "There was a minor scandal with a domestic worker. It was in the press and everything. That's why we had to leave. My mom couldn't take it anymore."

Alva just nodded.

"Anyways, what's your deal?" Zoey asked. "Why did you transfer midyear?"

"There was also a scandal at my old school. I got in trouble with the authorities."

"Shit." Zoey's eyes widened. "Did you call Chairman Mao bald or something?"

"No," Alva said. "I talked back to a teacher." She sensed Zoey would be unimpressed by HentaiLord; she'd heard her say anime was for nerds.

"That's still crazy. Why were you even in public school?"

"I went there since kindergarten. That's all my mom could afford. She used to teach English." That sounded so lame, unglamorous. "Before that she was an actress in L.A."

"She was in L.A.? Was she in any movies?"

"Yeah, she was the lead once," Alva said. "Back in the eighties, a movie about colonial Indochina. The set was in Cambodia. But then production broke down and the movie never got released. My mom decided to stay in Asia."

"Cambodia?"

"Yeah."

"That's weird."

"Why?"

"Wasn't it run by the Khmer Rouge in the eighties? It'd be like shooting in a war zone."

Alva had never learned about the Khmer Rouge at Mincai. She only knew that the textbooks summarily approved of anything Rouge, in North Korea and Vietnam and Cuba. "Maybe it was somewhere else," she said. "Vietnam or Thailand. Maybe I'm misremembering."

"Yeah," Zoey yawned. "It's all same same but different."

"What?"

"My friends who backpacked in Southeast Asia taught me that. It's, like, a tagphrase."

On-screen, a white-toothed blond girl in cowboy boots was shrieking after being told she was moving on to the next round. "Anyways," Alva said. "Now my mom married this businessman and they're gone all the time." She didn't specify that the businessman was Chinese. "There's usually no one home when I get back and I have dinner in front of the TV."

"Oh, Girlie brings me dinner here most nights," Zoey said. "My dad is the only one who cares about family meals, but he's never here."

Alva thought of all the parentless apartments in Shanghai, all the children in front of glowing screens.

"Wouldn't be this way in Churchill," Zoey said. Alva looked over and, at first, Zoey's profile was bored, serious, then they both burst out laughing.

## 23

February and March in Shanghai were cold, mud-colored. Alva stood hands forked over hips in the goalie box, watching the Yellow Sea turn to ink in the distance. She'd signed up because Zoey was a striker on the soccer team. After a couple practices, it became obvious Alva's foot and the ball interplayed with repulsive magnetism. Then Elisa, the goalie, quit because her parents wanted her to focus on Toastmasters' instead, and the coach put Alva on goalie training. Miraculously, she wasn't half bad.

Alva liked the practices. She enjoyed the sweat and the cleats and the whipping ponytails, the clinking of shin guards in duffel bags, the understated communication between teammates: no bullshit high school girl codes here, only shouts relaying the arc of the spinning ball, invisible lines guiding a mounting attack, the instinctual anticipation of where the leathered orb would land.

Because the SAS Pudong campus was so far out in the boonies, missing the after-school bus did create logistical problems. At first Alva tried getting lifts to the last subway stop on Line 2. But there were so many commuters crowding along the platform of Zhangjiang Hi-Tech station that, the first time she tried catching the train there at rush hour, she became trapped in a crowd frantically pressing ahead. She was pushed toward the platform's edge, with every other person focused on squeezing themselves back into the inner layers of the flow, away from danger, ejecting the weakest toward the precipice. It'd felt so precarious

Alva abandoned the idea of rush hour subway altogether—this was before a wave of deaths prompted the city to add guardrails to the stations.

When she told Sloan and Lu Fang about the soccer-home logistical conundrum, Sloan couldn't repress a nasty little smile. "A few months at the American School and you're already too good for the subway."

"You guys take taxis home from Puxi every day," Alva said.

"And Lu Fang already paid for your school bus. What a waste."

"I don't have a choice. I have to go to practice."

"No one's forcing you to be on that team," Sloan said.

"I like soccer, Mom."

"What position do you play?" Lu Fang interjected.

They both looked toward him. He was smoking his Double Red Happiness on the couch. Alva remembered the soccer jerseys buried deep in his closet. "Goalie," she said.

"It's good for young people to have a passion," he said.

Sloan sighed. "She'll grow sick of it by next month."

"I won't," Alva said. "I like it. The coach said it could be good for college."

"College, college," Sloan said. "She's in ninth grade, and already talking about college. That's how eager she is to leave me. She's already turning into a little American."

"I was always American," Alva said.

"How much do you need for the taxis home?" Lu Fang asked.

"Five hundred a week."

"Okay," he said. "I'll leave it on the hallway table."

It was an unabashed overestimate; the fare came closer to fifty yuan per trip. But Alva had gotten into the habit of factoring in imaginary inflation when asking Lu Fang for money—skimming the fat into a personal reserve she could spend on trips to Super Brand Mall, on higher-shelf imported liquor at Carrefour. Sometimes she looked up the prices of plane tickets online. It was an exercise in fantasy: the prices were exorbitant and she was a minor. But the reality of those six letters—PVG-JFK—made her both breathless from possibility and nauseous from dread. One day she'd go, and it'd be a true, complete, irreparable severance from China. After each flight lookup she closed the windows quickly, like she'd done something dirty, and scrubbed her search history blank.

One warm spring day, to save the taxi money, Alva exited the golf course gates and walked along the highways of outer Pudong, past the fields and satellite villages in the dusk. There was no apparent danger lurking in the villages, the peasants did not spring out of the rows of crops to attack her savagely. An old man ambled along the opposite side of the highway with an emaciated yellow ox, his hand resting lovingly on its flank.

Calves caked from dirt from the soccer field, Alva walked until she grew too tired and found a bus stop. The city center's skyscrapers were invisible in the distance. She had read somewhere on the internet that it wasn't true astronauts could see the Great Wall of China from space. What they could see were the yellow clouds of smog blooming over Beijing and Shanghai.

The air quality of Links Golf and Country Club was the freshest in the city, the vast seaside property seemingly immune to the drift of factory chimneys. For the past few months, Alva tried not to think about the smog shrouding Century Park, about the cram sessions and red neckerchiefs of Mincai. All of it was irrelevant now that she was at the Shanghai American School. And yet, when she looked back at the red roofs and green lawns of SAS, she sometimes felt an uneasy feeling. A feeling like guilt.

Gao Xiaofan's QQ icon was gray on her phone. She stared at it often but only talked to him occasionally, not wanting to seem too eager. Every few weeks she'd cave and ask for updates. Smiling and Proud Wanderer reported to HentaiLord: yes, Li Xinwei was still captain of the Communist Young Pioneers, and she'd scored highest in the whole district on the latest round of mock exams. There was a new Homework Delegate who didn't give anyone free passes. Teng Xin's dad was planning to send him off to a private school in Australia next year. And Gao Xiaofan himself—he was just trying to make it through the grade; the Chinese education system was no longer mandatory after nine years. He kept sending Alva rooftopping links.

She'd hated those videos at first. Now, she couldn't help but watch one after another on her phone as she waited for the bus. Shanghai was becoming the epicenter for rooftoppers in China. Most of them were active on CityX, which was full of video tours of Shanghai's skyscrapers by an army of trespassers, teens guffawing to escape guards, selfie sticks shaking over bird's-eye views. They stood on platforms smaller than the length of their feet, on mere spikes, lightning conductors, and for a second or two they'd let go of everything, holding only their phones, their selfie sticks, the city spreading infinite beneath their feet. One rooftopper shouted into the wind in one of his videos, "Why do I do it? Because I'm bored! Because this makes me feel alive!"

On the bus, the dot next to Smiling and Proud Wanderer flickered green. She typed:

HentaiLord: You're barely online these days

笑傲江湖: they keep us after school until dark

笑傲江湖: There's no question I'll flunk the zhongkao

HentaiLord: Why are you wasting time practicing for it?

Gao had encouraged her to break things open after all. He was the reason she was at the Shanghai American School. The least she could do was return the favor, help Gao Xiaofan see he could also stick a finger to the system he hated.

HentaiLord: I dare you to break free

She waited for an answer, but his little dot went gray.

## 24

Zoey Cruise's parents existed only in aristocratic hypothetical—Mister Daniel and Madam Julia, as Girlie called them. As the soccer season went on, Alva was at Zoey's almost every night. She'd never seen Zoey's parents, though, until the day Girlie buzzed open the door with a look of panic. "Miss Zoey, your father is back from Singapore. He wants to have dinner together."

"Shit," Zoey said.

Alva and Zoey were dirty in their sweat-soaked jerseys and grassy knee-high socks. Zoey dropped her Puma bag on the floor.

"I can leave," Alva said.

"No, you stay," Zoey shook her head. "Girlie, plan for four people, all right?"

Girlie seemed on edge and in no mood to argue. She nodded and jogged back to the kitchen.

"Are you sure?" Alva said. "I've been here so many times and haven't met your mom." Alva was sure Madam Julia monitored her comings and goings from the intercom; Girlie was always bringing elaborate playdate snacks of sliced fruit and finger sandwiches, room service courtesy of Madam Julia.

"You're not the rude one," Zoey said. "She is."

Madam Julia was always in her quarters working out. Alva imagined a fabulous, mermaidlike creature, toned and sculpted, buffed and polished. Except, as far as Alva could tell, this mermaid never ventured out of the Links Golf and Country Club. She assumed it had something to do with the Hong Kong lawsuit, some page 9 tabloid news Madam Julia had yet to live down. Alva had tried searching for Julia Cruise online, but most Hong Kong newspapers were across the internet firewall, and Alva had decided not to climb over. As long as she could come to the Cruises' company-provided villa, drink their Loire Valley wine, and eat cucumber-butter sandwiches, she didn't need to know. Zoey held the key to a fuck-allness Alva was watching herself take in and regurgitate. In this case, Alva decided, to rise above the gossip, to not know about the Cruise lawsuit, was required to maintain critical distance.

Zoey said Alva could shower and change in the guest room. The pressure from the showerhead was like a small waterfall, scathing hot, pummeling Alva's back. She inspected the shampoo and conditioner: not a word of Chinese, imported straight from Swiss thermal baths. They smelled like mint and lavender, clean and severe, unlike the gamut of coconut-mango-vanilla products Alva liked. She now saw her error: a predictable middle-class preference. She found a disposable razor in a drawer. With it she erased the black stubble growing out under her arms. The razor glided like a snail, leaving a trail of slime.

The guest bathroom was equipped with a white bathrobe and stacks of towels—were these possessions the Cruises moved from city to city, or did they come provided with company housing? Regardless, Alva was going to use them all. She fastened the sash of the bathrobe, wrapped her hair in a towel, and padded another around her neck. She left no cabinet door unopened, smeared on every lotion she found. The bedroom itself looked straight out of a home decor catalog, its walls a powdered baby blue, its king-size bed thickly blanketed with ornamental pillows. A perfect bedroom nobody slept in.

When she went downstairs, Alva found Zoey talking to a silver-haired man. He had ice-blue eyes and a domineering posture upheld easily by his height, and he exuded the assurance of a corporate executive who didn't need to labor to appear important.

"A pleasure," Daniel said, shaking Alva's hand. "I hear you are a mean goalkeeper. I'll have to come watch one of your games."

Zoey had changed into a Cornell sweatshirt, her hair up in a bun, adorned by a barrette only little girls wore. "Daddy, don't make promises you can't keep," she said in a singsong voice. She hugged her father around the waist and made a face at Alva from behind his back. It was weird, seeing a girl and a man touch like that, with such easy affection.

They all moved toward the dining room table. There was a bouquet of hydrangeas framed by candles in the center, and sets of polished silverware. Daniel turned to Alva, ran a hand through the perfectly crested gray wave in his hair.

"I just got back from Singapore. It really is an amazing country. An authoritarian state that pioneers green architecture."

Alva sat up very straight. "I've never been . . . sir."

"Please, call me Daniel. Well, it's worth visiting. It melds the incredible diversity in Asia. Have you traveled around the continent much?"

"No, sir."

"You don't need to call me sir," Daniel said, lowering his voice.

Girlie scurried in with a soup container. "Madam Julia is coming, sir," she announced.

"Thank you, Girlie," Daniel said. "You can set the tureen here."

They heard quick footsteps down the grand staircase. Alva braced herself for a sculpturesque society wife, but the woman who entered the dining room was short and plain, in black pants, a blue Oxford button-down, and close-cropped brown hair.

"We finally meet," Madam Julia said, sounding shockingly pleasant and normal.

"Thank you so much for having me—" Alva said, half rising from her seat.

Madam Julia waved her down. "Of course. Sorry I've been so busy; a dinner together is long overdue."

"The soup is a split pea and lardon velouté," Girlie announced, creeping around the table's edge. "The ribeyes will be out medium-rare in a minute."

Were there training schools for luxury maids in the Philippines? Polite society is what Sloan would call this—a real dinner party. Zoey looked bored. She only squirmed with obvious discomfort when Julia insisted they hold hands and say grace.

"Mom," Zoey said, "Alva isn't religious."

"I don't mind," Alva said.

Daniel speed-recited a blessing, and Alva whispered "Amen" with the rest of them.

When Alva opened her eyes, she found Julia peering at her with interest. "Your parents raised you atheist?"

"Not atheist," Alva said. "My mother just—she didn't ever talk about religion."

Daniel nodded. "The suppression of Confucianism has created a vacuum of spirituality in China."

"Her mom's *American*, Daddy," Zoey said.

"Oh, really?" Julia said. "Where in America is she from?"

"She grew up in the Southwest, then moved to L.A."

"For college?" Daniel perked up. "Our firm does some heavy recruiting out there—USC, UCLA. Lots of Asian Americans amenable to overseas work in China."

"Her mom's *white*, Daddy," Zoey said.

"Oh, how unusual," Julia said. "I mean, for your father to be Asian. It's usually the other way around."

"Did she go to Occidental then, or Pepperdine?" Daniel pressed. "I know some alumni there. What year did she graduate?"

"She didn't go to college," Alva said. "She moved there for acting."

"Ah," Julia said.

Daniel cleared his throat. "An actress! Was she in anything we'd know?"

"She was the lead in one movie, but it never came out," Alva said.

"What was the film about?" Julia asked.

"It was about a Chinese businessman falling in love with a white girl from a poor colonial family. In Indochina."

"Hmm. Like *The Lover*," Julia said.

"Poor colonials?" Daniel said. "Does such a thing exist?"

"Well, Marguerite Duras considered herself a poor colonial. The book is very autobiographical," Julia said.

She spoke articulately, evidently someone who'd received a good education. "Sorry, what is *The Lover*?" Alva asked.

"Oh," Julia said. "I thought you knew. It must be the book that movie was based on: Marguerite Duras's *The Lover*. That plot you described is the exact same."

Alva shifted in her seat. *The Lover?* Things weren't adding up and she had to backpedal. She didn't want to show her ignorance. "That is the name; I think I just forgot," she said.

"I didn't know about a canceled version," Julia said. "The French eventually made a beautiful movie of it in 1992. I remember reading the book in my French class at Vassar. *Je voudrais manger les seins d'Hélène Lagonelle* . . . I was so shocked by it then."

"What does it mean?" Zoey asked.

Julia blushed. "She wants to eat the breasts of another foreign girl."

Daniel bit mockingly into his steak. "The French are filthy," he growled.

"To quote my professor, the heroine wants to eat the erotic whiteness she is herself to the Chinese lover," Julia said. "Oh, I don't know. It's a lot of nonsense."

"So your mother lived in Asia and married a Chinese man, like in this movie?" Daniel asked.

"Yes, I guess," Alva said. The steak smelled rich and buttery, but she couldn't taste it. Why hadn't Sloan told her about the book, the other movie that was actually made, whose plot so neatly resembled their lives? Now she looked like an idiot in front of the Cruises. "Well, she actually only got married last year. To my stepfather."

"They don't get married in the book," Julia interjected softly. "He leaves her. Her family cannot take a Chinese man seriously, and his cannot accept a poor foreign woman. Also, she is fifteen."

"Ew," Zoey said. "I'm fifteen."

"So your stepfather is Chinese. What about your father?" Daniel asked Alva.

"He's Chinese too. But he's— I never knew him."

"Oh, I'm sorry," Julia said.

"I thought you were mixed," Daniel said. "Beautiful combination."

"Oh my god, Dad," Zoey whined. Julia smiled chastisingly.

"All right, all right," Daniel said. "These two are the compliment police. Apparently it's no longer allowed to call Chinese women beautiful."

Alva blushed into her soup. She knew it was Chinese women in general being discussed, but it still felt like praise. Usually it was Chinese people who called her mother beautiful. No one ever called Alva beautiful.

"So your mother raised you in Shanghai?" Julia asked, nodding at Girlie for a refill of wine in her thin, high-stemmed glass. Alva thought of the beer mug Sloan drank from, the effortful chitchat that reigned over their infrequent meals with Lu Fang. The Cruises were so jovial, so interested in Alva.

"Yes," Alva said, "I went to public school here."

"Why didn't she transfer you to international school earlier?" Julia said.

"We didn't have the money," Alva said, and only their stiff smiles helped her realize she'd been too blunt.

"Did she stay an actress?" Julia asked.

"No," Alva said. "She taught English. We lived over in Puxi."

"Must have given you such perspective," Daniel said. "That's what I always tell Zoey. That she should be more interested in the local perspective."

He'd risen to get himself another beer from the fridge. When he sat down, his knee accidentally bumped against Alva's.

"Speaking of local perspectives," he said, "what are your thoughts on this Olympic torch relay business?"

"Oh," Alva said. Since the new semester started, she'd barely paid attention to the news. She'd seen rumblings of the outrage online. "You mean the spitting on the Chinese athletes?"

"Yes, the boycott," Daniel said. "On account of Tibet, the Dalai Lama, human rights, the usual."

Julia sighed. "Maybe these teenagers don't want to talk about politics, Daniel."

"But she"—he gestured at Alva—"has the *local* perspective. I'm interested in hearing it."

"You already know the local perspective," Julia said.

Alva set down her steak knife. "Maybe people *should* boycott the Olympics."

Daniel blinked, surprised, and then he raised his glass. "I don't disagree," he said. "They've probably bugged the walls and will kick me out for this, but how else will the Chinese people ever know what the world thinks of their government?"

Julia placed her hand on his. "Daniel," she said. "You are being insensitive. And they *have* bugged the walls. So let's have dessert, and let this subject rest."

Daniel sighed, though he was smiling. Girlie brought over coupes of banana pudding. "Modeled after Magnolia Bakery's in New York," Julia said. "I've taught Girlie to replicate some of my favorite recipes."

"This pudding reminds me of Metro-North rides," Daniel said.

"Daniel commuted when we first got married," Julia said. "We had a little house in Old Saybrook."

"You lived in a *little* house?" Zoey clutched her heart.

Julia ignored her. "Do you like it?" she asked Alva. "It really is the best pudding. Have you ever had the original?"

"No," Alva said. "I've never been to America."

"Oh," Julia gasped. "We've been so rude, talking about it like—"

"No," Alva said. "I don't mind at all." She'd liked the way Daniel and Julia mentioned foreign names of towns, restaurants, and train lines as if it were natural Alva would be of this world, familiar with their references. "I'm taking notes for when I go."

"We're renting a property in the Hamptons in August," Daniel said. "I used to summer in East Hampton as a boy. Best beaches are on the Atlantic, Alva. If you like wild waves."

"I love wild waves," Alva said, though she'd never swam in any sea.

Julia smiled. "It'd be nice for Zoey to have a companion."

Zoey winked at Alva and pulled out a new piece of bubble gum.

They finished the meal over pleasant chitchat. Alva wondered if Sloan would ever let her go to America for the summer, if the Cruises were serious about taking her. Maybe Lu Fang could pay for the plane ticket, write the minor authorization letter. Maybe the Cruises themselves would pay for the ticket—it'd be nothing to them. She imagined herself walking with Zoey down the streets of New York, sunbathing at beach clubs in the Hamptons. Just like on *Gossip Girl*.

"Alva should sleep over," Zoey said after Girlie cleared the plates. "It's late and she lives far. Can she, Daddy?"

"Yes, stay," Daniel said. "We're not lacking in the guest rooms department. We'll have Girlie prepare a bed."

"Your parents will be fine with this, Alva?" Julia asked.

"I'll text my mom," Alva said. She took out her phone and typed to Lu Fang's number: *Sleeping over at a friend's house tonight at Links country club*

Immediately he responded: *Ask your mother?*

Alva put her phone in her pocket. "Yes, my parents are fine with it," she told the Cruises. "Thank you so much for having me."


"My parents liked you," Zoey said when they'd retreated to her bedroom. She took a bottle of Bombay Sapphire from her minifridge freezer and started mixing gin and tonics.

"I feel bad we talked about me the whole time." Alva sank into Zoey's velvet couch.

"They found you very interesting, I'm sure," Zoey said. "They think I don't have friends."

"Because of the lawsuit?"

Zoey turned toward her. "You really don't know?"

The way Zoey's shoulders untensed—it was like a weight lifted, that she could tell the story herself. "Our maid in Hong Kong sued," she said. "She found a legal organization that represented domestic workers and sued for physical abuse. My mom—she couldn't handle the publicity. That's why we had to move."

Alva couldn't imagine sophisticated, understated Julia striking a maid. But now she replayed how Julia watched Girlie's movements at dinner. There was a draconian grip hidden behind Julia's self-erasure; she was perpetually absent and yet always watching from the grayscale screens of the intercom.

"It was in the *South China Morning Post*," Zoey said. "They didn't name names but everybody in Hong Kong expat circles knew it was our maid. Dad paid to settle the lawsuit. Then he arranged a transfer, and that's how we ended up here."

"Was he upset with your mom?" Alva thought of Daniel's cordial repartee with his wife, how they chided each other charmingly. How performative it all seemed now.

Zoey wasn't listening. "Everybody at SAS knew when I came here," she said.

Her eyes were rimmed with red, and Alva worried she was about to cry. She scooted awkwardly next to Zoey, put an arm around her shoulders: American girls hugged. "It doesn't matter to me," Alva said. "I like your parents."

"You know, back in Connecticut we were solidly middle class." Zoey didn't shrug Alva's arm away. "Maybe upper-middle. We lived in the suburbs and I went to a private school. I was in sixth grade when my dad got transferred to Hong Kong, and everybody thought it was crazy we were moving to Asia. I missed my friends, but it was so exciting—even at the American Airlines lounge at JFK. I think that's when it hit us, in that JFK lounge: that we were going to be special from now on."

Zoey paused to take a sip of her gin and tonic.

"But something happened to all of us. In America my mom had a real job. Here she didn't need to work anymore. They hired maids and nannies and tutors and drivers, the company paid for it all."

"Your mom never leaves the house now," Alva said.

"It's the one realm she thinks is safe: this house. But it's leased, not even ours. It will be another family's the second we decide to leave. All she does is exercise on her stationary bike and rage-buy imported Ann Taylor clothes online. Her New York job used to be good, you know. I'm not sure she wanted to give it up and be an expat socialite in Asia. Now she's afraid of the outside—what people know, how fast things change. She wants to go back to America."

"She probably feels guilty," Alva said.

"Yeah," Zoey said. "Probably. But we're not moving. Not with the kind of money Dad is making here."

There was a Chinese saying Lu Fang liked: talk about 曹操 and 曹操 arrives. The door unlatched and Daniel peeked his head in.

"Dad!" Zoey yelped. "You could knock."

They held their gin and tonics, but it looked like they were drinking ice water.

"Sorry," Daniel said. He had changed out of his suit and into a slim-fitting black T-shirt. The sleeves squeezed his biceps in a way that made Alva take another sip of her drink, if only to look away. "Just letting Alva know that Girlie set up the guest room down the hall for her."

"Thank you," Alva said.

"Lovely to have you here. Julia says so too. You're welcome any time." He closed the door behind him.

They stayed quiet for a few seconds after he left.

"He likes you," Zoey said. "He probably thinks you're a good influence. And that we're going to sit here and braid each other's hair."

"We could, Z," Alva said. "Or we could get shit-faced." She raised her near-empty glass.

Zoey's thin pink lips stretched into a line. "Attagirl," she said in an exaggerated, guttural male voice, and they burst out laughing.

That night, as Alva lay in the plushest bed she'd ever sunk into, she checked her phone. As expected, neither Sloan nor Lu Fang had texted. Did her mother know she wasn't home, or was Sloan busy at some Puxi banquet? If she and Lu Fang didn't care, maybe Alva could stop living in that tacky Century Park apartment and move in with the Cruises entirely. There were so many rooms here. She and Zoey could be driven to school together, come home from practice together, copy each other's assignments while drinking wine and watching the CW.

Zoey had already talked about the Links clubhouse infinity pool that looked out onto the sea, which itself was too dirty to swim in. They'll work on their tans once it opens, Zoey had said, and go out in the city at night. Then, later during summer break, Alva could fly with them to JFK, American Airlines business class.

*You should reconsider being a colonial,* Alva wanted to text Sloan. *It's actually a pretty good life.*

## 25

Her mother's blond head wove through the throngs of diners huddling around the buffet stations. Sloan melted into the crowd here, at the Pudong Shangri-La Easter buffet, 699 RMB per person. Alva had asked for this for her fifteenth birthday. As a child, if she could have torn out the ads from *That's Shanghai* and licked them for sustenance, she would have. But of course it was something they couldn't afford. She'd told Lu Fang, offhandedly, and then watched the idea overtake his face.

Almost everyone at the Shangri-La was a foreigner, along with an army of mixed Eurasian offspring with brown hair, milky complexions, and dark eyes. The children chased one another around in their Sunday best, smudging ketchup on frilly dresses, screaming in English and French. The Chinese staff looked on, smiling obligingly, picking up dirty plates, mopping up spillages.

Lu Fang was walking back to their table, brandishing a crab leg midair.

"You have to go for the maximum price-value ratio," he said. "What do you think they do with the leftover food? Does the staff eat it?"

Alva swallowed the sip she'd stolen from her mother's glass of sauvignon blanc. "Probably not," she said.

"There's this poem—" Lu Fang began.

Alva sighed as he recited, "The spoiled alcohol and meat at the gates of the Zhu mansion sit stinking, while the frozen corpses line the street outside."

"Right." She stood and her chair rattled more violently than she'd intended. She didn't need his oblique opinions on her choice of birthday dining—not from a man who took her mother to three business banquets a week. She wanted to roam among the foreigners. She wanted the world to see that she was fifteen, and beautiful, and if she wanted to eat at the Shangri-La, she fucking ate there.

Today, she was wearing a new Zara dress, a pale pink shift that came down midthigh. She felt the eyes of expat fathers as she circled the food stations. One man in a Ralph Lauren polo repeatedly appeared by her side. Was he following her, brushing against her on purpose? She could feel him right behind her. She turned around to hand him the cheese knife. He said "thank you" and his hand, a big hand with hairy knuckles, touched hers. He smelled like woody cologne. She said, "you're welcome" and walked away quickly. It felt powerful: the buzz of the wine, the man's desire.

Maybe these men wondered if she was young enough to be someone's teenage daughter, or old enough to join a table where an older white man sat alone. She didn't want them to see the blond woman furiously downing her drink, and the paunchy Chinese man shattering a crab's carapace with his doughy hands. Her mother and Lu Fang looked uncomfortable, out of place in this clientele that seemed to consist of either jet-setting families or geriatric expat men and pretty Chinese girls.

Sloan used to call this kind of couple gold diggers and their Yankee sugar daddies. She'd taught Alva to disdain *those* kinds of unions, *those* kinds of families, *those* kinds of offspring. "That man will be *dead* by the time the kid is in middle school. Good riddance, as long as she has a green card in her back pocket."

Usually, when people assumed Alva's dad was the white one, she remembered her mother's disdain and was proud to narrow her eyes and set them straight. "My *mom's* the foreigner." That line always had great success, especially with the taxi drivers who wanted to know everything about Alva's ancestry. When they found out her mother was foreign, they said, "Well, your dad must be *good*!" Alva didn't tell them her dad was an unnamed squirt of sperm. She wished she could be as proud of him as the taxi drivers. But what did it mean, this *good*? It was like anyone chosen by an American woman must be a man among men, while the Chinese women who married white were silently scoffed at by all.

She sat down at Lu Fang and Sloan's table. Horrified, she realized that the other diners must think him her father. They looked like a family, and why would anyone assume otherwise? Even if they lacked the easy affection of the families surrounding them, the hair ruffling and gentle scolding, the intimacy of being a unit. Instead, they projected a sad rigidity, a joyless performance of a birthday. She wondered if others heard her call Lu Fang "Uncle Lu," if that explained how distant they all were, if that made this lugubrious domestic portrait any less pathetic.

Her plate was piled with smoked salmon, raw salmon, rare steak, caviar, four kinds of cheese engulfed by an advancing mush of goat curry. "You didn't have to get it all in one trip," Sloan said.

"She's doing good. You have to get the six hundred ninety-nine yuans' worth," Lu Fang said.

"It's obscene." Sloan nibbled at a smear of foie gras on a tiny cracker. "These expats could have a more authentic meal for ten yuan at the market in Chenghuang Temple."

"That complex is quite touristy, actually," Lu Fang said.

"That's true," Alva said. "No Shanghainese person actually goes there."

Sloan ignored them. "I'll tell you what it reminds me of—" She tapped a nail against her wineglass. "The Grand Hotel in Siem Reap."

Lu Fang wiped his fingers on the starched napkin and leaned back. Alva sighed. She knew this story.

"A few actresses and I heard about their Christmas lunch," Sloan continued. "So we decided to leave the set, take the day off, and see the Grand Hotel. There was a park right in front of the hotel, and an old woman sitting next to a stroller. The baby in the stroller had a head ballooning to twice the size of a normal human head. The woman was holding a sign in English asking for money. We all ran toward the hotel; I felt sick to my stomach. But once we got past the grand staircase, we forgot about the baby. The hotel was another world—foreign men in white linen suits, women in espadrilles gorging on caviar and champagne. We left so full our bellies were bursting. It was growing dark and the woman and her stroller and the deformed baby were still in the park. I took out a Cambodian coin and gave it to the old woman. And then, the baby, in a grown man's voice, because it was a grown man trapped in a deformed child's body, said, 'Miss, we only take American dollars.'"

Lu Fang groaned and shook his head.

"That's when I knew I was in a place too deeply corrupted by the West," Sloan continued. "They said that in Asia only China wasn't like that. But now it's changing here too."

Alva pushed her plate away. "What was the movie called?"

"What?" Sloan said.

"The movie you were there to shoot."

Sloan smiled her closed-lipped smile. "I don't think they ever finalized the title. It was so long ago."

"You know, the plot sounds a lot like *The Lover*," Alva said.

"I've never heard of it," Sloan said.

"And how come you were in Cambodia in the eighties? Didn't the Khmer Rouge—"

"There are no more beggars in the street of China," Lu Fang interrupted. "One way to eradicate poverty is by wheeling all the poor off your streets. Now, who wants another round of crab legs?"

Sloan and Alva both shook their heads. Sloan drained her glass and held it out for a waiter to refill, ignoring Alva. *The Lover* had clearly hit a nerve. Had her mother not known the book, or that another movie had been made? Alva wished they weren't fighting, so they could huddle at this table and laugh at the others, so she could tell Sloan about Julia Cruise and her snooty Vassar classes, about Beverly Steward's blue eyeshadow, the textbooks with pages so thick they gave you paper cuts and the soccer fields of evergreen plastic grass. But Sloan only pulled from her wineglass, and Alva stayed silent.

The check was brought to the table after Lu Fang returned, and he signed the hefty bill. "Happy birthday," he said.

Alva answered, perfunctorily, "It's nice to be all together as a family."

Lu Fang opened his mouth, and after a few seconds said, "Thank you."

He smiled at her, somehow horrifyingly, genuinely touched, so much so that Alva was forced to look away.

## 26

Girlie always made up the bed perfectly, the sheets wrinkle-free and white, even after the time Alva accidentally stained them with period blood. She had, of course, found fresh tampons in the bathroom cabinet: Tampax, an American brand, and they'd glided in so easily.

By the end of spring, Alva was spending most weeknights in the Cruises' guest suite. This morning, she opened a bathroom drawer and found a brand-new electric blue Maybelline eyeliner, which she applied copiously. She also spotted one of Zoey's sparkly barrettes. Alva clipped it behind her ear. Black roots were sprouting from her scalp, a sharp line demarcating her frizzy bleach job.

Downstairs, she was surprised to find Daniel, in a gray suit and sitting erect at the marble counter. "Mornin'," he said. "You're an early riser."

Alva climbed on top the barstool across from him. "I've been waking up at 6:30 A.M. my whole life."

"That's disciplined."

"That's Chinese school."

"Right. Militaristic." He pushed the tray of toasted bread and assorted jams toward her. "SAS is a walk in the park in comparison, isn't it?"

Alva slathered her toast with a fat glob of butter. "It's all right. The math is easy."

"Sure. Chinese kids are doing multivariable calculus in first grade."

"No." Alva bit into her toast. "Kindergarten."

He smiled at her joke. "Some of the young Chinese analysts at our firm . . . you'd think they are walking, human-size calculators."

Alva was surprised. "Chinese people work at your firm?"

"Of course."

"So you speak Chinese?"

"Well, no," he said. "We only hire the ones who speak English."

Alva nodded. Daniel was leafing through an English newspaper called the *International Herald Tribune*. The main headline said something about stock markets above the picture of a giant screen with red and green numbers. "This is what you do?" she asked Daniel.

"Yes," he said. "Let's say its health is crucial to what I do."

"Did you always know you wanted to do it?"

Daniel cocked his head. "Actually, no. I wanted to be an archaeologist when I was a boy. Like Indiana Jones."

"I've seen all the movies," Alva said. "I have *Kingdom of the Crystal Skull*, if you want to borrow it."

"Doesn't it come out in May?"

Alva sipped her coffee with her pinkie raised in mock sophistication. "I have the best pirated DVD supplier in the city. He's an expert on Bertolt Brecht."

"That's why I love China." Daniel sighed happily. "Anything goes."

He was folding the newspaper now, stuffing it into a leather briefcase. Alva didn't want him to leave yet. It was so easy to talk to him, to sit at this marble countertop with its continental spread and imagine every breakfast could be like this.

"Maybe I will borrow that DVD," Daniel said, pausing at the door.

"Then we can both be outlaws," she said.

She was grateful when he laughed again. He was looking at her barrette and she reflexively combed her fingers through her hair, shielding it.

"I like it," he said. "Is that Zoey's?"

"Um, I think so." She feigned uncertainty. "I just found it."

"Finders keepers. Zoey has about a million of them."

Yes, Alva thought, she does.

+ + +

That spring, she and Zoey went "out." The expat clubs in the French Concession all had similar names—Kandy, DKN, Factory. Alva learned that "out" was the dark, cavernous interior of Murals, the pool tables sticky with absinthe at Sport, the cocaine in the bathroom of Bonbon. Zooming under Yan'an Elevated Highway, holding on for dear life on the back of someone's motorcycle. Out was ceaseless, priceless, boundless stimulation, a high that permeated Shanghai's orange-glow nights. The question "Do you go out?" was secret currency in international school circles. If you met someone at a soccer tournament or Model UN, you'd assess if that person went out, and if the answer was yes, you saw each other out at some point, fifteen and glassy-eyed, young organs pumping chemical-laden blood.

In late April, one of Zoey's old Hong Kong friends, Gabe, visited Shanghai on break. They met on a French Concession street. Gabe was a tall white boy, dressed in head-to-toe gray.

"Alva's parents are in international trade too," Zoey said by way of introduction.

Alva had already taken a few shots on the subway from a plastic water bottle and solemnly shook Gabe's hand. Gabe was a freshman at Duke. She imagined him living in a fraternity house, rolling into bed with a blond cheerleader.

They rode the elevator to the top floor of the low-rise building. Migrant ladies scurried around with mops, and Alva realized they were clearing puddles of vomit, but the smell persisted, mingling with the fruity mist blasted from cold-air sprayers. "Does it always smell like this?" Alva asked Zoey.

Zoey shook the VIP wristband on her skinny wrist. "Open bar," she said. "Asians don't cope well."

They all did a round of tequila shots, and Alva mimicked the way Zoey licked the salt from the crook of her thumb and index finger. The bartender was a chubby white girl with enormous breasts on full display whenever she leaned down to scoop ice. Somewhere between rounds, when the bartender's wet fingers touched hers, it occurred to Alva that she'd never been served by a white person before.

But it made sense: this wasn't a *local* spot. Most girls at Kandy, she and Zoey included, were international schoolgirls. They wove their ways through the crowd, holding hands, eyelids heavy with glitter. They took pictures that they'd later upload on Facebook. So few *locals* had Facebook.

Most of the men at Kandy were older—expats and Chinese alike, some middle-aged, businessmen in suits. Everybody seemed very happy with the underage girls' infinite willingness to drink and shriek and dance as if their short fifteen years on Earth had culminated in precisely this moment, brains soggy with liquor, gyrating with abandon against each other, against the walls, against men who reached for their newly stretch-marked hips.

These men kept materializing near the circle where Zoey and Alva danced, even if Gabe was right there, awkwardly shuffling to the music. A tall, sweaty Scandinavian man came up behind Zoey and barricaded her in a grinding position. Zoey danced with him for two songs, the man's blue eyes awkwardly avoiding the rest of their circle until Zoey craned her neck back and kissed him, tongue sloppy with drink. Alva's heartbeat raced faster at the strange mix of terror and sexual thrill of this sight. Gabe glared at the floor.

At first nobody was dancing with Alva, and maybe it was because she looked too rigid, cautious. After a few more drinks her body grew into the music, and she felt hands creeping around her pelvic bone. She turned around. It was the man who'd been dancing with Zoey. Alva continued swinging her hips as the man pulled them closer to his crotch. She could only see his hairy blond knuckles and a gold ring. She felt something harden against her lower back, his belt buckle, maybe. He guided Alva's hand inside his pants and she touched the flesh of his hard cock. She yanked her hand back in a jolt. "Tease," he whispered, and then he was gone, absorbed into the crowd.

Zoey tugged at Alva's dress. "Bathroom break," she declared, and they left Gabe on the dance floor, walking past the pools of vomit to the bathroom hallway, where a migrant woman stood guard and told them they couldn't go in a stall together. "No together," the woman kept repeating, perhaps the only English words she'd been trained to memorize. Zoey rolled her eyes and pushed past her, pulling Alva along behind her into the stall.

"Why don't they want people together?" Alva asked.

"So we can't do this," Zoey said. She took a small pouch of white powder out of her bra. "You got a key?"

Alva fished her house key from her bra. Zoey used it to scoop a small line of the powder, pressed one finger into her right nostril, and inhaled with the other. She sniffed and sighed with relief.

Someone was banging on the bathroom door. "*Chulai! Chulai!*" the migrant woman was shouting in Chinese. Alva quickly copied Zoey's technique, sniffing up the powder as Zoey flushed the toilet. Then they opened the stall door, quickly walking past the furious migrant woman. "What," Zoey said in English. "We were peeing."

The woman shot them a death glare and was already banging on another stall door. "*Chulai! Chulai!*"

Alva's saliva was bitter. She asked, "Was that coke?"

"I hope so," Zoey said.

They threaded their way to the dance floor. "Where were you?" Gabe asked through clenched jaws. "This place is so fucking crowded."

"Then get a table," Zoey said.

She held Gabe's stare. Within seconds he walked away to talk to a man with an earpiece. Alva's mind was less cloudy after the boost of cocaine, and she took in the faces on the dance floor, white faces blue and red and orange beneath the strobe lights. Soon they were shown to a cordoned-off section. Girls in fake lashes the size of small brooms brought them sparklers and bottles of Dom Pérignon, Grey Goose, celery sticks and buffalo wings, and carafes of neon orange mixers. Gabe ripped off his VIP wristband and hurled it toward the dancing crowd below, like he expected them to fight to catch it, which they didn't. A skinny man in a vest poured Alva champagne. He had sunken cheeks that reminded her of Gao Xiaofan. She pushed that thought out of her head.

Gabe and Zoey were finally kissing. The skinny man who stood guard over their table was watching, too, his face entirely passive, like he was trained to watch but not see.

Alva looked around and saw the Scandinavian on a leather couch not far from them. He was with an Asian girl, and his hand was up her dress, fumbling between her legs. The girl's face was flushed and crimson, her eyes barely open. The skinny employee was standing to the side, eyes trained on the liquor bottles. Alva lunged toward the leather couch. "She's not even awake!" she shouted.

"She invited me here," the Scandinavian growled. Up close, he was broad-shouldered and greasy-haired, wrinkles framing his mouth.

"Get out of this area. It's VIP," Alva said, shaking her wristband at him.

The Scandinavian whistled and stood, smirking. "Rich little Chink," he said. "I could eat you."

Then he was off, shuffling down the stairs to the dance floor. The girl slumped across the banquette, mumbling. Alva turned to the employee, whose face registered no recognition. The slur had dissolved into the music, unabsorbed, but chinkchinkchinkchink clattered in Alva's brain like a broken EDM beat. "Did you hear that?" she asked the man in Chinese.

The vested man said nothing.

"You didn't stop him!" she said. "You were right there and he was—"

The man's mouth hardened. He shook his head almost imperceptibly. "My only job is to guard the liquor you purchased," he said.

He turned away, back toward the stage.

She trudged back to Zoey and Gabe's table. "We're tired," Zoey said. "I'll call Feng and we can get chicken sandwiches downstairs while we wait."

She smiled at Alva beatifically, lips swollen from kissing, Gabe's arm around her shoulders. Alva wanted to tell them about the Scandinavian and the word *chink* and the vested man's silence and the girl with her hiked-up skirt, but right then Zoey sighed and said, "This was such a fun night, wasn't it?" and Alva said, "Yes." They took the elevator down and sat on the curb of the sidewalk. They ate five-yuan sandwiches of chicken cutlets with grease-soaked iceberg lettuce and globs of mayo. Alva thought about whether it'd been wrong to leave the mumbling Asian girl there on that couch, whether she had friends coming, then Feng pulled up, they climbed into the Range Rover, and left.

## 27

Girlie came rushing out the door in her slippers, mumbling, "Susmaria-joseph." Zoey had fallen into a heavy sleep after they'd dropped Gabe at his hotel, and Alva had to help Feng carry Zoey once they reached the house. Feng shot Girlie a look, as if to say, *This mess is yours now*. Alva wondered whether they spoke the same language—Feng only elementary English and Girlie no Chinese, Feng's realm only Shanghai's roadways and Girlie's the interior of this prefabbed villa.

Zoey whimpered on the couch. This is what happens when you can't hold your liquor, Alva thought. She was drunk, too, but at least she was upright. "Help me take her to my room," Girlie said to Alva. They dragged Zoey down a first-floor hallway, past a walk-in pantry and the laundry room. Girlie's bedroom only had a single bed. On the nightstand was a picture of an older woman with her arms around Girlie. In the picture Girlie wore shiny lipstick and soft eyeshadow, her hair silky. With that makeup, Girlie looked young and pretty, not that much older than Alva. They dropped Zoey on the bed.

"Where will you sleep?" Alva asked.

"I'll watch her and make sure she doesn't choke." Girlie rubbed her eyes and sighed. Her cheap, billowing nightgown almost swallowed her bug-thin limbs. "I set up the guest room for you already. The usual one. You should go."

Alva went, not needing to be asked twice. She made it up the dark staircase by memory, fumbling toward a room that felt like hers already. She was relieved Zoey wasn't hers to take care of.

She slept poorly, her throat scorchingly dry. Finally, the sky between the curtains turned pale blue. Her phone said 5:45 A.M.

Before going downstairs, she counted the cash in her wallet. She was at least a hundred yuan short for a taxi ride back to Heavenly Peace. She found Girlie standing at the bottom of the staircase. They seemed to be the only people awake in the house. Breakfast pastries were already laid out on the kitchen island.

"Coffee, tea, orange juice?" Girlie asked, her upbeat inflection failing to hide her exhaustion.

Alva shook her head. "How's Zoey?" she asked.

"She threw up this morning," Girlie said. "Now she is back asleep."

Alva wondered if Girlie would tell Daniel and Julia about Zoey, so she could get some sort of tip. But maybe Zoey had preemptively taken care of this kind of thing.

"I can make you eggs," Girlie said.

"It's okay. I'm not hungry. I'm going to go home."

"Okay. I'll have the guards call you a taxi."

Alva clutched her wallet. "Girlie, do you have a hundred yuan I can borrow?" Her cheeks felt hot. She didn't know Girlie's wages, but surely, she could spare a hundred to lend. Girlie nodded silently and disappeared into the hallway. Alva picked up a croissant and felt sick looking at it, decided to wrap it in a napkin and put it in her bag. It was a real European pastry, not the sugary and meat-flossed knockoffs at Paris Baguette. Girlie reemerged and handed Alva two hundred-yuan bills.

"Just in case," she said. "Sometimes they charge foreigners extra."

Alva wondered if Girlie ever took taxis, ever left the confines of the Links Golf and Country Club. Did she have friends in Shanghai, did she wander the Bund, have drinks at French Concession bars? "It's too much," Alva shook her head, as her hands reached to accept the bills. "I'll pay you back next time I'm over," she said. "Just—please don't tell Zoey I had to borrow from you."

"Okay." Girlie wasn't smiling anymore. A car honked outside the window. Girlie went to the fridge and took out two more Evians. "You'll need this," she said.

"Thanks," Alva said. "I'll bring the money next—"

Girlie had already shut the heavy door.

The taxi driver eyed Alva wearily but nodded when she told him the directions in Chinese. He lit a cigarette and she opened a window. Under the morning light, dew on the golf course glittered like beads. Summer was near. Alva was nauseous. They sped back through the fields and shantytowns, to the wide avenues of Pudong. The driver shortchanged her. Alva was too hungover to say anything. When she walked through the door, she heard Sloan humming in the kitchen. She ran straight for the bathroom and locked the door, then threw up mouthfuls of bile.

When she came out into the living room Sloan was on the couch, leafing through a brochure. "Fun sleepover?" she asked.

"Yeah," Alva said.

"But you're sick."

"I think I got food poisoning."

"What from?"

"I don't know. The maid's pudding."

"They have a maid?"

"I'm going to lie down," Alva said.

"How old is Zoey's mother?" Sloan called after her. "Is she a housewife? Is the maid live-in?"

Alva shut her bedroom door. She lay in bed and listened to the noises of the compound coming to life outside the windows, children shouting, Shanghai's golden spring before a humid, suffocating summer. Inside the apartment, the television came on. "Is she all right?" she heard Lu Fang's voice.

"She was poisoned by the maid's pudding," Sloan said.

"Huh," Lu Fang said. "What about the art exhibit? We'd planned to go today. Is she too sick?"

Alva had completely forgotten about the impressionists exhibit at the Shanghai Art Museum. Lu Fang had mentioned it earlier in the month when handing her a new wad of taxi money and Alva had offhandedly said that sure, she'd be interested.

"Oh, fun," she heard her mother say now. "No, she needs to hold up her end of the bargain. She should have thought of that before running off to rich expats and stuffing herself sick."

"But if she really doesn't feel well—"

Sloan clapped her hands together. "Nothing is more restorative than a little *culture*."

## 28

Alva clutched her audio guide and drifted along the dark rooms, fighting nausea, trying to remember the names—Manet, Monet, Cézanne, Pissarro. She didn't like the blurry, smudgy landscapes, the lily ponds ever-present in every Shanghainese park. She paused only in front of those evocative of life in otherworldly cities—people dancing at a guinguette, the red lights of the Moulin Rouge reflected in puddles on a rainy evening. "A romantic vision," the audio guide said. "Take a step back, for it is only with distance that the composition's parts add up to a sum." But Alva couldn't take a step back. The room was too crowded. She bumped into Lu Fang.

"Do you know where 浪漫, the Chinese word for romantic, comes from?" he asked.

Alva nudged one ear free from the headphones. Lu Fang was always proving how cultured he was about the origin of words.

"Some people say romance, 浪漫, didn't exist in China until it was imported with Romanticism in the nineteenth century. But the poet Su Shi did technically use the word 浪漫 as early as the Song dynasty. Strictly speaking, it means 'flow of waves,' wild, unrestrained. That's even more romantic than romance."

Alva muted her audio guide, though she kept the headphones on to deter further commentary from Lu Fang. Sloan had caught up with them and stood shoulder to shoulder with him in front of a painting where a woman reclined naked amid a picnic spread. He cocked his head so that it almost touched Sloan's blond head. It was a small, quiet tenderness, one that seared itself into Alva's vision. Then she heard Lu Fang say, "You used to look just like that. Not a care."

"True," Sloan replied. "Back then I didn't have a care."

They stood still in front of the grassy picnic and Alva felt a violent seizure in her entrails. This time she didn't know if it was the rumbling of her hangover or the sinking sensation that she'd overheard something she shouldn't have, a new reality that had the potential to upend her own. Used to? Back then? Could they be talking about last year, early 2007, when Lu Fang had started visiting the apartment as their landlord?

Alva scrambled toward the EXIT sign glowing in the dark. In the bathroom she heaved over the toilet bowl. When she washed her hands, she stared at her face in the mirror.

Take a step back, the audio guide had said. Up close things are a blur, but they start taking shape once distance is placed between art and the beholder.

If Sloan and Lu Fang shared a long past that preceded her, then wasn't her own existence just a parenthesis in her mother's story with Lu Fang—and not vice versa?

She splashed cold water on her face. It didn't need to mean anything if Sloan and Lu Fang had a past. Sloan had a past with many Chinese men, her long string of "friends." But why then did she, after all these years, marry Lu Fang? Why did she not simply tell Alva they'd known each other, unless there was something to hide, unless there was something she didn't think Alva was ready to know?

It was then that the possibility hit her. The unnamed squirt of sperm. With horror, Alva thought of all the times she'd used that bratty retort with Lu Fang, "You're *not* my father."

In the mirror, Alva tried to find him in her own image. Up close her face was only a bunch of cells. Of course she and Lu Fang looked alike in some ways. It was true of her and any other Chinese person.

Sloan was waiting for Alva outside the bathroom. "You really are sick, aren't you?" Sloan's expression could be mistaken for concern. "Here. This is what I always take." In her palm were three fat red pills.

Alva said nothing, though she took the pills.

"Lu Fang appreciated that you made the effort to come today, even if you don't feel well," Sloan continued. Did she realize Alva had overheard and was now performing damage control? "See, if we can all get along, this is a good situation for all of us."

Alva walked toward the permanent exhibit wing, where the visitors were scant. Sloan followed her.

"I can talk to him about going on fewer business trips. And when your soccer season ends you can be home more often instead of holing up in that expat resort."

Alva stopped in front of a small oil painting in an ornate golden frame. She shoved the pills into her mouth. The still life depicted several faintly pink items wrapped in an almost translucent wax paper. "Alva?" she heard her mother behind her. "What do you say? I'm tired of fighting." She paused. "Partner?"

There was a note of hesitation when Sloan spoke that word, almost prude embarrassment. Sloan hadn't called her partner since the taxi ride on her wedding day.

"Alva!" someone shouted.

They both turned around. There were Daniel and Julia Cruise, impressionist pamphlets in hand. "Alva, I thought that was you," Julia said. "You came to catch the last day of the exhibition too? And this is—"

They all stood awkwardly before the painting. "My mother," Alva croaked. Sloan gave the Cruises a disdainful once-over. Julia was in a sleeveless dress that showed off her toned arms, though her face was still plain, makeup free. Alva knew her mother would notice, compare herself. Daniel looked, predictably, like an off-duty executive in khakis and a cashmere sweater. He stuck out his hand. "We are Zoey's parents," he said. "I am Daniel Cruise, and this is my wife, Julia."

Sloan took his hand, and Alva felt her mother stand up taller, suck in her stomach, tilt her head so her blond hair fell over her shoulder. "Sloan Collins," she said simply. There was a silence. Her mother didn't know how to conduct American small talk anymore. She looked cagey, uncomfortable.

"Thank you for having me over for the sleepover last night," Alva cut in.

"Yes, the girls had quite a night," Daniel said. "Probably didn't get much sleep, did you. We couldn't drag Zoey out of bed."

Sloan's smile was curt. Alva prayed for her mother to act normal, respectable, say something, anything. Julia cleared her throat. "What an exhibit, isn't it? To have shipped all this precious work to China. Daniel had free tickets from his company. I was an art history major in college. I couldn't let the tickets go to waste."

"Mm-hmm," Sloan finally said. "That would be bad. Tickets were hard to come by for the rest of us."

Alva wondered if by the "rest of us," her mother meant herself and other Chinese people.

"What is this strange little painting here?" Daniel asked cheerfully, winking at Alva, and she understood he was soliciting her help to change the subject, burying the strained small talk. She leaned closer to him.

"It's titled 'Still Life.'"

Daniel bent down to study the placard. "Rupert Swan. American."

"Oh, Swan," Julia interjected.

"You know him?" Daniel asked.

"Yes. I've heard of him. He's known for"—she sucked in her breath— "his 9/11 still lifes."

They all looked back at the painting. "What's wrapped inside—" Julia began.

Alva could see it now. The faintly pink objects in the parcels of wax paper had the shapes of hands and feet.

"I was supposed to be in a meeting at the Twin Towers that day," Daniel said. "But I missed the train I planned on taking into the city."

Julia took his hand and squeezed it. Alva felt the churn in her stomach again. The body parts in the painting made her want to be sick. She remembered watching the news with Sloan that day, how her mother had cried uncontrollably, and Alva had thought, She must really love America if she's this upset, and so Alva had made herself cry too.

"I was already in China when it happened," Sloan said.

"Alva told us you came here because you were an actress," Daniel said.

Sloan's nostrils flared with pleasure. "Yes," she said. "I studied acting in college."

Julia and Daniel nodded politely. Alva burned with embarrassment: they knew Sloan was lying. Alva had told them, so easily, that Sloan had never gone to college. Her mother didn't know how cheaply Alva had thrown her under the bus, spun their lives into an entertaining dinner anecdote, a Dickensian origin story. Thankfully Julia and Daniel were gracious enough to let the college point go uncommented. Sloan continued. "After I graduated, I was involved in an international movie collaboration," she said.

"Right," Julia said. "It must have been a disappointment that the production you were in didn't work out. *The Lover* is one of my favorites. What do you think of the movie that did get made?"

Sloan winced. "It was fine," she said. "*My* shooting took me to Asia, so I have no regrets. I can tell you this much after two decades."

"Oh, of course," Julia said.

"A great place to raise a daughter," Daniel said. "We've loved having Alva over. So interesting to have her *perspective*."

"—and so admirable of you to put her through the public school system," Julia said.

"I wanted her to be in touch with her Chinese roots," Sloan said.

"Alva told us she'd never been to America," Daniel said. "So we were happy to include her in our summer planning. It'll keep us from murdering Zoey. You know, teenagers on trips."

Sloan's smile froze. "Summer planning?"

"A stateside trip. I've had my eyes on a rental property . . ." Daniel sensed the wrongness in Sloan's face and coughed lightly instead of finishing his sentence.

Julia was squinting at Sloan. "All in the works, anyways," she said. "We're still a few months away. I'm sure you must discuss logistics first."

They know, Alva thought, that there's something wrong with her. They instantly sniffed out what others cannot, that *locals* cannot see in

Sloan. She wanted to find an excuse to make her mother disappear, remove this ticking time bomb from the Cruises' scrutiny, but right at that moment, Lu Fang turned the corner and entered the room. "There you are!" he exclaimed in Chinese.

They all stared at him. After a beat, he registered the Cruises and turned red. "Lu Fang," Sloan said in loud Chinese. "These are Alva's friend's parents. The soccer girl."

Lu Fang shuffled toward them. "Hello," he said in English. "How are you?"

Then, inexplicably, he made a circular gesture above his stomach.

"Bad food," he said.

Daniel leaned toward Alva. "Your . . . ?"

"My stepdad," Alva said quickly.

"Alva sick," Lu Fang continued. "Bad pudding. Are you okay?"

"He doesn't speak English," Alva said to the Cruises. "I told him how much I loved the Magnolia pudding." To Lu Fang she spat out in Chinese, "Stop."

"Well, we should get back to the exhibit before it closes," Julia said. "It was very nice meeting both of you."

Daniel nodded. "Alva, I'm sure we'll see you soon." He gave her shoulder a squeeze before walking away. For a second he brushed past Lu Fang, a whole head taller than him. And just like that they were gone, probably off to talk about this strange and uncouth family.

"Summer planning? Stateside?" Sloan said once they were out of earshot, enunciating each syllable through clenched teeth.

"It was vaguely discussed," Alva said.

"You're not going," Sloan said. "In case you were wondering."

"Why?" Alva said.

"You're not going with *those* people."

"What do you know about *those* people?" Alva said. The sickness roiled her stomach again. "At least they're educated. At least they know *The Lover* was a book. That there was another movie. At least they're not lying constantly."

"What?" Sloan said.

Alva pointed toward Lu Fang. "I heard you. Talking about *back then*. Why did you lie about not knowing him before?"

"I didn't lie," Sloan said. "You just never asked."

Lu Fang looked at them with confusion. They were yet again in an English fight, a fight he couldn't understand. "We can all calm down and take a taxi—" he began.

"She can find her own way home," Sloan said. "She certainly has enough taxi money now."

She pulled Lu Fang toward the exit and he cast a worried glance back at Alva. "I can get home on my own," she said in Chinese. Then they were gone and she sat down on the bench. She was sick to her stomach again, her thoughts scrambled. It didn't matter if the squirt of sperm was him. He wasn't a father. It didn't change anything: she'd still grown up in those Puxi rental apartments, she'd still been alone when her mother drank herself into stupors, she'd still asked for America every year and been told no. If he was her father, where was he then? She was fifteen now. She could choose the family she wanted. A family that gave her a bedroom fit for a five-star hotel, had a driver and a maid and endless airline miles, and spent summers in the Hamptons and would take her along.

Being a father meant showing up, offering something helpful. Even if Lu Fang was trying to make up for years of absence, it was too late.

Alva wanted to find Zoey and have a drink, sit comatose on the velvet couch in front of the CW. Her phone buzzed as if Zoey had guessed her thoughts kinetically. But when she pulled up her screen, the notification wasn't from Zoey.

It was a video link, and a message from Smiling and Proud Wanderer. In the past weeks, she'd logged onto QQ less and less, had nearly forgotten about him.

笑傲江湖: I dare you to watch this.

She clicked on the link. It showed a pair of red Nikes, scaling the rungs of a narrow rusty ladder on a TV tower. The Huangpu River snaked beneath, the glittering Bund, the squat mass of Super Brand Mall, the twin giants of Jinmao Tower and the World Financial Center. Squeezed onto a tiny platform at the top of the ladder, the Nikes shuffled left, then right, their heels above nothing, a ghostly shuffle-dance over the void.

# PART VI

# LU FANG

QINGDAO, 1994

## 29

Lu Fang couldn't forget a chart he'd once read: at age nine, an average American boy measured 135 cm and 28 kg. Minmin persisted below average in both categories. He had no interest in English and the only words that rolled off his tongue were *Chelsea, Liverpool, AC Milan.* Lu Fang indulged the purchases of soccer paraphernalia in hopes they would toughen his son's demeanor. But the problem was Ciyi: she chattered to Minmin incessantly, like a village woman, about news and radio programs and gossip from neighborhood committee meetings, which she'd joined after no longer needing to work. It drove him mad when Lu Fang heard Minmin ask, "Is it true that Auntie Wang confiscated so-and-so's television because it was a Japanese brand?" "Is it true that China invented spaghetti?" "Is it true that Chairman Mao's IQ was 184?"

It was like mother and son spoke a language Lu Fang did not, developed in his absence. For the past nine years, he had spent almost every weekend at the office. He asked Minmin to finish all homework before he came home from work—usually that wasn't before ten P.M., and by then the boy was fast asleep. Or pretended to be fast asleep. Sometimes Lu Fang listened in the darkness of Minmin's room, and no sound came at all, like his son was holding his breath.

For nine years Lu Fang began every day with a single purpose: to make money. There was something in the air in the Northeast, the rumbles of good fortune rolling up from Guangdong and Hong Kong, and suddenly everyone around him was talking about entrepreneurship, manufacturing, domestic consumers, and international partners. Xiao Qi had left the shipping company and gotten into electronics importation, and he advised Lu Fang, "There's no iron bowl anymore. Quit the nationalized enterprises and join the train of self-made bosses. The times are changing, brother!"

Xiao Qi was right: nowadays you didn't need a university degree to be a boss. So Lu Fang had taken a loan from the party secretary to cover start-up costs, reached out to a few old clients interested in Qingdao produce, and begun fruit exportation. His reeducation in Chuanxi came in handy when he talked to farmers. Client by client, product by product, he'd built his own import-export enterprise. He filled cargo containers with crates of Chinese pears he bought dirt cheap from farmers, packaged each fruit individually in plastic webbing, tied red bows around cardboard boxes that said: Premium Organic Qingdao Pears (VIP Gift Package). The farmers didn't know about the exorbitant profit margin; the clients didn't know there was nothing organic about the chemical fertilizer. Everyone was happy, and soon Lu Fang was shipping fruit baskets, plastic wrap equipment, and wholesale red ribbon rolls all over the Chinese seaboard, Japan, and Korea.

With money he could provide. Ciyi upgraded to Nivea hand cream, which she rubbed compulsively over her now-smooth hands as she watched clip after clip of party officials parading through rural schools, through machine factories, through the roiling waters of the brand-new river dams. Like the party officials, Lu Fang knew how to keep Ciyi and Minmin satiated with enough material comforts to discourage dissent— though he kept a tight grip on their budget. Most of his income went into a savings account he'd titled "Minmin's Overseas Fund." In five years, maybe seven, Lu Fang would have enough to cover the fees for several years of his son's foreign tuition, visa, and whatever it took to grease bureaucratic wheels. When he looked at Minmin, Lu Fang felt a self-sacrificial pinch to the heart: there would only be enough money to buy one person passage for an education abroad, and Lu Fang had long given up on that person being himself.

✦ ✦ ✦

Money paid off in other unexpected ways. When Sloan called, nine years since their last meeting, it was because Xinhua ran an article about the Haier electronics plant. Around this time Lu Fang was expanding from fruits to fridges. He'd been at a company banquet, invited through a Haier corporate liaison, and the Xinhua photographer had caught Lu Fang's face, a few pixels of smudgy ink in the back row.

His secretary had patched the call through from an unknown Shanghai number. The voice, its accents always flagrantly off, was instantly recognizable. "I found your company's number through an old Qingdao friend," she said. "Jim. The bar owner, remember? I thought to myself, 'That's Lu Fang, and he's made it to the national paper!' I was so happy for you."

After at last finding his voice, he said, "I can't believe anyone could recognize me from that blurry picture." But he liked the idea of being recognizable. "You're still in China?"

"I'm in Shanghai now."

Her voice stirred something in him, an old urge. "They recently opened a subway line in Shanghai, didn't they?"

"Oh, they did. It's fabulous. They also inaugurated the new TV tower. Lu Fang, it's so good to reconnect. I only half believed this phone number would work. There are so many Lu Fangs, it's fate I found you, isn't it?"

They talked for another ten minutes that first call, mostly Sloan explaining how she worked as an English teacher now, how there were all these schools demanding foreigners in Shanghai. She called again the next week, to ask if he had any good recommendations for bank services: she wanted to open a new savings account. On the third call she said schools were going on summer break and she'd be free every day. Free as a bird. It was an expression no one used in Chinese. There was even a popular song that had come out: *I am a little bird, and so I can't fly that high, no matter how hard I try.* That was the difference between them. He told her he wished he could take a vacation, but he was too busy.

"How about a business trip to Shanghai, then?" she said. "You're the boss, right?"

There was a long, expectant silence on the line. He imagined the starched sheets of a business hotel. A new branch in Shanghai, repeated trips, wife and son in a comfortable apartment in a distant northern city. That was the tale of many men he knew. Nine years ago he had decided to be a father, but money changed a man, gave him opportunities. "I've been meaning to see about expanding to southern markets," he said with some pride. But it then occurred to him the person she pictured was the wide-shouldered young swimmer she knew. Who said she'd even look at him nowadays, who said it was that kind of invitation at all? This pan-icked him, so he uttered the most neutralizing stipulation he could think of, "My son would love the excursion."

Sloan's voice didn't betray emotion. "Shanghai is a great city for chil-dren," she said.

# 30

When Lu Fang told Minmin they were going on a trip to Shanghai, his son glanced up from his exercise book and said, "Why?"

"So you and Baba can spend some time together."

"But why can't we all go together?"

"So you learn to be a man, and stop hiding behind your mother," Lu Fang said.

Minmin looked back down to his exercise book. Ciyi bit her lip and remained silent. Lu Fang had warned her this would be a father-son trip, no negotiations. With the rise of the family's fortune, Ciyi had become better than ever at normalizing injury. She'd declared it was a good idea, really, an excursion for Minmin, who had never seen much outside of Qingdao. "It's true you could use some time to get closer to him," she'd said. "He's so shy around you." She even packed her son's suitcase, se-lecting each article of clothing with exaggerated enthusiasm: this for an amusement park, this for sightseeing at the Chenghuang Temple, this for sleeping in the hotel bed. "You'll have such a good time," she said. By the end, as she hugged Minmin tightly and gently shoved him out the door, you'd think the whole trip was her idea.

For the seven-hour train ride to Shanghai, Lu Fang allowed himself the luxury of two second-class tickets. Eighty-six yuan meant the differ-ence between a window seat and the standing-only wagon. Minmin was quiet, cheek against the window, watching the scenery turn from yellow to green as they rolled south. An old man next to him loudly chewed boiled peanuts.

The teacher reports said Minmin was prone to reverie and lacking in motivation. "Unusually reserved," one teacher had noted.

"Where do you think this'll get you?" Lu Fang had said through gritted teeth when he read the reports and slammed them down on the table in front of a cowering Minmin. "This will get you nowhere. Do you want to go nowhere?"

Minmin was kicking the metal rods underneath his train seat. Lu Fang told him to quit it. His son stopped and stayed as rigid as a statue for the rest of the ride. It was so hard to tell what went on inside his little head.

They checked into a hotel in Xuhui District, a three-star establishment with shiny black marble floors. The girl who greeted them at reception had a pleasant face and called out to Minmin, "Little friend, do you want a sweet?"

She waved a piece of Rabbit milk candy. Minmin shook his head and whispered softly, "I don't want it."

"Thank you," Lu Fang rushed to say, "he's shy." He took the candy from the woman and put it in his pocket.

The room was standard business, newly renovated, a chemical smell faintly clinging to the furniture. There were two twin beds and a simple redwood desk. The room's one luxury was a small balcony overlooking the leafy street below.

Before Lu Fang stepped out on the balcony for a cigarette, he told his son to unpack his schoolbag and sit at the desk for his daily homework.

Minmin opened his thick summer workbook. "Baba, can I ask you a question?"

"Hmm?"

"If I finish tomorrow and Sunday's homework in advance, can I stay up for the World Cup final?"

Some cultivation of masculinity was healthy, but athletic fanaticism only resulted in distraction from more pragmatic paths. "Only number ones get into Harvard-Yale," Lu Fang said. "Not soccer fans."

Over the years, Lu Fang had chanted a steady refrain of Hafu-Yelu into his son's ears. A Chinese girl had gotten into Harvard a few years before and it'd made national news; the girl then published a memoir-tutorial titled *My Road to Harvard*. In the glamour shot on the cover, she held her acceptance letter out toward the viewer, her airbrushed face radiating a smugness that made Lu Fang's stomach turn. Still, he had no choice but to buy the book and set it on Minmin's desk. Never mind that Minmin had been seven. It was never too early to build ambition.

"But Brazil's playing," Minmin whispered. "Please?"

Lu Fang pretended he did not hear. As he expected, his son dropped the matter, and Lu Fang tried not to notice the boy's dejection as he bent over his workbook.

Sloan had proposed meeting at the Shanghai Botanical Garden. In the early afternoon Lu Fang and Minmin set out for the long walk from the hotel, and Lu Fang promised they'd find lunch on the way. "Tomorrow, then, can we go see the Oriental TV Tower? Or the Shanghai Zoo?" Minmin asked.

"We'll see," Lu Fang said. "We are meeting one of Baba's friends who lives in Shanghai. She might have some good suggestions about how to improve your English."

"It's a woman?"

"Yes, Lu Min, my friend is a woman."

They passed by a shopping complex selling electronics and mechanical parts. Minmin pointed to a Kodak shop. "What if I got a disposable camera for this trip?" His voice was so meek Lu Fang had to pull his hand and say, "What?"

"A disposable camera, since this is a special trip," his son said, louder. "Please, it's not expensive."

Minmin was looking at him expectantly. He wasn't one to ask for new toys. "All right, just this once," Lu Fang said.

He gave his son a twenty-yuan bill and waited outside the storefront, where rows of men squatted smoking, watching cars go by. Minmin ran back a few minutes later clutching an orange plastic camera. "Thank you, Baba," he said, breathless.

"Let's get walking," Lu Fang said.

He was unused to the traffic and chaos of a big city and held his son's hand tightly as they wove through the crowded sidewalks. The roads had four lanes and motorcycles zigzagged like mad between honking cars coughing out black exhaust. He spotted a stall of scallion oil noodles on a quieter side street. The noodles were dirt cheap and flavorless. Minmin was absorbed by his camera, flipping, and turning it, looking through the objective at his cracked bowl, the chopstick holder, a fly on the plastic tablecloth. He didn't dare click, not yet. Lu Fang could feel how badly his son wanted to take his first picture, but at the same time did not want to waste a precious shot. He appreciated the boy's self-restraint. But instead he said, "Quit monkeying around and eat."

The noodles turned to an oily mush in his mouth, a bad choice for a summer day. Shanghai was oppressively muggy, the kind of heavy moisture that bred mosquitoes and slick con men. Sweat dripped down Lu Fang's back and glued his shirt to his skin. The noodles made him heavy. He hoped his thickness wouldn't be too apparent; he'd stopped swimming long ago, after his company took off. As he and Minmin resumed their walk, he saw himself in the reflective surface of storefronts: a paunchy, provincial middle-aged man.

It was foreign, this insecurity. Until today, Lu Fang had been more focused on whether he looked appropriately rich than physically tasteful. He bought ostentatious suits made of shiny Italian fabrics at department stores. His leather loafers displayed big golden buckles. Some women didn't care about a thick waist if an Armani belt encircled it. He'd noticed these women—at business outings, KTV halls, a card slid under a door during a trip. Girls from Heilongjiang, Anhui, Hohhot. Lu Fang always said no: he wouldn't waste cash on would-be mistresses.

"Baba, wait here," Minmin said. They were almost at the entrance of the garden and his son had stopped in front of a large poster of Jiang

Zemin, in his trademark black-framed glasses and poofy combed-back hair, waving in front of the Shanghai skyline. Lu Fang watched in horror as his son angled his disposable Kodak toward their national leader's face. Before he could say anything, he heard the hard click of the camera.

"What did you just do?"

Minmin stared up at him, frightened. "It's the chairman in Shanghai. I thought Mama would like it." His arm was now bent behind his back, hiding the camera from Lu Fang's sight.

Ciyi was always praising Jiang Zemin—Good policy! Good leadership! And of course Minmin had learned to worship the man at school. Just like he venerated Mao Zedong and Zhou Enlai, Zhu De and Deng Xiaoping, and any men who would come thereafter. Lu Fang doubted Ciyi or Minmin could explain the nuances of these men's exploits and ideologies. But there was no point in having such conversations. Lu Fang envied his family, in a way. It must feel good to trust so deeply that deitylike men were at the nation's helm, steering them toward an assured future, and all they asked in return was faith.

"Don't waste a shot like that again," Lu Fang said.

"Sorry, Baba."

"A picture of a picture. Nonsense."

"I won't do it again," Minmin said in a small voice. Lu Fang could tell he was unsure what he did wrong.

Five years ago, when whispers of what had happened at Tiananmen first spread, Lu Fang saw illegal photos an acquaintance had smuggled over from a Hong Kong press. Taking in the blood, the white shirts, all those skinny student limbs dangling from stretchers, Lu Fang had sunk into a deep numbness. He was at his office desk, sitting in a big leather chair. They had recently moved into their newer, nicer apartment in the city center. His son was four and going to kindergarten. He had thought of Sloan then. She was probably long gone, back to America, watching this on TV news he'd never see. She'd once talked about such students— the ones circling petitions, asking for change.

And there, in his leather chair, Lu Fang had wept. He had once been a university student in Beijing, a train ride away. If he'd been born in a different time, would he have been there, sitting in the square? He wanted to believe it. In his own way, he reminded himself, he'd paid his dues, and this was something the young people today, born into a China they thought gleaming and open, had long forgotten.

Lu Fang didn't want his son to look teary or terrorized when they met Sloan, so he let the Jiang Zemin picture go. He wiped away a trickle of sweat from his temple. "Keep up so we aren't late."

Minmin broke into a trot, relieved that his father's temper didn't take a darker turn. A tyrant, he'd have her think, Lu Fang thought. It was like the conspiratorial glances Ciyi and Minmin exchanged when Lu Fang spoke too loudly or talked about Hafu-Yelu.

There were tourist groups waiting in line at the ticket kiosk, bands of children in red kerchiefs on school excursions from nearby provinces. He tried to spot the yellow hair by the gates. Even that exercise made his heartbeat quicken. She wasn't here yet. Minmin was frowning at the crowds. Despite his smaller frame, he looked a finer breed than those provincial students. His skin soft and light, his hair clean-cut. He wore a yellow-and-green Romário jersey that Ciyi had packed for him, his favorite.

"Lu Fang, Lu Fang!" a voice called behind him. He turned around. It was her, unmistakable, her hair still straw-yellow. She was wearing more makeup than he remembered, eyes heavily lined, her limbs thin in a short mustard dress. As she approached, he repeated to himself that she was beautiful, still beautiful.

"You're here," Sloan said, stopping a meter away from him. "And with this nice young boy."

"Yes, this is my son, Lu Min . . ." Lu Fang began, but his voice trailed off when she shifted a large swath of fabric from her back to her chest. And from that bundle emerged two white chubby legs. A baby, who blinked at Lu Fang and, with a sigh, burrowed her face back in her mother's bosom.

"My daughter, Alva," Sloan said. She smiled at Lu Fang's discomfited expression. "Did I forget to mention it?"

"Minmin, say hello to ayi," he said as deflection.

"Hello," Minmin said. He was staring at Sloan and her toddler with suspicion.

"I like your T-shirt," Sloan said. "Who is Romário?"

Minmin looked down at the ground and then up toward his father. "He's forgetting his manners," Lu Fang said. "It's a Brazilian footballer he loves. Lu Min, did a dog eat your tongue?"

"That's all right," Sloan said. "I know nothing about sports. Not since they got rid of the minishorts."

"Hah," Lu Fang said uncertainly. "And you, a mother now?"

"Just over one year old." Sloan patted the baby, who reared up her head again. She had large dark eyes and long eyelashes. And she looked, unmistakably—

"She's mixed?" Lu Fang said. He smiled with effort. "Her father is Chinese?" It would make sense why Sloan was still in China. Moved to a big city, married a Chinese man. A Chinese man younger, richer than Lu Fang.

"We'll have plenty of time to catch up," Sloan said. "Let me get our tickets first."

"Oh, no, let me—"

"Don't be ridiculous. I'm the host."

Sloan speedwalked toward the ticket office. She was much thinner than Lu Fang remembered. In his mind she'd been all soft flesh and curves. But the way she charged forward with absolute self-assurance hadn't changed. She swung her daughter to her chest and waved at the clerks inside the ticket office. The cluster of old women at the front of the line parted for Sloan and the baby, smiling and cooing.

"She just cut the line," Minmin said. "Isn't that rude?"

"Maybe she didn't see it," Lu Fang said.

"Baba, how do you know a foreigner?" Minmin asked. "Did you do business with her?"

"No," Lu Fang said, "she's a friend from a long time ago."

"How come you didn't know she had a baby?"

"What's with the questions? You're so chatty now when you were

mute just a minute ago. What an embarrassment. She'd be great to practice your English with."

Minmin pouted. "Where is she from?"

"The United States."

"Hmm," his son said, but he made no further comment. Sloan was
waving three tickets triumphantly. Lu Fang was still fixated on the baby.
Sloan's Chinese-looking baby. He tried to put that out of his mind.

The botanical garden's paths forked off and the crowds thinned. The
sounds of the city—traffic, construction—grew more muffled as they
advanced through a birch forest. Minmin was trailing some dozen meters behind them, distractedly looking at flora and fauna, his Kodak in
hand. "So you live in Shanghai with your husband?" Lu Fang asked.

Seeing his expression, she laughed. "No. I have no husband. Why,
should a lady my age be married?"

He had noticed the small lines around the corners of her mouth.
"You haven't aged a day," he said. "Is the father . . . around? Do you see
him?"

"Oh, no," she said. "There's no father to speak of. I just thought it was
time."

"Time?" he asked.

She shrugged. "To share my life with someone. You know, to be partners. Men aren't as reliable as babies. You're still with your wife?"

"Cohabitating," Lu Fang said.

Sloan nodded. "You look well. I mean, you look like you've done well
for yourself."

"I've been fortunate," Lu Fang said. "The company's not doing too
badly. It keeps me busy."

Minmin was catching up with them. "How do you like the botanical
garden?" Sloan asked him.

The boy stared at the ground. "Answer ayi," Lu Fang said.

"We have many parks back home," Minmin said.

Before Lu Fang could interject, Sloan said, "Yes, that's what I've always loved about Qingdao. The mountains. The ocean." She looked at
Lu Fang as she spoke.

The late-afternoon sunlight slanted into the gardens. "Do you want to see my place?" Sloan asked. The baby was sleeping in the bundle. "Alva needs to get changed. We can rest our feet, have a cup of tea."

Lu Fang studied his son, who'd been quiet for the past hour. "Yes," Lu Fang said. "Why not? How does that sound, Minmin? We'll visit Sloan ayi's home."

Minmin lowered his head. "Baba, I'm hungry," he said.

"I'll find you a snack at the apartment," Sloan said.

They exited the gates, and Sloan led them to an old compound behind a wall of gray concrete. The narrow alleys dripped with drying laundry hanging from crisscrossing ropes. There was the wet smell of a dysfunctional sewage system. They passed by a dark living room with open windows on the ground floor in which a couple of old men idled; its interior doubled as a snack stall. The men conversed in old-guard, incomprehensible Shanghainese. This was not where Lu Fang had envisioned Sloan living.

"This is my building." The entrance was unlit. The wall paint of the staircase peeled and curled, telephone numbers and advertisements sprayed over one another like an abstract graffiti montage—medical treatments, legal services, recruitment calls for the Falun Gong. The smell of mold reminded him of his old Qingdao apartment on Anwei Road. He saw Minmin scrunch his nose. The boy didn't remember that misery.

"Fifth floor," Sloan said apologetically. Alva was stirring and grunting. "Shh, we're almost home." She fiddled out keys. "I'm sorry it's not the most comfortable."

"Not at all," Lu Fang said before crossing the threshold of the door. But the inside left him speechless. He didn't expect her to live in such a state, not with a foreign teacher's salary. The room was small and dark, with barely any furniture. A few cardboard boxes with cloth draped over them passed as tables and chairs. There was a stove in the corner, beside a washbasin and a yellowing minifridge. He took off his shoes and ventured farther in. Through another door, there was a small bedroom with a mattress on the floor.

"Well, it's—" He struggled to find words. "It's—"

Sloan pulled two foldable stools from a closet. "Sorry. We don't have much space. I'll boil some tea after I get Alva cleaned up."

"Oh, thank you," Lu Fang said. Minmin stood awkwardly by the door and Lu Fang motioned for him to come inside. Sloan disappeared into the bedroom with Alva.

"She's poor," Minmin said softly.

"Shhh!" Lu Fang almost slapped his son. But Minmin was right, that was the word Lu Fang was choking on—this apartment reeked of poverty. He felt an acute embarrassment. He didn't know if he was embarrassed for Sloan—it was highly uncustomary to invite guests when one's place looked like this—or if he was embarrassed by the many times he'd offhandedly brought up his own good fortunes over the course of the afternoon. His own rent in Qingdao could probably pay for three tenements like Sloan's.

Sloan returned to the main room. "All clean now," she said. "Please, have a seat! Let's see what snacks I have." She opened the cupboard. "Well, ah, not much. Minmin," she called out, "do you like soda crackers?"

"Umm . . ." Minmin looked at Lu Fang uncertainly. "No."

"For heaven's sake," Lu Fang said. He opened his wallet and pulled out ten yuan. "Run to that snack stall downstairs and buy yourself something. I want you to come back immediately after, though. Don't go running around."

Minmin looked grateful to have an excuse to leave. Sloan shrugged in the kitchen. "It's a pretty safe neighborhood. Tea preferences?" she asked Lu Fang. "I have Lipton. Or . . ."

The door slammed. "Forget it," she said. She opened her minifridge and produced two green bottles of Tsingtao. "Old times' sake."

Lu Fang laughed. He sat down on one of the metal stools. "You still drink it," he said.

"It tastes like water, but it gets the job done." She emptied the bottles into two large tin mugs. "Have to keep up appearances now that we're parents." She winked.

"Sloan," he said, suddenly serious. "Don't take this the wrong way. But with a baby, are you . . . are you managing?"

The lines around her mouth deepened as her lips thinned. "I'm managing fine. I pay a neighbor to watch Alva when I teach classes."

"And you teach . . . full-time?"

"Technically, that's what my visa says. It's easy work. Put on a foreign movie, sing them a Beatles song. There's no textbook, and the kids are glad to have a break. But the schools are getting stricter now. The parents are asking for more, they complain about your teaching style. They want certificates, degrees, training. Perfect attendance. I changed jobs a few times."

"And that hasn't been too . . . disruptive?"

Sloan sat down on the stool across from him. "There are good and bad times." She took a sip from the beer mug. "I always find something else. Things are changing daily in this city. I'm happy to raise a kid here. I can't wait for when she learns how to talk."

Lu Fang put on a polite smile, though he did not understand. She acted as if this minimalist life, this squalor was a game, and not something to be taken to heart. "You're not thinking of going back to the States?" he asked.

"No," she said. "Alva was born Shanghainese. I know you've never understood it, but—China is my home now. I'm not a tourist."

"You're a marvel," he said. "Staying in China all these years, calling it your home."

"It is."

He didn't know what else to say, so he only nodded. They drank their beers in silence. She was studying him unabashedly, smiling. "Speaking of marvels, did you buy your dream car yet?"

He shook his head. "I took driving lessons. I have a license that I don't use."

"Strange," she said. "I always thought a car would be the first thing you bought."

Lu Fang laughed bitterly. "There were other priorities. A car has few uses here. We moved to a bigger place after Minmin entered school."

"Of course," she said. "Give him the best resources."

They heard footsteps of someone slowly climbing up the stairs. "You don't have to stay here long," Sloan said, getting up. "If he doesn't feel comfortable."

"He's very shy."

"Like his father," she said, and when she passed him, she drummed her fingers on his shoulder. He wanted to grab on to her wrist and pull her toward him, but she slipped toward the door. Minmin was outside holding a bag of ketchup-flavored chips, already open and half-eaten.

"Hi again, little friend," she said.

Minmin peeked inside the room with a mix of hesitation and visible disgust. He crunched his chips loudly as Sloan and Lu Fang, suddenly stilted, made small talk about his company. After some time Minmin walked to Lu Fang and whispered in his ear, "Baba, I have to pee."

"Oh." Lu Fang hadn't noticed a bathroom door in the apartment. He looked around.

"You have to go back into the staircase," Sloan said. "It's the door in the middle. We share it with the neighbors."

Lu Fang knew Minmin was squeamish about public bathrooms. He'd never noticed until today, but his son could be described as spoiled. Lu Fang decided to avoid further embarrassment.

"How about we all head out to dinner?" he said. "Minmin can use the bathroom there. Sloan, take us to a place you like. It's my treat."

"Oh, thanks!" Instead of deflecting, or saying the invitation was too much, Sloan lightened and stood up spritely. He forgot how American she could be. "Let me get Alva. I know the perfect place."

They stood before the shiny red sign and the golden arches. "I present you," Sloan said, "with Shanghai's first McDonald's."

Lu Fang knew vaguely of the American fast-food chain. It'd been in the news when the first flagship location had opened in Beijing. Sloan bent down toward Minmin. "I have a feeling you'll like this, little friend."

There were long lines of people standing in front of each cash register. It did smell delicious inside—of salt and fried chicken, sizzling burger grease. Sloan ordered Big Macs and fries for everyone, chicken nuggets and a milkshake. Lu Fang paid 65.40 yuan for the meal. Around them were young, fashionably dressed people, city people. The food came wrapped in paper and piled on a single tray.

"Didn't expect this, I have to say," Lu Fang said before he bit into his Big Mac. It tasted hot and salty, strangely satisfying. The tinge of something pickled reminded him of the vinegar-preserved radish he ate as a child in the winters.

Sloan shrugged, mouth full. "Right? You have to try it once." She shook the fry container in front of the baby. Alva's grubby fingers went straight for the fries. Lu Fang had a feeling the baby recognized and loved those yellow strips of potato.

"I used to beg my parents to take me to McDonald's for my birthday," Sloan said. "It was this superspecial treat."

Lu Fang turned to Minmin. "So what do you think?"

"It's not bad," his son said. Alva reached for his fries and he nudged the pack toward her. Lu Fang smiled broadly at Sloan. "If you study hard," he told Minmin, "you can eat at McDonald's in America every day."

Sloan laughed. Minmin said nothing and shook out a few fries for Alva.

At the four-seat table, in this crowded McDonald's full of young couples and parents with their small children, Lu Fang felt happy. The borders of his life faded momentarily. These cream-colored walls and brown wood surfaces must be the same in every McDonald's everywhere. They could be in California or London. It was the one place in China where the rest of the world was pouring in, and he could pretend he was where he wanted to be.

After dinner they strolled along the neon-lit Nanjing Road Pedestrian Mall. Minmin was walking ahead, drinking the last of his milkshake. The meal had softened him. He looked like he was having fun, or comatosed by the fast food to the point of appeasement. He was still clutching his Kodak in the nook of his arm. Alva was fast asleep against Sloan's chest despite the lights and the noise. Sloan caught Lu Fang staring.

"Past her bedtime," she said. "We should probably head home soon."

Lu Fang thought about Sloan returning to her compound in Xuhui District, to that mattress on the floor. Minmin slurped the milkshake loudly as the last liquid rattled up the fat yellow-striped straw.

"Our hotel is not too far from the center," Lu Fang said. "How are you getting home?"

"It's a few stations down the metro line they opened," Sloan said. "Then I'll just walk."

"Do you—" He checked his watch as if it was unspeakably late. "Do you want to come stay at the hotel?"

Sloan and Minmin both stopped walking. Sloan looked back and forth between Lu Fang and his son. "Well, that's kind, but I don't want to intrude on your vacation."

"Not a bother. It's a business hotel," Lu Fang said. "I'm sure they'll have spare rooms."

"The lobby looked busy," Minmin said.

"Why not," Sloan said. "It's very generous of you."

"Do you need anything from your apartment?" Lu Fang asked. "For the baby?"

"I've packed spares." Sloan tapped the baby bundle. "And I'm sure there's a toothbrush at the hotel. As long as no one minds seeing me in the same dress tomorrow!"

"It looks good on you," Lu Fang said, a reflexive compliment that slipped out before he remembered Minmin.

Lu Fang hailed a taxi and they all drove back to the hotel. Minmin didn't utter a word the whole ride. The reception said they did have spare rooms, a room on the same floor as Lu Fang's, in fact. When the receptionist asked, Sloan had her passport open and ready.

When Lu Fang shut their room door, Minmin said, "How much is a hotel room, Baba?"

"Why do you ask?"

"Is she going to pay you back?"

"Don't be small-minded," Lu Fang said, "We are more fortunate. That's why I offered."

"Mama wouldn't like it," Minmin said.

Lu Fang opened the balcony doors and pulled out a cigarette. A gentle rain was falling on the rooftops. Five balconies to the left, Sloan was cradling a sleeping Alva against her chest and gave him a small wave before returning inside. He imagined slipping out later tonight, knocking on her door. But the sight of Minmin getting into bed reminded him of why he'd brought his son on this trip. He was a father and a husband, a successful businessman from Qingdao. That, he thought to himself without conviction, was a respectable life, not to be thrown away so carelessly.

## 31

At breakfast the next day, Sloan said she would serve as guide while they explored the city. It astonished Lu Fang, that easy assurance she felt that Shanghai was hers. With Minmin and Alva in tow, they boarded the ferry and headed east across the Huangpu River. They waited in a mass of pedestrians, cyclists, men in suits straddling motorcycles. The ferry gates opened and the wave rushed in—Lu Fang pulled his son against his body with one hand and grabbed Sloan's with the other, their contact hidden among the density of the crowd. It felt instinctual. Their fingers interlaced as they stumbled forward, carried by the horde onto the ferry. With her own spare arm she clutched Alva. Minmin looked back toward him, and in a jolt Lu Fang released Sloan's hand. Soon enough their bodies pulled apart as people spread across the two floors of the ferry, trying to find a railing to hold on to. With a roar the boat departed.

They went to the back and watched the trails of white spray. Across the riverbank, the pearls of the Oriental Pearl TV Tower were two metallic pink spheres. "It's Shanghai's new pride. Do you think it's beautiful?" Sloan asked.

"Do you?" he said.

"No. It's kind of ugly."

"I've heard it's based on a poem," Lu Fang said.

Sloan smiled. "Of course you have."

"Lu Min!" Lu Fang called out to his son. The boy didn't seem to hear.

"Lu Min," he shouted louder. "Come here. Let's hear the pearl line from 'Ballad of the Pipa,' by Bai Juyi."

Minmin walked over and recited robotically, "'The sound of pearls, big and small, falling onto a jade platter.'"

Lu Fang tried to ruffle his son's hair but the boy slipped away, back toward the roaring motor.

Lu Fang bought them tickets—forty yuan each—and they boarded the elevator that would take them up the TV tower. The Pearl had a large, carpeted viewing surface, where they could see the city stretch, dense and squat to the west, sparse and flat to the east. Lu Fang and Sloan stood side by side and looked out.

"Would you ever live here?" Sloan asked.

Minmin was on the other edge of the viewing platform. They both glanced toward him.

"The city has its appeal," Lu Fang said. "I wonder what an apartment here costs." He leaned his forehead against the glass. "Probably much more than in Qingdao."

"You'd fit in here." Sloan's hand was on his back, a brushing moment.

He was aware of the fabric of his white shirt against his skin. The leather wallet weighing down his pocket, the sagging of a body worn by meat and nicotine.

"Schools here are probably much better than Qingdao's," he said.

"Probably," she nodded. "And with more foreign teachers too."

Lu Fang stretched his arms along the glass sphere. "Looking at all this, it makes you think. Inside China, this is the place to be. It's growing by the day. It could be worth investing in a property, renting it out . . ."

Minmin wandered back to them and squeezed past a delegation of middle-aged women. "Ba, can we go?" he asked, still clutching his Kodak, unused since Jiang Zemin. The women started to whisper. One of them, who wore a "TOUR LEADER" armband, stepped toward Sloan. "Can we take a picture with you?" The tour leader shoved her camera toward Lu Fang.

"I—" Sloan began, but the tour leader interrupted in English, "Beautiful lady. You take picture with us."

"All right," Sloan said. The squadron of women squeezed around her. She looked like a movie star with a fan club, Lu Fang thought as he pressed click. After the flash, the matrons dispersed with nods and whispers of "thank you" and more "beautiful, beautiful."

The tour leader stayed in place. "Do you have a camera I can use? For your family picture," she said.

"Oh, it's all right," Sloan said. She turned toward Lu Fang. "They think we're a family."

"Let's get a shot. We might as well," Lu Fang said. "Minmin, give the lady your camera."

"I'm saving the roll," Minmin said, the Kodak hidden behind him.

"It's really fine," Sloan said.

"Lu Min," Lu Fang said calmly, "give her the camera."

His son handed over the Kodak. The tour leader received it graciously, told them to gather closer. "Beautiful family," she said in English. A flash, a mechanical whir. Lu Fang thanked the woman. Minmin sped off across the carpet. Lu Fang shot Sloan an apologetic look and followed his son into the bathroom. Minmin was already in a locked stall, though no sound came from it.

"What's wrong?" Lu Fang said, squatting outside the stall.

"It's *my* camera," Minmin said.

"It's only a picture."

"I don't want that picture on my camera," Minmin said. "We're not a family."

The toilet flushed. Lu Fang sighed and walked back out to the main floor. "Is he all right?" Sloan asked.

"He'll be fine," Lu Fang said. "He's shy, but he's got a temper."

"He doesn't like me."

"He's a kid. He doesn't know you."

When Minmin finally walked out of the bathroom, Sloan told him, "I'm sorry. It's all because they wanted a picture with me. It happens to me a lot in China."

"Why?" Minmin asked. "Are you famous?"

Sloan grimaced and shifted Alva up her chest. "You could say that," she said.

Sloan said Goubuli meat buns would cheer up Minmin. Goubuli meant "the dog ignores," and the franchise on Nanjing Road was popular with tourist families crowding the edges of the room, gawking at the bamboo steamers carried over by frenzied waiters. Bottles of vinegar spilled on the tables as people shouted in different provincial dialects.

"Do you think there's some kind of system here?" Sloan frowned.

"I think you wait around until there's an opening, and then you duel to the death," Lu Fang said.

"Maybe we should flag down a waiter."

"They're ignoring everyone."

"Can we go somewhere else?" Minmin said. "I'm hungry."

"Oh, but we've come all this way," Sloan said. "Let me try something."

She took a step onto the dining floor, until she stood directly in the path of a hurtling young waitress in a white shirt and an ill-fitting vest. The waitress was carrying a towering stack of bamboo steamers that leaned like the Tower of Pisa and did not see Sloan until they were face-to-face.

"Can we get a table?" Sloan said in English.

Utter bewilderment came over the waitress's face. Sloan tilted her head and waited. The waitress's eyes flitted from Sloan to the tables. She craned her neck toward the cash counter and shouted, "Manager Zhou!"

Next to Lu Fang and Minmin a family also watched the proceedings, bemused. The father was short and missing a front tooth. "The laowai is getting the manager," he whispered as if narrating the scene. "For the laowai they'll call out the manager."

The manager squirreled out from the backroom, irate, a fat man with a golden nameplate. "What?" he barked.

The waitress motioned toward Sloan and scampered off with her bamboo tower.

"Could we get the next table?" Sloan repeated in English. "We've been waiting a while. Ta-ble."

"Hmm?" The manager's eyes were about to bulge out of his head. Then he waved his hand as if announcing defeat. "OK, OK!" he shouted, possibly the only two letters he knew in English. "Xiao Huang, when that table leaves, reserve it and seat her there."

"*Xiexie, xiexie!*" Sloan chirped, though the manager was already hurrying back to his office.

She returned to Lu Fang and Minmin. "Matter of minutes," she said. The waiting crowd broke into protests. "No way," the father with the missing tooth hissed. "We've all been waiting."

If Sloan heard, she pretended not to. A few moments later a harried waiter came to escort them to a table. "We were here before them!" Lu Fang heard someone shout. The commotion in the restaurant drowned out his cries. "She did it again," Minmin whispered, and Lu Fang could only nod.

They ordered and promptly were served the meat buns, which tasted average. Sloan ate with great gusto and Alva shredded the buns to get to the MSG-sauced meat within, leaving a pile of spongy white bread all over the table. She processed five or six buns this way. Lu Fang made no comment. It was then that he heard the hiss. "Traitor dog!"

He paused, looked around, then continued eating. He thought he might have misunderstood, but then heard it distinctly again.

"Traitor dog! Think you're better than us because you're with a foreign devil?"

Minmin had obviously heard as well and nervously fidgeted with the scroll of his Kodak. There was no doubt who the insult was directed toward. Lu Fang turned to face the room. "Who said that?" he asked loudly. The conversations quieted.

"What is it?" Sloan said. "What are you doing?"

"Who said that?" Lu Fang thundered, louder this time. Even Alva stopped eating, her fist holding a white tuft of bun midair.

"Calm down," Sloan said. "Why are you making a scene? What happened?"

Lu Fang was shouting now. "Stand up if you're a man!"

There was a scuffle in the crowd, and the father with the missing tooth stepped forward. His family was still waiting along the wall. "Me! And so what? I don't have to answer to a traitor dog!"

Before he knew what he was doing, Lu Fang was lunging at the man, knocking him to the floor, and he felt the pellet of fists, tasted blood in his mouth. People were screaming. He was yanked away from the other man. Someone was shouting about the police, and the manager was rushing to him, dragging him toward the back office as Lu Fang howled. "Say it again!" And the man, who was also being pulled away, shouted, "Traitor dog! Sellout! Devil worshipper!"

At the table, Minmin was crying silently. Sloan looked horrified, hands covering her mouth, shrunken in her chair. Alva was in her lap, watching the commotion intently, though she didn't appear perturbed. This was Lu Fang's last sight before the office door closed behind him.

"You'll stay here," the manager told him, "until we tally the damage of the broken plates. You're lucky we're not involving the police since you're with a laowai."

Lu Fang breathed heavily. He wouldn't be called a traitor dog for— for what? Had he betrayed his country in the eyes of his fellow countrymen? She was the one who'd cut the line, with such confidence he'd assumed she'd done it a hundred times before, and it had never turned awry. But the anger—it'd been directed at him. He'd let his guard down, thinking that in a big city like Shanghai being with Sloan would only attract stares of envy. He'd forgotten some would see it as a betrayal. Brownnosing with the foreign class, who treated China like their playground. He remembered a picture in Minmin's history book, a sign at a colonial park in Shanghai not far from where they were now: CHINESE AND DOGS NOT ALLOWED. But that was sixty years ago. Only the worst jingoists would think sharing a meal with a foreigner meant selling out your country. And yet it stung. Lu Fang hated that it stung. His son who parroted his mom's patriotic phrases, who was middling in his English classes—had his son thought of him as a traitor dog this whole trip?

The manager returned. "Three hundred and thirty-six yuan," he said to Lu Fang. It was a ridiculous sum, but he was in too much pain to argue. He handed over the money.

"Your, erm, wife and children preferred waiting outside on the street," the manager said, a trace of pity lacing his tone.

Outside Sloan and Minmin stood a good distance apart, silent. His son's eyes were red.

"I'm sorry," Sloan said.

Lu Fang sat down on the curb. His jaw, where he'd been hit hardest, was burning. "It's not your fault," he said, even though it wasn't true. "It's just the way things are."

"We should get back to the hotel," Sloan said. "It's been a night. At least we tried the buns." Her tone rang too light, too deranged, too American. Before leaving, he noticed the Kodak abandoned on the curb. He was too tired to scold his son. He picked it up with a sigh.

Lu Fang's ribs hurt. His ripped skin burned. They walked by reception with the least fanfare possible—successful, respectable businessmen didn't get into fights.

In front of Sloan's hotel room, she paused awkwardly. "Maybe you should come in and I'll help you clean those wounds," she said.

"I'm all right—" Lu Fang tried to decline, though it sounded forced. He did want to go with her. He didn't feel like fighting the urge anymore. He gave the room key to his son. "You go while Sloan ayi and I talk."

"Talk about what?" Minmin said.

"Nothing to do with you," Lu Fang said. Minmin took the room key and turned away. "Be in bed when I come back!" Lu Fang called out after him. "We have an early train tomorrow."

Sloan's room smelled like lemon spray and talcum powder. "I have to get Alva to sleep," she said. "You should go start a bath."

When Sloan lifted Alva out of the bundle, she saw Lu Fang and started shrieking. Lu Fang walked into the bathroom and closed the door, muffling the cries. He scraped the bathtub with his finger: it came back gray. He took a towel off the rack, wetted it, and started scrubbing.

It hurt his back, and he thought of his wife, all the years she'd scrubbed tubs. When it looked clean enough, he turned on the faucet and let the hot water flow. He took off his slacks, his shirt, his socks, his underwear. He folded every item and stacked them on the fake marble countertop. The mirror grew fogged from the steam. A large bruise was spreading across his upper right abdomen. The train was at 7:40 A.M. the next day, just in time to get Lu Fang back for an afternoon meeting. He'd have to explain the split lip.

He lowered himself into the scathing hot water. It burned, but he was already burning. His skin was the color of fish belly in the bathwater. He reclined his head on the porcelain and closed his eyes. He heard the door open and shut.

When he opened his eyes, Sloan was undressing. She was so thin the knobs of her vertebrae jutted sharply. Her breasts sagged. Her body was different, yet still familiar. She lowered herself into the tub. It was too small to fit one person comfortably, let alone two. She lay back against his chest. The water turned gray from the dirt on their skin.

She smelled the same. Their bodies had their own rhythms: his erection was growing against her lower back, even if they hadn't exchanged a word. She didn't turn around. She lifted her hips to guide him inside her. She had to try a few times. They rocked back and forth, jerkily, as quietly as they could, the gray water sloshing. At one point he let out a groan. Outside the bathroom a wail started up again. "You woke her," she said. She resumed rocking forward and back, faster now. "Let's finish." "Okay," he said. They both breathed heavily, wanting and not wanting to be done. He felt the despair again, in the sloshing of the gray water, the sample-size shampoo at the edge of the bathtub, the white funereal light overhead, their respective children, now alone in separate bedrooms of this three-star business hotel. He couldn't finish. "It's enough," he said.

Sloan didn't answer. She took a towel, thin and worn, from the rack. She was gone for a few minutes and the wails stopped. When she came back into the bathroom, Lu Fang was still in the tub. The water was cold by now, and his teeth chattered.

"The guy who owned the bar, the one with long hair. Jim," he said.

"What about him?" She tightened the towel across her chest.

"Did you sleep with him?"

"Excuse me?"

"And those students in Qingdao? Did you call them too? And the men in Shanghai who no doubt chase after you? Did you see them in the newspaper too?"

"What's come over you?"

"Why did you call *me*?"

She wetted a piece of tissue and started rubbing furiously under her eyes.

"You called and I came," he said. "I came with real . . . real feelings. So I want to know."

"I called because I saw your picture and missed you."

"Me specifically?"

"Yes," she said. "I was lonely. With Alva, it's harder than I thought."

"If it's this hard," he said, "you could go home."

"My home is here," she said.

This time he didn't hide the impatience in his tone. "But why?"

"My baby's Chinese."

"Then the baby's father should help you. Is there an issue? Is he another . . . married man?"

She resumed rubbing off her mascara in the mirror, swiping under one eye, then the other. But the tears surged faster than she could dry them. "I only want to be less alone, Lu Fang. The truth is that I'm hanging by a thread. I keep losing jobs, and of course it's not hard to find another, all these foreign language schools hiring, but I'm not as young and bright and shiny as all these college grads doing their stint in China. They're letting so many foreigners in now, there are always fresher arrivals."

Lu Fang was quiet. It was hard to find compassion for her predicament when she could flash her face as a business card, find a job by virtue of her mother tongue being the world's linguistic currency. "Why do you keep losing jobs?" he asked.

"I miss classes. One day I showed up to teach hungover and they said I was still drunk. Maybe it was true. It's my fault, I know. I drink too much. I went out to bars after work. Yeah, I slept with a few people. Some were Chinese and some were not. I forgot about the pill. I was drinking a lot and there were nights—I can't remember them. I didn't know I was pregnant; I didn't even know what the baby would come out looking like. Those men—I thought about who the father could be, and none of them mattered, they all either wanted something from me or moved on to the next foreigner, a younger, newer version. When Alva came out Chinese, though—she became my anchor. Before her I almost couldn't go on. Now I'm a mother, raising a Chinese daughter, and I want to do it well."

They looked at each other in the foggy mirror. "I'm sorry," he said. "I think you can be a good mother." He closed his eyes. "What do you need? I can give you some money. If that's what you want. I can help you out once, but—"

She held up a hand. "Alva and I will be fine. Seeing you in that newspaper picture, so successful—it's true I was curious. I thought that with the years, with the circumstances, things might be different between us. But you brought your son. And as soon as I saw him I understood. It's him, Lu Fang. He's your reason."

In the cold bathwater, a shiver ran through him. "I want him to have advantages," he said. "I want him to speak English. To get out."

"He speaks some English," Sloan said. "He told me, in English, outside the restaurant: *You're a bad woman.*"

"Oh." Lu Fang didn't know how to respond—somehow, he couldn't feel angry at Minmin. "He shouldn't have said that," he finally said.

She handed a towel to Lu Fang. "He's not that shy after all," she said.

They went back into the unlit bedroom. He could see Alva's small body sleeping beneath the covers. Lu Fang and Sloan lay down on the other bed, and he hugged her to his chest. "This is nice," she whispered. "This is enough." He nodded, unable to speak, silent tears seeping into his pillow. Alva's breathing was loud and regular. They may have drifted into sleep this way, or at least Sloan may have, because when Lu Fang woke some hours later, the moonlight outside sliced brightly into the room from the balcony windows, and Sloan stayed immobile, her eyes closed. She stayed this way as he left the room, closed the door behind him.

## 32

He knew what the next day would look like. He would meet the South Koreans in his office. He would work late; he would go home. Minmin would tell Ciyi about Sloan and the weekend, Ciyi would be suspicious. Lu Fang would tell her to forget it, that it was only an old acquaintance. He would go to work—and life would go on. Life would go on.

When he got back to his own room, the lights were off. There were no sounds, not even breathing. The beds were empty. Minmin ran away, he thought. He imagined his son in the streets of Shanghai. He was about to turn around and run downstairs when he heard a voice coming from the balcony.

*Cafú. Still no score.*

He opened the balcony doors. Minmin was sitting there, feet dangling between the metal rods, holding a small portable radio to his ear. Ciyi's radio. The soundwave sputtered. It was the World Cup final. *Baresi with a header. The Italians are doing a very good job of forcing the Brazilians out wide.*

"What are you doing?" Lu Fang said. He tried to rid his voice of the panic he'd felt. To give it threat and gravity. "Why aren't you in bed?"

*Dunga for Brazil. Romário plays it back.*

"I'm sorry, Ba," Minmin gasped, only now realizing his father's presence.

"We have to wake up early," Lu Fang said. "And the train—" But he noticed how puffy his son's eyes were from tears. He sat down next to

Minmin, slipped his legs between the railings. The night air was fresh, the city uncharacteristically still.

"What's the score?" Lu Fang asked.

"Zero-zero," Minmin said.

*Romário claimed it was a foul, but the referee wasn't fooled by it. Albertini has the ball—*

Lu Fang felt for the pack of cigarettes in his shirt pocket. "But who's going to win?"

"Brazil," his son said without hesitation. He stole a glance at his father, who was exhaling a plume of smoke. "Should I keep it playing?"

The radio crackled. *Here at the Rose Bowl in Pasadena we are still waiting for a goal as we approach halftime—*

Lu Fang nodded. They could hear the roar of the crowd in Pasadena. Lu Fang let himself imagine the men in blue, the men in yellow. The arc of the spinning ball, the spectators' tandem cheers. Halfway across the world but in real time. Apolloni got a yellow card for tripping up Romário. Everybody wondered whether Roberto Baggio of Italy would score a goal. When the referee blew the halftime whistle, Minmin asked, "What were you doing in her room?"

*Was Roberto Baggio injured too badly? Would he save Italy?* "Talking," Lu Fang said. But he knew what Minmin was really asking. He chain-smoked as they waited for the game to resume. *Ninety thousand people at the Rose Stadium, listen to them!* The screams blurred into a wave of white noise. Father and son sat nearly motionless and listened to the second half. Bebeto missed a great pass by Romário. The legend Baggio finally went for a shot, narrowly saved by Tarrafel. For the first time in World Cup history, the commentator announced, there would be penalty shoot-outs.

"I don't like that American lady," Minmin said.

"I know. You told her."

"I'm sorry," Minmin said. "Am I in trouble?"

The radio burst with howls. An Italian, Albertini, scored the first goal of the match.

"No," Lu Fang said. "You're not in trouble."

Romário evened the score for Brazil. *Brazilian fans have started jumping around. Evani scores another for Italy, but the Brazilian goalkeeper, Tarrafel, blocks the next attempt—*

From the night came cries of others in Shanghai who had gathered to follow the match. Minmin sat still. There was so much bundled up in his son's thin frame, so much held back, such emotion swallowed. The screams from the field were so loud it seemed like the radio might explode.

"Are you going to leave Mama and me?" Minmin asked quietly.

Lu Fang put one hand on his son's shoulder. *And Roberto Baggio of Italy is now his country's last chance against the Brazilians. It's a simple equation now.*

"No, of course not," Lu Fang said.

*And HE MISSES!* the commentator screamed. The crowd erupted in Pasadena. *Roberto Baggio misses! Brazil wins the World Cup!*

Minmin fell back flat against the cool balcony tiles. Dawn was breaking at the horizon, and Lu Fang pulled the last cigarette out of his pack. There were distant shouts in the city. Minmin's narrow chest heaved up and down, and suddenly, he pumped one of his small fists, a smile spread on his lips. Lu Fang would always remember that smile. "I knew they'd win, Baba," Minmin whispered.

Lu Fang took his son's hand and pulled him to his feet. "Come on," he said. "We're going home."

# PART VII

ALVA

SHANGHAI, 2008

## 33

She'd planned to meet Gao Xiaofan at the Haoledi KTV complex at Thumb Plaza, the preferred location for local students to conduct their illicit romances. Its labyrinthine hallways and glass-slotted doors yielded glimpses of singers basking in the glow of TV screens. For most teenagers, it was the closest semblance to privacy outside the home.

When Alva stepped through the automatic doors, Gao was waiting on the lobby's leather benches, hunched forward, elbows propped on knees, scratching his head like he was shaking off dandruff. It took him a second to recognize her. Her dyed yellow hair still looked like hay no matter what conditioner she used. Did she look good? She hated that this was the most searing question on her mind, when it was staggering that Gao Xiaofan was even physically here, in this Haoledi, after standing on top of one of Shanghai's tallest structures with only his toes.

"Well, fuck," he said, rising from the bench.

"I can't believe you're actually doing it," she said. Of course they didn't hug like her new schoolmates did. Instead they shuffled awkwardly toward the reception counter. He'd been the one to suggest the meetup after he sent her the link, and she'd thought of little else all week.

"You look different," he said.

He took in her soccer jersey and shorts. She'd come straight from practice. She noticed his eyes dwelling on the sharp lines of her calves, the bare skin of her thighs. "I play goalie," she said quickly, suddenly shy.

He reddened a little too. "Let's pick a room," he said.

They busied themselves looking at the list. Alva pointed to a mid-range one: a small VIP room. The employee named the price and Gao didn't move. Alva was usually the one to wait after a bill appeared, but she recovered and reached for her wallet. "I'll get it," she said cheerfully.

An employee was showing them the way to their room when Gao said, "Can we stop by the KTV store first?" They perused the row of snacks, and he chose a small bag of salted peanuts, like a kid picking the least expensive trinket in the toy store. Was he hungry? Alva grabbed two bags of chips, chocolate Pocky sticks, and a Snickers. He used to eat them after lunchtime basketball at Mincai. "I'm always ravenous after soccer," she said, and paid for everything.

The employee left them in a room with a wraparound couch and a giant TV screen. The microphone made a dull thud when Alva picked it up.

"How long have you been—" she began.

"I stopped going to school two weeks ago," Gao Xiaofan interrupted. The disco light shone little red and green diamonds across his face. "I thought they wouldn't care. But Ms. Song called my dad. I think she was actually worried. My parents threw a fit. My mom cried for three days straight, I swear."

"What did you tell them?"

"That I never had a future with school. It was only going to get worse from there. Trade school, or a high school for migrants? I'm never going to Qinghua or competing in the white-collar market, that's for sure." He shook his head. "The rooftoppers—they're doing something different. My parents don't understand, so they kicked me out."

She scooted closer to him on the couch, close enough to see the corners of his mouth droop. "It's no big deal. I got a job at a construction site behind Yanggao Road, the new office complex they're building for Taiping Insurance. They let us stay in the barracks."

Alva had seen those long blue rows along the edges of giant pits. "Have you ever done work like that?"

"No. And it pays like shit. There are ten migrants for every shitty job, and they told me to take half pay and keep quiet about my age."

He brought his hands to his skull, digging his thumbs into his temples.

"Hey," she said. "That video you took. Wasn't it a little ... dangerous?"

"You don't get views unless you're bold. Plus, it's only dangerous when you think you're safe."

"So you'll be really careful."

He laughed. "You're the one who dared me, HentaiLord. Did the laowai school make you tame?"

"No," she said, stung. "I'm going to America, actually. I've been putting a plan together."

"Yeah," Gao said. "I guessed, from the dyed hair."

Alva reflexively touched her ponytail. "It looks bad."

His fingers were coated with salt and red dust from the peanuts. He leaned closer to her. She thought he was going to run them through her hair. Instead, he reached for the TV remote and turned up the sound of the automated loop of karaoke tracks. He was wearing the same pair of red Nikes, one of them tapped the floor with a nervous beat.

"I dare you," she said.

He looked at her with saucepan eyes. They were both blushing, though it was hard to tell in the disco lights.

"Put on 'Stubborn' by Mayday," he said.

She bent over the control screen and found the song. Mayday was a famous Taiwanese rock group they'd all loved at Mincai. When she turned from the display screen, he caught her face with his hands. Then their lips were mashing together, and "Stubborn" was blaring. She tasted salt and peanuts, then withdrew her tongue, afraid it was too much. His hand was on the side of her ribs. He pressed it there awkwardly. The light projector on the ceiling was stuck, flashing the diamonds in one jittery ray, a pizza slice-shaped beam.

Finally, he pulled back. Alva felt saliva at the corners of her mouth. She wanted the kiss to continue. She leaned in again until her lips touched his. It wasn't a kiss, just soft tissue against soft tissue, neither of them moving. He let out a sigh that sounded like a whimper.

"Can I ask you something?" he said.

She sat back. Outside, in the hallway, an employee hurried past, shooting them a wary glance through the glass panel. "Of course," she said, her body loose with crackling heat.

"A favor," he said.

"A favor," she repeated.

"The construction site I mentioned earlier—truth is, they fired me. I can't do the lifting, I can't hold a drill."

"Oh."

"Without the construction dorms I have nowhere to stay. Some of the rooftoppers, though, they are starting to make money from their stunts. Some of them are living in this group apartment in Puxi, a crew, and the rent is cheap, but . . ."

Alva stared at the disco light. "How much?" she said.

"Anything. I'll pay you back."

"And what are you going to do?"

"I told you. There's a whole community. People pay wagers online. I just need some start-up funds to get settled, and then I'm going to be a real rooftopper, make big money with big stunts. I'll pay you back."

"I only have a few hundred on me right now," she said.

"A couple thousand yuan to get started, that's all I need."

She thought about the stash in her room, money she'd been skimming off the taxi fund, saving for a plane ticket to America. "I don't have that kind of money," she said.

"You go to the American school."

She didn't answer. Quietly, she moved sideways, took out two hundred-yuan bills from her wallet, and set them on the table. She'd been saving them to give back to Girlie the next time she went to the Cruises. She kept forgetting.

She thought he'd press for more. He reached for the bills without making eye contact. "Stubborn" was still playing on a loop. She tried remembering Gao as the first boy she'd ever really liked, surrounded by Mincai's red bricks, playing on the basketball courts, hunched next to her in the back row of a cybercafe, the boy she'd poke with a pencil and give a free pass on homework. The wetness she still felt on her lips now tasted sour.

"You know," she said, "I actually liked you."

He couldn't look at her. He was still clutching the two hundred-yuan bills. "Don't take it that way," he mumbled. "I asked because we're friends."

She got up, walked across the room, cracked open the door. The noise from the hallway, echoes of dozens of songs at different tempos, all came pouring in at once. "But were we friends?" she asked.

Gao waved his hand, looking not at her but at the video, like he was picturing himself as an audience member in the concert pit, waving a glowing phone on a warm summer night in Taiwan. "We were, Hentai-Lord," he said. "Fox and dog friends."

"I hope it works out for you, the rooftopping," she said. "But I don't think I want to talk to you again."

He smiled sadly. "Sure, Alva," he said. "I dare you not to."

## 34

In early May came the day Zoey had advertised: the pool at the Links Golf and Country Club opened. Soccer season was almost over. They both told the coach they felt ill so they could go sit poolside. The days were getting hot and damp, presaging the infernal humidity of summer.

Zoey was debating going to a music festival held at the city's edge, one with bands Alva had never heard of—VIP tickets went for one thousand yuan. It was advertised as the Chinese Coachella.

Alva had seen the pictures of the real Coachella online, all palm trees and bleached blond waves, like the California of her mother's stories. She imagined Sloan as a teenager, barefoot in the desert, smoking a fat joint and dancing among long-haired men in loose shirts. The Chinese Coachella, the flyers said, would feature a "desert dance floor" made from a cubic ton of imported white sand.

"What if it's only *locals*?" Zoey mused. "I'm not sure that many people are going."

"I'm sure *people* are going," Alva said.

She was staring at the pool's unnaturally beautiful blue, sipping on rum mixed into the pineapple juice the attendant kept bringing over. Alva drank faster than Zoey and had to stop herself from finishing the last third of her glass while Zoey was still sipping the foam at the top. Alva liked the haze, the way the sea stretched beyond the edge of the infinity pool. Here there were no Gao Xiaofans, no construction noises, no parents to avoid. It was hard to believe they were even in Shanghai.

She splayed her toes against the waterproof cushion. She didn't care what Zoey decided about the music festival: if Zoey went, she'd go. The semester was almost over and the Cruises were flying to New York at the start of summer break. Alva had tried asking Zoey offhandedly if they'd booked their plane tickets yet, and Zoey said it was always last minute, depending on her father's work schedule. What Alva really wanted to know was whether they would seriously take her along. Alva had looked up the Hamptons on her computer. With Google Earth street view she could see the clothing boutiques and ice cream parlors and picnic tables with chipped paint, where blurry-faced American children sat holding enormous wafer cones.

This was now the only summer she could imagine. It was impossible to contemplate staying in Shanghai. She couldn't remain stuck in Lu Fang's apartment. She'd been avoiding him. Every time they crossed paths in the hallway she averted her gaze. She'd been trying to forget the impressionist exhibit, the "back then," the possibility that she was issued of him, that she was already living with the parts that added up to her whole, and what a sad, misshapen collage it had turned out to be.

"I'd miss you if you went away," Alva reached toward Zoey, interrupting her midsentence. Alva realized she had no idea what Zoey had been talking about. She felt Zoey's fingers interlace with hers.

"Drink some water," Zoey said.

"I'd miss your craziness," Alva said.

"I *do* want you to come along. I'll talk to my dad—"

"Do something crazy right now," Alva said.

Zoey smiled. Two middle-aged women were lying on lounge chairs in the shallow end of the pool. Zoey walked to the deep end and dove in. Then, before she reemerged, her emerald-green bikini top bopped up in the water, followed by her tropical print bottoms. With a gasp she resurfaced and hurled them toward Alva. They both screamed with laughter. The women looked over, their faces shielded by large sunglasses, and resumed their conversation. The waiter at the pool bar squinted at Zoey. Alva held up the dripping wet swimsuit pieces. She saw herself and her mother coming out of H&M fitting rooms in bikinis, Sloan sucking in her stomach, saying, "Imagine we're on a beach in Honolulu." But this was not a real memory. Why had her mother lied about her history with Lu Fang? Alva felt the reflux of rum and pineapple seared with acid creep up her throat. She tossed the wet fabric back into the pool. But Zoey wasn't waiting to receive them. She was swimming deep underwater, a pale, wavy blur.

When they got back to the house that afternoon, they found the living room overtaken by giant canvas bags of stuffed animals. Julia was sorting through them. Zoey didn't seem surprised. "I need to shower," she said, pulling at her wet hair. She ran up the stairs, voice trailing, "Alva, let's watch *American Idol* after."

Alva stood in the sea of bagged animals. "What are these for?" she asked.

Julia was wearing a bright yellow T-shirt that read BIG LOVE OR-PHANAGE. "It's a place where I volunteer," she said. Messy strands escaped her ponytail. "We're doing a toy drive. Give me a hand? I need to take those to the lobby."

Alva grabbed one of the big canvas bags. She had thought Julia only left the house to attend galas. She noticed for the first time that Julia had a delicate silver cross around her neck.

"It's an orphanage run by a Christian charity," Julia said, noticing Alva looking at the cross. "A lot of little girls."

"Oh," Alva said. She ran her tongue over her teeth. She could still taste the sandy sugar of her drink. "Because their parents . . . ?"

Julia nodded. "Sons are best."

They dragged the canvas bags to the front door. Alva picked up a pink dog, its fur matted and musty, loved by another child, or maybe long forgotten in a shop window. "What happens to the girls?" she asked.

"We work with an adoption agency in America," Julia said. "It's usually the younger ones who find a home."

Feng materialized at the door, wordlessly taking the bags. The Range Rover's engine hummed in the driveway. "Xiexie," Julia said to him in

Chinese. He nodded and his expression behind his sunglasses softened almost imperceptibly.

"Thank you for your help," Julia said to Alva. She jogged after Feng toward the car. The back of her yellow T-shirt spelled 爱, the Chinese character for love. Alva tried to find something wrong with the picture so she could make fun of it with Zoey later—Julia the spoiled expat wife, the maid-hitter performing charity work—but she was too tired, the hangover already settling in.

"Hey!" she called after Julia. "I hope they like them."

That weekend, the soccer season culminated in a tournament held outside the Jinqiao community mall. Alva was running warm-up laps when she saw Lu Fang hovering near the metal bleachers where they'd all left their gym bags. He waved and Alva motioned for him to move away from that area, where the assistant coach, Ms. Su, was studying a clipboard. He didn't get it, though. Zoey was ahead of Alva, her light brown ponytail whipping back and forth, and soon all the girls would reach the bleachers, disperse and hydrate, and wonder who this slightly idiotic-looking man was, in his black polo and tacky aviator sunglasses. Alva sped ahead so she could be the first to intercept him. It was too late. Ms. Su had glanced up and was smiling uncertainly at Lu Fang. Alva arrived just in time to hear Lu Fang tell Ms. Su in Mandarin, "Hello, teacher. I am Alva's parent."

Ms. Su's face froze with a confused smile. She was a thirtysomething Asian American woman, native to Ohio, who had followed her husband to Shanghai. "*Dui bu qi*," she said. "I don't—"

Alva rushed over. "Sorry, sorry," she told Ms. Su. "She doesn't speak Chinese!" she hissed to Lu Fang in Mandarin.

"Oh," he fumbled. "Sorry."

"No need to apologize," Ms. Su said graciously in slowed-down English. "You are Alva's father?"

"Yes," Lu Fang said after a pause, red in the face.

"He's my stepfather," Alva said quickly.

"Well, it's very sweet of you to come cheer on the team," Ms. Su said. "The section for parents is over there, if you want to join them." She pointed to another set of bleachers across the field. Lu Fang's gaze followed her fingers to a group of foreign parents with baseball hats and coolers, and only then did he understand he was in the wrong place. He nodded three times in a row, almost bowing. "I'll walk him over," Alva told Ms. Su.

Lu Fang followed Alva down the white edge of the field. The other girls were looking at them. "How come you're here?" she asked.

"You talked about this last week," he said. "I thought . . ."

"Where's Mom?" Alva interrupted.

"She . . . she was tired and wanted to sleep."

"You don't need to lie. She's still mad at me."

"Yes," he admitted. "She doesn't like you making plans for America." They were almost by the parents' section, where expat moms in sleeveless shirts were rubbing sunscreen onto their freckled arms. Alva was grateful the Cruises weren't among them: Daniel was on a business trip to Hong Kong, and Julia wouldn't leave the house for this. "Well," she breathed in deeply. "So what do you think, then?"

"About what?"

"The summer plan."

"It's not for me to say," he said.

"They'd pay for everything there," Alva said. "I'd just need help with the plane ticket. And then you and Mom can have the apartment to yourselves, I'd be out of the way." She closed her eyes and pictured them at the museum again, heads leaning against each other. *Not a care back then.*

Lu Fang took off his aviators and rubbed his eyes. "It's not up to me," he repeated.

Alva swallowed hard. "If you were my actual father, would you let me go?"

"Alva—"

"I heard you at the museum. I know that you've known each other a long time."

"Yes, I knew your mother when she was young," he said.

She couldn't bring herself to ask the actual question. "Everyone here is watching their *children*." She gestured toward the bleachers. "Why are you here?"

He blinked, put his aviators back on. "My son loved soccer," he said, his voice soft.

Right then the referee blew the warning whistle, and Ms. Su gestured for Alva to hustle to the goal box. A son? Lu Fang had never talked about a son. Alva stared down at the cleats she'd picked out at Decathlon earlier that semester with Lu Fang. He'd known about cleats. Now it made sense: the jerseys, the Nikes. Because of his son.

"I lost touch with your mother for many years," Lu Fang said. "You were born during that time. I don't know anything about your father."

She'd mangled the grass clumps underfoot and realized she couldn't meet his gaze, her head pressed down by a heaviness that felt eerily like disappointment. It was the disappointment of an answer within grasp, then slipping away like smoke. Finally she looked toward the other end of the field, where Ms. Su was windmilling her arms. Alva mumbled, "I have to go."

"Do your best," Lu Fang said. He climbed to the bleacher's top row, a distance removed from the other parents.

During the game Alva dove into the mud, slammed her body down to barricade the shots, but she kept crashing in the wrong direction. The balls zipped past her the other way, one miscalculation after another. She didn't know why she was so out of sorts—had she really wished that he was her father? She didn't want him to be. But she couldn't shake the rising bitterness that Lu Fang had so categorically said *no*, he was here not for Alva, only because his *son* loved soccer. Of course no one was here for Alva. Of course Lu Fang had another family, of course he had a son. Did Lu Fang ever see him? Did *Sloan* know him? Did they visit him on their trips?

She didn't look his way a single time during the game. Her team lost 5–2 and didn't move onto the next round. Everyone was in a bad mood, and after they shook hands with the rival team, Zoey turned to Alva and asked, "*That's* your stepdad?"

Lu Fang was still sitting there, alone on the highest row. "That's the ATM," Alva said loudly. She didn't care if he heard. Zoey laughed. Alva asked the rest of the team, "Milkshakes at Blue Frog?" A few girls nodded. They straggled toward the mall, and Alva made a few nonsensical hand gestures at Lu Fang, motioning for him to leave. He nodded, or she thought he did. As the girls walked into the mall's chilled interior Alva looked back again and saw Lu Fang standing at the edge of the now vacant field, holding one of the soccer balls with the American School emblem printed on it. He set it down and gave it a gentle kick. Then he started walking toward the bus station, alone, his head bowed low.

## 35

Alva didn't go home after the milkshakes. Instead, she took the subway across the river to Puxi and wandered along the old nongtangs. Kids at the American School called Pudong and its plain wide streets "Pu-Jersey." "If Pudong is New Jersey, where nothing interesting ever happens," Zoey had explained, "then Puxi is Manhattan." Alva tried to see the Manhattanese Puxi through the eyes of her new classmates. Foreigners loved writing novels on the triads and cabarets of flapper-era Shanghai. You wouldn't know this standing in the quiet lanes on an early summer dusk, the sunlight slanting onto mossy stone tiles. In the heart of Puxi there were patches like this—ghostly, lonely, where the roars of motorcycles faded in the distance and a window creaked closed. And if this was the real Shanghai, then Alva felt alone in it. The compounds where she and her mother used to live, near the botanical garden and the train station, were razed and gone. So Alva walked toward a mall—warm lights and shops, the comfort of commodities, the proximity of human masses. Malls were the only refuge when a disquieting solitude of the city seized you. To grow up in an Asian metropolis is to learn to love malls.

Alva rode the escalators to the top floor of the Xuhui Friendship plaza. She paused in front of a Brazilian steakhouse, a popular chain Lu Fang had taken them to before. There was a heavy glass token you set on your table: the green side meant keep it coming, the yellow side meant no more for now. Lu Fang hadn't flipped his token to the yellow side over the course of the entire meal, even when it was clear he was straining to swallow the mouthfuls of cooling fat. "What if something good comes along?" he'd said.

Before today, she hadn't even considered he might have another family, a child. She'd assumed he was another average man busy mining China's economic boom. A man so average she'd never imagined her mother could actually love him. Is that why it stung so much, she'd been foolish enough to consider the possibility that he was her father? Of course he wasn't. They were only a pretend family, a tangled web of transactions.

How often did he see his son, his real family? Maybe he missed them. Now she thought back on things she could no longer ignore without feeling guilty. How he stayed up late by himself most nights, watching Hollywood action flicks while chain-smoking. How he went alone to FamilyMart to replenish the soft-drink rack. How his overusage of poems and proverbs sometimes struck Alva as brilliant.

She walked to a bench overlooking the escalators. The mall was lively on a Saturday night. She sat watching people come and go, until the throngs thinned, and the stores dimmed, and guards started circling the floors. They were so many people in the city, but did they feel as she did, floating atoms never a part of anything real? From the mall's bay windows, Shanghai's dense forest of skyscrapers lit up in the night. Maybe Gao Xiaofan was on a roof, watching car lights course through elevated highways like rivers of gold, watching the entire city, watching her.

She took the subway back east over the river. On the corner of Yingchun Road, she looked for a white van full of plants and the DVD man, but he wasn't there. She headed toward the fluorescent lights of the twenty-four-hour FamilyMart, with its shelves full of cucumber-flavored chips and silk leggings and fish ball stews and liquors and lubricants. The clerk who rung up Alva's bottle of on-sale Ballantine's didn't say a word, even if by now she knew his face and he knew hers.

She walked out of the cool interior of the FamilyMart, into Shanghai's already humid night air. And the van was there, as if it'd materialized out of the dark, parked in its usual spot, the DVD man smoking next to a giant snake plant.

She went up to him. "Did you just pull up?"

"No," he said. "I've been here."

She shifted the FamilyMart bag behind her, the plastic crinkling. It was likely futile; he'd probably seen her stand in front of the small selection of liquor, seen her reach for the Ballantine's. She needed to find another corner store soon, be more careful. Careful about what, though? Not getting caught? No one was out to catch her.

"You haven't come around in a while," the DVD man said. A toothpick stuck out from his lips. "I've seen your classmates, but you don't go to that school anymore, do you?"

"How do you know?" she asked.

His meaty face, beneath his usual buzz cut, was oddly serene. His thick, dangling earlobes reminded her of Buddha.

"I know a lot about people in this neighborhood," he said. "Years on this corner and you see people go by, you know who likes to pick out what kind of movies. You," he continued, "besides watching American trash, think a lot about that fancy German, Brecht. You want to know where the movie ends and the truth begins." He chuckled. "Your mother, she likes the big movies with beautiful actresses. Elizabeth Taylor. Brigitte Bardot. Movies they don't make anymore."

"She still comes by?"

The DVD man nodded. "With the man from Dongbei. Mr. Sad."

"Why do you say he's sad?"

"Isn't he?" The DVD man snapped a sickly stalk off a peace lily plant. "He always picks one of two kinds of movies. Hollywood action blockbusters, and the kinds of early Wang Jiawei and Jia Zhangke so bleak they'd make you cry."

"I've never seen him watch those," Alva said.

"There are things you only watch in private," the DVD man said.

She thought about this. "Do you have a movie called *The Lover*?" she asked.

"*The Lover*?" He picked at something between his teeth, pensive. "I don't have it here. But I could get it for you."

"Maybe later," she said.

"Maybe later then." The DVD man's eyes gleamed in the dark forest of potted plants. "Better get home, girl. It is strange to be out shopping at this hour of the night."

Alva clicked on Gao's username before going to sleep. The Smiling and Proud Wanderer already had a few dozen followers on his rooftopping account.

Gao Xiaofan's latest picture was a selfie of him lying on a roof, shoulder blades against the ledge. He wore a disposable medical *kouzhao*, a standard face mask. In another picture he stood on the rusty ring of a conductor needle. Lightning could strike, the foot could slip. The pictures made her feel sick to her stomach.

She Baidued the tallest buildings in Shanghai. Their names all had "trade" or "financial" in them. Whether she gave him money would have made no difference, she told herself, he still would have become a rooftopper. She studied the eyes above the disposable face mask. These weren't the glazed-over and bloodshot eyes of Gao Xiaofan at Mincai, after an eleven-night binge at the cybercafe. There was, she had to admit, something alive about them.

## 36

Zoey told Alva to meet at the Biyun mall's underground parking so they could get a ride to Chinese Coachella. She'd decided it was worth going after all, and Alva had peeled away one thousand yuan from the amassed savings of Lu Fang's taxi money to order a VIP pass. The amount she'd saved was pocket change compared to the tens of thousands of yuan it would cost anyway. So she spent more at H&M buying a fringed suede dress that looked like the pictures she'd seen of the American Coachella. When she arrived in the parking lot, Zoey was wearing a tight minidress of black sequins and heels—an odd choice for dancing in a cubic ton of sand.

"Where's Feng?" Alva asked.

"It's his day off," Zoey said. "Don't worry, I've made alternate arrangements."

A few minutes later, a Range Rover screeched into the garage lane before them. The driver was a young Chinese man in a starched white shirt. He did not speak to them. In the back seat, they discovered a bucket containing a bottle of chilled champagne. Zoey popped open the bottle. The bubbles overflowed and fizzed out between the sequins of her dress.

The car pulled on the highway, westward toward the interior. Alva could read the road signs in Chinese. "Zoey, this isn't the direction of the music festival," she said.

"I know," Zoey said. She patted Alva's hand, fingers ice-cold from the champagne flute. "Surprise! We're not going there. I got us invited somewhere better. Somewhere *fancy*."

The thousand-yuan VIP pass sat heavy in Alva's purse. Just like that, it'd become a worthless piece of paper. Her mouth was dry. She'd already finished her champagne. She reached into the ridges of the car door and, sure enough, found a tiny bottle of Evian water.

It was a long trip. They drove past the gray buildings and factories into the tea plantations and rolling hills of the Hangzhou prefecture, soft and golden in the setting sun. As the car powered up a winding road on a mountain dense with bamboo, Alva tried to catch a glimpse of a building in the impending darkness. She could see nothing through the canopy. Then, out of nowhere, an ornate house with white columns and French windows and balconies materialized, white walled and red roofed, a classic European replica. Although the rural barracks they'd seen on the way were barely illuminated by streetlamps, the entire mansion was aglow, shooting light out of every window.

Alva expected security and guest lists, but there was no one at the heavy metallic front door. "We can just go in?" she turned to Zoey. Zoey nodded. "Anyone who's driven here is already on the list. We ain't in Pu-Jersey anymore, Toto. We are far up Mogan Mountain."

Alva felt a pang of insecurity. Mogan Mountain was famous as a site for ensconced villas built by past-century elite. And she was someone with no fortune, no famous last name, no grand connections except for, apparently, Zoey.

Zoey's cold fingers grazed Alva's neck, tucking the label of her dress under the back of her collar. "The whole world doesn't need to know it's H&M," Zoey said.

And they went inside.

"People come to me and say—I adore brunch at the Westin. I say, please! Free vodka with your caviar? No self-respecting five-star establishment would propose that, except in this country."

A white man wearing a double-breasted suit held court in the foyer with a cohort of well-dressed blond women and one Chinese man. The Chinese man, who kept patting the sweat at his temples with a napkin, nodded emphatically. "Vulgar," he said with a British accent. "Classically vulgar."

The white man waved his hand, which was tattooed to the second knuckle. "It's hard for some first-timers in Shanghai to navigate what's on offer. That's why I created an elite concierge service for business travelers. We have a 'realize your wildest dreams' vibe, kind of a Dubai branding. Of course, the legal environment here is actually more *pliable* for the pursuit of wild dreams."

"One eye open, one eye closed," a woman said.

Zoey pulled Alva across the room, not introducing her to anyone. The floor was tiled with mosaics, the mirrors framed with brass. The furniture made Alva think of words like *parlor* and *boudoir*. She hadn't expected so many older adults, all of them obviously moneyed. "Who are these people?" she whispered.

"Everybody that matters," Zoey said, pausing their march. "That fat Chinese guy? He owns half the private art museums in Shanghai."

Everywhere around them there were whispers in Chinese, whispers in English. A silver fox was showing off his nearly unaccented Mandarin to three Chinese women, sending them into peals of laughter. Alva tried to hide her disappointment. "This is what I imagined embassy events to be like," she told Zoey. "My mother never wanted to go."

"This is a lot more exclusive than those, Alva," Zoey said. "Your mom couldn't come even if she wanted to. This is the Sino-American Philanthropy Network. My dad is on the board."

Alva didn't reply. Was Daniel here? In the most ostentatious sitting room, a man in a tuxedo was climbing on top of a massive oak table. He clinked a spoon against a crystal glass.

"A-hoy, a-hoy! Welcome, *huanying*!" he cried. "Please, if I may have your attention."

A Chinese woman in an evening gown repeated the sentence to the crowd in Chinese. People filtered into the salon from elsewhere in the house. Alva and Zoey were definitely the youngest in attendance, though

Alva noticed a few other young Chinese women. They looked like they'd gotten the same plastic surgery modeled after Fan Bingbing.

"Great philanthropists are gathered here today, folding the crème of the Chinese business community into the crème of the expatriate business community. As you may know, this is an emergency event in response to the recent earthquake in Sichuan. A week and a half has elapsed and we are already counting a tragic fifty thousand casualties. But people are still under rubble, and the clock is ticking."

A fundraiser? Zoey knew Alva had no money to give.

The man in the tuxedo had a mustache shaped like the character 八. He gesticulated toward a young Chinese woman sitting on a nearby couch, who wore a dress stitched from a million chiffon ruffles. She smiled gracefully at the impending introduction. "We are fortunate to have Miss Xi Lipeng here today—though most of you may know her better as Lily Xi, rising star at Red Cross Shanghai. Lily has generously sponsored this chance to come together in the wake of a great tragedy, which has so profoundly touched many of us."

Lily Xi rose and bowed. "Xiexie, xiexie, dajia."

Zoey handed Alva a glass of wine from a tray a sullen waiter was circulating around the room. "That woman's dad is big in the government," she said. "Like, *big*."

"Thank you, Lily," the man in the tuxedo said. "Please come speak to Lily, myself, or any of our board members if you would like to discuss a . . . special contribution. In case you don't know the board of the Sino-American Philanthropy Network, we have Miss Alice Fan here. . . . Please wave—"

An Asian woman with permed hair stood and gave the Queen's salute. "Mr. Daniel Cruise—" And then Alva saw him, standing against the wall across the room. He unfolded his crossed arms and raised a hand, the silver wave in his hair falling slightly with the movement. Alva curtsied at him mockingly from the crowd, and he smiled. "—and Charles Zhe, who recently joined the board as McKinsey Shanghai's youngest partner." Murmurs arose as a round-cheeked young man in glasses stood and bowed slightly. The man in the tuxedo dismounted the table and raised his glass. "Now back to the celebra—the fundraiser!" he shouted. "Xiexie!"

Zoey turned to Alva and licked her lips. "Time to get the party started."

"Your dad got us here?"

"He wants me to get involved with charity. He said to invite you too."

Someone had dimmed the lights of the room, and a vaguely tropical soundtrack played from hidden speakers. A banner above the central table spelled WENCHUAN EARTHQUAKE DISASTER RELIEF. "Are you having fun? I brought you here to have fun." Zoey sounded drunk. "It'll be a different kind of fun in New York."

The Cruises had booked the tickets to America for late June. Zoey had already rattled off all the things they were going to do: shopping in SoHo, lox omelettes at Sarabeth's, concerts at the Bowery, meeting up with her old Hong Kong friends who had an apartment by NYU, beach clubs in the Hamptons, and . . . hearing Zoey talk about these plans produced both the most amazing and saddest feeling in Alva. She still had to figure out how it was all going to happen. But Zoey didn't need to know about the backstage struggle.

"You want a shot of this?" Alva produced a nip-size Bombay Sapphire from her purse. "In case the old people finished all the wine out there."

"Alva, this isn't a place where they'd run out."

Alva shrugged and took the shot herself. The mansion was abuzz, people conversing in small cliques in dark rooms. In one, people were dancing, softly, lethargically, with middle-aged head bops and none of the mating call urgency of a nightclub.

There were fragments of serious conversations, most of them about business, scarcely any about politics. Here it was referred to in passing, with knowing smiles. The mansion was crawling with foreigners who liked to play Chinese, showing off their linguistic acquisitions or "insider" knowledge. Foreigners who liked doing exactly what Sloan did. She overheard a Chinese woman telling a white man, "Oh, John, your Chinese is *so* good."

"Daddy!" Zoey squealed in the little girl voice reserved for her father.

Daniel was leaning against the staircase. He'd taken off his suit jacket and was holding a glass of something luxuriously amber in hand.

"My two VIPs," he said.

He pulled Zoey in for a paternal embrace and kissed her on the cheek. Then he opened his arms toward Alva as well, and she leaned closer. His fingers pressed against the bare skin of her shoulder blades, and he kissed her on the cheek too. She was a little drunk and liked the pressure of his fingers on her skin. Then suddenly it was gone, and he was turning away. "Have fun but be careful, all right, girls? Whenever you get tired, there are bedrooms upstairs reserved for board members and guests."

"Okay, Daddy," Zoey called after Daniel. She turned to Alva, smirking. "Bullshit. We're staying up until sunrise."

"Let's go dance," Alva said.

They chose the room with what sounded like old-school hip-hop, where the crowd was slightly younger. Charles the-youngest-partner-at-McKinsey-Shanghai Zhe was there, talking to men in suits in the corner. Alva and Zoey, coupes of something frothy in hand, started grinding back to back and getting low. They had the shamelessness of teenagers, knowing that for every measure of embarrassment or provocation, they had the advantage of youth. Alva beamed at Zoey, laughed when half of the contents of Zoey's coupe went sloshing onto the Arabian carpet. She heard Zoey say she needed to wash the stickiness off her dress, and Alva tapped her left nostril with a finger, inquiring, and Zoey shook her head, no more; it was true—they'd done two lines each already and the plastic pouch had been flung into a bamboo bin full of icy, jasmine-scented hand towels. *I'll be right back*, Zoey mouthed, and Alva nodded. She closed her eyes and felt the fringes of her H&M dress whip against her thighs as she swayed from side to side.

There was a hand on her shoulder and when she turned she recognized one of the businessmen who'd been talking to Charles Zhe. He was Asian, with tan skin and thick, straight eyebrows, some gray in his stubble. He was saying something to Alva. She couldn't hear him over the music. He was pointing to a doorway that led to an adjacent room, where more men in suits were sitting on couches around a low glass table. She cupped her ear and the man leaned closer. His breath was warm as he said, "Come have a drink," and she nodded and followed him into the other room. The suited men were smiling, their faces greasy, and there was a bottle of Lagavulin on the table. Alva counted the men, nine of them, one white and the others Chinese, all in nearly identical suits, all with button-downs of such nice-looking material, and there was a woman, too, one of the Fan Bingbing lookalike Chinese girls sitting on a businessman's lap. Alva turned toward the door, scanning for Zoey, but she was nowhere to be found.

The businessman with tan skin said, "Come with us for a minute, we won't eat you." The men in suits were all staring. The path of least resistance was to sit and then leave. She didn't want to offend them. Then she heard someone say her name. Daniel Cruise was beside her, hands on her shoulders. "I have to borrow my daughter's friend here for a second," he told the men. "Of course, Daniel," the man with tan skin said, his expression utterly neutral. The other men wore similarly indecipherable smiles.

"I was searching for you girls," Daniel said as he led Alva out of the leathery parlor.

"Zoey was just here," she said.

"By the looks of it, you've had a little too much to drink." He still had one arm around Alva's shoulder, steered her toward the brightly lit hallway. "I recommend a little time-out, because fraternizing with that group of bankers wouldn't have been the best of ideas, I think. What's so funny?"

Alva was giggly. She only got this way when the buzz was hitting right. "You said time-out," she said. "Like I'm a little kid."

"Oh god. We've got a more serious case than I thought," Daniel said, though he didn't seem mad. "Let's get you some water."

He wasn't steering her anymore, and she wanted him to wrap his arm around her again. But then she thought, I am great at walking in a straight line, so she concentrated on that so he wouldn't think she was drunk, and like this she followed him up to the second floor, where no music was playing, and you couldn't hear the reception downstairs. At the end of a long hallway was a library with an old-fashioned bar in the corner. Daniel bent down behind the bar, filled a large glass of water with ice cubes, and handed it to Alva.

"It's great that you're helping with the earthquake," she said.

In truth she'd barely paid attention to the news, which they'd first heard during the last period on Monday when Ms. McCoy, the history teacher, said those who wanted could pray for the children of Sichuan. The praying had made Alva deeply uncomfortable. News of the earthquake was only beginning to spread from those who'd received the alerts on their phones. Many of the children trapped under crumbling school buildings had moments ago been just like them, sitting out their last class. What good did prayers from the American school do them now?

"It's tragic," Daniel said, pouring himself a finger of scotch. "Those kids? Thousands dead and more missing. This is the most difficult period." He took a sip. "The two weeks after, when you can't be sure whether someone declared missing in the rubble is dead or alive. They are still pulling them out, at least those who've managed to survive this long without food or water."

"I know what you mean," Alva said. "It's all the not knowing."

Her brain felt like a loose mass, an island floating in liquid. Daniel came to sit in the armchair across from hers. "That's why we're hoping to funnel funds directly to search-and-rescue, not down layers of bureaucracy so that all the provincial cadres can fatten their wallets."

"Disasters are lucrative," Alva said.

Daniel looked impressed. She finished her water in one drain and set down her glass.

"Right. Put a Chinese businessman next to a Western one opening his checkbook," Daniel said, "and they'll be trying to outzero each other in no time. We learned this about the psychology of donations. China is a nation with a very young culture of philanthropy."

He stretched out his long legs. The tip of his shoes almost touched Alva's feet. "Countries forge their identities in tragedy. This earthquake will be one. Look at 9/11, or Madrid in 2004, London in 2005—we live in an age of disasters. China hadn't yet lived through its great modern tragedy. Since '89, I mean."

Alva didn't know what he meant by "89." She decided to nod and play along. "When I first heard about the earthquake it was like I could feel the ground shaking," she said. "I felt so terrible about it."

The truth was that on Monday night she'd gone with Zoey to play billiards at Johnny Sport's and drank absinthe with boys from SAS Puxi. Nobody mentioned the earthquake.

"Empathy is good," Daniel said. "It's so easy to be insensitive to the suffering of locals. The Chinese state's greatest trick is the foreigner's illusionary freedom. They want to keep us fat and happy, apolitical, docile and captive, just like their people."

Alva nodded again, *us*, eyeing the wooden bar. Already the water made her feel like she was losing her buzz. Would it be bad if she got up and poured herself something? She didn't think he'd mind. Daniel was talking to her adult to adult. She sprang to her feet, less spritely than she'd thought, asked "Can I?" with nonchalance, prepared herself for the off chance of a fatherly *is that a good idea*. He said, "Help yourself."

She found the bottle at the bar, poured a finger in her glass. In the freezer there were ice cubes shaped like globes, which cracked like the earth splintering when she dropped them in her drink. She pressed her lips to the rim slowly, knowing he was watching.

"I like that dress you have on," he said. "It's different."

She did a half-spin, the skirt lifting and the fringes fanning out against her bare thighs. "I thought I was going to a music festival."

"Zoey mentioned. I'm glad you're here instead."

Alva came back to her armchair, crossed her legs, then uncrossed them. Daniel's legs were still stretched out, even farther it seemed, and this time she made sure the toes of his leather loafers touched the side of her sandaled foot. She took a sip of the scotch and exhaled. It was smoky, tasted of grown men. "Julia doesn't like coming to these things?" she asked.

"She's sworn off public functions," Daniel said.

"Because of the lawsuit."

"Yes," Daniel said. "Zoey told you about that?"

"I can't picture her hitting someone," Alva said. The words just came out, her lips were syrupy slick. "She's so calm and put-together."

Daniel tilted his head. "Who, Zoey?"

"No, Julia. Your wife."

He seemed puzzled. "Did Zoey tell you Julia was the one who got in trouble with the maid?"

Alva froze. Did she? Alva couldn't remember. It'd always been implied, hadn't it? That Julia was the one disgraced, hiding in shame at the Links Golf and Country Club. "No—" she began, trying to backtrack, but her brain was slow. "Zoey—"

"Zoey was young," Daniel said. "Barely a teen, and the move to Hong Kong was a big transition. Julia and I were gone a lot. We didn't know. We were shocked when the maid's legal service sent us the pictures. It was only a child's teeth, really, but they did leave marks. Zoey said she didn't know she was hurting her, that she was playing."

Alva sank into her armchair. "Right," she murmured. So, Zoey had hurt her maid. It was bad, but not as bad as thousands of children dead in rubble. Alva was fighting to make herself feel the tragedy of even that disaster, really feel. Maybe if she watched the news on TV, saw the footage, she could cry.

"I hope you don't judge Zoey too much for it," Daniel said. "It helps her to have you as a friend. I'm very glad you're thinking of coming stateside with us this summer, if it works out with your parents. When we ran into each other at the museum, I thought that maybe your mother was a bit anxious to let you go."

"She's fine with it," Alva said. "It's just the plane ticket—"

"That's on me. Happy to do it," Daniel said.

It was so easy. He hadn't retracted his foot from hers. "Why did you take me away from those businessmen?" she asked, feeling brazen. She was already finishing the last of the scotch in her glass.

Daniel smiled sadly. "What do any men want from a pretty girl?"

All she heard was *pretty girl*. She got up to get a refill at the wooden bar. Daniel did nothing to stop her. He was putting himself in the range of fire, wasn't he, giving her compliments like this? Like how he had called her a *beautiful mix* before at dinner. "You think I'm pretty?" she asked him, sitting back down.

His eyes were wide. "Alva," he said, his tone chastising. But she knew. She knew she was winning at something, the way his right hand was nervously playing with the golden ring on his left hand. She wondered where Zoey was at this precise moment, maybe kissing a sandy-haired foreigner somewhere in the house. Zoey told Alva that she'd had plenty of sex, starting in eighth grade. The first time in Hong Kong, on one of the expat yacht outings, in the cabin with an older boy. "You just get it over with," she'd said. "Then it's demystified. And you fuck whoever you want."

Alva didn't know if she wanted to get it over with, but there was a pulsing in her lower abdomen. "Your knee," she said to Daniel. "At dinner. Your knee always bumps into mine." Like the way the eyes of expat fathers followed her at the Shangri-La—none of it was an accident.

He sighed, set down his glass, stood up. She'd gone too far, she thought, he was leaving, and this would be a huge embarrassment. He took a step toward her, knelt down in front of her armchair. And then his hands were on her thighs. He kissed one thigh, then the other. "Tell me to stop," he said. She opened her mouth. No words came, only a whimper, which seemed to have a great effect on him because he said again, with an almost pained expression, "Tell me to stop."

But she didn't. He gently dragged her hips forward so they were at the edge of the armchair. Her knees were splayed, like Sharon Stone in *Basic Instinct*. She watched what was happening below her waist like it was a movie. He was kissing up her thighs, then pulling down her underwear, and then there was his tongue, probing her like she was something to unseal. She opened her legs wider. It felt good, and strange, but it only took a few more seconds for it to start to feel slimy, alien. He stopped, looked at her like he could sense her hesitation. There must have been some expression on her face because he got up and leaned over her in the chair, his lips now hovering right above hers. His breath smelled like sex.

"Did you want that?" he asked. It was a polite question, though there was something shaky and rushed in his voice. "Did anyone do that to you before?"

"No," she said. "It felt good. I just—" She didn't know how she felt.

He wiped his mouth with his sleeve, found his drink, and took a sip. Maybe she tasted terrible, and he had to wash it away. Suddenly he was across the room from her, and Zoey's father again. "There's a bedroom right down the hall," he said. "If you want to rest." She nodded, pulled up her underwear, and stood. This time when she tried to take a step, she did wobble.

"Jesus," he said. "Take my hand."

His grip was strong. She let herself be led and seconds later she was sinking into a very soft bed. Daniel closed the door, shutting out the distant sounds from downstairs. He sat next to her, rubbed his fingers up and down her spine. She put a hand against his chest. She wasn't sure if she was pressing against it, pushing him away, or merely resting it there. Her fingers slipped between two buttons of his shirt, and she felt thick hair and solid flesh. "Attagirl," he said. "I'll get you some more water and aspirin."

She could hear him in the bathroom now, running the faucet, opening cabinets. In a moment he'd be gone, and maybe she'll have ruined everything by cutting things short, by chickening out on the verge, and then how would she ever go to the Cruises' house again, how would she go to America with them? Her mother's words resurfaced, *Sometimes, when an opportunity presents itself, you have to play the part.*

Daniel was giving her water and an aspirin. She swallowed it and almost felt like crying from the feeling of his hand stroking her back. Her mother used to do something similar when Alva was sick. But this stroking was different. She drank the water in small sips until there was none left. She felt the dance of his fingers along her spine. Then he slinked one strap of her dress down her shoulder, then another, and still she said nothing. You are fifteen and this is living life, she thought. She would be like Serena or Blair or those girls on TV. Powerful. Like Zoey. Like Daniel. She could be powerful like Daniel. If he wanted sex with her, if this was the kind of bad thing that gave you power, then she could feel the same power too, in a mirror-image world.

She let herself fall back onto the mattress. When she was horizontal, he pulled down her dress completely. She didn't need to move, only lift her hips slightly. Anything can happen in this country, she thought. Everything changes so fast, going up like the skyscrapers Gao Xiaofan climbed and crumbling down like those schools in the earthquake. She didn't want to move, but just let it happen to her. One second Daniel was kissing her neck, the next she felt pain, the cold sensation of gel, the cough syrup scent of strawberries. She closed her eyes and let him move in and out until the burning became dull. He made deep noises and she stayed silent, trying not to think about Zoey and if she'd be mad, or about the Fan Bingbing lookalikes downstairs, and whether the men saw them all as one and the same.

His thrusting was becoming faster, rougher. "I'm pulling out," he said, and then he was upright on his knees, looming over her. She felt soreness between her legs and something wet and hot landing in spurts on her stomach. With what sounded almost like a wail he sagged down on the bed next to her. She didn't move, not wanting the horrible liquid on her stomach to drip and spread. "Oh god," she heard him say.

She felt stunned, like her body had fallen asleep. "Can I have some tissues?" she asked in a quiet voice. He reached over to the bed stand, ripped out a chain of Kleenexes and handed them to her. She used them to sponge her stomach until only slick, wet spots remained. "I won't tell anyone," she said. "We can be careful this summer."

"This summer?" His voice cracked. "Oh, Alva."

"This summer in America," she said in a fog.

She could hear his long, shaky inhale. "Oh, Alva," he said again. "I'm not sure if that's a good idea anymore."

"It's not a good idea?" she repeated.

"I'm sorry," he said.

Alva's mind was strangely blank. All she wanted was for this moment to end. She couldn't hear what he was saying, even though he sounded distressed, maybe even in tears. All she understood was that there would be no flight to JFK, no plane ticket after all. No more nights at Zoey's. No more soft sheets, no more fresh pastries and eggs fried by Girlie. She closed her eyes. She felt so far from a place she could think of as home— and wasn't sure such a place even existed.

The next morning, Alva woke to an empty room. There was a splitting pain in her head, the previous night's events murky. She could remember the outline of them, and, with a pang, the dissolved possibility of flight, no more summer, no more New York.

The mansion was quiet, as if everyone had gone, and she was the only person left in the mountains. It burned when she peed. A thin ribbon of blood swirled in the toilet bowl. She pulled on her fringed dress and went downstairs. It smelled like espresso and bacon. Chinese staff in gray uniforms were cleaning the rooms, picking up broken glass and garbage. They didn't look at her.

The brilliant morning light filtered through the green forest outside. Zoey had sent a text: *Did you fall asleep somewhere?? Left with an early car.* There were more black cars in the driveway. A man asked if she needed a ride back to the city. "Is it free?" she asked. He looked at her scornfully and said yes, taking in her disheveled hair, her short dress. She knew she smelled foul, like sweat and alcohol and cough syrup lubricant.

As they sped back toward Shanghai through the tea fields, Alva wondered if a lot of money had been raised for the earthquake victims. If what she had done made her compromised, or mature, or if both were the same. She tried casting the previous night as an age-defying, *Graduate*-style affair, one she'd later look back on with some distance, laugh off as a wild anecdote. But there was only the hollowness in her gut, and the memory of warm, wet liquid dripping down her stomach.

She told herself there were worse things. There were people still trapped under the rubble in Sichuan. Gao Xiaofan's red Nikes perched on a tiny ledge, ready to slip at any moment. Lu Fang's late nights in front of the television, chain-smoking, watching sad movies in solitude.

Sloan whom she'd betrayed by wanting to go to America, and now there was no more America. Alva thought of how fast things changed all the time, how pausing to wallow only left you in the dust as the world moved ahead and converged around you. She thought about how, in a movie, someone might take her hand and say, *You're a woman now*, and how untrue that would be.

# PART VIII

# LU FANG

DANDONG, 2003

## 37

The train from Dalian to Dandong zipped through the bare country-side. Occasionally a smattering of factories, with their dense rows of bar-racks, broke the rhythm of rolling brown earth. Lu Fang had seen these structures raised and razed countless times, back when he was a child and his mother took him to run errands in the nearby cities.

"We're about to pass through my hometown," his mother used to announce every time they rode by Dagu Mountain. The characters of 大孤山 meant Great Lonely Mountain. In earlier years, the wagons were full of sleepy passengers, local students and farmers with exhaustion in their bones. Tonight, Lu Fang was surrounded by soldiers headed back to the border bases along the Yalu River.

When the train rolled into Dandong, four young soldiers in the next row stood up. He waited until all the men in green left before finally rising and stepping off the train.

Old Two, his brother, was waiting on the platform. They shared a brief, silent clasp. Old Two had aged better than Lu Fang, brows thick and eyes still sparkling, grown in heft where Lu Fang had grown in paunch. They were both tall, like many men of the north.

"I heard about Minmin from Ma," Old Two said.

"He's fine," Lu Fang said. "He has an English class tonight and Ciyi will bring him tomorrow. When did you get here?"

Old Two shivered in a padded military coat that had once belonged to their father. He said he'd made the trip from Guangdong the week prior. His wife and baby had stayed behind and would spend Chinese New Year in the South with his in-laws. His wife's father was in poor health, and they hadn't wanted to risk buying three fake tickets from the resellers, *yellow cows* who lingered outside the stations, peddling often nonexistent seats on sold-out New Year trains. Any tickets, even fake ones, were expensive.

They walked across the big plaza with the Mao Zedong statue. "I remember coming here the day Chairman Mao died," Old Two said. "September 9, 1976. Everybody on the plaza was already crying, so I cried too."

"You always were a crier."

Old Two laughed. "Dandong has changed so much, but some things are the same. The 17 bus is across the street," he said. "Remember?"

"I'm tired," Lu Fang said. "Let's just get a taxi."

After they hailed one, Lu Fang asked Old Two to ride in the front seat. He wasn't sure if he could name the streets to take them home.

"The night scenery is much improved," Old Two said, pointing to an illuminated gate in the distance. The driver chimed in, his thick north-eastern accent friendly and familiar, "They turn on the lights for the tourist season."

"Tourist season?" Lu Fang asked.

"To see the North Korean border," the driver said. "The Yalu River boardwalk tourist complex. You can rent binoculars and take pictures. Ten yuan, a good deal."

The taxi dropped them off in front of a compound of tall brutalist housing towers. The elevator's upward ascent was surprisingly powerful, and the two brothers watched the numbers blink as they rose from the ground, hearts pressed against their separate chambers.


The next day, Lu Fang's wife and son arrived on a late train. As soon as they were in the door, Ciyi oohed and aahed in front of Old Two's display of multicolored fireworks. She shed a fur-trimmed coat, her cheeks glowing from her ten-thousand-yuan spa membership. Minmin, a tall, pale boy at seventeen, was wearing the latest Nike Shox sneakers, a gift from Lu Fang for his birthday. They were bright red and the thick springs in their heels gave him a few additional centimeters in height, much needed since Minmin always stooped, as if his spine couldn't quite find the will to right itself.

The bags Old Two had brought from the South spilled over with sparklers, rockets, and fireworks that would bloom and trickle like a waterfall of sparkles. He said these usually required legal resale permits, powerful stuff, only purchasable because he had a buddy at the factory.

Old Two had buddies everywhere. He'd been a gap-toothed kid who ran around the city in feral packs, a small-time hustler, a bush schooler. "Look at your uncle," Lu Fang had told Minmin many a time. "Do you want to become like him?"

Out of decorum, he couldn't say *become like me instead*—but he did have grounds to be proud. In the past year, Lu Fang had become a millionaire. A millionaire in China in 2003 was hardly a rarity, feeding off the decay of the old system, nourished by raining subsidies. No one batted an eye at a millionaire in Shanghai or Qingdao. But in his hometown, a border outpost like Dandong, Lu Fang could still claim triumph. He hadn't come home an imperial scholar, but he was an international businessman after all.

"How far up do they go?" Minmin asked quietly, bent over the firework packages. It was the first sentence he'd spoken since arriving.

"A hundred meters at least," Old Two said. "All of Dandong will be able to see them. Hell, the North Koreans will see them too."

That night they sat on pink plastic stools and ate plates of boiled dumplings Lu Fang's mother had spent all afternoon making. "You won't guess what's in them," she said. "Fennel."

"It's her new discovery," Old Two said. "She didn't know this vegetable existed before."

He poured vinegar and sesame oil into a bowl of raw garlic, dipping sauce for the dumplings. There was also a bowl of cold minced jellyfish. Minmin picked up his chopsticks. Yet he wasn't eating. "Do you want some seaweed?" Lu Fang's mother asked. Minmin said no.

For his mother, Lu Fang thought, seafood was not shellfish or clams or delicacies; it was whatever you would scavenge from the ocean. The things washed up on sandy shores: mounds of kelp, and massive jelly-fish dead on the beaches of the Yellow Sea. Minmin's generation did not know this definition of seafood. Lu Fang decided he would go to the supermarket the next day and bring back premium shellfish, shrimp, crawfish, and crabs. His son used to love crab.

"How's school, then?" his mother asked Minmin. "It's gaokao year, isn't it?"

"It is," Minmin said. His plastic stool scraped against the tiles. "I'm going to lie down."

"The train trip," Ciyi said quickly after he left. "He's always had motion sickness."

"He's doing fine in school," Lu Fang said. "He's taking supplemental classes and preparing for the TOEFL. That's the English exam to go abroad."

"You'll let him go abroad, after . . ." his mother began. Ciyi held a finger to her lips and glared toward the bedroom door.

"It'll be good for him," Lu Fang said tersely.

Old Two gave his brother a can of lukewarm Harbin beer, which they divided into ceramic bowls. Lu Fang had grown to like his beers icy, but in the backwaters, people still did not believe in drinking anything cold. When they were young, their mother made them boil the Coca-Colas they'd saved up to buy. Lu Fang would fume into his flat, warm cola, the taste ruined. Old Two would pat him on the arm and say, "It's still sweet, brother."

Lu Fang wanted to believe that. Still sweet after it'd gone flat. Life was like that. Business was good, more than good, and he had the money to fix things. To buy his son a new Lenovo desktop computer and the latest Nikes, to bid his colleagues returning from abroad to bring back noncounterfeit soccer jerseys from the teams his son used to love. But

Minmin rarely watched soccer anymore. And he no longer wore jerseys. Lu Fang found them in his son's closet, intact in their plastic pouches.

After the meal Old Two reappeared with a bottle of Bordeaux wine with a shiny gold label. He motioned for Lu Fang to try it. "I thought you might like it. It's just as good as the imported ones." The spelling on the bottle was all wrong. Lu Fang didn't want to tell him there was no such thing as a domestic Chinese Bordeaux. Old Two smiled and said, "I bought a *case* of these from a buddy."

At nightfall on New Year's Eve, Lu Fang's mother came out of the kitchen, wiping her flour-covered hands on an apron. "A Fang, Old Two, Minmin—time to invite the ancestors home. Ciyi can stay and help me with the dumplings."

"Of course, Ma." Ciyi's smile was pinched as she rolled up the sleeves of her cashmere sweater. "What do you want me to do?"

"Knead the pork and garlic," Lu Fang's mother said. "Make sure you use your hands."

The men put on their coats. "I've got a lighter," Old Two said, producing a lime-green Bic. Minmin carried stacks of yellow paper. Lu Fang accepted a long metal stirring spoon from his mother.

"Don't be long," she said. "And remember, don't look back."

Lu Fang, his brother, and his son walked outside into a light snowstorm. They exited the compound gates down a long, dark street, looking for a dry spot to burn the paper money. Minmin pointed to a patch of concrete beneath the awning of a closed shop. "Here," he said. Old Two squatted and built a nest with the paper, shielded the Bic's flickering flame in his palm. The papers quickly caught fire and he stepped aside to let Lu Fang stir the yellow cut-out coins with his long spoon. It was the same ritual every year. "*Laomulao*, come home for the New Year," Lu Fang muttered. "Laomulao, we're here to invite you."

There were little fires like theirs glowering in the distance, shapes of bundled humans fuzzy through the sheets of snow. Soon their paper money was only dying embers. Minmin kicked at a flyaway piece of smoldering paper with his Nikes. "Don't soil your new shoes," Lu Fang said. "They didn't fall from the sky." Minmin made no reply. Lu Fang gave the flashlight in his pocket to Old Two. "You lead the way back," he said, "Minmin can go in the middle and I'll close the line. Laomulao," he started chanting, "come home for New Year."

"Laomulao, we invite you," Old Two repeated, starting the walk home, the flashlight's beam leading the way.

"You don't want to *see* the ancestors," Lu Fang's mother had told him and Old Two when they were kids. He remembered keeping his neck very tense so that he didn't make the mistake, even a subconscious slip, of looking back. The fear made him think he could actually *feel* his great-grandfather and grandfather and father, roused from the dead, trailing behind him.

But the ancestors didn't care about the paper money burned for them. What use was it to worship those already dead, to hope they would watch over you, to play the charade of paper money, paper houses, and paper cars? His fortune wasn't a gift from the dead. If Lu Fang was now a millionaire, it was because he stayed at his office until midnight, because he'd shuttled between cities and laughed with clients until his face hurt.

The blizzard was gathering strength. He returned his attention to Minmin's silhouette. His son was nearly as tall as Old Two. Too bad he hunched. But soon Minmin would get better, stand up straighter. After Lu Fang paid for his passage to an American university—it would be a liberation. After the gaokao, they may talk again about the treatment the doctor recommended. Lu Fang hated that doctor, with his frameless rectangular glasses and his diplomas on the wall: a doctor of *psychology*. This doctor didn't know Minmin had always been a quiet child, even if he'd grown more withdrawn and solitary in recent years. Lu Fang shouldn't have bought him that computer. Minmin rarely left his room after that. But depressive *disorder*? "Nonsense," Lu Fang had told the doctor at that first diagnosis. "Melancholia is a common affliction. We've always had it. We've always lived with it. My son only needs to toughen up and get through these studies. Then he'll go abroad and have a very different life. See if that won't *cure* him."

The doctor had shaken his head. Ciyi sat beside him, red-eyed and blowing into a tissue, saying nothing. "We all know why we're here," the doctor had reminded him softly. "If it happens again, that future will not exist."

Tonight would go well. Tonight there would be prayers in front of blackening pork and waxy fruit for the Lord of the Furnace. They would eat the dumplings the women prepared, drink special edition baijiu Lu Fang had been saving in his suitcase, and end with a game of poker that Lu Fang would let Old Two win. Lu Fang would tolerate the squalor of his mother's apartment for the next few days and try to forget that he had once lived under blackening moldy ceilings and rusting pipes. Minmin had all the opposite luxuries, grew up with more resources than a child of Lu Fang's generation could dream of, and yet. The Yalu River and its dirty, brown currents of discontent flowed through his veins, as it had through his father's veins, through the veins of all men of this border.

The cold wind whistled between the sooty housing towers. Laomulao, Lu Fang chanted. Follow us home, Laomulao. Protect us, Laomulao. The flashlight's beam cut through the curtains of snow. Do not linger with the dead, do not look back.

Lu Fang looked back. He saw no one behind him save for the dark outline of a lonely mountain.

## 38

When they opened the apartment door they were greeted by the fragrance of fried sweet potato balls and braised pork knuckles. Ciyi sat in front of a hundred neatly lined dumplings, ready to boil. Steaming dishes crowded the table, chopstick pairs neatly set. Lu Fang noticed, with satisfaction, that the shrimp and crab he bought had been placed at the center of the display.

"Let's drink something good," Lu Fang announced to the kitchen. He went to the bedroom and returned with a bottle of reserved Maotai. It was a special edition, from a set of five he'd bought to gift to clients. "Special liquor for a special year," Lu Fang said.

Old Two examined the bottle and whistled. "This is good stuff, brother." His unopened domestic Bordeaux was still sitting on the table.

"A toast," Lu Fang said as he poured himself a glass. "It's been a good year for business. And this next year—well, it's going to be the most special year to date. Minmin is graduating from high school."

Minmin stared down into his bowl. "I've talked to a friend who runs a visa agency, and study abroad opportunities are good if we're willing to pay full tuition," Lu Fang said. "And some extra for the visa. But it won't be a problem, Minmin. Ba will take care of it. Soon you'll be calling us from Niuyue! Or Lundun! Or Luoshanji!"

"A bright future," Lu Fang's mother said. Minmin's longish bangs, a cut fashionable with young people, hung over his eyes. He took off his glasses and wiped them with his shirtsleeve. His sleeves were always long and loose, the fabric stretching over his fists. Ciyi leaned to caress her son's hair, but he shrugged her away.

"The first to carry the Lu name to university!" Lu Fang said loudly. He didn't need to remind anyone here that he'd in fact been the first to do so. He refilled his glass with the Maotai.

"I was always too dumb!" Old Two offered. "Ganbei."

The brothers downed their drinks.

"Ciyi, you're ripping those shrimp to shreds," their mother said abruptly. "Don't chip those pretty nails."

Ciyi's fake fingernails were fuchsia and oblong, with small shiny plastic specks glued into flower patterns. She'd been furiously mangling the orange-and-white flesh of the shrimp. Lu Fang contemplated his wife: Ciyi's translation of their new wealth into displays of pure gaudiness was her own capitulation. Lu Fang never took her to business meals or client trips, not with her unshakable Yunnan accent. But although they disagreed on many things and never touched each other anymore, they were aligned in their understanding that their son should only have the best options ahead.

"Ma—" Lu Fang turned to his mother. "Do you remember when we had to buy food with ration tickets?"

"What?" his mother said, cupping her ear. "Ration tickets!" Lu Fang shouted. She nodded, not looking Lu Fang in the eye. She was like an old turtle or another of these animals, proud but spiteful. "Grain tickets for grains, meat tickets for meat, tofu tickets for tofu," Old Two said.

"It is thanks to Chairman Mao," their mother said, "that we have built our characters to be honest and simple people."

What a line! How many times did Lu Fang and Old Two go to bed hungry because of those meal tickets? But maybe that was how she'd rationalized her life, with this kind of selective amnesia. Maybe amnesia was the only way to go on in the new China. He swallowed the food with difficulty. Although he'd spared no expense, his mother had also cooked hormone-pumped chicken thighs the size of turkey legs, which she probably thought symbolized the progress of their nation.

"They don't have meat like this in America." His mother pointed to the chicken. "What will Minmin eat there, cows? Tough and tendony—"

"Those are Chinese cows," Lu Fang cut her off. "American cows are fat and soft—"

"Trying to watch the CCTV gala," Minmin said.

"I've got something better than the gala," Lu Fang said. "Something to bring a little actual progress to this household."

"Now, A Fang?" his mother said. "Let me clear the plates first."

Lu Fang motioned for her to stop. His cheeks felt warm from the Maotai. "Here's for you, Ma. To stop pinching pennies. Get yourself some health supplements." He took a hefty red envelope out of his suit lining and handed it to his mother.

"There's no need for it," she said. "The heavens will decide if I live or die."

Lu Fang ignored her. "And Old Two—I know it's not easy down south. This has ten thousand yuan, so invest wisely, pay off your debts."

Old Two nodded at the envelope. "Brother, that's generous."

"And here's for you, too, of course." Lu Fang distributed the last two envelopes to his wife and his son. "Because times are changing for our family."

Ciyi finally got ahold of Minmin's hand and squeezed it.

"It's been a good year," Lu Fang said. He noticed his son didn't even make the pretense of counting the amount in the envelope. "I broke a million yuan. It's natural to share with family."

"A million. That's big," his brother said. But Old Two's usual cheer hung thread-thin. Their mother said nothing. Ciyi stood and started stacking the dishes. Minmin only stared at the TV screen, then rose and went into the bedroom, without a word of thanks.

While Ciyi and his mother finished clearing the table, Lu Fang clasped Old Two on the shoulder and refilled his cup. "Drink up," he said. "So I can milk you dry at poker." For the past few years Lu Fang clamored for poker after the New Year's Eve meal; he'd learned Texas Hold'em at a client dinner and loved the clinking sounds of the chips.

"We're starting now, Minmin!" Lu Fang called out in the direction of the bedroom. No reply came.

"Is he all right?" his mother whispered.

"I'll set up the tokens," Old Two said.

Lu Fang walked to the bedroom. "Come play," he said. "What's wrong?"

His son was lying down with his arms folded behind his head, staring at the ceiling. "I don't want to," Minmin said.

"Up," Lu Fang said. "We need three people at least."

"Why don't you ask Ma or Nainai?"

"They don't know how to play," Lu Fang said.

"You've never taught them."

"I'm in a good mood," Lu Fang forced a smile. "Now be a man, and get up."

"Ba," Minmin said, "I can't."

"You can. Just try," Lu Fang said through clenched teeth. "All I ask is that you try."

He returned to Old Two at the poker table and waited. A minute later, Minmin emerged from the bedroom. Lu Fang set down a glass in front of the empty seat. He'd filled it with a finger of Maotai. "A special treat for you, son," he said. He'd expected Minmin to fumble and refuse, but his son sat down, lifted the cup, and drained its contents.

Lu Fang dealt the cards. "De-ke-sa-si style," Old Two said. "I've seen it in the gambling halls down south. Did you know they've got a version where they play 'black'? You never look at your cards and you bet. Everybody has to pay double if you win."

"Never heard of it," Lu Fang said.

"Chinese invention," Old Two said.

Lu Fang laughed and leaned toward his son. "Your uncle might have more money if he wasn't playing *blind* poker in gambling halls."

Minmin said nothing. "Hey, to each his style," Old Two said. But he flipped up the corner of his cards and looked at them.

Ciyi, her kitchen duties fulfilled, returned to plant herself in front of the television. Lu Fang's mother also came in, pulling plastic sleeve covers off her arms. She stopped in front of the table. "Are you giving your son alcohol?"

"Just a glass," Lu Fang said. "The greatest poets were all alcoholics."

"Is Minmin a poet?" his mother said.

"Ge's talking about himself," Old Two said.

Ciyi tapped her nails on the couch. "Come sit down, Ma."

"That stuff is worse for you than the Yalu River water," the old woman mumbled.

Minmin folded his hand, adding his cards to the pile. Lu Fang groaned.

"You win, brother," Old Two said.

Lu Fang raked in the chips. "Minmin, it's no game if you fold so early every time. Your uncle never has good cards."

"I don't have good cards," Minmin said.

"Then bluff," Lu Fang said. "Bad cards, good cards, you play. That's the point of the game. You *play*."

"Folding *is* playing," Minmin said.

"You have to learn to play," Lu Fang repeated, his words slurring a bit too much for his liking. "When you're in America, you'll floor them all with how good you are at Texas Hold'em."

"Sure." Minmin refilled his own cup with Maotai.

Lu Fang dealt another round of cards. Minmin lifted the corner of his, then threw them to the side.

Lu Fang tried to suppress the rising anger inside him. "If you're going to do this, let's play with real money," he said. "Does that motivate you, Lu Min? Maybe if everything wasn't handed to you, you'd start *trying*."

"Real money. Is that a good idea?" Old Two said. "I'm guarding some earnings here."

"There's no point in playing for fake," Lu Fang said. "I just gave you money. Both of you. Take that as your buy-in. But if you lose, you give back what you owe me."

Lu Fang's mother called from the couch, "We're all a family, there's no business taking money from each other."

"A Fang," Ciyi chimed in. "It's time to put away the Maotai."

"If Ba wants to play with money, let's," Minmin said. The alcohol gave a pink flush to his cheeks. "Deal, Uncle."

Old Two hesitated, but Lu Fang nodded. "Deal."

After Old Two had finished dealing, Lu Fang looked at his cards: a pair of queens. A good hand. He doubled the blind. Minmin threw in his chips, then sat back and folded his arms. He hadn't touched his cards.

"Playing black, Minmin?" Old Two said. "It's double if you win."

"I know."

"And double loss if you lose," Lu Fang said.

"I know."

Old Two put in his chips, then flipped over the cards in the river: 9, 10, K. He whistled. "Nothing for me here," he said. "I'll leave you father and son to it."

Lu Fang pushed a stack of tokens forward. "Raise to two hundred." Minmin set down an identical stack, still without looking at his cards. Lu Fang nodded toward Old Two. The next card was a K. Two pairs was good. The odds of his son having something better was low, especially in a blind scenario. Minmin's hair was all over his face, hiding his eyes. "All in," he said. He pushed forward his entire stack of chips.

"You owe me real money if you lose, son," Lu Fang said. "I hope that's understood."

"It's understood," Minmin said.

"I'll match." Lu Fang set most of his chips at the center.

Old Two flipped the last card. It was a Q. Full house.

"Open," Lu Fang barked at his son. "Let's see where your blind playing got you."

But Minmin took his two cards, still not looking, and pushed them to the middle of the stack. "I fold," he said softly.

Lu Fang stood up so violently that his glass of Maotai toppled and spilled over his tokens. "Are you trying to insult me?" he shouted.

"Sit down," Ciyi yelped.

Minmin took the red envelope out of his jean pockets. He unlatched the string and emptied its contents, bills and bills of pink Mao Zedongs, onto the table.

"Take it all."

"Minmin," his grandmother called. "Don't."

Lu Fang grabbed a handful of bills and shook them at his son. "This money is what pays for your Nikes. For the bedroom you live in and the computer inside of it. For your school and all your expensive tutors and TOEFL classes and for the chance for you to one day—"

"I haven't been going to the TOEFL classes," Minmin said. He was smiling strangely. "I haven't been going to any of my after-school classes."

"That's impossible," Lu Fang said. "You're lying. Your college entrance exam is months away. You're going abroad."

"Who told you I wanted to go abroad?" Minmin said, his voice a whisper.

"You are going abroad," Lu Fang repeated. "You're getting a foreign degree."

"Yeah, Ba, a foreign degree. From Hafu-Yelu? I don't even speak the language. I never did."

"If you try to learn, you will—"

"I've tried, Ba. You know I don't want to, but you refuse to see."

Minmin rolled up his sleeves. Old Two and Lu Fang's mother looked away from the faint pink scars on his wrists. Ciyi stood up from the couch, face white as a sheet.

"Have some pride, son," Lu Fang said. His head was spinning from the Maotai, from the colorful tokens on the table, from the crisscrosses of flesh he'd willed himself to forget since that night he'd found Minmin, since the hospital, since the doctor of psychology's thin, admonishing lips. "Roll down those sleeves. Youth has ups and downs. School is tough now, but at least you can go to school. Your mother never did. I had to leave university. You have all these opportunities we never had—and it's an insult to us all that you'd throw them away."

Minmin rolled his sleeves back down. "Okay," he whispered. "Okay. Mama, do you also want me to go abroad?"

Ciyi's face was wet with tears. She and Lu Fang had been over this fight many times, and he shot her a death glare. She had to swallow hard before saying, "Minmin, Ma only wants you to have a better life than ours."

"So you also want me gone."

"I want you to be . . . better," Ciyi said.

"I don't understand," Lu Fang said. "We've given you everything, we've given you a happy home—"

At that Minmin laughed, though he wasn't really laughing. "A happy home?"

"I was making money," Lu Fang said. "For you."

"But you never wanted this family," Minmin said.

"How can you say that?" Lu Fang was shouting now. He'd given up everything for his son, even his own happiness, just so his son could throw it all away, disrespect him, discredit all he's done. "Get out," he ordered.

"It's not your house," Minmin said. "It's Nainai's."

"Who do you think bought this fucking house?"

"A Fang—" his mother called.

"My money bought this apartment. My money bought the apartment you live in. My money bought the lives of all you parasites," Lu Fang thundered. Old Two was staring at the bottom of his cup.

"A Fang, let him be," his mother said.

"*Let him be?*" Lu Fang's chest was about to explode. "I've worked my whole life so that our lives are different. To get away from this goddamned place. And I should *let him*? Be the smallest possible person he can be?"

"The only times I've been happy," Minmin said, "were the times away from you."

Lu Fang lurched toward his son and shoved him in the direction of the door, so hard that Minmin stumbled back and crashed into a commode. Ciyi screamed. Old Two wrapped his hand around Lu Fang's arm, roughly this time, pulling him back. His mother was shouting Lu Fang's name.

Minmin got up, slowly. "I'll get out," he said. He went to the door, pulled on his shoes and coat. He bent over Old Two's bag of fireworks, clutched a box to his chest, and closed the door behind him. Ciyi was crying. She scrambled toward the exit to go after their son. "He's *sick!*" she shouted at Lu Fang. "You can't push him. He's sick."

"Stay back," Lu Fang said. "I'll get him."

He stuffed his feet into his shoes and ran to the elevator in the hall. He didn't know what he wanted to do—chase his son down and beat some sense into him, banish him, or drag him back into the house. He wasn't sick. He was just weak-willed. They'd all had much harder lives, lives they actually had to survive. Maybe it'd been wrong to spoil his son, to give him a life without obstacles. It'd made a worm out of him. That's what he would tell the doctor, Lu Fang thought.

When he stepped out of the building, he saw Minmin's silhouette near the compound gate. Lu Fang started running. His leather shoes squeaked in the fresh snow.

Somewhere on the next block something exploded. It was midnight. Firecrackers detonated everywhere. He could see Minmin rounding the corner of the street, merging onto the larger avenue that lined the hill stacked with junk car parts and trash. He followed the footprints of the Nikes, the pattern imprinting itself in his brain. He was out of breath, a sharp pain shot through his side. He didn't know how long he ran and he didn't know what he would do if he ever caught up with his son, but the violence that'd seized him in the apartment waned with each huff forward. What had Minmin meant, the happiest times were away from him? Lu Fang was on the esplanade now, by the shore of the Yalu River. No one was out at this hour and firecrackers thundered all around. The opposite bank, North Korea, was dark.

The Nike footprints continued, freshly pressed. Finally, they stopped at the base of the broken bridge, the border crossing that had been bombed by Americans, never repaired. Lu Fang squinted. Through the curtain of falling snow he could see the shape of a person on the bridge. With great effort he hoisted himself over the barricade. Usually there would be guards. They must have gone patrolling for the New Year, to make sure nothing was burning. The broken bridge was an impasse that stopped midriver. As he came closer, he saw Minmin standing at the end of it.

His son was hunched over something on the ground. At first Lu Fang couldn't see what it was. Then he recognized it. His son was shielding the flame from the green Bic lighter. The fuse from the fireworks box glowered and burned with a hissing sound.

"Get back!" Lu Fang screamed. "What are you doing!" Minmin turned and saw him, took one step away from the box, then two. The fuse slithered like a snake as it shortened. Lu Fang stopped a few feet from his son.

"Come home," he said. "We can talk about this."

Minmin looked at the river. "You know, Ba. I've had time to think it over throughout the years. Ever since you took me to meet your foreigner."

Lu Fang nearly stopped breathing. "What?"

Minmin turned around to face his father. He was smiling sadly. "After seeing you with her, I understood why you always draw 囚 on the table. That's what you are. A prisoner of a family you never wanted. A life you never wanted."

Lu Fang stood, dumbfounded. "I'm not—"

"You don't have to be a prisoner," Minmin said. "None of us do. I wake up every morning thinking: there's no need to keep on. I don't want to go to school. I don't want to go abroad. I was scared to admit it for so long, Ba. I was so scared of the thoughts in my head, the weight on my chest, and you and Ma acted like nothing was wrong, and I was so scared that I would always have to pretend, that it would never end."

The fuse had burned all the way. With a boom, the box released an upward charge of white light, the whistle of a rocket, and father and son looked to the sky after the trail of smoke. The fireworks exploded in the night overhead, and it was just like Old Two had said, trails of gold trickled down like the tears of a weeping willow, shimmering downward until they faded, and all that was left was the falling snow.

"Minmin. Ba was only doing what he thought was best—"

His son tilted his chin toward the dark landmass across the broken bridge. "They are admiring the fireworks too. From the other side."

"Minmin, Ba will listen to you—"

But Minmin was leaning against the metal railing of the viewing platform, looking down to the black waters again. "Don't worry, Baba," he said. "I was born wrong."

"Minmin—"

Minmin crouched down, took off his red shoes, and lined them up neatly in the fresh snow. "These were a nice gift, Ba," he said. "I don't want to spoil them." Then, with a sharp inhale, he hoisted himself onto the platform, legs dangling over the edge. For a split second, Lu Fang saw him on a Shanghai balcony again, cradling a radio that sputtered *the crowd is going wild in Pasadena*—

"I fold, Baba," Minmin said softly. "I'm sorry. I did not want you to see."

Lu Fang lunged, but it was too late. Minmin didn't make a sound when he hit the black waters. Or, if he did, it was drowned out by the explosion of fireworks erupting all over Dandong.

All that surfaced in Lu Fang's brain in that instant, amid the deafening symphony of blasts, was that he'd never taught his son how to swim.

# PART IX

# ALVA

HAINAN ISLAND, 2008

## 39

They were finally on summer vacation. The Chinese character for vacation was 假, also the character for "fake," and if Lu Fang were awake she would've asked him if he thought that was on purpose. It was the last week of August, and they were on a plane to Hainan Island. What more to celebrate a month of being locked in the apartment, of non-stop Beijing Olympic footage—a tropical vacation! Her mother and Lu Fang were sleeping, heads stacked and mouths agape. He'd spent the past weeks in the office, working increasingly late nights. Sloan's new manicure was pastel blue. Alva dozed off and next thing she knew they were deboarding onto a tarmac of hot asphalt. Her contacts were peeling—the Ballantine's she kept in her thermos did that, sucked the moisture from her eyeballs. She blinked behind her plastic sunglasses the whole drive between Sanya airport and Yalong Bay. The warm air slapped at her face. She couldn't taste its salinity, though, couldn't admire the colors of the tropical flora lining the highway. For a split second, she thought of the wild, gray Atlantic beaches of the Hamptons. She wanted to scream, but no sound would carry across that great a distance.

Slats of wooden fans whisked the air of the cavernous lobby. Sweat dripped from Lu Fang's temples as he leaned over the reception desk. There was a problem: the three of them were sharing a standard room, double beds.

"We booked the one-thousand-two-hundred-ninety-nine-yuan family suite," Sloan said.

The receptionist tapped slow strokes on the keyboard. "The reservation system shows a standard room—"

"Then your reservation system is wrong," Sloan said. "Lu Fang? Can you tell them?"

"My wife is very upset," he said.

Alva scoffed. Is that how they conducted all business negotiations? No one wanted to get in trouble with a foreigner in China. Every white face concealed the imperial reach of a distant Western government. There was a Chinese expression for this—

"Paper tiger," Alva said out loud from her wicker chair.

No one heard her. The receptionist's face was scrunched in a frown. "It must be our mistake, but standard doubles is all we have left."

Sloan's pastel nails tapped impatiently against the counter. "Aren't we entitled to some form of refund? Compensation?"

The receptionist tore off two pieces of paper from a stack. "Coupons for our restaurant," she said.

Sloan opened her mouth to say more, but Lu Fang was already reaching for the coupons. "This will do," he said.


The room's two large beds faced a blocky TV. "No sea view." Sloan was circling the room, lifting the balcony curtains. "Not even that. That wing over there—that must be where the suites are."

Alva dropped her bag on the floor and sank into a bed. Headache gathering. She had finished the Ballantine's she'd smuggled in her thermos. Sloan's ankle-length beach dress was made from some delicate, silky material. She looked good, slim. But Lu Fang's eyes were on Alva. Why was he always looking at her? "I'm going to the beach," she said, standing up.

"All right," Lu Fang said. "But meet us for dinner soon."

"Mm-hmm," Alva said.

She followed a path lined with blooming frangipani down to the beach. People were amassed there to catch the sunset—families squeezing

tightly for a group shot as someone yelled "One-two-three-CHIAY-ZI."
A thatch-roofed shack displayed a few dingy liquor bottles, and Alva's
muscles untensed. A girl was working behind the counter, her skin
shades darker than everyone else on the beach.

"Rum and Coca-Cola," Alva said without preliminaries. Coca-Cola,
*kekoukele* in Chinese—可口可乐, pleasing to the mouth and worthy of
joy! She noted with disapproval that the girl was using an actual jigger to
measure the shot. "Double, okay?"

The girl nodded. "Room number?" she asked.

"Can I pay directly, with cash?"

"It'll be a hundred and twenty yuan."

Not cheap. But that didn't matter now. Her stack of plane ticket
money was worthless. The Cruises had long ago flown to JFK, without
her. She felt around her pocket for a crumpled wad, peeled away six
orange Maos. Glass in hand, she went to sit on the edge of a plastic
reclining chair farthest away from the crowd.

The brown liquid sloshed. This had to be downed quickly, like
medicine, so the buzz could be felt faster, though it wasn't really a buzz,
more a cancellation of her migraine. She'd mastered these measure-
ments toward equilibrium.

Alva closed her eyes but it was still there. The feeling of hot, slimy
spurts landing on her stomach.


It was only when she'd gotten home the morning after the fundraiser
that she'd thought to look up the likelihood of getting pregnant with
the pullout method. The internet confirmed it was a surefire way to get
pregnant. She read story after story of girls who'd fallen for Neanderthal
schemes. There were also endless lists of home remedies: wearing a tam-
pon soaked with hand sanitizer, drinking enough hard liquor to make
sure the embryo would overdose septically on the spot. Then there was
something called plan B, which you could get in pharmacies.

Alva hadn't been sure plan B existed in Chinese pharmacies. If it did,
they wouldn't sell it to her, an underage girl.

If her mother had been around, maybe Sloan would've come home with a pill that solved everything. Or, if they'd been in America, there would have been any number of solutions. In this moment she hated her mother. In America, she thought, people like Daniel Cruise would think twice before taking young girls to remote mansions. But here, men like him knew they had impunity precisely because they weren't in America, because here there were no laws that applied to *them*, at least as long as the people they were doing bad things to were unimportant and disposable.

That morning after the mansion party, she'd walked herself to the pharmacy in Thumb Plaza. It had been empty except for two women behind the counter in white lab coats, each looking at their phones. Alva had crept along the aisles of medicine—jars of dehydrated herbs and animal parts and petrified antlers and rare roots, rows of dietary supplements and cough medicine and tiger balm and heated pads but of course there was nothing, nothing at all related to contraceptives. She stopped between two aisles. She willed herself not to cry.

She walked to the counter and said to the women, "Can you help me?"

The older of the two women looked up from her phone and, seeing Alva's face, asked, "What is it, *guniang*?"

Guniang meant "girl," an old-fashioned address hardly anyone used in Shanghai anymore; everyone now went with the slick and Westernized *xiaojie*—"Miss." Alva tried to hold the composure of her eyebrows, her cheeks, her mouth, to say the words even if they would get her in trouble, "I need a pill. A pill for—in case I'm—"

The two women stared at her. "Are you over eighteen?" the older one asked.

"No."

So it did exist. But out of all the things not sellable to minors, cigarettes and drugs and the countless bottles she'd purchased from wine shops and supermarkets and corner stores, this was the one thing they'd refuse her.

The second woman was returning from the back room. She held a small white box that had "Yasmin" printed on it in English letters. She slid it across the counter. "Don't wait," she said. "It's less effective the longer you wait."

Alva shoved the box in her pocket and set down a hundred-yuan bill. The younger woman shook her head. "No use."

The words barely escaped Alva's throat, "Xiexie." The women were looking back down at their phones. As she walked out, Alva heard one tell the other, "Just a child."

*Just a child.* But it wasn't true; she was unlike the little kids around this resort, coddled and venerated by their parents. Something broke and suddenly you were no longer a kid, you were out on your own and nobody asked you questions, nobody paid attention.

Alva tilted her glass for the last drops of her drink. Her arms had turned from golden to a shade neither white nor tan. She dug her nails into her stomach. It was flat and weak, empty.

She took out her phone and typed in the familiar website. The Smiling and Proud Wanderer had over thirty thousand followers now on CityX. He'd upgraded to a professional account where he could accept virtual coins. "SHOW YOU ARE AFRAID OF NOTHING," a commenter had written.

Alva remembered what Gao had said. Rooftopping was the freedom of letting go. She wanted to ask him if he really thought it was freedom—but they didn't talk anymore, even online. When had she lost them all, one after another? She and Gao didn't talk, she and Li Xinwei didn't talk, she and her mother didn't talk, she and Zoey didn't talk. Well, Zoey was trying to talk to her.

"Another one?" a voice asked.

It was the girl from the bar, pointing to Alva's empty glass. Alva hesitated. She caressed the crumply bills in her pocket. "Fine," she said after an exhale.

The cooling sand filled the cracks between her toes. She felt calmer now. She remembered her dinner appointment, where she'd pretend nothing was wrong. Nothing was wrong.

The resort's gardens were eerily empty, basking in the nascent darkness as she walked to the main building. It was the hour when vacationers dusted off sticky sand and wriggled out of wet swimsuits. Happy families on 假日, false time. Four rapid knocks on the door—no one came to open it. She knocked again, louder. Did they leave the room to have dinner without her? What time was it? Suddenly she heard footsteps, and Lu Fang was standing in the doorway, rubbing his eyes.

"Your mother's in the shower," he explained without apology.

He was in his boxers, his legs thin and hairy beneath a soft, protruding belly. Once she would have stared at it in disgust or said something sharp-tongued and nasty about the room, hit him where he was weak. Instead she lay down on the bed closer to the balcony, which they'd let her have, and turned on the TV. Lu Fang furtively pulled a T-shirt over his head in the corner of the room. She made sure she didn't look his way.

Once it was her turn for the shower, less than a third of the shampoo was left in the complimentary hotel tube. She clawed at her scalp, struggling to work the meager gel into foam, then squeezed out an entire fistful of the L'Oréal conditioner Sloan had brought from Shanghai. Alva stared at the goopy white liquid in her palm and squeezed the bottle's contents straight down the drain until it was empty.

The resort's main restaurant was called Coconut Grove, possibly after the few sickly trees adorning the beachfront lawn. The entire seafood section had prices listed per pound, not per dish. Lu Fang ordered only a sea bream—a stingier choice than usual. "Let's order some wine to go with it," Sloan said.

"Pretty expensive bottles for Australian," Lu Fang said.

"I thought it was a honeymoon."

A shadow came over Lu Fang's face. In such moments, Alva pitied him—she recognized the effort he put into serving up what was expected of him, despite the many imperfections of the situation. Today, something was wrong. He was tallying the cost of what they ordered, she realized. Were they in trouble?

"I spoke with the front desk and they can give us a discount for one of their tour packages, to offset the mix-up with the room," Lu Fang said. "We could go to Tianya Haijiao tomorrow."

Alva exhaled with relief. No, he was still paying for a tour. But she had seen pictures of Tianya Haijiao. It meant "edges of the sky, corners of the sea." It was just a beach with some large rocks with the characters Tian Ya Hai Jiao carved in red. There were a lot of those in China—sites where tourists flocked because some official agency had engraved a rock.

"It's a tourist trap," Sloan said. "Another photo op for the crowds."

"And what's wrong with that?" Alva said, forgetting the train of thought she'd had seconds earlier. She could say it; her mother couldn't. She hated it when foreigners made fun of Chinese tourists for taking pictures, for flooding the Louvre or some historical site, ruining it for everybody else. Why were they the cause of ruin? Why did Chinese tourists have a lesser right to photography than a midwestern family making their children pose with Mickey Mouse at Disneyland? "You like being in pictures, don't you?" She pointed a finger at her mother.

"I don't like being in pictures more than the average person," Sloan said.

"There are nine sites total in the tour package," Lu Fang said. "I think the three-day option provides the best value—"

"I don't want to go," Alva said.

Lu Fang and Sloan both stared at her. Her rejection was too direct, she hadn't even pretended to play the game, to at least proffer an excuse. It was true, all said and done, she didn't want to go, she wanted to stay here and ride out the stay in a rum-cola haze.

"Are you not feeling well?" Lu Fang asked. "I've already told them to reserve a private van, it'll be air-conditioned—"

"You should go, the two of you," Alva said. "This was supposed to be *your* honeymoon, no?"

Lu Fang looked to Sloan, who downed her glass of wine and said nothing. Alva knew a packaged tour was the last thing her mother wanted to do, but she didn't actually have the gall to back out. Someone needed to maintain a semblance of effort here. But it was tiring. Everybody was tired.

The seafood came. It was possible to eat entirely in silence. The bill came out to seven hundred and eighty yuan, the waiter announced. Lu Fang had already shoved forward his credit card and three coupons before the young man could finish speaking.

# 40

A nearly intolerable part of the standard double: the sight of the two of them beneath the sheets together. They did not touch; he curled toward the wall, she faced the opposite way, eyes shielded by a mask. The first rays of sunlight crept into the room. Alva was awake. She was still horizontal, but the hangover would hit the moment she sat up, and she'd need something to combat the migraine. She missed FamilyMart.

Outside the hotel gates there was nothing but the newly built highway. No sign of city life, only equidistant arrangements of hanging bouquets, sun-bleached billboards with hammer-and-sickle backgrounds promising new policies of economic prosperity.

Along the resort's open hallways, the breeze still had the cool undertones of night. The velvet morning light pained Alva. So did the relentless exuberance of birdsong and insect buzz drifting in from the garden, in which peasants in straw hats and orange uniforms watered birds of paradise. She retreated to the relative deadness of the business center, paid a sleepy employee for an hour-long internet session, and compulsively checked CityX. There was one new post from Smiling and Proud Wanderer. He balanced on his abdomen along the edge of a skyscraper, arms extended over negative space and fists clenched. SUPERMAN, a commenter wrote. Gao had replied to a thread: "Tomorrow 6 P.M.—LIVE STREAM."

She hated it but knew she would watch the live stream. She already knew. Her hands were shaky again. She left the business center with much of her hour remaining.

The breakfast wing was bustling. Her mother was there—the back of her blond head unmistakable, never a good Waldo—and indeed there was Lu Fang, too, at a table on the terrace, already sweating large pit stains. The day had begun heavy and overcast. He saw Alva and waved.

"Our tour starts soon. What will you do with your day?" Lu Fang asked when she sat down.

"Wait for its end," she said, and he looked genuinely concerned for a second, so she added, "Swim, I guess."

"You have to watch out for the ocean," he said. "If you don't feel well—"

"It's time for the van," Sloan interrupted, rod-straight like she was taking a ride to an execution site. Chairs scraped and Lu Fang mumbled something about being careful and Alva's nose was in the bitter watery coffee—Sloan would have aspirin in her toiletry bag, or—yes, she might as well skip to the good part. The beach bar would be open. The moment Lu Fang and Sloan left, Alva was already speedwalking down the path, and within minutes she was lying straight on the sand, a sweaty glass of sloshing brown beside her.

There was a movie reel Alva replayed in her head: Daniel Cruise is sleeping next to her when she wakes up in the mansion on Mogan Mountain. She contemplates his sleeping form and long eyelashes and salt-and-pepper hair, and thinks, *this is my lover*. She wants to giggle at the grandiosity of that word, how little she understands it. He reaches for her in his sleep. Then she is in an American Airlines plane, and she and Zoey are eating from identical trays full of little plastic containers, and Daniel is with Julia in the row ahead, reading newspapers, and Alva thinks, they don't know. When they touch down in New York she sees the whole city glimmering, the surrounding sea a deep blue, the skyscrapers sinking into it. And in a clapboard house by the sea he comes into her room when Julia and Zoey are elsewhere, and he says, *again*, and he says, *don't be afraid*, and she is not.

In this movie she is not herself. In this movie she doesn't reek of alcohol and he doesn't say "Oh, Alva" with pity in his voice. In this movie she doesn't go to the pharmacy by herself and swallow the pill that kills all doubts only to find something else growing in her stomach. A black webbing that tells her: it should not have happened. A black webbing like *shame*.


"How long are you here for?" the girl asked when she returned with a new glass of rum and Coke for Alva.

"Four nights."

"Where from?"

"Shanghai."

The girl nodded. "We get a lot of guests from Shanghai. But you are not Chinese?"

"I'm half Chinese." Except in Mandarin there was no good way to say this. The closest thing was: *I am half a Chinese person.* "And you? Are you from here?"

"From the island, yeah."

Alva glanced at the girl's name tag. It said Joyce, in English, surprising given the uniformly Chinese clientele. Some places did this to look upscale, globalized. The girl noticed her staring. "I'm Su Lin," she said. "These name tags were handed out to us at random."

"Do people call you Joyce?"

"No," she rolled her eyes. "I can't even pronounce it." She made Alva repeat the word and whispered it to herself, *Joyce, Joyce.* "Does it mean something?" she asked.

"Joy, like happiness," Alva said, though she was guessing.

"Then it's a good name," Su Lin said. "I was lucky to get this one."

Alva squinted against the sun. "You don't get many foreigners here?"

Su Lin plucked off her name tag and traced the letters with her index finger. "They don't come to this resort. They like the other side of the bay, a beach called Dadonghai. The riptides are dangerous, and Chinese tourists avoid it. As long as you don't swim, though, it is the most beautiful place on this island. All the foreigners are there."

Alva didn't quite remember how, after settling the bill, she found herself hailing a motorized rickshaw outside the hotel. But an hour later, she was at Dadonghai Beach, a windswept bay with clearer waters than the ones along the nineties-built resorts of Yalong. Su Lin was right: all the foreigners were indeed here, spreadeagled under thatch-roofed parasols, mostly Russian, meaty men with hairy backs, tall blond women in rhinestone swimsuits, children with hair so pale it gleamed white in the sun.

She'd wait five minutes, she decided, before she took out the plastic bottle again. Su Lin had poured five shots into the Farmer's Spring water bottle. Alva had already had a few swigs when the motorcycle stopped at intersections.

She propped herself up on her elbows. The azure waves appeared gentle, placid. Around her the foreigners were heavy with somnolence, low murmurs occasionally overlapping with the sounds of tides. A few recliners away there was a red-haired teenage boy sitting while hugging his knees, each knob on his vertebrae visible, his pale back covered with moles.

Alva looked down at her own strange body, the stretch marks of puberty running across her hips, the soft white breasts inside the triangles of her bikini. There was an on-and-off switch in her brain: when she let the sense of violation rush in, it crushed her with a radiating sense of nakedness. Or she could drown those feelings into oblivion, anesthetize them with enough ethanol, and the body was just a body, a teenage girl's body, indelicate, commonplace, normal. Anatomically nothing had been taken from her; a membrane broken, a fracture did not equal loss.

She reached for the plastic bottle. She watched the young man again, the lines and grooves in his musculature. He was now standing, running his hand through his hair, dusting sand off his calves. He looked around, restless. His eyes swept past Alva, did not stop to take her in. He stretched and walked toward the water.

He didn't even pause to consider her. Suddenly the black webbing pulsated in her gut again, hot and desperate. She recognized that sweeping gaze, it was the one in Zoey's eyes every time she scanned the clientele of a bar. It meant the young man thought she was Chinese, backdrop, *local*, nothing to see, identical and interchangeable.

Alva was at the water's edge. She wanted the young man to turn around and see her, on her own, contextless, behold her. He didn't turn around, though, and instead started swimming, fast strokes cutting perpendicular to the waves. Alva imagined that entire beautiful body sucked into the ocean. She considered following him. She thought about herself disappearing. This summer, there were movies she watched for the first time, only to realize she'd seen them before, deep into a drunken night. For hours she'd read, listen, watch things she'd never remember. Her brain knew more than she did. She still hadn't cried; she didn't remember crying, but perhaps she'd cried all the moisture out of her body during those lost hours, and that's why she woke with a parched throat and peeling contacts. The Alva of those hours may be another person entirely. The Alva who was now despairing for the white man to stop and LOOK AT HER; this wasn't the Alva she knew.

She had to get away from the shore. She turned away from the water, ran to her recliner, gathered her towel and sunglasses and the crunched plastic bottle she buried deep in the bag.

She was swaying by the highway, waving her arms at a rickshaw, and then zipping past barracks and dirt yards where chickens squawked, and soon found herself standing in the frangipani-scented hotel lobby again, handing the driver pink Maos by the fistful. And the reception employees looked on, eyebrows raised, and she was stumbling toward their standard room. Of course the room was empty, because they were gone on the tour, and she was alone again, alone with her body, with the terrible feeling wrapping itself around her entrails. Her breaths were so short she was heaving. But by the time she sank into her bed, the switch in her consciousness flicked again, and already she remembered nothing.

◆ ◆ ◆

They returned, carrying the leathery smell of cars, and Alva woke to the sudden blare of an HBO film as one of them turned on the TV. They were not speaking to each other. Lu Fang locked himself in the bathroom. Sloan kicked the ugly sporty sandals off her feet with vengefulness; she was like a volcano wanting to erupt with complaints, and for a moment it looked like she might turn to Alva and speak, then remembered it'd be a capitulation. There was a flush of the toilet and movement in the shower. Alva didn't know what time it was, only that the sky outside was a dusky mauve.

The adults were absorbed in a heavy silence she couldn't understand. Again Alva felt the dread that something was wrong. When Lu Fang came out of the shower and asked, "What did you do today?," she said, "I don't remember," and she realized it was true. The pain in her head drilled her like a jackhammer, and she barely heard him mumble about dinner, "something quick, maybe the lobby café."

The lobby café was cheaper. Dinner was ham-and-cheese sandwiches, ordered and eaten in under fifteen minutes. Sloan asked for an amber ale. The garden was thick with the buzz of crickets and the hiccups of frogs. Periodically, vans rolled up to the entrance and unloaded tourists who still carried whiffs of the airport and other cities. Alva wanted to be like them, to arrive fresh. Instead, she folded the crust of her sandwich over and over until it frittered, and still the adults weren't talking.

Sloan etched tear lines in the condensation of her beer glass and broke the silence. "I don't think I'll go on the tour tomorrow."

"As you'd like," Lu Fang said.

"You could see about canceling it."

"It's already paid for, so I'll go alone."

Sloan swatted at her calves to fend off mosquitoes. Red welts were forming on her white thighs. "Damn it," she said. "You don't have to go alone. Just ask for a refund given the error with the room—"

"There was no error with the room," Lu Fang said. "I booked the cheapest one." With this statement he stood. His flip-flops snapped against the cream-colored marbled floor of the lobby. Alva had never seen him walk away from her mother. Suddenly she was seized by a cold fear: he'd had enough of them. He would make them pay everything back.

She turned toward her mother. Sloan rested her neck on the ledge of the couch, staring straight up at the ceiling. Alva knew this posture. It was the same one she remembered from her childhood days, when Sloan explained that Mommy felt sadder than usual and drank in front of the television and the most insignificant detail triggered a torrent of tears. Alva could feel the all-consuming loneliness emanating from her mother, knew she wasn't enough to abate it, and retreated into her own small enclosure of solitude. Now she understood what the alcohol did to Sloan. It was a way to make time pass when emptiness crept around your heart and constricted it until it was about to explode.

"Mom," she heard herself say. And Sloan immediately said, "Partner," like she'd been waiting for Alva to say something all along.

Alva scooted closer to her on the couch. She could see each pore swelling on her mother's thighs, little spider veins exploding beneath her mother's near-translucent skin. "Partner," Sloan repeated, pulling her into her arms.

"Are we in trouble with Lu Fang?" Alva asked.

"I don't know," Sloan said.

Alva closed her eyes. "Maybe we can go to the ocean together tomorrow," she said.

Sloan's fingers were caressing her hair. "Yes," her mother said. "We've never done that."

There was more to say but the truce hung fragile as spider's silk, and they both knew not to disturb it. They rested their heads against each other and listened to the crickets sing.

## 41

The next morning Sloan and Alva went to the breakfast buffet and folded stolen pastries and rolls into napkins. They bought a bottle of Malibu at the gift shop. Neither of them spoke about the months of glacial silence; there were no quibbles about the appropriateness of Alva's drinking. They asked the concierge to call them a car to Dadonghai Beach.

Lu Fang had left by himself early that morning. It was a radiant day, the sky cloudless. In the car, with the windows rolled down, Sloan's blond hair flapped wildly in the wind. After the taxi dropped them off, they followed the beach path to the fine white sand of Dadonghai, and Sloan let out a contented sigh. "Feels like a real getaway now," she said.

Alva directed them to the same set of thatch-roofed lounge chairs where the foreigners had unfailingly shown up for another day. She didn't tell Sloan that she'd been here before. They spent the next two hours pouring the Malibu into flimsy plastic cups swiped from the hotel sink. There were only the sounds of waves, seagulls, the murmurs from one sun-dazed laowai to another.

"This is where all the foreigners come," Sloan said.

"It is *nicer.*"

"They can sniff out the nice stuff—"

"Like wild boars sniffing out truffles."

Sloan laughed. Alva missed hearing her mother laugh.

"Was the sightseeing that bad?" Alva asked.

Sloan sighed. "You narrowly escaped the world's worst tour."

"Was there really nothing pretty?"

"I lived in L.A. I've seen beaches—" Then, finally, her mother caught herself. "I'm sorry. I know you're upset you didn't get to travel with your friend this summer."

It was almost too much to hear it said out loud. Alva let her hand dangle off the lounge chair, fingers combing the hot sand. She blinked back the dryness of her contacts.

"But letting you go with a family of strangers—"

"It's okay," Alva said. "It's too late. There's no use talking about it."

"They were so arrogant," Sloan said. "They have advantages we don't. I never wanted you anywhere near that world for a reason."

"I'm not talking to Zoey anymore," Alva said.

Her mother lifted her sunglasses and looked at her. "What happened?"

Alva took another gulp of Malibu. Malibu was the name of a town in California and also tasted of coconut and sugar. *What happened* was a question that made the black webbing inside her pulsate. "We grew apart."

Grown apart was a perfectly acceptable adult term for the way teenage allegiances expired over a period of eventless separation. Zoey didn't seem to understand this. She sent "????" after "???" when so many of her messages to Alva went ignored. She'd been friendless all too long and persistent and wanted to know what was wrong, and Alva couldn't explain why she could never go to her house again, not with Zoey's mother's calm brown eyes peering through an electronic surveillance system or the horror of sitting across from her father. In any case, they were in New York, and the sand was sticky between Alva's fingers.

"Maybe that's good," Sloan said. "To keep your distance from them. From that lifestyle. Getting used to comfort only makes you more vulnerable."

"But we got used to comfort too," Alva said. "With Lu Fang."

Sloan lowered her sunglasses. "Maybe we did."

"Did Lu Fang tell you anything more about why he booked that room?" Alva asked.

"Things are—" Sloan began. She cleared her throat and reached for the Malibu. "There are rumors about the market. The manufactured housing parts we were investing in may be less in demand—"

Alva exhaled. So it wasn't her fault. "Why did he bring us here if business is bad?"

"There was no refund for the plane. He said getting away might be healthy for you."

"Healthy for me?" Alva blinked.

"We can see you haven't been doing well."

And yet, Alva thought, you still weren't talking to me, not until I spoke to you last night. Then she wondered what they'd seen. She hadn't tried very hard to conceal it. The Ballantine's sat atop her pile of old Mincai uniforms back home. Sloan went on. "He thought this time away, the three of us being together—that it'd do us good. But he's getting phone calls from the mainland nonstop, and I spent all of yesterday stomping around these tourist sites while he was in the van talking to investors and honestly, partner, I'm not sure what's going to happen."

Alva closed her eyes. If Lu Fang lost his money, if the well that paid for the Century Park apartment and international school and taxi rides and expensive haircuts and golf trips dried up, would the whole premise of their arrangement crumble? She thought of him, a lone figure on the soccer field. She might have been too silent while her mother droned on, she might've subconsciously tuned it out, fallen asleep, because when she turned toward her mother's lounge chair, she found it empty. With a terrible presentiment Alva looked to the water. Sloan headed like an otter toward the waves, darkened blond head a small dot.

She'd never told Sloan about the riptides. She sprung to her feet and ran toward the water, footsteps clumsy, shouting "Mom!" Sloan could not hear her. Alva flung her arms wildly. The water was to her ankles when suddenly her gravity gave way and she was down sideways in the shallow tide. Scaping the skin on her knees, drinking in seawater. She tried pushing herself against the sand but her vision was filmy and she was coughing and coughing, the muscles in her arms like jelly. She heard shouts from the beach. Now surely everybody was looking at her, except she could only see blurry shapes, and suddenly her mother was emerging from the waves, running toward her. "What happened? Did you fall?"

"You can't swim here," Alva managed between gasps.

"What are you talking about?" Sloan was helping her sit on the wet sand.

"There are riptides. I forgot to tell you."

Sloan narrowed her eyes and turned toward the ocean. "Oh, partner, it was fine out there. I'm a good swimmer."

"Don't go back in."

They limped back to their chairs. Alva couldn't stop hiccuping. Her mother was patting her back. "God, partner, how much Malibu did you have?"

It was gone; she'd finished it. But that didn't matter. Her mother ripped away by the tides—that would have been a tragedy. That was what mattered. "Mom, you have to be careful," Alva said between gasps. Her mother didn't respond. She hugged Alva tightly, so tightly that the hiccups shaking Alva's body became sobs. It struck her now, how careless her mother had always been. Alva recognized the panic she'd just felt, the same hot knot of fear on the nights she'd waited as a child for her mother to come home, afraid she might not, afraid she'd fallen over some edge out in the city's darkness. The many times Sloan had passed out on the mattress after so many beers, not a sound coming from her, and Alva huddled close, listening to her mother's breathing. That didn't happen anymore, not since Lu Fang moved in. She wanted her mother to hold her now and say in return, *Partner, be careful. Don't go out too far.*

Her mother had come running when she was sideways in the tides, when she'd lost her balance for good. Her mother had kept her promise. She had always come home. Alva felt Sloan's hands moving up and down her back, the same calming stroke she'd used when Alva was a child. It felt so good to be nestled against her skin again, her warmth. She could tell her mother. She needed to tell her mother. They were partners.

"The sleepovers weren't sleepovers," Alva said.

"What?" Sloan stopped stroking her back.

"I thought it might prove something about myself—"

"You're not making sense."

"Prove that I could do it too."

"Do what? What did you do?"

"It was a fundraiser in the mountains and there were all these rooms upstairs and I did it. For the first time."

Sloan stared blankly at Alva, shielding her face from the sun. She cared so much about her skin not falling prey to age, but in this moment there was something worn about her. "Oh, partner," she finally said. "Don't overthink it. Fifteen is—I did the same thing when I was fifteen. It's part of growing up."

Alva was still hiccuping. "He got me away from all these other businessmen."

"Alva—" Sloan's hand was gripping her shoulder harder now. "What do you mean, businessmen? These aren't teenagers?"

"He was old."

"Did he force you?" Sloan's face was drained of blood. It was an almost beautiful pallor. A pallor of true rage, of true motherhood. Her fingers digging into Alva's arm hurt. It was a good kind of pain, the kind that made the flesh matter. Her mother would fight for her, would obliterate those who hurt her. "Were you drunk? Did you know him? Alva!"

"I knew him," she said. "I thought he liked me." Now she was saying it out loud, and her mother was holding her, and she wouldn't have to face it alone. "It was his idea for me to go on their trip, to fly with them and spend the summer. But you wouldn't buy the tickets. Then he offered—"

"Wait," her mother said. "Who offered? This man, this man who took advantage of you, is he—"

"He'd talked about all the things they'd take me to see in New York, and I just thought—"

"Oh, Alva."

"I thought he liked me and that it could help if I gave him what he wanted, but in the end he took it all back. I didn't know he'd take it all back."

"Poor girl," Sloan said. But there was something off with her tone, the way she said *poor*. A stiffness had crept into her embrace. "That horrible man from the museum? That expat father whose house you're always running to—"

This could not be happening. There was anger in her mother's voice, and strangely it seemed partially directed at her.

"I told you about those Chinese women," Sloan said. "I've always warned you. Oh, Alva, what did you do?"

"What did *I* do?" Alva closed her eyes. Moments ago, she'd felt like there was hope. Now she saw Sloan wasn't treating her as a child, that maybe she would never again be a child. Goose bumps crept along Alva's arms, her neither-here-nor-there skin cold and clammy. She felt a hollow disappointment spreading over her, searing shame. She was alone and grown and had somehow done the worst thing a Chinese woman could do—*whored* herself out to a white man. Her mother didn't say it out loud, but she might as well have. In a violent jolt, Alva shrugged off her mother's arms.

"You did it too," Alva said. "You did the exact same thing with Lu Fang. You said you had to play the part."

Her mother only stared, ghostly pale. "We'll have to talk about what to do with you. Only in China would this happen."

Alva's head was pounding. "*Only in China?*"

"It's my fault." Sloan was looking down now. Fat tears splotched on the plastic recliner, like a faucet turned on. Alva found this incredible, because even she, Alva, wasn't crying, and she felt no desire to comfort her mother. "I should never have stayed," Sloan said. "It did something to me. To us. I became someone I didn't want to become, and you're turning out the same. Oh, Alva." She was weeping now.

Alva stared ahead at the sea. She gathered the towel more tightly around herself. "Mom," she said. "Why did you dye your hair blonder and blonder over the years, even though it's brown?"

"What does that have to do—"

"Is it because you think it gets you more attention?"

Her mother blinked back tears. "I—"

"You want to be desired, you dated all these Chinese men. But when I tell you a foreigner took advantage of me, somehow I'm the sellout."

"I'm only saying this society—here in China, those expats, they—"

But Sloan couldn't go on. The sun was halfway down the sky, and Alva shivered in the hotel towel, even though the air was wet and warm.

"But you're not Chinese, Mom. You're one of *them*."

The way her mother looked at Alva then, it was like she'd broken something into a million pieces, like a distance was so rapidly expanding between them it could never be bridged again. They were both silent for a long time. "Let's go," her mother finally said. They gathered their empty bottle and wet towels. Everything's changed and nothing's changed, Alva thought. She'd told her mother the most important, devastating thing that'd happened to her, and somehow it had turned into a fight, one that proved her mother could never be trusted. She looked at her watch: it wasn't even four. Once they got back to the hotel, Alva decided, she'd go to the business center. Somewhere in Shanghai Gao Xiaofan was scaling a building. For that she had to get back, she thought while holding her hand up against the sun, marching through the burning sand toward the highway behind Sloan. She couldn't miss Gao Xiaofan's live stream. He was the only person not trying to get out, but up. Up, he'd said, where you could look down at it all.

Alva slept in the car back from Dadonghai. In the lobby, when Sloan started going on about sobering up, Alva just slipped away like a slippery fish, toward the beach shack where there was an employee who wasn't Su Lin. Alva said she'd gotten a plastic bottle filled before, Joyce did it for me. The employee was an older man who glared at her as he poured. Alva charged it to the room. There was no point in hiding anymore. Then she went to the business center.

The holding picture for Smiling and Proud Wanderer's live stream was grainy, one of his most popular shots, his red Nikes dangling above a bird's-eye panorama of Shanghai. Alva had tried on Lu Fang's forlorn pair back in the apartment, walked around the living room in restless laps. The sneakers were too red, too springy, too big. They were surprisingly heavy.

At six, the feed sputtered to life.

A webcam had been set up on another roof. The lens had a clear view of the top of a skyscraper, the glass windows of the office building glinting in the waning, orange-gray light of a smoggy dusk. A perfectly bisected shot: smog, office. The number of viewers in the bottom right corner of the screen grew from two digits to three.

Now here was Gao Xiaofan, crouching over the ledge. He was wearing a face mask but she could recognize his eyes, the way his hair fell into them. Commenters typed HI in the live stream chat. She typed in Hi gxf. She knew she was breaking a dare. But unlike the rest of them, she knew his real name.

He started doing push-ups on the concrete slab of the ledge. His arms were skinny. His feet so big with the red Nikes. He was proud of these shoes, she could sense it, and the boyish vulnerability of this pride nearly killed her. She wished he'd stop doing the push-ups, he only had to wobble sideways for it to be over. The commenters were saying PULL-UPS, 3,000 coins for OVER THE LEDGE. Gao Xiaofan stopped the push-ups to glance at his phone, then looked straight at the webcam and nodded.

Alva typed NO in the chat, but he'd already tucked his phone away and was lowering himself on his stomach, scuttling backward so that first his feet went over the drop, then his legs, then his thighs, until he was perpendicular folded over the ledge like a human angle. NO she typed again, but her message was instantly drowned in new comments. He'd started scuttling his abdomen inch by inch, his arms tense, until his chest and head were also over the ledge, his whole body hanging vertical against the exterior of the tower. Only his bent fingers gripped the edge.

He turned his face toward the camera. His arms bowed and performed his first pull-up, his upper body tense. One was enough, she thought, then he lowered himself down again, slowly, flat against the windows, his biceps shaking. He did another, more effortfully, this time barely raising himself over the ledge. The comments were stacking so fast she couldn't read them. She could only put her finger on the screen, on his body, which was back to the hanging position, and she said it out loud, "NO." He tried to pull himself up a third time. A tremor ran, almost imperceptibly, through his right hand.

He hung still for a second, like he was coming to a rest.

He looked down. When it happened, it was just the blur of his body falling. Then there was only the ledge, only the windows of the empty office building, only the sound of the wind.

## 42

Alva didn't remember leaving the business center. When she woke, she was on a recliner and everything around her was dark, and someone was shaking her. The only light was the other hotels blinking along the bay. Farther still, distant horns signaled the comings and goings of night cargo. The face in front of her was Lu Fang's.

If this were a movie, she'd realize in those initial hazy seconds that it had all been a hallucination, a recurring nightmare of lost hours. But it was all coming back to her now—her mother's disgusted eyes, the back seat of a taxi, the live stream, Gao Xiaofan falling, how she'd screamed at the computer. It had happened. She blinked at Lu Fang.

"The reception called about a commotion at the business center," he said. "Alva—how much have you been drinking?"

"How much?" she repeated. The empty Farmer's Spring bottle was right next to her. She didn't want any more at this moment. "Gao Xiaofan, he fell," she said.

Lu Fang was kneeling in the sand beside her. "Who?"

"It was a video online. A live stream. He was hanging from a roof. And then—" Before she could realize it, a sob tore through her. "He slipped." Another sob. "Or he let go."

Lu Fang was silent for a moment. Then he said, "These videos online, you can never trust them."

Above her, there were palm fronds like the ones she'd stared up at as a little girl, at the botanical garden near her house. "His name was Gao

Xiaofan," she said. "He liked video games. He got in trouble at school. He wanted to be a rooftopper. He asked me for money, and I didn't really give it to him. After that we—after that we did not talk."

"Gao Xiaofan," Lu Fang said. "Was he one of the boys from the car?"

"He has the same—"

"Nikes."

"Yes," she said. "You remember him."

Beyond the palm fronds there were stars you couldn't see in the city. She remembered Lu Fang on the balcony and Gao Xiaofan in the parking lot, the perversity of drunk children for whom everything was play. The blinking ninja avatar that blew apart and came together, started another game. She always thought Gao Xiaofan was like that little pixelated ninja. The Smiling and Proud Wanderer who always survived.

"Maybe it wasn't real," she said. "Maybe he's laughing somewhere about it."

Lu Fang was silent. The stump of cigarette crinkled between his lips.

They stayed like this, not speaking, he on the sand, she on the plastic. When she finally looked at his face, she saw it was shiny with tears.

"He was just a kid," he said.

She finally grasped what she should have known for a long time. The reason he chain-smoked alone in the night. The person who really owned the green-and-yellow jerseys stacked in the closet, whose feet had run in those worn Nikes. His son had liked soccer, just like her.

"Your son," she said. "Is he gone?"

Lu Fang didn't answer. They listened to the low roar of the tide. Eventually he stubbed out his cigarette in the damp sand.

"He would have been twenty-three this year," Lu Fang said.

"Sorry," she said. And she did feel sorry.

"And I'm sorry too," he said. "I'm sorry about your friend. And this—" He pointed to the plastic bottle. "I'm sorry I didn't notice until now. I would have stopped it. You know what it's done to your mother."

She nodded. Lu Fang knew nothing of her shame, how much of herself she'd given up. In the darkness of the mansion at the fundraiser. How differently she remembered Gao Xiaofan's lips on hers, how fast she'd flinched when he asked for money. For help. She wanted to stop now, to rewind, to be a different person. She said to Lu Fang, "You must miss him."

"Every day," he said.

"We haven't made it easy for you. My mom and I."

"Your mother—" he said. "One day you'll understand how in her way, she tried."

Alva smiled sadly. "She is lucky to have you, to always defend her."

He stood up. "Not just her," he said. He extended a hand, and she took it. They turned away from the black waves, steps falling into tandem, and began walking toward the room with no sea view.


When Sloan opened the door and saw their faces, she didn't ask for an explanation. She put on a kettle of boiling water and slipped out of the room. When she returned, she carried three cartons of Master Kang instant noodles from the gift shop.

The boiling water hissed out from the kettle into the three cardboard cups. The little plastic sachets of dehydrated vegetables and dried beef cubes fell like confetti. The flavor paste oozed out of the silvery pouch, fat neon orange. They waited the mandatory minute as the shriveled meat grew bloated, as the salty broth mollified the yellow bricks. This was countless childhood dinners, when her mother handed her a five-yuan purple Mao and Alva ran down to the corner stall where the old man with no teeth handed her a two-pack wordlessly. This was a Sloan and Alva meal.

As they ate, cradling their bowls on the hotel beds, the TV screen for once black, Alva thought the standard room wasn't so bad. Lu Fang's cell phone buzzed on the table, but for now they buried their faces in the steam of their noodles. Her mother did not know about Gao Xiaofan, and Alva didn't want to talk about it, not right now, because Lu Fang knowing was enough. And Lu Fang didn't know about the mansion, the cough syrup smell, the pill. They knew so little about one another. They each had puzzle pieces that might never lock into a flat, smooth whole.

Lu Fang's cell phone buzzed again.

Staring into her chemically red broth, Alva imagined Lu Fang pleading with investors, fighting for what he'd built over the years, now at risk of dissolving into embers. If they returned to bankruptcy, their lives wouldn't be too different from what they'd known before renting Lu Fang's apartment, before things got comfortable. Maybe her mother wouldn't mind going back to that other life, the one she found so freeing. Maybe that was why Lu Fang didn't want to answer his phone, why he wanted this moment of them all together, instant noodles in a standard room, to last a bit longer.

The phone vibrated again, and Sloan said, "Pick it up, Lu Fang."

He took it onto the balcony. They could see him nodding, head bowed. When he came back in, he said, "It was the bank."

"And?" Sloan said.

"They're going to take the apartment."

Alva waited for him to say, *We'll rent a smaller one. And you'll return to Chinese school. And your mother will go back to teaching English. But I'll be here.*

He was looking at Sloan, like he was waiting for her signal. Sloan took a deep breath and said, "Then we're going back." She looked so despondent, so pale. Alva thought she might faint.

"It's okay, Mom," Alva said. "We've done it before."

"I don't mean Shanghai. I mean America."

Alva stared at her mother. "But you always said we had no one there."

Her mother gave her a pained look. Then, suddenly, Alva knew what Sloan was about to say. Maybe she'd always known, deep inside, that there'd been another option. One obfuscated and held out of reach, the highways and strip malls and cul-de-sacs where Sloan's parents had died tragically young. A land where she had no one, a land with nothing to offer.

Sloan was turning to Alva and saying, "Your grandparents in New Jersey . . ."

Alva looked toward Lu Fang to confirm he was hearing what she was hearing. He stared back at her and she saw immediately that he knew, that he'd known all along.

PART X

# LU FANG

SHANGHAI, 2005

## 43

The mermaid reminded Lu Fang of her: a self-satisfied smile. Beckoning from every street corner in Shanghai—he'd have to look up the number of franchises. Starbucks green. That's how he'd come to think of it. But before the coffee chain popped up everywhere in China, he'd have called it the color of pine. Darker than the translucent, luminous green of Qingdao bottles.

He checked his phone. He'd been sitting here for nearly two hours. Ten more minutes and he'd leave.

There were so many shades of green in the Chinese language—the green of peas, tea, olives, apples, forests, moss, meadows, gray lakes, crystal, jasper, jade, peacocks, beetles, ink, tenderness. But there were other, more elusive versions, too. He flipped over the receipt for his frappuccino (thirty-six yuan) and wrote:

苍翠 (deep emerald)

绿油油 (the shiny lushness of grass blades at their prime)

灯红酒绿 (wine green against the debauchery of red lanterns)

翠色欲滴 (drippingly verdant, like a dewdrop at the tip of a leaf)

一碧千里 (the singular, thousand-mile greenery of grassland filling the horizon)

万古长青 (evergreen, like the eternity of ten thousand years)

青 meant green. 青年 meant youth: the tender green years. 青春: the green spring of life. A spring his son never lived past. What to call this period Lu Fang was in now—the chill of early autumn? He was fifty-six.

"Lu Fang!" the familiar voice called.

He stubbed out his Double Red Happiness and checked his phone: 10:28 P.M.; two more minutes and he would have left. He didn't yet look up. She would be forty-four by now, an unlucky number.

"I didn't know you meant the Starbucks across from the Langham—there are at least three on this street, I must have gone into every one of them."

She pulled back the metal chair and it scraped against the stones. Finally he looked. Her heels were too high, the beige suede stained with grime. And her hair—every strand ill, bleached to death and back, brown roots sprouting beneath it all. Only now did he realize the blond hair he'd so admired was the product of a chemical dye. The word that entered his mind at this moment was 枯黄, a withered yellow.

She was watching him take her in, eyelids heavy with smudged eyeliner. "Lu Fang. You could say something."

"It's late," he said.

"Not by Shanghai standards. The night is just starting. Come on, where do you want to go? Sit somewhere, have a drink, catch up. It's good to see you."

She was trying but failing to hide her drunkenness, the words slurring. The Sloan he used to know could hold her liquor. That Sloan would not want him to see her like this. "It is late," he said. "Perhaps it is better if we catch up another time."

She straightened her spine, as if reminding herself that uprightness conveyed control. "I'm sorry. I was looking forward to this."

"I was too," he said. He wanted to back away, a polite retreat from the wreckage. It'd been wrong to contact the foreign teacher agency and ask for her email address. He should have left this Starbucks table long ago after she was late an hour, then two, known something wasn't right. And yet he'd stayed because he'd thought there was nothing to lose. The least he could do now was not leave her drunk in the middle of Xintiandi.

"Let's get you home," he said. "Where do you live? Still near the botanical garden?"

"It's not even midnight," she protested.

He reached out to hold her by the elbow because she was teetering. "It's better to rest at home," he said. Like this he supported her toward Madang Road to a line of waiting taxis. "But it's early," she kept saying, too loudly. A couple whispering goodbyes forehead against forehead stopped and stared. He could see the face of the driver of the first taxi in line, watching Sloan with equal measure disapproval and hesitancy. When Lu Fang opened the car's back door the driver pointed at her and shook his head.

But Sloan was already slumped on the back seat. The driver's face made it clear that Lu Fang would have to get in with her, or there'd be no ride. She was holding an arm out toward him. "Come on, Lu Fang. We'll drop you off. Are you staying at a business hotel? We can drop you, and then I'll go home."

What could he say? She was looking at him, the driver was looking at him. He felt the lateness of the hour, how tired he was.

He sighed and got in. The taxi driver snapped down the green 空车 sign. "I'm not exactly staying close by," he said.

"I don't mind. Though if you're worried about—I'm not trying to follow you home, nothing like that."

"I understand," he said. The driver's face had taken on a falsely neutral professionalism. "Pudong," he told the man dryly. The driver said nothing. It would be a big fare.

"Thank you," she said. "Are you staying in Lujiazui? The hotels there have nice views over the river."

"I'm not staying at a hotel," Lu Fang said. "I bought a place in Pudong. Century Park."

"Oh! Nice area for a family."

Sloan leaned forward, her cheek almost pressed against the plastic partition around the driver's seat. "I know the roads, I can tell the driver what route to take." She stage-whispered to him, "I don't like them to rip me off."

The driver narrowed his eyes at Lu Fang in the rearview mirror. "Put on the radio, will you?" Lu Fang told him.

The driver pushed a button and a pop song came blaring on. Sloan clasped her hands together.

"Li Yuchun, from that *Super Girl* singing contest. Alva loves watching it."

Alva. He could still hear the baby's wails from the last time he'd seen Sloan, when they lay in the gray water of the business hotel's bathtub. And of course he never forgot Alva sleeping on the floor mattress of that dingy one-room where Sloan had taken him. His son had run downstairs for a snack, unable to stand the sight of their misery. "Where is she now?" he asked.

Sloan rested her nape against the banquette. "What do you mean, where? She's home."

"Home alone?"

She twisted her mouth. "Well, yes. She's twelve. She doesn't need a babysitter. She's very well-behaved, you know, very studious. A regular little adult. She probably finished her homework and put herself to bed by now."

"You leave her alone at night often?"

"No," she said. "There are guards at the entrance of the tower. She's not scared. She's twelve," she repeated. "Can you believe it?"

"It's been a long time," he said.

"You had this proverb for the passing of time. I can't remember it."

"Day to night like shooting arrows, sun to moon like a shuttling loom."

She laughed. The car took a sharp turn and she tilted toward him like her head was going to meet his shoulder, then she pulled back. "Remember the story you told me about Chang'e on the moon?"

She slid toward the car window. "You can't see the moon tonight. You can never see the stars in Shanghai, the sky is always orange. There used to be stars in Qingdao."

They descended from the South-North Elevated Highway, a gray snake skirting by housing towers, so close you could peer straight into the grimy kitchens and flickering TVs.

"Another eleven years," she was muttering. "Do you do it on purpose? You plan it out? Like Chang'e and Houyi, once in a moon cycle?"

The driver honked loudly at a car merging lanes. She was confusing tales. "That's the story of the cowherd and the weaving fairy," Lu Fang said. "By most accounts, Chang'e and Houyi never see each other again."

"Oh," she said. "That's not a nice ending. No wonder I didn't remember."

They were descending down the Yan'An tunnel. He thought of the Huangpu River roiling overhead, all those cubic tons of sandy waters.

Her face was so close to his again. "Your son must be off to university now, right?"

"No," he said. They were still underwater. The Yan'An tunnel was interminably long. "Minmin drowned in a swimming accident two years ago."

The radio's signal had been cut off—there was only white noise. In the rearview mirror, the driver lowered his eyes.

"Lu Fang, I am so sorry," Sloan said.

He'd memorized the prayers and blessings, the appropriate responses to condolences. 节哀顺变—"restrain the sorrow and adapt to change." Yes, he would restrain his sorrow. He'd gone to the temples. He'd laid wreaths of chrysanthemum at the grave by Dagu Mountain. On the first day back to work, he'd walked from the entrance of his company's office, past the desks of dozens of employees, to the room with the view of the Yellow Sea, and picked up the phone and called his client as scheduled. His office door was locked. The client was in Singapore—and as Lu Fang recited the shipping rates of cargo options, he looked west at the sea and started sobbing so hard he could no longer speak.

They were emerging in Pudong now, on the other side of the Huangpu River. The sleek skyscrapers of Lujiazui rose like giants. Sloan was silent. Lu Fang wondered how well she remembered his son. He no longer had a family. After Minmin's funeral, Ciyi handed him the divorce papers, over which she'd cried so much her signature was smudged. "You're free now," she'd said. Though they both knew it didn't matter. Their son was dead, and from now on they'd both be 凶s, bound to a mutual tragedy.

They'd packed away Minmin's room, vacated the Qingdao apartment, and she'd moved back to Chuanxi, the village where she'd grown up. Lu Fang's mother had passed not long after Minmin, and his brother rarely spoke to him, laboring to raise his own family in the south. As he cleaned out the remnants of his previous life, Lu Fang had kept the jerseys and shoes; the only thing he wanted to remember was the beatitude on Minmin's face when his son had lain on the cool balcony tiles in his yellow-and-green shirt. A moment that belonged to the two of them alone, father and son. Earlier today, Lu Fang had walked by the site of the nondescript business hotel where they'd stayed on that trip, but it'd been razed and replaced by a shopping mall. He'd walked away, dazed.

"I couldn't stay in Qingdao," he said.

Her hand squeezed his. "It's okay to need a fresh start," she said.

"A fresh start." Fresh starts in the autumn of life. There were freckles on the back of Sloan's hand, or maybe they were age marks. "Did you really find one when you came to China? After your parents' accident?"

They turned onto the wide, empty lanes of Century Avenue. The radio came back on, a Taiwanese-accented pop hit. "That can't really compare," she finally said.

"Death is death," he said softly.

She lowered her head. They curved around the iconic metallic sculpture on Century Avenue's main roundabout, a gigantic aluminum sundial called Light of the Orient. Finally Sloan said, "They're retired in New Jersey. I hardly ever talk to them. They don't even know about Alva."

Strangely, he felt no surprise. All those years ago it was her hair he'd seen first, hair the color of light. He'd never thought about its veracity, though in some ways it never mattered. The tales she told about America, her unhappy childhood, her parents' deaths, the L.A. days, the movie set. China as the country of pure renewal. He'd wanted to believe in her optimism. He'd have believed anything she said back then, while believing none of it at all.

She was nervously scrunching up her hair. She spoke very fast. "My parents are serious, middle-class people. They never supported me going to L.A. after high school, and in retrospect they were right. I didn't get any callbacks. Back there, it felt like I was not only average, but less than average. I paid for acting classes, and they were so expensive. I didn't tell my parents I was renting a tiny apartment and waitressing at the twenty-four-hour Chinese restaurant downstairs. They hired me because I learned a few Chinese menu items and it made the boss laugh. The customers got a laugh out of me listing the Chinese dishes. The boss lady always wagged her finger at me and said, 'Slow! Slow!' The customers thought it was my name. One night a drunk customer told me, 'Slow, don't worry so much, you are a pretty girl. In China they would think you are a very pretty girl.'"

The car glided along the dark lawns of the Pudong People's Government complex, past the vast plaza of the Shanghai Science and Technology Museum.

"I spent all my savings from waitressing on a visa and plane ticket to China. They were right. The first week I landed here, people took so many pictures of me. Entire classes of children would walk up and ask to take my photo. Like I was famous. Like I was a movie star. Everybody was always looking at me."

"Yingchun Road," Lu Fang said to the driver. "Garden of Heavenly Peace. The next right."

Sloan sniffled. "I'm sorry I lied. I thought if I said I had nothing in America, no one would try to make me go back. I could pretend I was this whole new person here, someone who wasn't average."

The taxi crawled to a stop in front of the accordion gates of the compound.

"You're not average," Lu Fang said.

"My hair is fake, my name is fake," she said. "Sloan is a nickname I gave myself. If you look at my passport, my real name is Sally. I'm brown-haired, brown-eyed Sally. I am something here. There I would be nothing."

She was gazing at the sleek new buildings of the compound, the neat stacks of snacks at the well-lit twenty-four-hour FamilyMart on the corner of the block.

"You've lived in China for twenty years. You've raised a daughter," Lu Fang said. "If you went back to America, you still wouldn't be nothing."

"Lu Fang," she said. "I really am sorry about your son."

They were both jolted by the sound of a car door slamming. The driver had walked onto the street, in the direction of the FamilyMart. The meter was still running. A man was selling DVDs in front of the convenience store. They could see the driver bent over the stacks, examining the covers.

For a few moments they were silent. Then Sloan said, "Years ago, I watched this movie called *The Lover*. It's about a white girl in Asia and a Chinese man falling in love. It's set in colonial times. She was poor and he was a businessman. They don't end up together; they can't, they know it could never be more than a fantasy. I thought, that's us. That's me, that's Lu Fang. All these years I pictured myself as her, and I told Alva that's the one role I got in my life, a foreign woman who falls in love with a Chinese man but who is never chosen. Who will always be a foreigner—that was my lead role."

Something loosened in Lu Fang. He remembered the late afternoon they spent driving in the orchards, young, exhilarated, the warm wind and smell of soil. It had truly been one of the happiest moments in his life. Once, he would have chosen that to be his every day. But then life passed over them. Look at him now, paunchy and hollowed by grief in the back seat of this taxi, and at her, with her hair dye and her sad, drunken eyes. It didn't matter that her name was Sally, and her hair was brown, and her parents were alive in New Jersey. It didn't matter that she'd lied. It didn't matter because in the past twenty years they'd reinvented themselves, the whole nation ran on reinvention. And there was a little girl home alone, and a little boy in a river. And finally, he had a choice.

There was a distant jingle, the FamilyMart automatic doors opening, the driver walking back toward them. Sloan leaned her head back on the seat. The gates of Heavenly Peace loomed outside his window. He could get out, and she'd go home to her daughter, ships crossing once again in the fog, and history would repeat. He could wait out the next chapter of his life, with a million-yuan apartment, an empty two-bedroom without

Minmin, a two-bedroom for a family. Or he could invite her inside. He wondered if there was still space left in him for a family.

The driver opened the door. "Is this the final destination?" He held it open, inquisitive. The meter blinked up another red number, waiting for Lu Fang to say the word.

PART XI

ALVA

SHANGHAI, 2008

# 44

Lehman Brothers collapsed two weeks after their plane returned from Hainan Island. It was Lu Fang who checked his BlackBerry and said, "It happened."

"What?" Alva asked.

"America," he said. "It's falling apart."

Sloan said nothing.

"I've been sensing it for months," he said. "My company won't be the only one. Just watch."

They watched. The news channels buzzed with alarm: Western markets were going down the drain. There was no escaping the sudden frenzy that'd overtaken Shanghai—the hushed phone calls and triple-checking of Hong Kong accounts, the cutting of losses as things tipped into free fall.

The only fall Alva thought about was that of a boy from a skyscraper. But the rest of the world couldn't care less about him. The identical broadcasts across the CCTV channels praised the strength of the Chinese economy. The Hangsheng Index was already climbing back up. The Western world had shot itself in the gut while China would carry on, unscathed. Except for those sectors too heavily reliant on international trade. Meanwhile, grim-faced expats got one last Bund drink before a scheduled flight, fleeing from a city where only the *locals* were left, a density they contemplated with horror and resentment.

Without the expat package, China suddenly lost its appeal. Then the

108-yuan cocktails in the French Concession started tasting expensive, the international school tuition seemed astronomical, and household maintenance without an army of local servants simply impossible.

*Impacted* was the euphemism that circulated in the Shanghai American School. Alva hadn't returned, Lu Fang and Sloan agreeing she could take some time off, that they'd make preparations. But the impact was inescapable: old classmates gossiped on Facebook about the expat families falling like flies. Alva heard that Zoey had quietly gone to the administrative office to sign transfer papers. She wasn't alone; the fallout tumbled into view: executive villas would be reclaimed by the real-estate developers, companies composed of men's last names could no longer afford leases and tuition packages, entire families were to be repatriated.

*Where are you?* Zoey texted Alva. *We lost everything. Please text me back.*

On a weekday Alva took the subway to Jing'an District and walked by the glass tower that housed the company with many men's names. There was stylish Scandinavian furniture and plum blossom art on the ground floor, hefty metallic initials affixed next to the revolving doors. She'd looked up Daniel Cruise's page on their website, the wave of silver in his hair perfectly dynamic even in stillness. Moving trucks lined the street outside the building, and uniformed men carried large boxes from the freight loading deck. Ergonomic chairs and enormous computer monitors, Waterford crystal whiskey tumblers, along with the expats themselves, all shipped back across the Pacific to their corporate owners. She stood by the revolving doors for a while before turning around.

In Apartment 803 of Building 38 in the Garden of Heavenly Peace, far from the green lawns where the pop of golf balls had momentarily given way to silence, bags were being quietly packed as well. Trips to the American consulate were made, papers signed, passport photos taken, all safely stowed away in the Box of Important Things. Tickets to Newark were booked. Two adults, one child, one-way. Sloan could have commented on the deserved downfall of the parasitic neocolonials, but she stayed silent. They didn't talk much about her parents, the house where they'd stay in her hometown of Colts Neck, New Jersey.

This was not the departure from Shanghai Alva had imagined. She had never pictured fleeing the city, part of a flock of migratory geese who'd overstayed their welcome. Shanghai was her world. The only nature she knew were its willows and man-made lakes, the only sky its milky orange canopy. She'd been raised to the beats of its drills and the swings of its cranes, to the glow of its neon lights and the density of its crowds. Here China converged, and toward China the world now converged. It was her own beating heart.

Her nerves fluttered every time she walked by the FamilyMart. Soon she'd be in America, where she couldn't stroll into a store and pick up a Ballantine's, a fish ball in brown broth. She couldn't zip along elevated highways on motorcycles or watch the next season's movies, recorded in dark theaters on shaky handheld cameras. That was the opposite of freedom. Sometimes at night she lay still in her bed and the tears flowed, and this time she would remember these tears, how easily they came from a deep well within her body. She felt sick at the thought of leaving. But there was so little left. Gao Xiaofan was gone, Li Xinwei and Zoey too. Lu Fang had cleared the stash out of her closet, wordlessly, the bottles clinking in a trash bag. This was also the city where Alva had lost her way. The black webbing still pulsed in her stomach, faint.

She only knew that, before she could really arrive anywhere anew, debts had to be settled.

She took out her phone, took a deep breath, and dialed Zoey's number.

Girlie's eyes were red-rimmed when she opened the door. There were towering piles of cardboard boxes in the foyer. Alva didn't need to ask. She could guess that like most domestic helpers, Girlie would be sent home. Feng would be sent home. She nodded to Girlie and headed upstairs, but instead of swerving toward Zoey's bedroom, she went right. She knew this house like it was her own. This was the aisle of the hallway with the master bedroom. She pushed open the door she'd never dared touch before. Inside, there was Daniel, alone, bent over a large Samsonite suitcase.

"Zoey, I told you, we're not shipping extra boxes," he said.

Alva remained still in the doorway until he looked over. His temples were sweaty, and his silver hair, usually gelled gracefully, fell across his forehead in disarray.

He tried to hide his surprise. "Alva."

"Just saying goodbye," Alva said.

The room was stacked with cardboard, clothing strewn in piles all around. Daniel's eyes darted nervously toward the door—Julia must be somewhere in the house. Then he seemed to compose himself. "I appreciate you not telling Zoey. It's better that way."

"Better for you?" Alva said.

"For you too. The expat circles in this city are small. You still have years in school—you don't want a reputation."

"A reputation?"

He laughed dryly. "Oh, come on," he said. "I know what you and Zoey got up to on weekends. You think Feng never told us about those extra hours?"

He sighed and checked his watch like this conversation was delaying him from something more important. But Alva knew he had no appointments. He was home. The firm with many men's names had shipped out their entire office. "You knew what you were doing," he said.

"You did too," she said.

He sat down on the bed and ran his fingers through his hair. "I was trying to help you. And you came on to me, and I know I shouldn't have responded the way I did. I already said I was sorry. Something came over me in the moment and—"

He stared vacantly ahead. She tried not to remember the cough syrup smell, the slick, goopy liquid dripping from the side of her stomach.

"I lost control," he said.

"The strawberry gel," she said. "You had it ready."

"God," he said. Then he said it again, louder. "You want an apology? Sorry. There. Again. I shouldn't have. I shouldn't have done any of it."

"Would you have done it if we were in America?"

He stared at her. "We aren't in America," he said softly. For a moment the thought seemed to soothe him, and his mouth hardened. "But I had dinner with the consul just a few months ago."

She knew this piece of information was meant to make her feel small, powerless, and it did. She kept her face a wax mask. This unsettled Daniel. "Compensation," he said. "If you want compensation, I can give you money. But please leave my family alone after that."

Before Alva could reply, he disappeared into the walk-in closet. She heard fumbling, and he emerged with a stack of green bills. It was a heavy wad, thicker than any amount Alva had ever seen.

"Take it. Take it if it's what you came for," he said as he tossed the cash at the floor in front of her. And then he sank onto the bed, hunched with his head between his legs, his fingers laced against his nape. He was a bug curling into a ball, fending off the world's blows. "And let it be settled," he said. "God. I cannot wait for this, all of this, to be over. I don't know what China turned me into."

Any second now, and the tears would be flowing furiously, silently from Alva's eyes. She stared at the stack of green money. The man on it wasn't Mao. It was at once the most meaningful and meaningless thing in the world. And yet here she was, bending down. Picking it up. She knew what she would do.

"This country turned you into nothing," she said. "Nothing you weren't already."


Zoey was in her bed staring at the ceiling, surrounded by a labyrinth of crates. The furniture was still in its usual place, items that never belonged to the Cruises, that would be cleaned and covered in dustsheets and used by the next expat family that would ride the wheels of fortune into the Links Golf and Country Club.

"You didn't answer any of my messages," Zoey said, still parallel to the ceiling.

"I had a bad summer," Alva said. She sat on the edge of the bed. "I was drinking a lot."

"Oh," Zoey said.

"I've been drinking a lot this year."

"I guess we both have."

"Me more than you," Alva said. "And sometimes it—" She stopped. She stroked the comforter. She'd always loved how soft this material felt. "It doesn't matter," she said. "We're all leaving now."

"What?" Zoey squinted. "You're leaving too?"

"My stepfather's company went bankrupt. My mother's parents are in New Jersey. We're going there."

"We'll be in Connecticut," Zoey said.

They sat in silence for a while. No one said, *so we'll see each other*. No one said, *so we can still be friends*. Alva ran her finger along the velvet one last time.

"Good luck with the move," she said.

Before she reached the door, Zoey called out, "I'm sorry I didn't watch out for you more."

"I'm sorry too," Alva said. With that she closed the door lightly behind her.


Finally, she knocked on Girlie's door.


Lu Fang was waiting outside the Cruises' villa in a rental Toyota van. Alva got in the passenger side. "Debts settled?" Lu Fang said. Alva nodded. When she started crying, he kept his eyes straight on the road ahead. The guard didn't wave when he lifted the barrier, no doubt thinking Lu Fang was an employee, a hired driver, a mover. They rolled past the rural barracks, back onto the highway.

"Your mother is the one who taught me to drive," Lu Fang said after a few minutes.

"What?" Alva said between two hiccups. "When?"

"A long time ago."

The maglev train roared past them on the elevated tracks running along the highway. It was a speed train of the future, a train that floated.

It only went one place: the Pudong airport. Where they would go tomorrow and board an Air China to Newark. Alva imagined herself in that train, floating at three hundred miles per hour, toward the future, 未来. That which hasn't arrived.

"Did Mom know him?" she asked. "Your son?"

"My son?" Lu Fang reached into his pocket and handed her his wallet. "Look inside," he said. Alva knew that bloated brown leather wallet so well, had seen Lu Fang hand over bills from it so many times.

"On the left," he said. "In the second slot. There's a picture."

Alva found a worn piece of paper, a hard shiny Kodak print gone soft with years. It was folded in four. She carefully unfolded it. In the picture there was a family standing against the backdrop of the city. Then she recognized the yellow hair, her younger mother. And Lu Fang, thinner, also younger, in a white button-down. To the side, there was a Chinese boy with a sad face. And against her mother's chest, a baby with a mop of black hair, gazing at the camera in a half daze.

"You met that summer," Lu Fang said. "He liked you, in a way. He gave you some of his fries."

Because he kept his eyes straight on the road, she could only see Lu Fang's profile, his slight smile. It was a smile so full of sorrow. She wanted to tell him she remembered his son. But that would have been an untruth, and she was not her mother. Instead she folded the picture carefully and put it back in his wallet.

"Lu Fang," she said. She handed him his wallet, and for the first time, she took in his worn face, one with lines digging their ways down the edges of his lips, a face more like her own than her mother's. She felt herself choking up again. "I'm scared. About America."

"I am too," he said, his eyes back on the road.

"Why?"

"I will be jobless, a nearly sixty-year-old Chinese man. It's hard to imagine life at these grandparents' who never knew about us, counting on their charity until we find our footing. You are young, but I will have to begin again, and I am tired. I do not speak the language. I've heard enough from those who have returned from overseas, the indignities that await. These old bones of mine have taken enough. And I am afraid of how much I will miss China."

"I'll miss it too," Alva said. "I didn't want to leave this way."

They were silent until they got off the exit toward Century Park. Then he said, "One of my favorite books is Yu Hua's 活着. *To Live* in English. I always thought it was a mistranslated title. 'To live' in English is active. But 'living,' maybe, is a better translation. To go on living because it's the neutral condition. When I was young, I used to think I would only be truly alive if I got out, saw the world, but that was long ago. I lost my son. I lost my will. But when your mother came into my life again, I thought . . . so much has happened, yet I am still alive. No matter where we are, we will carry our sorrows and fears, but if we are alive, we can look out for one another. Here, or there."

Outside the windshield, the gates to Heavenly Peace opened with a slow mechanical whirl. Alva stayed quiet. She did feel less fear.

"Thank you for driving me," she finally said. "Maybe one day you'll teach me." And his face lit up briefly, almost imperceptibly, but she knew it did. Before she slipped out of the car, she said, "I really love poems too. You know one I think about a lot?"

野火烧不尽, she began,

and he joined in to finish the line,

春风吹又生.

## 45

She had a last errand to run before going home. She walked toward the FamilyMart. She could have drifted through the automatic doors with her eyes closed, guided only by the jingles of the bell, and found the ridged neck of the familiar bottle. Instead she peered into the green interior of the van, where the DVD man was stroking his Buddha earlobes.

"You're here," he said. "I've been waiting for you."

"Do you have it?" she asked.

He bent sideways, half disappearing behind a bush of potted rhododendron. When he reemerged, he held a thin cardboard rectangle between his fingers. Beneath the words *The Lover* was a stick-thin white girl with scrawny pigtails in a fedora hat, and a Chinese man in a luxurious white linen suit, eyes cast downward toward the girl's nape, a leery half-smile on his face.

"I burned it for you," the DVD man said.

Alva handed him two purple Maos. He shook his head. "It's not worth a cent," he said. "It's a terrible story."

"Thank you," Alva said. She put the money back in her pocket. "I'm moving away."

"I know," the DVD man said. "I see everything." Then he leaned back into his wicker chair, deep into the foliage of snake plants and banyans, and resumed seeing.

✦  ✦  ✦

She pushed open her mother's bedroom door. Lu Fang was out on a last trip to the furniture outlet mall to resell his redwood tables and chairs. The apartment was almost all cleared out, even the beds, and Sloan was sitting on a mattress on the floor, arranging belongings into boxes and suitcases. It was a sight Alva had seen many times, when they'd moved every year or two, when they slept on the same mattress, where Alva copied characters along grids as Sloan sipped a beer and distractedly stroked Alva's hair.

At Sloan's feet sat the Box of Important Things. Four dark blue booklets were laid out, the golden eagles regal on the covers. Alva sat next to her mother on the mattress and reached for the passports. They'd all gone to the consulate—to get the paperwork for Lu Fang and their own passports renewed. The two old passports had their back corners cut off. Alva flipped them open. A small Chinese girl and a young white woman. The old passports were as pristine as the new. The small Chinese girl now a teenager with dark eyes, hair dyed black again, clipped behind both ears. The young white woman now middle-aged, cheeks sunken, lips so thin they disappeared. The names read *Alva Collins* and *Sally Collins*.

Alva had never thought of her mother as Sally, though she'd seen the name many times as a child. "Sally Collins is dead," Sloan used to say. Like her parents had been and her entire history had been. Like the possibility of America had been.

Alva set down the passports.

"You'll understand when you get there," Sloan said to the wall.

Alva made no response.

"Why I hated Colts Neck. Listen to that name."

Alva had Baidued Colts Neck. She read about the Colts Neck Fair on Buck Mills Road, seen pictures of Uncle Sams on stilts, pubescent girls in jean cutoffs waiting in the cotton candy line, the pumpkin and custard pies at the Country Food Market. On Google Earth she zoomed in on the brown fields outside Laird's distillery, all those barns and silos, the endless gray stretch of Route 18. All along the country lanes were big houses on big fields, and Sloan said the grandparents lived in one of these big houses, that they would stay there while she and Lu Fang looked for work, and maybe Alva could enroll at Colts Neck High for the spring semester. Alva had also searched for pictures of Colts Neck High. It was nowhere near as nice as the Shanghai American School. She typed in Sally Collins, Colts Neck High. She found a digitized copy of a yearbook, 1978, her mother's hair frizzy and brown, her teeth braced. The caption beneath the picture only said *Sally Collins*, no quotes, no positions. Just plain Sally Collins.

"I know you've seen all those movies," her mother said. "That you think growing up in America is the best thing in the world. But it wasn't for me. It wasn't at all like the movies."

Alva thought of the childhood she had imagined for Sloan, the collage from romantic old westerns and road-trip Americana. "You weren't from the desert," she said. "You didn't wear cowboy hats and go to saloons like Thelma and Louise."

Sloan shook her head. "No. I came from the suburbs. My father managed a supermarket chain and my mother volunteered at the church. We took vacations to Florida."

"You weren't poor," Alva said.

"We weren't poor. My upbringing was—comfortable, Alva, unchanging, the same refrain year after year, week after week. School. Church. Boys and Girls Club. Summer camp. School. Church. And I wasn't especially good at school, or especially pretty, or especially interesting. It seemed to me that everything interesting in the world was happening outside of my life. I was a boring girl growing up in New Jersey in the 1970s. I wanted to be an actress and I did go to L.A., but I didn't have what it took to stand out."

"And then you came to China."

Her mother slowly turned the pages of their old passports, empty save for a chain of residency permits. "Some years it was so lonely that I almost cracked. I know I was here for the wrong reasons. Being a novelty, feeding on attention, that wore thin. I couldn't stop, yet I had no other purpose.

Until I had you. Walking around Shanghai with my baby—something was different. I know sometimes it didn't seem this way, but you made me happier than anything. You kept me alive. You gave me another role here in China. I would stay and be your mother. I had a partner."

That's what Alva used to think: they were partners. Alva had wanted to hear her mother's raspy laugh, wanted her mother to take her to a park, to a secret pool, to a pirated DVD stall, to a flower-and-bird market where parrots sang, to a ferry ride on the Huangpu, to the Bund at low tide. But what if she was only the by-product of a fake story, a staged performance her mother had put on in China, a reenactment of some romanticized colonial tale? Could a person live out her life in a foreign country as performance art, give birth as performance art, raise a child as performance art? Was that why they'd never left China—because it was Sloan's stage?

Now Alva tucked the DVD copy of *The Lover* in the Box of Important Things, its plastic shrink-wrap still unopened. They both stared at it. "This is the movie you were never in," Alva said. She didn't need to watch it to know their lives were nothing like the movie. That the only true story their lives were based on was their own. Unlikely partners. Loose in Shanghai, watching another storm burst. Then someone else had entered their lives, and they'd all lost sight of one another.

"Do you really love Lu Fang?" Alva asked.

"Partner." Her mother pulled her into her arms, and though her touch was foreign, her smell was familiar. "It's the three of us now."

"Over there—he will be an outsider," Alva said. "It'll be so much harder for him than for us. I don't want to lose him."

Sloan squeezed Alva hard, then let her go. "No matter what happens," she said, "we'll make sure he doesn't feel like an outsider with us."

"No," Alva said. "We won't let that happen anymore."

"No," Sloan said. "Not anymore."

Their last night in Shanghai, Alva went to the garden of the compound and sat on a bench, watching feral cats chase each other in the darkness.

She took out her phone and logged onto QQ. It was there again. The little green dot next to the username Smiling and Proud Wanderer. She had to catch it at the right time. Most of the time it was gray. But for a few weeks now she started noticing how it blinked back to green at strange hours, sometimes for seconds only.

The feral cats emerged from the bushes, chased each other across the plaza, disappeared into a rustle of leaves. They were so quick on their feet; it was unimaginable that they'd let themselves get caught. Nine lives. The Smiling and Proud Wanderer was a game player; he always pressed start again.

She looked up toward the apartment. A red dot glowered in the darkness of the eighth-floor balcony. She raised her hands toward it, and it danced back at her.

She thought about what her mother used to say when she woke with a bruise and Alva asked her if it would stay there forever.

"I'm fine, partner," Sloan would say. "Every bruise fades."

"Every single one?" Alva would ask, tracing the blue and purple clouds on her mother's white skin.

"Yes," her mother said. "Every single one. And then everything is new again."

The eighth-floor balcony was dark. Tomorrow it would no longer be theirs. Tomorrow they would hand over papers, clear borders, embark. Not 人, not 从, but 众. Alva allowed herself to picture a man, a woman, and a girl, sitting huddled at an airport gate. A Chinese man, a foreign woman, a half-and-half girl.

Facing the outside world, they would be a family. That she knew was true.

## ACKNOWLEDGMENTS

I am grateful to my agent, Hillary Jacobson, a force of nature, and to my infinitely wise editor, Jessica Williams, for believing in this book. I am also thankful to the team at William Morrow for their care and attention—Julia Elliott, Eliza Rosenberry, Laurie McGee, and so many of their indispensable colleagues. To Lucy Morris at Curtis Brown, for her insights and championing of this novel in the UK. To Josie Freedman at CAA, for bringing this story to the shores of LA.

This book would not have come to life without the insights and friendship of my classmates at the GrubStreet Novel Incubator program—John McClure, Juliet Faithfull, Kasey LeBlanc, Sara Shukla, Nicole Vecchiotti, Cameron Dryden, Michael Giddings, Joan Nichols, and Susan Larkin. And our fearless, brilliant teacher, Michelle Hoover, one of the hardest-working literary citizens I know.

I revised this book surrounded by exceptional nature thanks to the Studios of Key West, Salty Quill Writers Retreat, and Willapa Bay AiR, and the wonderful, generous staff at these residencies, especially Bree Anne Buckley, Jeff McMahon, Chris Ross, and Cyndy Hayward. Whitney Scharer and Alexander Lumans, you were the best second readers I could have asked for. Thank you to Garth Greenwell and my classmates in the workshop "What Sex Can Do," one of the most exceptional classes I've ever taken, where chapters of this book were shared and discussed. Stephanie Ji, Lü Xin, Lillian Fitzmaurice, Jessica Tsu, Yan Chengdan—I am grateful to you for interviews and conversations about this book's contents. The writers at 5 George Street provided light in dark times—thank you to Uri Bram, Jehan Azad, and especially Sylvia Bishop for your invaluable comments. I'm grateful to Iwalani Kim for her sharp insights. And thank you, Rachel Barenbaum, for being a guiding light about the publishing world.

I would not have found this path without the teachers of writing in my life. I am grateful for Jennifer Kao and Patrick Carroll at SMIC; Mary Fulton, Kevin O'Connor, Jeff Domina, Lewis Robinson, and Catherine Tousignant at Phillips Academy Andover; Anne Fadiman and Caryl Phillips at Yale University; and Stacy Mattingly at GrubStreet. The Pauline Scheer Fellowship at GrubStreet and Kitty Pechet, along with the Writers' Room of Boston, provided invaluable support and working space. Thank you to my colleagues at *Off Assignment*—the inimitable Colleen Kinder and Anya Tchoupakov—who welcomed me into the literary ecosystem and whose dynamism sustained me, and this book's revisions, through the pandemic's early phases.

The courage to commit to writing full-time would have eluded me were it not for the support of Jadon Montero and Frances Marshman during formative years. I'm grateful to my grandparents, Andrée and Jacques Rey Lescure, and Li Guihua and Wang Mingjun, for nurturing my love for the most important places in my life. To my stepmother, Ginger Jiang, and my little sister, Oceana Wang, for showing me Shanghai through new eyes. And to my father, Wang Defu, and my mother, Isabelle Rey Lescure, for the story still being written.